Robert

Hope you enjoy

the book,

DECEPTION

My best wishes

GENE BOFFA

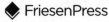 FriesenPress

Suite 300 - 990 Fort St
Victoria, BC, V8V 3K2
Canada

www.friesenpress.com

Copyright © 2016 by Eugene R. Boffa, Jr.
First Edition — 2016

ISBN
978-1-4602-9115-3 (Hardcover)
978-1-4602-9116-0 (Paperback)
978-1-4602-9117-7 (eBook)

1. FICTION, ACTION & ADVENTURE

Distributed to the trade by The Ingram Book Company

In memory of Warren Murphy,
it has been an honor and privilege to have called him my friend.

For
Ron "Haig" Shaljian
&
Gene "Charko" Ciarkowski

Thank you for all the years of friendship.
You both have helped me navigate the road of life.

Other books by Gene Boffa

The Deed, a Mac Daniels Novel

ACKNOWLEDGEMENTS

There have been many who have given freely of their time and advice for which I am grateful. I may have left a few names off and I apologize.

My wife Pat, who's the first reader of all my manuscripts.

My son Michael, the doctor whose advice has helped me keep Mac and Astrid alive and healthy after they get shot.

My son Gene and daughter Jessica my favorite critics, who are always on hand to give constructive criticism and advice.

Ken "Bak" Johansen one of Jet Blue's finest pilots who was very helpful and generous with his time and advice, but had to learn from Mac Daniels how to fly backwards.

Dave Scelba CEO of SGW Integrated Marketing Communications for all his time and advice.

Leo Montes de Oca of Changebridge Productions for trying to make me look good in the photo.

Cesare Pari EVP of SGW Integrated Marketing Communications for his work on the cover design.

Robert "Bible Bob" Cavalero of Catholic Book Publishing who has always been there with a wealth of excellent advice.

Lexye Aversa the global guru with her travel event company Professional Touch International in Palm Beach Gardens, FL, who plan all the great trips for Astrid and Mac as well as for my family.

Tony Seidhl of TD Media.

And to my wife's cat, Mombo who sat on my lap every night as I wrote this book.

"A military operation involves deception. Even though you are competent, appear to be incompetent. Though effective, appear to be ineffective."

The Art of War, Strategic Assessments
Sun-tzu
Fourth century B.C.

CHAPTER 1

AUGUST 6, 1945

Twin Mitsubishi MK4A-11 "Kasei" 14-cylinder radial engines, producing 1,530 hp each, pulled the Mitsubishi G4M along at a cruise speed of 175 knots two hundred feet above the calm Pacific Ocean. The "Betty", as the Allies called G4M, was the main twin-engine, land-based bomber used by the Imperial Japanese Navy Air Service in World War II. Its Japanese crew normally had a contingent of seven men (main-pilot, co-pilot, navigator/bombardier/nose gunner, captain/top turret gunner, radio operator/waist gunner, engine mechanic/waist gunner, and tail gunner), and the plane was unofficially called the "Hamaki," Japanese for cigar, in honor of its rotund, cigar-shaped fuselage.

This flight was different, very different. There were only two crewmembers, the pilot and co-pilot, and the bomb bay was empty as were the gun turrets. Missing from the tail turret was the 20 mm type 99 cannon; from the nose turret, the waist positions; and the top turret, the 7.7 mm machine guns. The aircraft was stripped of everything that was not necessary for flight.

Kaigun (Naval) Chūsa (Commander) Koichi Koboko glanced over to his co-pilot Kaigun (Naval) Chui (Sub-Lieutenant) Fumio Tanaka. Tanaka's hands balled up on his lap, his eyes locked on the horizon, as if he dared not look away or the plane would drop into the sea. Koboko reached over and tapped Tanaka's shoulder. Tanaka jumped, his face reddened, embarrassed by his actions.

"Take the helm and hold the course and altitude," ordered Koboko.

Without looking at his commanding officer Tanaka locked his hands onto the wheel and a very slight smile appeared on his boyish face. He let out a long breath. He was flying, but where to, he wondered, and why on this plane? This flight to nowhere had gone on for hours. *Hold the altitude* he thought, *any lower and we would be swimming.* This could not be a combat mission. Trained to follow orders and not to question, it took all the courage he had to say, "Sir, may I ask, what is the purpose of our mission?"

Koboko looked out the side window at the endless sky and barren sea. He did not immediately answer his sub-lieutenant. He too questioned this mission, but the Imperial Army General Staff Office and the Ministry of War, both of which were nominally subordinate to the Emperor of Japan, the supreme commander of the army and the navy, had conceived this plan.

The scheduled co-pilot for this top-secret mission was not Tanaka, but Koboko's long time friend Akio Sato. But Akio had died along with most of the senior pilots when the Allies bombed the airfield. The plane escaped destruction by pure chance. Recently painted in jungle camouflage and covered by netting, it had been parked off the field. Koboko had decided to fly the mission solo when seventeen-year-old Tanaka, a newly minted sub-lieutenant, arrived at the airfield. Immediately assigned to the mission, Tanaka stepped off the truck, and with his duffel bag still in hand, climbed into the plane and buckled in, and they were heading into the wind for takeoff.

Koboko turned to Tanaka and asked, "Do you know what sarin is?"

"No, sir," was the quick reply.

"The war does not go well, Sub-Lieutenant. The Allies control the air and sea. They bomb us at will. What ships we have are useless and they will most likely invade our homeland. Every day they drop leaflets telling us to surrender or face destruction."

"We will never surrender," yelled Tanaka. "We will fight them in the streets to the death."

Koboko shook his head. "They will win. We have no ability to fight without bullets, without tanks. Many of them will die but many more of us. This mission may be able to stop the invasion and perhaps give us an honorable peace."

"What are we going to do in this unarmed plane, sir?"

"We are going to land on a small island, north of Peleliu."

"Peleliu?" exclaimed Tanaka.

Koboko shook his head. "The Battle of Peleliu, where we fought the devil dogs," he said, referring to the First Marine Division of U.S. Marines. "We lost a small airstrip there but we had secretly built an airstrip on another coral island. That is where we are going. The strip is cut across the island, ninety feet wide."

Tanaka unconsciously looked out the window at the wings. The wingspan of the G4M was eighty-two feet. This was going to be a dead-on landing or they would be dead for sure.

Koboko knew what his co-pilot was thinking; the same thing he'd thought the first time he flew there. It was a tricky landing. As they approached the landing, he had to suppress his grin when he thought about Tanaka. Across the top of the airstrip were bamboo and netting covered with palm leaves that blocked out the view from the air. It was like flying into a tunnel... which it was. He had to touch down at the end of the beach where the sand lightly covered the concrete runway, just a few yards before the trees. Sometimes when the waves were up they would break on the landing gear. Three large rocks were arranged on the beach in a straight line, indicating the midpoint of the runway. Once inside the tunnel there was a centerline to follow. In the middle of the island, cut into the jungle on one side of the strip, was a work and living area. Living on the island were mechanics, a communications specialist, and a civilian weapons specialist. On the other side of the strip were a fuel depot and a storage facility for the weapons.

"What is sarin, sir?"

"I'm not sure exactly sure myself. It is some type of liquid that turns into a poison gas. We have a German weapons specialist on the island who can answer your questions. It was discovered in error. It seems they were trying to create a stronger pesticide and ended up with a poison gas. The Germans delivered it by submarine. That's all I know about that shit."

Tanaka turned to look at his commander. "Sir, are we going to use the sarin?"

"I hope so. It may be the only way to end the war."

"Do you know how it works, sir?"

"All I know is, if you breathe sarin in, you die. Even if you do not breathe it in, the vapor concentrations may immediately penetrate your skin and you die. A soldier's uniform will absorb sarin and hold it for about thirty minutes after exposure to the gas, which can lead to the exposure of other soldiers. Even if you absorb a non-lethal dose, without immediate medical treatment, your brain suffers permanent damage. Even at very low concentrations, sarin can be fatal. Death may follow in a few minutes after direct inhalation of a lethal dose. We are going to bomb the Allied headquarters. We may be able to kill over one hundred thousand people. This will allow us to show the Allies we have this new weapon." Looking for the right words, he hesitated, and then he said, "... weapon of mass destruction."

After that, the cockpit was silent. Neither man spoke. Both realized the horror of killing so many with one bomb. The plane flew on for another hour.

Koboko broke the silence, "I will take over. We should see the island shortly. Tighten your belt."

As if by magic, the island appeared on the horizon. Koboko dropped the flaps, and reduced the power to both engines. The plane began to lose altitude. He further dropped the flaps and again reduced the power. The plane was now seventy-five feet over the water. He dropped his main gear, and the wheels locked down. Finally, he was at full flaps and now at stall speed of 120 km/h (75 mph). Koboko lined up with the three rocks. A few minutes later, he set the plane down on the leading edge of the runway. Tanaka said nothing, just sat frozen in his seat as the plane ran down the runway and slowed to a stop.

The brakes locked, the wheels chocked, and the engines wound down. Koboko exited the plane, followed by Tanaka. The men who had been living on the island greeted the flight crew and Koboko introduced Tanaka to them. The mechanic climbed on board to retrieve the supplies and the precious mailbag.

Tanaka spotted the cases, all marked with the swastika. There must have been at least two dozen, maybe more. He could not read German but saw that there were different markings. He immediately understood the two chemicals. Behind the cases was bomb casting, lined up in rows like soldiers waiting for the order to kill. He walked over to the row of boxes and picked one up. He was surprised how light it was.

"What are you doing?" said a voice in Japanese with a German accent.

"Just looking," replied Tanaka, "just looking."

"I am Oberleutnant (Senior Lieutenant) Gunther von Stern. I am in charge of the sarin project."

"How does it work?"

The oberleutnant thought for a second. Finally, he said, "There are two chemicals. Each by itself is harmless. Put them together and you have sarin; a nerve gas that kills. Sarin degrades after a period of several weeks to several months. So, we keep the two elements apart until we are ready to use them. The elements within the bomblets are kept apart and placed into the bomb castings. The castings hold about one hundred and twenty-five bomblets. The chemical reaction takes place when the bomb is deployed. The deployment action removes the barrier between the chemicals, so they can react with one another. Then there is a bursting charge to aerosolize and distribute the gas. It is simple, no?"

"No, but let me get settled in. Do you play chess?"

"Ja."

The communications specialist pulled Koboko aside. He reported that communications with the headquarters of Field Marshal Shunroku Hata's Second General Army had abruptly shut down.

"When did this happen?" asked Koboko.

"About 08:15 Hiroshima time, sir."

"Well, we will just stay and wait for orders. All we have is time and time is the most valuable thing a man can spend."

CHAPTER 2

ONBOARD A NORTH KOREAN AN-2

PRESENT DAY

Hamhung, South Hamgyong Province, North Korea, located on the east coast, is the second largest city in North Korea. It is also the home of Yonpo Air Base; operated by the Korean People's Air Force and the main base for the Antonov An-2, a military transport nicknamed "Annie" by the Russians.

The An-2 looks like a plane from the past that managed to escape into present time. It is a single-engine biplane, with a Shvetsov ASh-62IR 9-cylinder supercharged radial engine delivering 1,000 hp, giving the plane a cruise speed of 120 mph.

North Korea has a number of these so-called transports, with wooden propellers and canvas wings, giving them a low radar cross-section and therefore a limited degree of "stealth." In a war, they could possibly be used to parachute or deliver Special Forces troops behind enemy lines for sabotage operations.

In the morning, the Annie took off with a two-man crew and one passenger for Ho Chi Minh City, Vietnam. There the cargo and passenger would transfer to a chartered jet operated by Cubana, the national airline of Cuba. The jet would then fly to San Julian Air Base located at Pinar del Río, Cuba.

It was a quiet, uneventful flight in perfect flying weather, and Miguel Antonio Ricardo was actually enjoying the flight, relaxing and reading his book. Ricardo was a special courier of the Cuban government and was on his way back to Cuba. He was taller than his Korean pilot and co-pilot by several inches, standing at six feet two inches. His tanned skin made his blue eyes stand out. His features were chiseled—movie star handsome. He had a short beard and dark black hair. He was anxious to return home, having spent several days in North Korea. This, he knew, was not a place for a vacation. He was the only person seated in the body of the aircraft and that did not bother him. Ricardo had all the company he needed—strapped in on the six front-facing, bench-style seats across from him, were six lead canisters of weapons-grade uranium. Each weighed about five kilograms, or eleven pounds.

The pilot opened the curtain, leaned back, and yelled to his passenger in Spanish, "We're landing. Fasten your seat belt."

Ricardo pulled the strap and continued reading. The pilot dropped the flaps and reduced power, and as the plane slowed to thirty-five mph, it hit the ground and rolled to a stop. It taxied to a prearranged parking place and the pilot shut down the engine. Ricardo unbuckled his belt, stood up, stretched, and waited for the pilot to open the door so he could transfer his cargo to the waiting jet.

From the window, Ricardo saw a fuel truck driving toward the plane. He did not see the Cuban jet. "Captain," he said to the pilot, "Where is my plane and when do I get off?"

The co-pilot answered, "I am coming down to let you out."

Ricardo turned toward the door. The co-pilot followed behind, but instead of opening the door, he pulled out his nine millimeter BaekDuSan, the North Korean copy of the Czech CZ-75 pistol issued to pilots. He stuck it into Ricardo's back.

"What the fuck are you doing?"

"Sit down and shut up," ordered the co-pilot, shoving Ricardo toward the seat. "Buckle up." As soon as Ricardo sat down, he handed him handcuffs. "Cuff your right hand to the arm rest," he ordered.

Ricardo complied. "What are you doing? My country is one of your few friends."

The co-pilot smiled a toothy grin. "Your country may be, but you are not."

While the plane was refueling, Ricardo saw the pilot of the chartered Cubana flight running toward the plane. The Korean pilot saw this and radioed something, which Ricardo did not hear. Several armed guards stopped the Cuban pilot before he reached Ricardo's plane, forcing him back to the Cuban jet.

After the Annie was refueled, it took off heading east. Four hours later, the co-pilot came back to Ricardo. "Are you ready to go swimming?" he asked with a laugh as he opened the cabin door.

"Why are you doing this?"

"Orders from the Supreme Leader," he said, referring to Kim Jong-un.

"Why?"

"You see that?" the co-pilot said, pointing to the canisters. "They are filled with sand— sand for which you paid fifty million euros." With that, he started to laugh.

Ricardo figured it out. He was dead. Kim had agreed to sell the uranium to the Cubans, who had a deal to sell it to a few Middle Eastern countries. North Korea did not have enough hard currency, so they'd sold him sand, which would never reach Cuba. They were going to kill him, fake a crash, pocket the money, and no one would know better. "Fuck you and that pint-size little shit you call leader."

"No fuck you," the co-pilot replied, throwing the key at Ricardo. "Get up."

As Ricardo un-cuffed himself, the co-pilot pulled his CZ-75. Ricardo did not move but sat there. The co-pilot made a mistake, grabbing him by the jacket and pulling him up. Ricardo flew into the man, knocking him down and grabbing the pistol with his right hand. The pilot heard the racket, looked back, put the plane on automatic pilot, and climbed out of his seat, reaching for the AK-47 hanging on the wall.

Ricardo and the co-pilot rolled on the floor. Ricardo got his hand on the pistol and forced the co-pilot to squeeze off a few shots. One of the shots hit the pilot, who fell backwards into the yoke. In a dying reflex action, he squeezed the trigger and the AK-47, being on full automatic, sprayed twenty-five 7.62x39mm rounds throughout the cockpit before the pilot fell to the floor. Ricardo and the co-pilot rolled over toward the open door. Realizing this, the co-pilot let go of Ricardo to grab for the legs of the seats. One more roll and they both would be out of the plane. It took a few long seconds, but Ricardo grabbed seat legs too, and both men managed to stay in the cabin.

Raising his pistol, the co-pilot managed to get to his knees. Ricardo kicked the weapon from his hand. Both men were now on their feet.

The plane was losing altitude. The co-pilot threw a right hand, which Ricardo stopped with his left and with his right he grabbed the other man's elbow, snapping the arm. He then kicked his left knee, cracking the cap. The co-pilot fell to the floor, taking Ricardo with him. Both men were now half out of the cabin with their feet hanging in space. Ricardo took advantage of the co-pilot's broken arm and pulled on it. The pain caused the man to release Ricardo.

"Asshole, it isn't sand, but the real shit. We swapped it out. Your Supreme Leader will have to go fuck himself," Ricardo said as he pushed him out the door.

Ricardo crawled back into the cabin and picked up the CZ-75, sticking it into his waistband and making his way to the cockpit. He pulled the pilot back off the wheel and buckled himself into the co-pilot's seat. Glancing over the instrument panel, he saw the damage. He was flying blind; no compass, no avionics. He hoped the radio would work.

Changing the frequency, he keyed the microphone. "Coach," he said, using the call sign of his contact, "this is Shortstop. Please come in. Coach, this is Shortstop. Please come in."

There was no response. He changed the frequency and tried again. "Coach, this is Shortstop, come in please. Come in."

A metallic voice came on. "Shortstop, this is the USS Ronald Reagan, you are on a restricted channel. Please change frequency."

"Fuck restricted, this is Shortstop and you are Catcher."

"I repeat—this is the Ronald Reagan and you are not authorized to broadcast on this frequency."

"All right, Ronald Reagan this is my emergency identification (EID) Nuco 429 Page. Repeat Nuco 429 Page. Notify your captain that you have an EID Nuco 429 Page."

After a few minutes, a different voice said, "This is the captain. We are authenticating your EID."

"Sorry Captain, I do not have time. You have orders to allow a Cuban chartered flight, call sign, "Reliever" to land. The flight is terminated. I repeat—terminated. You are the Catcher and I am Shortstop. There is no time. I am flying blind. I need your civilian passenger, call sign Coach."

The captain understood. "Roger that."

"This is the Coach. Shortstop are you all right?"

"No, I am not. I am flying fucking blind. See if you can pick me up and give me a direction. I have no compass, but I'm flying easterly. If I land this crate in the water, I don't know long it will float."

"Will do. I received a heads-up from our Cuban pilots. What happened?"

"When we got to the airport, the Supreme Leader decided to double-cross us. They took off and didn't let me transfer the stuff to the jet. They planned to send me swimming."

"Do you have it?"

"Yes, it's all with me. If you don't get here, the shit, along with me, will be on the bottom of the ocean."

"When you get here we can go through this. The captain has an E-2 Hawkeye up looking for you. It should pick you up. Stay put."

Ricardo threw down the microphone, talking to himself: "Stay put? Where the fuck am I going?" Then he noticed the fuel gauge was dangerously low. *Now what*? he thought. Looking out the window, he saw that some of the rounds had punctured the fuel tanks.

Back on the radio, he said, "Coach, this is Shortstop, I am going down—the fuel is gone. I'll stay with the plane as long as possible. Find me fast."

The plane flew on for another twenty minutes. There was no response from the Reagan.

The radio died, the engine stopped, and Ricardo tried to hold the nose at the horizon so that the plane would go into a gentle glide. As the plane dropped, he saw an island. He couldn't make it, but with luck, he would be only a mile or so off shore. He could swim, if the sharks didn't get him.

Even though the ocean was calm, it didn't help. The An-2 has fixed landing gear and as soon as the wheels hit the water, the plane started to cartwheel, tearing off the wings. The plane would not float for long.

Back on board the Ronald Reagan, the captain said, "Mr. Haig, we think we have a location and when we get in range I'll launch a helicopter, but for now we'll launch a couple of Hornets."

"Thank you Captain." Concern showed on Ron Haig's face. The words of the captain, "We *think* we have a location," did not rest well with him.

"To tell the truth," said the captain, "I was anxious to see the Cuban Lear 24 land on the deck."

"Our pilots are former naval aviators with plenty of experience. The Lear is twelve feet shorter in length than the sixty-foot Super Hornet."

"But the Lear needs five thousand feet of runway and our deck is little more than a thousand."

"Captain, I will tell you a secret—our Lear has a tail hook."

"This must be important, Mr. Haig. What is on board? Gold? The navy usually doesn't turn over a super carrier to the CIA."

"Captain, you don't want to know what's on board. May I have a room for a private call?"

The captain stepped out and Haig used his secure satellite phone. When he pressed a preset number, the phone rang at Langley.

It was answered on the first ring. "Ron how did it go?" asked Dr. Cornaci, the director of the CIA.

"Not sure, sir. The shortstop had to do an unassisted double play. The other team tried to throw out the shortstop, but it did not work. We are in control of the game. Just need to find where the shortstop is playing."

There was silence on the phone. Finally, Dr. Cornaci spoke: "It's true, a military operation involves deception. Keep me posted. We can't lose an all-star shortstop."

Ron Haig nodded his head in agreement, hung up, and said to himself, no better player than Mac Daniels.

CHAPTER 3

A DESERTED ISLAND; PART OF THE REPUBLIC OF PALAU

The water was pouring in on Daniels. Quickly, he rummaged through the plane, finding a knife and some line but no life jackets or raft. There were a few maps, and although they were written in Korean he thought they might be helpful. The two box lunches he definitely wanted. The plane was taking on more water and the nose was going under. He grabbed his duffel bag and tossed his clothes out. He loaded the bag with the treasures he'd found and threw in the CZ 75. From the pile of his clothes, he threw in his running shoes, sweat socks, baseball cap, and sunglasses. He stripped down to his shorts, slung the Kalashnikov over his neck, tied the line to the duffel bag, and secured it around his waist. He took a deep breath before the plane was completely submerged.

Through the broken window, he pushed through but could not make it to the surface. His duffel bag got caught and held him fast to the sinking aircraft. He saw the floor of the ocean coming toward him. The plane hit the bottom. Daniels dove back into the plane and freed his duffel bag. Pushing off the aircraft, he swam for the surface, stroking and kicking as hard as he could to overcome the weight of the Kalashnikov and the duffel bag. He needed what was in the duffel bag. He could not cut it. Finally, he broke the surface and gasped for air. Using the combat sidestroke, he started toward the island, pulling the duffel bag behind.

It was a steady and methodical stroke as Daniels paced himself, ignoring the drag of the duffel bag and the weight of the Kalashnikov. Ninety minutes later, he felt the sand, stood, and waded onto the beach. He dropped to his knees to catch his breath, pulled the duffel bag onto the beach, and fell back. The sky was clear. He was hoping to see a helicopter. He lay there for a few minutes collecting his thoughts.

Trained as a Navy SEAL, Daniels was a highly trained, skilled operative. He knew how to survive. He was a member of the Special Activities Division (SAD) of the CIA's National Clandestine Service (NCS), responsible for covert operations known as "special activities."

Within SAD, there are two separate groups; one of them is the Special Operations Group (SOG) known for its tactical paramilitary operations and the other is the Political Action Group (PAG). PAG is responsible for covert activities related to political influence, psychological operations, economic warfare, and cyber warfare. SOG is generally considered the most secretive special operations force in the United States. They are involved in operations with which the U.S. government does not wish to be overtly associated. If they are compromised during a mission, the government may deny all knowledge.

Daniels knew what he had to do, but first did a quick recon of the area. He thought he might be lucky and find the island inhabited. He slipped on his pants, a shirt, running shoes, hat, and sunglasses. In one of the box lunches there were some sandwiches sealed in plastic. He tore one open and ate it. He hid the duffel bag and the AK in the bushes as he did not want to walk in on a pool party carrying the weapon, but he tucked the CZ 75 in his waistband. He started down the beach in what he believed a southerly direction. Being the optimist, he hoped he would find a nice resort where he could have a cold beer and call Haig on the Reagan. Thirty minutes later, he turned around and headed back toward where he'd hidden his stash. There were no signs of life, at least in that direction. Once he came upon the site, he discovered everything was gone. He was not alone. The order of survival just changed.

Heading north, he encountered an opening into the forest. He stepped in. The ground was hard. Kneeling down and using his hands, he swept away some sand and was amazed to see there was concrete underneath. He ventured further into the forest, and there, tucked into a makeshift hanger was a Mitsubishi G4M.

"Holy shit, a Betty!" Daniels blurted out. This must have been some type of Japanese base.

"Hōrudoappu."

Daniels turned toward the voice. "What the fuck?"

Standing there was an old man in a tattered Japanese uniform, holding the Kalashnikov and pointing it at Daniels. The old man was repeatedly raising and lowering the barrel. Daniels recognized the sign and slowly raised his hands.

"Anatahadare."

Daniels shook his head from side to side and shrugged his shoulders.

"No Japanese." The man just looked, not sure what to do. Daniels had the CZ 75 but he decided not to use it. This man, he thought, had been there his whole life and there was no need to end it now. Daniels saw that the safety was still on the AK and decided to sit down. Slowly, he sat down on the hard surface. He waved his hands downward. The soldier got the message and sat down some ten feet away from Daniels. Daniels very slowly pulled up his shirt, with two fingers slowly pulled out the CZ 75, and threw it toward the beach. He lifted both arms and hands outward to show there was no more. The soldier laid down the weapon.

"The war is over," said Mac Daniels. "The war is over."

The soldier just sat there, not moving. Finally, he said, very softly and slowly in English, a question he clearly feared to ask, "Who won?"

"We did. It has been over a long time." Daniels felt sorry for him. His whole life spent on this island and only to find out it was all for nothing.

"I must prepare," said the soldier.

"Prepare for what?" asked Daniels.

"For my death. It is Seppuku or as you might call it, Hara-kiri."

"I know about this. Your government pushed the idea of the Samurai Bushido code that said that it was better to die than to suffer the humiliation of defeat. But you are a hero. Your emperor will receive you. Please," said Daniels. "Please, it is time for you to live."

The old man just sat there. His face had tanned over the many years, the lines and creases showing the years. He had no beard on the sides of his face, but had a stringy, salt-and-pepper goatee. Surprisingly, his hair was cut short.

Daniels went on. "Your emperor ordered a cessation of the war and no mass suicide. Your emperor was treated with respect for his courage and his order applies to you—no Hara-kiri."

Shaking his head as if he did not believe or just did not want to believe, the old man asked, "Who are you? Where did you come from?"

I am Lieutenant Commander Bill Cody, United States Navy. I was flying when I had trouble and crashed at sea. And who are you?"

"I am Naval Sub-Lieutenant Fumio Tanaka."

"You speak English very well."

Tanaka let out a sigh. "I was born in California. My family returned to Japan right before the outbreak of the war with you."

"Is there a place we can sit and talk?" asked Daniels. "I am sure you have many questions and I have a few of my own."

Pointing to the plane, Tanaka said, "The plane is my home. When everyone else died, I moved into it. There is fresh water, fruit, yams, and I catch fish. You are welcome to enter."

Daniels stood and as he did, he noticed the cases, all marked with the swastika. Pointing he asked, "What is that?"

"It's the elements of sarin. Let's go..."

Daniels cut him off, "Hold on Sub-Lieutenant. Sarin? What were you going to do with it?"

"Bomb you. Let's go and talk. I am sorry I ate your food."

"I now have a question. Where are we?"

"Good question," laughed Tanaka. He looked at Daniels. "This is the first time I laughed in many years. As to your question, this is a small island, north of Peleliu. I believe that is where your Marines were engaged in a costly, losing battle."

"I am sorry Sub-Lieutenant, the Marines won."

Daniels knew that the island of Peleliu was part of Palau; officially the Republic of Palau, an island country located in the western Pacific Ocean spread across 250 islands and forming the western chain of the Caroline Islands. He now had an idea where he was.

"Will they come for you, Lieutenant Commander?" asked Tanaka.

"If they had me on their scope they will be here in a few hours. If not, you and I will become good friends until they find us or we get out of here."

"Scope?"

Daniels avoided the question. "How did you manage to stay here, waiting like you did?"

Tanaka was silent and then said, "The fates have given mankind a patient soul."

Daniels nodded his understanding, "Come on we have much to talk about. You have quite a hideout."

"Hideout?" Tanaka thought for a moment. "Are you talking about a place to hide? Let me show you." He led to a spot behind the plane and pointed to the ground. "Look," he said.

Daniels saw nothing. "Look at what?"

Tanaka smiled. He picked up a small log, which was a handle to a trap door covered with years of palm fronds. Daniels looked down into the cave. It was filled with munitions and several rows of bombs. "They are the sarin bombs," said Tanaka.

"Leave the door open," said Daniels. "I am sure the authorities will want to empty it out. They will never find it if you close the trap door."

Tanaka nodded his consent. "That's where they all died. Let's go to the Mitsubishi."

Daniels followed him to the Betty. "Who died?"

Tanaka did not answer, he just said, "Mitsubishi is a good plane. Are they still flying?"

"No, they make and sell cars in America."

"Strange, very strange."

CHAPTER 4

ONBOARD THE USS RONALD REAGAN

"Mr. Haig, the Hawkeye picked up a blip. It was on the screen for a few seconds when it dropped off. We have an idea where it went down. I launched a pair of Hornets that should be over the area in less than twenty minutes."

"Thank you, Captain." Haig used his secure satellite phone to call Dr. Cornaci. "Doctor, they think they have a fix on him."

"Wonderful, Ron. I am with Admiral Charko," Cornaci said, referring to the Director of the National Clandestine Service, and the "DD" or the Deputy Director of the CIA, Ron Haig's immediate superior. Haig was the Deputy Director of the Clandestine Service. "You are on speaker. Was Mac chipped?" he asked, referring to a GPS microchip implant.

"Admiral," said Haig, acknowledging his boss. "No Doctor, we decided that it was too risky. Kim is too paranoid. Mac would have been scanned and probably given a colonoscopy before he would get within fifty feet of the little leader."

Admiral Charko spoke. "Ron can you pick up the uranium or are you going to need special equipment?"

"Not sure yet, Admiral. I have three members of a SEAL team with me. Depending on the depth of the water, they can retrieve it. If it's really deep we can fly in Winnie the Pooh."

"Winnie the Pooh?" asked Dr. Cornaci. "Please explain."

"I'm sorry, Jon," chimed in Charko. "Ron is referring to an atmospheric diving suit...an ADS. It resembles a suit of armor with a large head, thus the Winnie the Pooh nickname, and it maintains an internal pressure of one atmosphere. The ADS can be used for very deep dives of up to 2,300 feet for many hours."

"Learn something every day," smiled Cornaci. It was his university background speaking. Prior to accepting the position of director of the CIA, Jon Cornaci had been the president of a prominent Jesuit university in the northeast. While he was not a spy, he was an excellent administrator and held in the highest regard for his ethical approach to life and business. The president hoped that Dr. Cornaci's sterling reputation would polish the agency's graying reputation.

"Ron, what went wrong?" asked Charko.

"The operation from our part went according to plan. Mac intercepted the Cuban courier and we have that man's body here on the ship on ice. Mac got into North Korea, as the Cuban courier. Oddly enough, they had a similar appearance and with make-up and Mac's new beard, the resemblance was remarkable. Mac delivered the passwords to the bank accounts and an attaché case full of hundreds to Kim himself. Mac picked up the canisters of the uranium and went to the airport. He was supposed to transfer to one of our planes repainted as Air Cubana. Two top former navy pilots who work for us were to fly him out and land on the Reagan. I was to take custody of the uranium and then drop the plane over the side, and report the accident. Kim had other ideas and they didn't let Mac change planes. They too had the idea to fake a crash and that way the Cubans would not ever realize they'd been tricked. The Korean plane, an Antonov, a military transport, took off with no flight plan filed. Most likely Mac killed or disabled the crew, but from his last message, he was going down. He apparently crashed the plane somewhere east of us."

There was a knock on Haig's cabin door.

"Enter."

A young sailor put his head into the room. "Sir, the captain said that the Sea Hawk," he said, referring to HH-60H Sea Hawk, "will be lifting off in fifteen minutes. He thought you would like to be on board."

"Please notify the captain I would be pleased to be on board and will be up in ten minutes. Thank you." Haig went back to the call. "It looks like they found him."

"Ron, set up a video conference call when you get back."

"Yes sir, Admiral." Haig disconnected the call and went up to the flight deck. A blue shirt led him to the helicopter and handed him a life jacket and helmet. Some of the ground crew had extended the four rotor blades, while another member of the ground crew was checking the tail rotor. Haig took a center seat in between the two door gunners, strapped in and plugged in the communication leads so he could hear and speak with the crew. A few minutes later, the blades began to spool up and the carrier-based helicopter lifted off.

The chopper moved away and the ship soon disappeared. Haig asked the pilot, "Where are we headed?"

"The Republic of Palau," he replied. "The Hornets saw oil traces in the water about three miles off one of the uninhabited Palau islands. We'll fly over the wreck and see if we can find your boy."

An hour later, the pilot called to Haig, "On the port side."

Haig changed seats with side door gunner and could see the outline of the sunken aircraft. "What is the depth of the water?" he asked.

"About forty feet."

The pilot turned the helicopter in a clockwise direction around the wreck. This put Haig in view of the beach. He saw a glint from the beach. Something was shining. He smiled—it had to be Mac.

"On the beach," said Haig.

"Got it," said the pilot.

The Sea Hawk made a direct line for the shining object.

CHAPTER 5

A DESERTED ISLAND, PART OF THE REPUBLIC OF PALAU

Tanaka took Mac around his island. To some it might have been a paradise. For Tanaka it was a prison without walls. Mac asked him why he did not attempt to leave and Tanaka's answer was simple: "We were ordered to stay, but then they all died. It was terrible. I had no fuel and I could not fly by myself."

They continued walking, and Tanaka went on, "I suspected the war was over but I thought that Japan was victorious. No one could successfully invade Japan."

"What happened here?"

Tanaka explained, "Oberleutnant Gunther von Stern was instructing us how to load the little metal," he hesitated, looking for the English word, "bomblets into the bomb castings. They used to work in the cave. One day I was on the other side of the island, fishing, and when I came back they were all dead. On the floor of the cave was a broken bomblet. I did not touch the bodies; Gunther had told us a person's clothing could release sarin for about thirty minutes after it has been exposed to the gas. The next day I buried the bodies and I have been living, no…just existing here until you happened to come here."

They walked around the island ending up at Tanaka's home, the Mitsubishi bomber, where they talked some more. Daniels told him about the war and answered his questions.

Tanaka said he was from a village near Hiroshima where his parents and younger brother and sister lived. Daniels withheld the details about the atomic bomb. Tanaka gave him a cup of coconut milk and some fruit, apologizing profusely for eating Daniels' food. He explained it had been a long time since he had anything other than fish and fruit.

Daniels heard the distinct whooping sound of the rotors and knew immediately that rescue was at hand.

Tanaka heard the sound too. "What is that?"

"Our rescue, Fumio. It's a helicopter."

Puzzled, Tanaka asked, "What is a helicopter?"

Mac thought for a second. "It's easier for you to see than to explain," he said. "The good news you will soon be on your way to Japan. Maybe you'll find your younger brother and sister. I hope so. You have much to see and catch up on. My boss," Daniels hesitated, needing a name, he said, "George Hayes, will probably be on the helicopter. He is a pain in the ass and will be mad at me for losing an airplane. He will chew me out but I try to ignore him. Behind his back, I call him 'Gabby.' You're going to land on an American aircraft carrier. I am sure the captain will be there to meet you."

Daniels explained the protocol for entry onto an American warship. The sound of the rotors got louder and he stood up. "Let's go."

"I will be out in a few minutes. This is a joyous and sad moment. This has been my whole life," Tanaka said, waving his arms around the aircraft, "I need to change and clean up."

Daniels understood.

Daniels was standing on the beach as the copter set down, Haig jumped off with the side gunners, bent down to pick something up, then jogged up the beach to Daniels. He was about four inches shorter than Daniels but much thinner. Ron was losing his hair and doing a comb-over to cover the bald spot. It was always a source of teasing from Daniels.

"Thank God you're okay," Haig said. "Let's go."

Daniels said, "Cody, Bill Cody, explain later."

Haig knew better than to ask questions. He just nodded.

"Wait, I have to show you something. You're not going to believe this." Daniels led Haig back into the jungle. "Well," he said, pointing to the airplane.

Before Haig could respond, Naval Sub-Lieutenant Fumio Tanaka climbed down in his double-breasted, dark-blue, full dress tunic with his blue trousers, which had a gold stripe. His footwear was homemade scandals, and around his waist was his Imperial Japanese Navy officers' model 1883 dress sword. He was clean-shaven.

Haig was speechless. Tanaka stepped up to him and saluted. Haig's mouth was open in astonishment. He nodded his head.

Daniels returned the salute. "This is the first time, Sub-Lieutenant, that Gabby is speechless." Turning to Haig, he said, "Mr. Hayes, this is naval Sub-Lieutenant

Fumio Tanaka. Sub Lieutenant, this is Mr. George Hayes. He is not in the military so he did not return your salute. It was my honor."

Haig finally spoke. "Sub-Lieutenant, I don't know what to say."

Daniels turned to Haig, pointing to the cases all marked with the swastika. He opened one for Haig to see. In it were rows of metal balls slightly larger than a baseball. "Sarin bomblets. They fit them into bomb castings and when they hit the ground, the gas escapes and people die. We have to get this shit out of here." Calling to one of the side door gunners, he said, "Sailor, please grab a case of this and be very careful. It's nerve gas."

"Holy fucking shit," was all the gunner said.

Haig shook his head as if to clear it, "This is the Twilight Zone."

They led Tanaka to the Sea Hawk and Tanaka stopped and stared. "Does this really fly?"

The side gunner keyed his mike, "Sir, do you see this?" he asked the pilot.

"Affirmative," was the one-word reply.

Haig said to the door gunner, "Seaman White, this is Sub-Lieutenant Tanaka."

Daniels mouthed the word, "Salute," and made the hand gesture.

The gunner saluted and Tanaka returned it. The gunner helped Tanaka into the Seahawk and strapped him in.

"Give us a few minutes," said Haig.

Daniels led him back into the forest. "By the way, Ron, how did you find me?"

Ron handed Daniels the CZ-75 he picked up. "Why the fake names?"

"Because when he gets back to Japan I don't need my name in all the papers. I'm sure the press will be looking for Bill Cody to interview and the same goes for you.

"Gabby Hayes?"

"It was better than Dale Evans. What about the uranium?"

"It's in forty feet of water. I'll send the SEALs back to retrieve it."

"Let's go before we get accused of an invasion. This is a foreign country."

Soon after, Tanaka sat upright in his seat as the Seahawk skimmed over the sea. Haig was on the radio with the captain of the Reagan and told him about Tanaka.

The Reagan came into view. Tanaka could not believe his eyes. "It is as big as my village," he said. "The airplanes have no propeller."

The Seahawk landed and Haig and Daniels jumped out. The side gunners helped Tanaka out of the Sea Hawk. On deck were all personnel not required to be at their stations. Tanaka saluted the American flag, and then he saw his flag flying; the red globe on the white field, the "rising sun" off the mast. He saluted and then turning to the captain, he saluted again and said, "Permission to come aboard, sir."

The captain returned his salute. "Welcome aboard, Sub-Lieutenant."

Tanaka drew his sword and handed it to the captain as a sign of surrender.

The captain held up his hand. "Keep it Sub-Lieutenant, you are not a prisoner but an honored guest. I would like our doctors to have a look at you and then is there something we can do for you?"

"Yes, sir, could I have a cup of tea?"

With that, the crowd on the deck cheered and applauded.

Tanaka was led away. The captain told Haig that in the morning, the navy was going to fly Tanaka to the Philippines and from there, Nippon Air would fly him to Tokyo. "We'll have the docs look him over, feed him, and send him home. My God, what a waste of a life. I hope he has some family left."

The Sea Hawk side gunner was standing there with the case of the sarin bomblets. "Sir, what do I do with this shit?"

The captain and Daniels turned to the side gunner.

"Oops, sorry, sir," said the red-faced gunner. "I was addressing Mr. Cody."

Daniels told the captain that he had sarin bomblets and wanted them tested. The captain directed the gunner to bring them to ship's magazine for storage. He told Daniels that he would have the bomb disposal unit look at the bomblets and get a report back as soon as possible.

"Captain," Haig said, "we need the video conference room. I'm sorry but it'll be off limits to all but Mr. Cody and me."

"I understand. No apology necessary."

"One more thing, Captain, I'll need another Seahawk to fly my boys to do some underwater salvage. We'll be bringing back a special cargo. I believe you have the sealed orders I had delivered to you. I suggest you open them in your cabin and then we can talk. This is top secret."

Haig and Daniels were led to the video-conference room. On the return flight on the Seahawk, Haig had called Admiral Charko from his secure satellite phone to report the rescue of Daniels. He'd briefly told the admiral about the sarin and the location of the crashed aircraft. The admiral wanted to know if they could salvage the uranium. Haig told him it was not an issue but that he was concerned about the chemicals, which were in foreign territory. The airplane, he reported, was in international waters. Charko suggested a small landing party could retrieve the chemicals, but Dr. Cornaci suggested that this matter needed more thought. They'd agreed to discuss it on the video conference call with thepresident.

Before the video conference call could begin, Haig's phone buzzed. "Haig here."

He handed Daniels the phone. "The admiral wants a word."

"Yes sir."

"The identity of our Korean asset is TSSCI," Charko said, referring to Top Secret/Sensitive Compartmented Information. "I don't want to discuss this on the conference call. Is our asset safe? Can the switch be traced to our asset?"

"We took all reasonable measures to protect the asset, sir," said Daniels. "He was hundreds of miles away on vacation with his family and without access to a computer when the switch happened. During the night shift, as planned, a supervisor had the canisters filled with the sand. The workers had no idea what was going on. They just filled the canisters. The computer generated the labels that were applied to the sand-filled canisters, which were placed into the storage racks. Prior to our asset going on vacation, he managed to queue the numbers, so when the labels were printed they contained the numbers of the..." he hesitated, "the real stuff. When the day crew received the order to send the canisters out, they took the real stuff. If anyone checked the logs, all the canisters are accounted for. If they find out about the switch, they would have no way of knowing which canisters have the sand. They would have to go through all of them and that is highly unlikely. Our guy is safe."

Charko was quiet for a moment, and then asked, "If he's caught, he won't last long under their torture, then this whole thing becomes public and we'll be in a shit storm, not to mention a possible war. Will he do it?"

"Yes sir, he is prepared to take his own life before he is captured. He knows we will get his family out and provide for them."

"Very well, Mac. Good job, now let's get this conference call out of the way."

CHAPTER 6

THE WHITE HOUSE

Even though it was Sunday, at the request of Dr. Cornaci, the president convened a special meeting in the Situation Room, a 5,000-square-foot conference room and intelligence management center in the basement of the White House, which is run by the National Security Council. The Situation Room is equipped with secure, advanced communications equipment for the president to maintain command of U.S. forces around the world. It was built in 1961 by President Kennedy and is staffed by senior officers from various agencies, including the military, which stands watch on a 24-hour basis, constantly monitoring world events.

Sixteen different intelligence agencies advise the president, however, today with the president there were four representatives from the intelligence community. To the right of the president sat Maud Evens, the assistant to the president for National Security Affairs, commonly referred to as the National Security Advisor. The president, without confirmation by the Senate, appoints the National Security Advisor. Sitting next to Adams, was Frank Green, the director of National Intelligence; the head of the Intelligence Community, overseeing and directing the implementation of the National Intelligence Program and acting as the principal advisor to the president, the National Security Council, and the Homeland Security Council for intelligence matters related to national security. Sitting across from Adams and Green were Dr. Jon Cornaci, the director of Central Intelligence (DCI) and the deputy director of Central Intelligence (DD) Admiral Charko.

"People, can we get started?" said the president. "I have something to do today. It is Sunday and even the president is entitled to a day of rest." In fact, the president and Maud Evens were on their way to Jersey City to play golf with the local politicians at the famous Liberty National Golf Course across from the Statue of Liberty.

Dr. Cornaci nodded to Admiral Charko to begin.

"Mister President we ran a covert operation in North Korea which was successful but with slight implications. Operation Deception..."

Director Green interrupted Charko, "You mean serious implications, Admiral. Anything you do with North Korea could be very serious."

Charko continued, "Well, our operative..."

Now the president interrupted him. "Is this operative Mac Daniels?"

"Yes sir."

"It figures," said the president. "What did he do now? How many more innocent people did he kill this time? Don't tell me he started a war with the North."

"Mac and Haig are going to call in and give us a report to tell us what happened but..."

"Why can't this be done at Langley?" asked the president.

Dr. Cornaci answered, "He is somewhere in the Pacific, Mister President and Daniels doesn't come to Langley."

The President turned red and yelled, "What?! You're his boss, what do you mean he doesn't come to Langley?"

Charko volunteered, "Mister President, Daniels is somewhat of the legend at Langley but I don't think anyone, a very few, sir..." he thought for a moment, "perhaps five or six of us have ever met him. I know him as I recruited him."

"Don't tell me, Jon," said the president, "that you never met this criminal."

"I met him, Mister President," said Jon Cornaci. "Right before I came to Washington, Daniels came to my home in Jersey City. My wife Annemarie answered the doorbell and there he was. He introduced himself as a member of the World News Corporation and showed me his identification. He said he was there to interview me. Well, my wife made him a cup of coffee and he stayed for dinner. When my wife finally left us, he told me the truth. He also told me that I should improve my security. He told me he doesn't come to Langley and explained why. Honestly, Mister President, my wife and I found him quite charming."

The president was truly exasperated and shook his head. "I don't believe it. You entertained an assassin, a murderer, a criminal in your house."

"You know, Mister President," said Charko, "Daniels once managed to get into the White House and serve your predecessor breakfast in bed. He has his way of doing things. He's quite efficient and probably one of the most lethal people in the world. You should be glad he's on our side."

"I don't believe it," said the president. "I just don't believe it. This man should be in jail. Anyway, let's get on with it. What happened?"

Charko told the president the details of Operation Deception. He detailed the plan to purchase the uranium, the Korean switch from uranium to sand, and the switch back to uranium. He told him about the North Koreans trying to fake a plane crash. "The uranium," he said, "is being transferred to the Reagan where it will be secured until the Reagan comes to port." He also told the president about Daniels' discovery of the sarin chemicals and about finding Tanaka.

The president just sat there, stunned.

Maud Evens asked, "How do you plan to get the chemicals off the island? This is a sovereign country. You cannot send in a landing force."

Now the president jumped in. "No one will set one foot in a foreign country. We are going to notify the secretary of state and let him handle it through the appropriate diplomatic channels. We will do it properly."

Dr. Cornaci asked, "Mister President, I hope you don't think we would do it improperly."

"No Doctor, you wouldn't, but the military has a way of doing what it wants when it wants."

An aide interrupted the meeting and said the video-conference was about to begin. The president nodded and the screen came to life.

In the room on a large screen appeared Mac Daniels and Ron Haig. Haig spoke first.

"Surprised to see you, Mister President. Director Green, Miss Evens, Dr. Cornaci, Admiral thank you for taking the time on a Sunday for this call. I would like to give you our assessment on the situation. We feel that the operation was successful and the salvaging of the uranium is underway as we speak."

Director Green asked, "How are you explaining or intending to explain the fact that the uranium didn't show up in Cuba without implicating us?"

Now Mac Daniels answered. "We were supposed to transfer the uranium to one of our airplanes, fake a crash, and then return the body of the Cuban courier to Cuba, but now the plan is changed a little bit..."

The president interrupted, "The body of the Cuban courier?"

"Yes, Mister President, I had to kill him and we have his body in the refrigerator. We were going to soak it in the ocean for a while and then return it to the Cubans, but now we can't do that because of the real plane crash. I'm going to float a story about the crash of the Antonov somewhere over the trenches, which are so deep it cannot be salvaged. We will float the Cuban body and the body of one of the Korean pilots, which is still strapped into the sunken aircraft.

The Philippine Navy will hopefully find them and return them to their respective countries. The copilot unfortunately is truly missing."

The president asked, "Where is he?"

Daniels answered, "I really don't know. I threw him out of the plane before it crashed."

The president just shook his head. "How much money did this cost us?"

Daniels smiled, "That's the beauty of the operation, Mister President. I wired $50 million to the North Koreans to buy the uranium, but it was actually the Cubans' money, which they had received from various Middle Eastern countries."

"You gave the North Koreans $50 million?"

"Well, not really, Mister President," said Daniels. "I wired the money and gave Kim's people the account numbers. As soon as they opened the account to verify the funds, the pass code they used actually transferred the money and through various transfers around the world, it all ended up in the agency's account. I hope that North Koreans will be mad at the Cubans, the Cubans will be mad at the North Koreans, and the Middle Eastern countries will be mad at both of them—a perfect deception."

Director Green said, "Mac, if the North Koreans find out we were behind this it could set off a war."

"We have that covered, Director," replied Daniels. "World News Corporation will report the crash through its Philippine office. According to the story, the plane went down over the trenches. No one will ever be able to look for the uranium; it's much too deep. The nice part of this was the North Koreans were going to fake a crash anyway, so they're stuck with the story. They'll think that the Cuban put up a fight and the plane crashed. The pilot was shot and his body will confirm that. We'll drop some oil and debris in the water. Everyone will think it was lost, which is what we want. We've taken much of their uranium off the market. Believe me, there was enough of it to build a few nukes and plenty of dirty bombs, and we have their money."

The president nodded, but Daniels was not sure if it was a nod of agreement or disgust.

He continued, "There will be stories in the newspaper about Tanaka—hell, he'll be a hero in Japan and will end up on every talk show in the world. I'm sure he'll tell everyone about me. He won't talk about the sarin. He was ashamed of what he was going to do, and if he does talk, the sarin will be off the island. I gave him a false name. He thinks I'm a naval aviator who had an accident. The story will fly. No one should put two and two together. The trenches are far from the island."

"Did this cost us anything else?" questioned Director Green.

Well," said Daniels, "I also gave Kim himself—that little piss-ant piece of shit..."

Director Green spoke, "Mr. Daniels that language is inappropriate."

"Oh, I'm sorry Dr. Cornaci, I apologize."

The president fumed.

Daniels continued, "I actually handed that little"...catching himself, "leader a case with $10 million in hundred dollar bills, however, most of them were high-grade counterfeits laced with chemicals. Within several hours after he opens and exposes it to the air, it will start the chemical process to dissolve the paper. The next time he opens the case he'll find nothing but scraps of paper. He's going to be really pissed. Excuse me, upset, especially at the Cubans. Let's hope we've broken the Cuban-Korean relationship, at least for now."

"You seemed to have pulled it off, Daniels," said Director Green. "I sure hope so. Because the Reagan will be participating in the South Korean war games. Kim sees that as a threat and if he ever ties us in to losing the uranium and the money, well, God knows what he'll do."

"What about the sarin chemicals?" asked Haig.

"I'm ordering the secretary of state to run it through diplomatic channels. We don't need you to be involved," said the president.

"Why, the secretary of state?" asked Daniels. "We're here now. We could land a few Seahawks with a couple of dozen Marines, load the chemicals, and be off before anybody knows it. We don't need this stuff falling into the wrong hands, Mister President."

"That's just it, Daniels. You break the law and you're not doing it under my watch. This is a sovereign country and we're going to respect the sovereignty. We're going to allow them to remove it. It is not our problem. Do you understand? This is an order from your commander-in-chief."

"Yes, sir."

The connection went black on the president and his aides. Daniels looked at Haig, "It's not our problem now, but it will be. Mark my words, Ron. Fuck this. I have to call Astrid."

Haig knew Daniels was right, but this was an order directly from the president.

Back in the Situation Room, the President stood up and started to leave, and then he turned and asked, "How is Daniels going to get the World News Corporation to cooperate?"

"The World News Corporation is owned by Astrid Reed. Astrid Reed, Mister President is Mac Daniels' significant other," said Charko.

"It figures."

CHAPTER 7

ATLANTA, GEORGIA

NEXT DAY

The World News Corporation building stood proudly overlooking downtown Atlanta. All of Atlanta was looking up at its eighty stories of mirrored glass and steel. The reflection of the sun made the building look like a burning flare. World News provided information to hundreds of millions of people around the world through its films, radio, newspapers, magazines, Internet, television, cellular phones, and cable television. The crown jewel of the World News was its popular cable television channel, Wolf News. At the helm of this electronic information conglomerate was Astrid Reed, the chief executive officer and majority stockholder, making her one of the richest women in the world.

After Astrid had finished her master's degree at Harvard, she went to work for the company, learning every aspect of the business. By the time she was twenty-nine, Astrid was first executive vice-president, reporting directly to her father, Harrison Reed, the founder of the company. Her mother had died when Astrid was only three. Spending her life at her father's knee, she was always learning. After his sudden death in Hong Kong, Astrid assumed the mantle of power and took over. The board of directors knew immediately that she was her father's daughter. A bunch of stuffed white shirts could not bully Astrid. Well qualified, smart, and creative, she was also a real beauty. Fair skinned, not a blemish or freckle, Astrid's skin was soft and smooth as silk. Her flaming red hair cascaded over her face, which made her deep emerald green eyes seem larger than they were. At five-foot-seven, with long legs, Astrid had a perfect shape, and she worked hard to keep it, working out every day in her private gym with her personal trainer.

Astrid's penthouse apartment was part of her office suite. A workaholic, she would stay in her office apartment rather than go home at night. Showering, she dressed in blue jeans, a light-blue, button-down shirt and running shoes, looking more like a delivery person than a chief executive. Pulling her hair up and clipping it off her shoulders, she was ready for work. Glancing at the clock at exactly seven, right on time, her phone buzzed.

She picked it up. "Yes, Viv, I'll be right there. Put the coffee on."

Vivian Berkstrom was Astrid's executive assistant and the mother she'd never known. When her husband died, Harrison Reed hired her as a nanny for Astrid. Astrid never knew it, but Vivian reminded Harrison Reed of her mother in looks and manner. Since Vivian's grown children were living in different states, when she was staying over in the apartment, she was in at seven and left at seven, never complaining about the hours or the stress. Astrid could count on her to be there. Astrid loved Viv and the feeling was mutual.

Astrid stepped off her private elevator into her private office. Her elevator made only five stops; the basement parking garage, the lobby, her office on the seventy-ninth floor, her apartment on the eightieth floor, and the heliport on the roof. The elevator worked only by thumbprints; Mac Daniels's and hers.

Astrid had a corner office. Two walls were floor to ceiling glass. The wall across from her desk held several large, flat-screen televisions, all on different news channels. One of the giant screens was a computer display. Surrounding the televisions' screens was a collage of photos of Astrid with the world's famous people: kings, queens, presidents, and movie stars. On her large U-shaped desk, there were two phones; one for business and the other a special encrypted satellite phone to which very few people had the number, besides Daniels. When the bat phone, as Viv called it, rang, it was always Mac. Behind Astrid's desk was a credenza covered with pictures of Astrid and Mac. No one but Vivian came into her private office. Astrid held her business meetings in the many conference rooms. Her relationship with Mac was special and she needed her privacy. If she admitted others to her office, any one of them would easily know that Mac was her "someone special."

Astrid flopped on her couch, her feet up on the coffee table, and Viv handed her some coffee. Astrid took a sniff of the aroma and sipped the hot brew. "I'm now ready."

"Before we start, Missy," said Viv, giving her the look only a disapproving mother can give, "button your shirt before you fall out. I don't have to sit here looking at your, what's the word, ladies."

"Oops," said Astrid buttoning her shirt. "That was an accident. But that's not fair. When Mac is here you don't tell him to button up."

"Honey when he's here he can sit around naked. Oh my God, I don't believe I said that."

"I'm going to tell him what you said."

"Don't you dare. By the way, have you heard from him?"

"No, but I will, I just know I will. Let's get to the day's schedule."

The phone rang, and Viv looked, over to the ringing, "It's the bat..."

Before she finished Astrid was at her desk and picked it up on the second ring. "Mac?"

"Who else, babe?"

"Well, it could have been John or Harry or Peter or Paul..."

"You need a good spanking. Only trouble is you would like it."

"Ok, just Peter or Paul. How are you, sweetheart?" she asked. "How did it go? Please tell me you're all right—no new scars, marks, or bullet holes."

"I'm great, Astrid. Safe and sound. Mission somewhat accomplished."

"Can you tell me where you are?"

"Somewhere in the South Pacific. I need you to do something for me, and if you can pull it off I can get home real soon."

"You're trying to bribe me and it's working. What do you need? Never mind, what do you want? No, ignore that question too. I know the answer to those questions. What is it, Mac?"

He told her what he could about the plane going down and about his finding the island and Tanaka. He did not disclose to her anything about the uranium, but he wanted a story on all the news outlets, especially about the plane crashing over the trenches. He stressed it had to be from the Philippines office from an undisclosed but reliable source. There should be no mention of the United States. She understood. This was not the first time she'd provided cover for him. She asked questions about Tanaka, and he told her to send him a number of someone in the Philippines' office, and that when Tanaka was on the way, he would call and give the person a heads-up but no other information.

"You'll be the first one to get pictures and a story."

"Hell with the story, when will I see you, Mac?"

"Somebody is horny. How about I send you some glossy eight by tens of me in living color."

"I don't need to see your shortcomings, darling."

"Nobody likes a wise ass, Astrid."

"You love my ass."

"That's beside the point."

"You want to roll on my ass?"

"Why not, as long as I can play farmer and plow your field. Better yet, how about brunch and you're the buffet table?"

"This is turning into phone sex."

"I know and I'm getting a woody here on a ship. This is not good."

Then speaking loudly so Viv could hear, Astrid said, "By the way, sweetheart, Viv would like to see you naked. Honest to God that's what she said."

Viv's face turned red.

"At least somebody appreciates me."

"When are you coming home? I miss you."

"Babe, you have no idea how I miss you. I should be out of here in a few days. What would you like to do?"

"I want to go someplace hot where we can do nothing. I mean it, sweetheart, I want to do nothing."

"Ok, Astrid, you got it."

"I'm going to call Lexye and see what she can do for us," said Astrid, referring to her travel agent and friend, who made discreet and private travel plans for the couple.

"Let me know and I'll be there, Astrid. I'm reachable on my cell. I'm looking forward to sitting by the pool, making love, drinking vodka punch, making love, drinking vodka punch, going out to some great restaurants, making love, and going to sleep and then starting all over again. No phone, no Ron Haig, just the two of us doing nothing."

"Do you mean you want to get me drunk and just have sex with me?"

"You're so romantic, Astrid. How could you say such a thing? What would ever give you such an idea?"

"You're a sailor and I know what you're thinking, Mr. Daniels, but you know I love you and it sounds great, doing nothing, just lying by the pool with you. I need a good rest and I'm sure you do too. Mac, this girl is in love with you."

"Call you when I get stateside. Astrid, you are my first thought and last thought, always. I promise we'll spend a few days doing nothing. Love you, babe."

CHAPTER 8

ONBOARD USS RONALD REAGAN

NEXT DAY

Haig was standing on the tower outside of the primary flight control center run by the air boss. Daniels appeared and handed him a mug of coffee.

"You look a hell of a lot better now that you've shaved," said Haig.

"Feel a lot better, too. The beard made me want to scratch, but those blue-colored contact lenses were hard to take. In a day or two, the dye should wear off and my skin should be back to normal. It was a bitch getting the latex prints off," Daniels said, holding up his fingertips.

"I'm sure glad I had them, though. They must have printed everything I touched. It's a wonder they didn't print my dick. Astrid would be embarrassed," he said laughing at his own joke.

Haig shook his head.

"I'm anxious to get out of here. Maybe I can grab a flight to Guam and from there to Hawaii and then a flight back home. Looking forward to putting my prints on her..." He didn't finish the sentence. "By the way, how did the sub-lieutenant do?"

Haig told him that Tanaka had been given the royal tour of the ship. "The crew got him some shoes; they cleaned and repaired his uniform, polished his sword, and shined his brass. He looked like he just stepped out of a time machine. The captain showed him television and he spoke to the Japanese prime minister. They're going to give him a parade and a lot of back pay."

"Well, I'm sure in some of his interviews he'll mention us. When did he leave the ship? I was so tired last night—slept like a baby."

"They flew him home early this morning. He couldn't believe he was flying in a plane without a propeller."

"How are the news stories going?"

"Astrid did a good job. Plenty of news about the plane crash near the Mariana trenches. I just hope the little leader up in North Korea buys it, otherwise there'll be hell to pay."

"Did we get all the uranium?" asked Daniels.

"Yes, it was an easy job. The plane was only forty feet down. It's all safely stored on board."

"What about the plane?"

"It was dragged off by the helicopters and dropped in some deep water. The Philippine Navy found two bodies, which we conveniently dropped in front of them. The bodies are being returned to Korea and Cuba. So far so good."

"What's going on with the sarin?"

"The captain said it was still lethal when the components were mixed. The bomb squad threw one of the bomblets and when it landed, it broke open and the gas escaped. Thankfully it was vented off the ship. Regarding the removal, the last message I had from Admiral Charko was that the secretary of state will be contacting the president of Palau, who will have to deal with it and have the chemicals destroyed."

"Who's running the operation?"

"Don't know, Mac. We should be running this, but we take orders." Haig saw the look on Daniels' face and corrected himself. "I take orders, you take suggestions."

"Mark my words, some asshole will fuck this up and we'll be back looking for the sarin.

CHAPTER 9

WASHINGTON D.C.

SAME DAY

The Department of State is located in the Harry S. Truman Building. The Truman Building is located in the Foggy Bottom neighborhood at 2201 C Street, NW, a few blocks away from the White House. In his seventh floor office, Secretary of State Terrance Hertz had just hung up with the president. He turned and faced Senator John Bartlett IV, an American blueblood who happened to be the chairman of the United States Senate Select Committee on Intelligence (sometimes referred to as the Intelligence Committee or SSCI). The committee is dedicated to overseeing the United States Intelligence Community—the agencies and bureaus of the federal government of the United States that provide information and analysis for leaders of the executive and legislative branches. The senator had heard only one side of the conversation, but he'd heard enough to raise his interest.

"Terry, what was that all about, if you don't mind me asking? Sarin gas? Who is this president you were talking about? I don't believe I'm familiar with that particular president or his country. Where the fuck is it? What's this all about?"

"Well, John, it seems a navy pilot crashed and made his way to some remote and apparently deserted island. Along with the chemicals to produce sarin gas, the pilot found a Japanese soldier who was still fighting the war. The president didn't want us to send in a landing force to remove the chemicals, as it might be perceived as an unauthorized intrusion, so I'm going to call the president of Palau and tell him what our pilot found on one of his islands. I will offer to help. By the way John, the information came from the CIA."

"The CIA? What were they doing there?"

"Be damned if I know, John. That's more your area than mine."

"I saw something on the World News Cable," said the senator, "about the Japanese soldier. Some story, all those years waiting for orders..."

The secretary interrupted him, "Waiting for orders to gas MacArthur and whatever else they could hit. Thank God they never received the orders to gas us."

The senator thought for a moment. His eyes narrowed and he raised his eyebrows. "Why didn't the CIA pick the sarin up?"

"John," said Terrance Hertz as he poured two shots of Jack Daniels straight up and handed one to the senator, "it was the CIA that brought this to the president. Dr. Cornaci had the smarts not to step onto the island without getting presidential clearance. The president has no confidence in the CIA. He thinks the National Clandestine Service, especially the Special Activities Division, is a bunch of thugs, and I am inclined to agree with him. That's why I was going to call the president of Palau."

"Holy shit, none of this came before my committee," he commented. "Why?"

"Believe it or not John, it just happened."

"I'm going to look into this."

The senator took out his cell phone, calling his chief of staff, Dick Edwards. Edwards answered on the second ring. "Yes, sir."

"Dick, I want to follow up on some sarin gas found on the island of Palau. I also want to talk with Dr. Cornaci about the CIA's involvement in this sarin gas. Why didn't the navy report this up the chain through naval intelligence? Why wasn't General Bellardi or his chief of staff Colonel Starges in on this?" he asked referring to Lieutenant General Tony Bellardi, the director of the Defense Intelligence Agency (DIA), the military's version of the CIA.

"I don't know the answer to your questions, Senator," said Edwards, "but I'll find out. I heard the news about a Japanese officer who had been on the island, but nothing came across my desk about sarin or the CIA. I'll look into this and report. Give me a few days."

"Do whatever you have to do. Something smells, Dick."

"Should I pay a visit to Langley?"

The senator replied, "If you think so, then do it. God damn, I hate those sons of bitches at the CIA. There nothing but trouble makers."

Turning to the secretary of state, he said, "Terry, do me a favor. Hold off that call for a day or two. I want Dick Edwards to look into this."

Secretary Terrance Hertz never missed a chance to kiss the ass of a powerful senator of his own party. He was considering running for his party's nomination for the presidency and it would pay to have John Bartlett IV and his millions of dollars in his campaign war chest. Looking at his watch, he said, "Well, it's the middle of the night there and the sarin sat there all this time, I guess a few more days won't hurt."

■ ■ ■

Dick Edwards had been the senator's right hand for more than ten years. This position gave him the ability to gather much information, and he needed to keep his boss in the know. Knowledge is power, especially in Washington. Many in the nation's capital suspected that Edwards was the brains in the office. Senator John Bartlett IV was a master politician, glad handing, kissing babies, and at the right time kissing the president's ass, but a senior senator serving four terms did not have to be smart, he needed to hire smart and that was what Dick Edward was … smart.

Something bothered Edwards, besides the fact that his boss had it out for the CIA and would take any opportunity to embarrass them. If the senator had his way, he would merge the agency into the FBI; nevertheless, Edwards thought, *What is the CIA doing and how do they know about the sarin on Palau? There's no reason for them to be there, especially on a deserted island. Who is this pilot who happened to find this island and why isn't this a navy matter?* The senator was right, something smelled.

CHAPTER 10

INDONESIA

SAME DAY

The cell phone rang, and Amr Ibn Taher at first thought it was his alarm. His hand crawled across the small bedside table, finally finding the phone. When he flipped the phone open, the glow lit up the dark room. Rubbing his eyes, he saw it was five o'clock in the morning. The satellite-encrypted phone identified the call as restricted.

"Who is this?" demanded Amr.

"Allāhu Akbar," the voice said.

"Allāhu Akbar," replied Amr. "But who is this?"

"Aswas Rajul."

Amr Ibn Taher bolted up in his bed. The name brought him to attention. No one knew his real name; they just called him Aswas Rajul. It was Arabic for "brave man." Legend had it that Osama bin Laden had named him. He had been one of the few who'd had direct access to bin Laden and had been on the way to bin Laden's compound when the Americans attacked. He'd seen it all.

Amr Ibn Taher was born in Al-Ahsa, the largest governorate in Saudi Arabia's Eastern Province, in the biggest city of the governorate, also called Al-Ahsa. For many years, he had fought against infidels coming to the Holy Land—the birthplace of the prophet. Bin Laden had recruited Amr and he had been with him in Afghanistan, fighting the Russians. When he returned to Saudi Arabia to recruit more freedom fighters, bin Laden introduced Amr to Aswas Rajul and ever since that day, he'd been taking orders from Aswas Rajul.

Amr was in Indonesia recruiting young extremists to join Al Qaeda. He needed to recruit loyal followers who would follow him to death and go back to Afghanistan with him for further training. Amr had not received the full plan from Aswas, but knew that if necessary, he would die a martyr's death in the name of Allah.

"Do you know the Island of Palau?" asked Aswas Rajul.

"Yes, it is a small island several hundred miles from here. It's where the Japanese soldier was."

"My sources tell me the Americans found sarin bombs. For some reason they have not notified the authorities on Palau. We have to act quickly. I want some of those bombs and we may only have a few days. Take the next flight to Palau and take a room at Palau Royal Resort in Koror. The hotel has a marina, so rent a boat and get over to the island. I will text you the coordinates of the island for your GPS. Do whatever you have to do but get me those bombs. I will meet you at the hotel in a few days. Use any of the passports and credit cards you were given except the one with your real name."

"I will be on the next flight."

"I want those sarin bombs," said Aswas Rajul.

"For use against the Americans?"

"We will see. We will see."

CHAPTER 11

PYONGYANG, NORTH KOREA

TWO DAYS LATER

Kim Jong Un became the leader of North Korea in 2011, having inherited his position from his father Kim Jong-il. His life and even his birth date and early childhood are shrouded in mystery. Just as secretive is his marriage to Ri Sol-ju, who, according to intelligence reports, has been tentatively identified as Hyon Song-wol, a former singer for the Pochonbo Electronic Ensemble, a musical group popular in North Korea. In 2012, Ri made several public appearances standing next to Kim Jong-un, causing speculation about who she might be. On 25 July 2012, North Korean state media announced that she was actually Kim's wife, saying she was "his wife, Comrade Ri Sol Ju."

Ri Sol Ju is a petite, pretty woman with short black hair and dark eyes who often wears Western-style dress. She is college educated and has a degree in science. Her father is a university professor and her mother a doctor. While she has all the trappings of a modern day woman, she knew that when her husband was upset, it was time for her to assume the traditional Korean role of a submissive woman, and today the Supreme Leader was very upset.

She followed him as they walked in silence from Ryongsong Residence, the main residence located in the Ryongsong District of Pyongyang. An underground tunnel connected the residence to the national headquarters. From the residence to the headquarters was a seven-minute walk. The Supreme Leader's hands were folded behind his back and his head was bowed as he walked toward the elevator.

The national headquarters building was only four stories high. The tunnel running beneath it was four stories below the ground. Kim and his wife stepped into the elevator and quickly rose to the top floor opening into the Supreme Leader's spacious office. Waiting for him was General Cheon Won-hong, the minister of the State Security Department of North Korea. This was an autonomous agency of the North Korean government reporting directly to the Supreme Leader. It was established in 1973 and served as the secret police of North Korea. It also was involved in the operation of North Korea's concentration camps and various other hidden activities. It was reputed to be one of the most brutal secret police forces in the world and has been involved in numerous human rights abuses.

Cheon Won-hong hopped to attention as the elevator doors slid open. He bowed his head as Kim paraded across the office to take his seat behind a large wooden desk. Ri Sol Ju took a seat to his side.

"Do you have a report?" asked the Supreme Leader.

"I do, sir."

There was silence in the room. Kim's wife spoke. "Minister Cheon," she asked, "what is your report."

Minister Cheon began, "Our agents in Cuba had access to the autopsy report, and Miguel Antonio Ricardo was dead before his body was in the water. No water was found in his lungs. We took copies of his fingerprints and they match the fingerprints we had here on file. There is no doubt that the man who met with you is the Cuban agent and he died in the airplane crash. Our doctors did an autopsy on the pilot, who died of gunshot wounds. The body of the copilot has not been found. It appears that Ricardo put up a fight during the flight. The pilot and most probably the copilot were shot and then the plane crashed, killing Ricardo. The depth of the water prohibits any type of recovery."

Kim didn't say anything, just opened the drawer of his desk and took out a bottle of Johnny Walker, his favorite drink. He took out two glasses, filled the glasses, and nodded to Minister Cheon to pick one up.

The minister wondered if this was poison.

Supreme Leader smiled. "Drink," he said.

Minister Cheon took a swallow. It tasted good and then he took another sip. The Supreme Leader took a large swallow and put the glass down. Minister Cheon felt a sigh of relief.

Finally, the Supreme Leader spoke, "I am glad the water is too deep for recovery. What will the Cubans do about the fact that the uranium was not delivered?"

"I am told they want their money back. They took money from the Middle Eastern countries. Since uranium wasn't delivered, they feel the money should be returned and returned quickly."

Kim started to laugh, his wife joined in, and soon all three were laughing. Through the laughter Kim said, "Let them dive for it. If they want, we can sell them some more sand at a discount. We have plenty of sand for them."

"Supreme Leader, the Americans and the South Koreans are going to start war games right in our backyard. The Reagan, with its battle group, will be conducting flights in the area. What are your instructions?"

Kim thought for a moment, weighing his options. "Let's fire a couple Nodongs," he said, referring to a missile in the North Korean arsenal.

"Where should we fire them, or at what?"

Supreme Leader took another drink, tapped his fingers on the desk, and asked, "Do you think the Americans had anything to do with the crash of our plane?"

"I don't think so, sir. I really don't, and if they did what would they have gotten—buckets full of sand?"

"Make an announcement that we are going to test our missiles. This should keep the Americans away from our borders. After all, they don't think we have accurate technology and would worry that a missile could accidentally hit their aircraft carrier. Accidentally on purpose." He started to laugh again.

CHAPTER 12

KOROR, PALAU,
THE PALAU ROYAL RESORT

ONE WEEK LATER

Aswas Rajul sat on the balcony of his hotel room. He was transfixed by the ocean as the waves gently rolled up to the beach. It was so soothing. He led a double life and both were hectic and uncertain. He relished these few moments.

"Rajul, Rajul," said Amr Ibn Taher, snapping him out of his trance.

"I'm sorry Amr, I was lost in thought."

"What are we going to do with the little sarin bombs? They are like hand grenades. Use them in our fight against the Americans?"

"Yes and no, but are the crates hidden safely?"

"I do not understand yes and no. I think it is your Western upbringing when you talk. My answer is just, yes. When I was on the island, I found a cave. The door was open so I hid the crates in the cave. The cave was filled with guns, bullets, and a lot of stuff from the war. Japanese must have built the cave for storage. When I closed the hatch cover, it became impossible to detect. When do you want me to go back to the island and get the gas?"

Rajul smiled. "Yes, they will be used in the fight for Islam but not by us—by ISIS. We cannot beat the Americans with military might. Do you know who has the largest air force? The Americans. Do you know who has the second largest air force? The American Navy and Marine Corps. Do you know who has the nuclear submarines armed with missiles? The Americans. You want to fight them?"

"But why am I recruiting? What are we doing?"

"The way to defeat the American is economic downfall and a revolt from within. When Americans cannot get food or gas, then we will win. There is a plan, but it is not our time yet. Before Bin Laden was martyred, he put together a master plan with what they call cutouts. When I need money to fund the operation there is a procedure I follow and the money comes. I do not know who sends it, but it arrives. Be patient, my friend, be patient."

Rajul took out his smart phone and started to do a search. "Here it is," he said. "I have made arrangements for you to be picked up. In two days, a ship with a captain friendly to us will be stopping at these coordinates." He showed Amr the cell phone. On the screen were the coordinates. 7°30'35.1"N, 133°28'09.0"E

"Where is this?"

"It is about one hundred miles east of Palau, and due east of the Philippines, in the Sea of the Philippines. You cannot return to Palau with the gas. It is too risky. The nearest country to Palau is the State of Yap, part of Micronesia. It's about 500 miles from here. You will not make it. I will send you the coordinates; plug it into your GPS. You will meet the ship and the captain will take the cargo on board. You will return here and then catch a flight to Pakistan. The ship will travel on to North Korea and eventually back to its home port in Syria."

"What is the name of the ship?"

"The Sails of Allah."

They both sat there for a few minutes saying nothing. Finally, Rajul got up and said, "I'm leaving. If you need me, use the satellite phone. You shouldn't have any trouble. Everything is paid for. It is critical that you meet the ship.

"Allah be praised."

"Allāhu Akbar."

CHAPTER 13

OCEAN BEACH HOTEL, MIAMI FLORIDA

SEVERAL DAYS LATER

Mac Daniels had flown from the Reagan, to Guam, to San Francisco, and finally on to Miami, Florida where he met Astrid. Lexye had arranged for a suite at the Ocean Beach Hotel in the South Beach area of Miami. Both of them sat by the pool and as Mac had promised, his cell phone was off, upstairs in the room safe, locked away, and Astrid had the combination.

Lying side by side on a large, two-person lounge with a large pitcher of vodka punch, Mac was dozing off and on, and Astrid had her nose in a novel and was sipping her drink. Other than lying by the pool and going out for dinner, for the past three days they'd done nothing. This was what Astrid wanted to do—absolutely nothing. She needed this rest and she knew that Mac did, too. Only he was too stubborn to admit it.

"Mac, did I tell you that Aunt Sarah is coming over? I invited her for a few days. I have her in the room next to ours."

This woke up Mac immediately. He sat up, looked at her and said, "You're kidding me?"

"No, darling, how can we come to Florida and not see Aunt Sarah?"

Mac's mother and Sarah Gaccione were sisters. Sarah and Marie Daniels' maiden name was Bellardi. General Anthony Bellardi was their brother, Mac's uncle. Sarah was the oldest, and then Tony, followed by Marie. Sarah had retired to Florida with her late husband Jerry. It was unfortunate that Jerry had passed away in the early years of their retirement. She called Naples, Florida her home.

Sarah was seventy but didn't have a wrinkle on her face, nor for that matter did Marie or Tony. Mac teased his father that the lack of olive oil gave him the wrinkled look. Mac favored his Italian ethnicity with his dark eyes and dark complexion. His

Irish ancestry gave him his chiseled features. Sarah was the family matriarch, the family psychologist, and the family advisor on all matters pertaining to love.

"There goes my sex life," groaned Daniels as he lay back and closed his eyes.

Astrid was a little tipsy and she leaned over, stuck her tongue in his ear, and pinched his nipple.

"Ouch."

"I never say ouch." She ran her hand down his stomach and slipped a few fingers under the top of his bathing suit.

He grabbed her hand. "Come on," he said, "if this is the last time I'm going to get laid, let's do it right."

"This should be a new experience."

Mac opened the door to the room, and Astrid stepped in first. He turned to the lock and double bolted the door. As he did, she pulled down his bathing suit. He turned to face her, but she was down on her knees and took him into her mouth.

He reached down and lifted her up, "I said I wanted to get laid." Daniels carried her over to the bed, gently placed her down, and untied her bikini top and then the bottom. Their bodies locked into each other's arms, and their tongues explored each other's mouths.

He rolled her over onto her back, started to kiss and lick her neck, her breasts, her nipples, and licked, and kissed his way down, until he was entrenched between her open legs. He ran his tongue down each side of her groin, exploring her. She was warm, wet and moaning. She began to hold her breath, until she couldn't hold it any longer and let out a scream, "Oh, God. Oh, my God."

She was well-tanned and the contrast with her white lines turned him on. It was a picture of perfection. He didn't stop.

"Oh God, oh God, oh, my God," she said over and over then screaming, "My love." Almost exhausted and wet with perspiration, she pulled him to her, held him and in a whisper said, "I had an out of body experience."

He smiled at her, "I'm not done with you."

"You're right. I want to do something to you," she said, breathing hard.

"I can't say no to that."

She took her bikini top, tied it around his right wrist and tied it to the bedpost, then took the bikini bottom, tied it around his left wrist and tied it to the other bedpost. She squatted over him and let her body down and onto his. No part of her body touched his except for the penetration, and slowly she moved up and down, up and down and occasionally, her ass hit his thighs. Finally, she began to lose control and began to move faster, harder, pounding away. She could not stay off his body; she dropped down onto him and screamed as her body shuddered. Mac tried to get his arms free to hold her but he couldn't. Finally, she let out another scream and fell forward, her swollen nipple in his mouth. He made the last thrust upward and joined her in total ecstasy. They lay there, her arms around him, holding on to him for dear life. She did not want to let go.

"Untie me so I can hold you," he said.

"No. I like it this way. I am finally in control."

"You are always in control."

She stayed on top of him, holding him, their bodies still connected. They stayed like that, and neither moved. Finally, the phone rang. After several rings, Astrid slowly reached across the bed to answer it. "Yes, fine, no problem. Thank you."

"What was that?" asked Daniels.

"It's the front desk. Aunt Sarah is coming up."

"Oh shit."

Astrid pulled the sheet up over Mac leaving him tied to the bedpost. She took a towel from the bathroom and wrapped it around herself.

"Untie me Astrid. Astrid, don't fool around. I don't want to rip your suit."

"Don't tell me you're modest. You're covered."

The doorbell rang Astrid went to open it. Daniels wiggled his hands trying to get free and then he heard Sarah's voice, "Darling, so good to see you. How are you my love? Where's my nephew?"

"This way, Aunt Sarah."

Sarah stood by the bed looking at Mac tied to the bedpost covered in the sheet. She started to laugh. "Do you always make love with Mac tied to the bed, Astrid?"

"Only when I need to keep him under control. You know how these horny sailors are."

"Aunt Sarah, I have been tied here for three days, help me." Mac managed to get his hands finally free, grabbed the towel, and gave it a yank, causing Astrid to turn toward him, displaying her bare ass to Aunt Sarah.

Sarah looked. "Nice tan. I think I'll go to my room and let you two get dressed so we can go out for dinner." She laughed all the way out the door.

Mac grabbed Astrid, pulled her down across his lap, and was about to give her a playful slap when the phone rang. This time Mac answered. "Yes, Aunt Sarah?" There was silence on the other end.

"Mac, it's Ron. Why didn't you answer your cell?"

"Because Astrid locked it in the safe. Ron, my hands are full," he said as he patted her ass. "Why the call? Remember I'm on leave."

"The director wanted me to tell you that the twenty-four cases of sarin have been safely removed and destroyed."

"Ron, there were thirty cases."

"Are you sure?" He hesitated, and then he continued, "I'm sorry. If you said there were thirty cases, there were thirty cases."

"What about the munitions in the cave?"

Haig looked over the manifest. "I don't see any munitions on the manifest, Mac."

"Fuck! Ron, there were cases of arms, bullets, and various ordinance. They were in a cave. I left the trap door open. No one could have missed it. Someone fucked up."

"What cave, Mac?"

Mac let out a sigh. "You know, Ron, I am going to enjoy my time off. I'm here with a beautiful woman. I'm going to have a nice dinner with her and my Aunt Sarah. I have an idea; let the president straighten it out. I'll call you tomorrow."

"Mac?" The line was dead.

Haig thought for a second. He knew Mac was right. In fact, Mac had warned them. But there are some things that were just out of your control.

■ ■ ■

Sarah, Astrid, and Mac went to a little Italian restaurant in South Beach, walking distance from the hotel. Astrid and Sarah talked the evening away, catching up, two friends having a good time. Mac sat there smiling at them and enjoying the evening but his mind was elsewhere. Six cases of sarin were missing. He assumed the worst. Someone had gotten them and he knew they were going to use them—most likely in the United States.

After dinner, they walked back to the hotel together, stopping for a gelato. Sarah's room was right next door to Mac and Astrid's. She entered her room, and turning she said, "Keep it down in there. I need my beauty rest."

Astrid and Mac were standing on the balcony wearing the hotel robes and enjoying the evening. The moon was low in the sky making the ocean glimmer. "It was a great dinner honey," said Astrid. "I know you were trying to enjoy it but you were far away. I know that look, Mac."

"You know me too well," he said, smiling at her. He knew she was right. He was far away; his mind was on the other side in the world on the island of Palau. *What happened to those fucking cases,* he thought?

"I have an idea," Astrid said, "let's go to Palau. I'm sure they have a wonderful hotel on one of those islands and we can pick up our vacation and you can go check on your cases of sarin."

He turned toward her, pulling her close, and sliding his hands under her robe. "You're not wearing underwear," he said.

She pulled the cord on his robe. "Neither are you."

Their robes fell to the floor. They kissed. He picked her up and carried her to bed. "I thought Aunt Sarah said to keep it down."

"It's more fun to keep it up, sweetheart," Astrid said with a smile.

"Did I tell you I love you?"

"Yes, but you can say it again. Mac, how do they say 'I love you' on Palau?"

He smiled. "They say, I love you."

She rolled her eyes and shook her head. "You're an ass. But I love you."

CHAPTER 14

THE DESERTED ISLAND

TWO DAYS LATER

The Gulfstream G650's two Rolls-Royce engines, each producing a maximum thrust of 17,000 pounds-force, allowed the aircraft to cruise at a speed of 650 miles per hour at fifty thousand feet. Its top speed was 710 miles per hour; almost supersonic. From Miami to Babelthuap is 9,200 air miles and the G650 had a range of 8,000, so they put down in Hawaii for a refueling. It was now on its landing approach to the Roman Tmetuchl International Airport on Babelthuap Island, Palau. Astrid looked over and Mac was sound asleep in the recliner. She was amazed at how he could sleep on the plane. It was time to wake him. She leaned over and kissed him gently on the lips. A big smile came across his face.

"You want to fool around now?"

"It's time to get up."

"I am, babe."

Astrid shook her head and rolled her eyes. "We'll be landing soon."

"You're no fun."

Ground control directed the Gulfstream to park on the tarmac by the General Aviation hanger. Two custom agents came on board to check the passports. One agent went up to the cockpit to clear the flight crew, and the other agent went to deal with Astrid and Daniels. Astrid handed her passport to the agent, who looked at it, studied the picture, and looked at her face.

He asked, "What is the purpose of your visit?"

Astrid replied, "Vacation. I'm here to enjoy the beach and the sea."

The agent turned to Daniels, who handed him his passport. The agent repeated the ritual of studying the passport and looking at Daniels' face.

"What is the purpose of your visit here, Mr. Mac Arthur?"

"Vacation and a little rest and relaxation."

The agent handed the passports back to Astrid and Daniels. "Welcome to Palau. You should have wonderful weather, enjoy yourselves."

After clearing customs, Mac rented a car and drove to Koror where they had a room at the Palau Royal Resort. They were on the top floor; a corner room with a balcony overlooking the ocean. The bedroom had two double beds.

"Which one do you want, Astrid?" asked Mac.

"The one you're in."

Astrid had once confided to Sarah that she always felt safe sleeping in Mac's arms. She would put her head on his chest, her leg over his, and his arms around her. It was a good feeling and this is the way she fell asleep.

"What do you want to do, Mac?" she asked.

He gave her a look, and then smiled. "How about a boat ride?"

"A boat ride? That's not what I expected from you. Sounds good. Let's do it."

They changed into their bathing suits, tee shirts, and running shoes. Astrid had a beach bag and Mac gave her his Ka-Bar, a knife, with a seven-inch carbon steel clip point and leather-washer handle.

The United States Marine Corps first adopted the Ka-Bar in November 1942 as the combat knife. Many SEALS carry the SOG SEAL 2000 but when Mac had completed his SEAL training, his Uncle Tony had given him his Ka-Bar.

She was about to ask him if it was necessary, but then thought better of it and put it in her bag without comment. There was no use. He loved that knife. She knew there were several things a SEAL never left home without; one was his knife and the other was his dick.

The hotel concierge arranged for a boat rental. At the marina there was a thirty-foot Scarab, outboard, center console, with twin engine Yamaha F-300, XCA sport-fishing boat waiting for them. Each engine put out 300 horsepower, which could push the Scarab over sixty miles per hour.

The rental agent gave them the walk around and the details on the boat. Astrid took the helm and Mac cast off the lines. Astrid navigated out of the slip through the marina and out into the ocean. Mac took a seat next to her. She pushed the throttles forward and the Scarab planed out and was soon doing fifty miles per hour. She had a GPS setting in her phone and set course for the deserted island. Mac spent his summers at the New Jersey shore so boats were second nature to him. Astrid was not a boater until she'd met Mac and with a few lessons, she'd taken to it like a duck to water. Over the years, she had perfected her skills and could handle most any pleasure craft. Most of the time Mac just sat back and enjoyed the ride.

Two hours later, the island came into view. Astrid cut the power. They were about twenty feet off the shore. The depth gauge read five feet. "It's getting shallow Mac."

Mac walked up to the bow and peered over. "There's a reef. Circle the island so I can find the spot where I came onto the island."

Astrid maneuvered the boat into the wind and moved south along the beach. Mac saw the place where he first came ashore. "Over there, Astrid," he yelled.

Astrid piloted the boat a little farther south then turned in to the island. As she got close to the beach she cut the power and raised the engines to get the props out of the water and the boat beached itself. Mac jumped over the side and took the anchor, dragging it onto the beach. Astrid jumped over the side and followed him ashore.

"Here," she said, handing him his Ka-Bar.

"Thanks, Babe," he said as he tucked the sheath into his waistband of his bathing suit. He stood there for a few seconds, then he started for the jungle. "Astrid, are you coming?"

"Be right there." Astrid looked around the beach and something caught her eye. "Go ahead, Mac, I'll catch up with you."

Mac moved down the runway. The Mitsubishi was gone. He could see that it had been dragged toward the other side of the island. The sarin crates were gone. He knew that and it was expected. He wanted to check out the hidden cave. He stood there looking, trying to find the spot that Tanaka had found so easily. He walked the area, dragging his feet through the palm fronds.

"You looked like a little boy playing in the leaves," Astrid said as she walked up the runway.

"Join me. I need a little help."

"Sure, but what are we doing?"

"We're looking for a very small log that is a handle to a trap door."

For the next few minutes, the two of them walked through the palm fronds, shuffling their feet. "I found it Mac."

Mac cleared the area and lifted the handle. Looking down into the cave, he saw the munitions were still there. He also saw the markings in the sand where the containers had been stored. He let the trap door fall shut, shaking his head, and muttering, "Fuck."

"What is it Mac?"

"Someone was on this island before the authorities came and stored the chemicals in the cave. After the authorities left, they came back and now someone has a very deadly weapon of mass destruction. If the fucking president had only let us take care of this. Fuck."

"Mac, I think we may be in luck."

"How's that Astrid?"

"Come with me." Astrid started to jog back toward the beach with Mac in tow. She ran up the beach to a spot, stopping, "Look," she said.

In the sand was the fresh mark of another beached boat.

"Mac, this is a deep groove. Whoever beached the boat didn't have much experience in boating. It looks like they powered up onto the beach. From the markings I bet this was a deep "V" hull; a cabin cruiser."

"I think you're right, Astrid," said Mac as he waded into the water. Looking down he said, "There are marks on the coral. If it was an inboard, he may have bent a prop. Good job, Astrid."

"Let's go, Mac, maybe we can find him."

"Hold on, Astrid. You can pilot the boat but you cannot chase an armed terrorist. There could be a lot of them. So let's do this right. It's a big ocean and chances are we won't find them, but if we should be lucky, we call it in. Deal?"

"Deal," she said. "Okay, let's go."

They ran back to the Scarab and Astrid hopped on board. Mac ran the anchor back to the anchor locker and pushed the boat off the beach. Astrid lowered the engines into the water, started them, and slowly backed into a little deeper water. She swung the boat around and pushed out to sea.

"Where to?" she asked.

"The marina."

She pushed the throttles to the stop and the Scarab raced back toward Koror. Mac was on his satellite phone to Haig. He told Haig what he discovered. "Ron, do we have any birds in the area? I'm betting that the boat I am looking for is between the island and Koror. There are no major land masses within 500 miles of here."

"Even with a couple of satellites up, this is like finding the needle in the haystack."

"Get back to me in case you do find something." Mac turned to Astrid. "Want me to take the helm for a while?"

Astrid shook her head, "I'm fine Mac. No need for a midfield handoff."

He leaned over and kissed her.

"What's that for? Don't even think about it now, Mac."

"That's because you're a genius. Listen."

Mac dialed up Haig again. "Ron, Astrid figured it out. There's going to be a mid-ocean handoff. Check all the shipping lines—not the majors but the small lines. See who has ships in the area. Get back to me."

He kissed her again.

CHAPTER 15

CIA HEADQUARTERS, LANGLEY, VIRGINIA

SAME DAY

The analysts were busy at their computers, running the shipping lines, checking ports, customs list, and security reports. After a few hours, they had it down to three ships that would be in the area. Haig looked over the list. He picked up his office phone, pressing Admiral Charko's extension.

Lila Cooper answered.

"Lila, its Haig, is he available?"

"He's with the director," she told him.

"Thanks," he said, hanging up. He then dialed the director's extension. Helen Benton answered.

"Helen, I need the director."

"The admiral is in with him."

"I need them both."

"Come on up," she said.

Dr. Cornaci's office was on the top floor of the building. Haig's office was on the floor below. Haig ran up the stairs and down the hall to the director's office. He entered the outer office and Helen told him to go right in.

Haig knocked and walked in.

"What is it?" asked Cornaci.

"Mac has a lead on the missing sarin."

Charko looked at Haig then at the director. Cornaci nodded. "Tell him, Admiral."

"The president does not want us on a wild goose chase. He told us that there was no evidence that not all the gas was taken off the island. The secretary of state, who has been in contact with the president of Palau, has assured us the island is clean. The president is not a big fan of Mac Daniels and truthfully he would like him out of the clandestine service and out of the navy."

Haig was shocked. "What does he want to do with Daniels?"

Charko cleared his throat. "Put him in jail."

"This is crazy. The president must be nuts. If Mac said there were thirty cases, there were thirty cases. Admiral, you know Mac."

Cornaci answered, "I'm not firing him. Daniels is one of the most decorated naval officers and an officer of this agency who has done more for this country..." He stopped for a second, his face reddening. "No fucking way."

That caught everyone's attention. No one had ever heard the director use the "f" word.

The director continued: "What do you have, Ron?"

Haig told them what had transpired. He handed the director the list of the three ships. The director looked it over, and then handed it to Charko.

"Which one, Ron?" asked Cornaci.

"Two ships are going to Hawaii. We can have them inspected when they enter U.S. waters. The third ship, the Sails of Allah, is going to North Korea. I would target it with a satellite and see what happens."

Cornaci smiled. "See what happens? You mean have Mac Daniels board the ship and then see what happens?"

"To tell the truth, it fits the profile. Mac said there were thirty cases and twenty-four were recovered. There's a half-dozen missing. He said there was a boat on the island and it only makes sense, looking at the geography, that a boat that could be beached would not have the range to make it to any other island than Palau. The closest place would be Yak and that is 500 miles away. Small boat couldn't make it. It would have to meet some ship somewhere and hand off the cargo. My opinion sir; track it and let Mac intercept it."

Admiral Charko asked, "How do you intend to intercept it without causing an international incident?"

"I'm sure Mac could find a way."

Charko shook his head. He looked at the director. "Knowing him, he'll blow it up. Well, Jon?"

There was a long silence in the room. The director clasped his hands in front of himself as if he were praying. He closed his eyes, rubbed the bridge of his nose, and finally spoke. "The president gave us a direct order to drop it." He went silent again for a long moment. "Isn't Mac on vacation? If my memory serves me correctly, he's a boat enthusiast. Tell Mac to enjoy his vacation, have some fun and perhaps he should rent a boat and do some deep-sea fishing."

"I'll make that suggestion to him," said Haig. "I'm sure he'll appreciate your good wishes."

"Do what you can do to help him, Ron. Sure he'd appreciate it. And for God's sake, please don't let Mac start a war."

"I'll get on it right away, sir," said Haig.

Cornaci and Charko stood up. "We have to go. We don't want to keep the senator waiting," Charko said.

Both Cornaci and Charko had been summoned to testify in a closed-door session before Senator John Bartlett IV, chairman of the Senate Intelligence Committee.

Haig looked at them both and said, "Good luck gentlemen."

■ ■ ■

Haig ran back to his office and called down to Mike Golef's office. Mike was an attorney, but playing with computers was more fun than drafting documents. One of his clients was a start-up technology company, which had made him an offer he couldn't refuse. What he did not know was that the company was a CIA front. Mike had finally ended up at Langley, running the most advanced technology department in the world. He was having more fun, he often said, than he deserved. He was making a generous salary with great benefits and he knew his service to his country was invaluable.

After a few rings, Mike answered the phone. "Golef," he said.

"Mike, it's Ron. I need to see you."

"I suppose you need to find Mr. Daniels? Why can't he leave his locator beacon in?" he said, referring to the long-range beacon that is implanted in the body.

"I know where he is, Mike. I need you to find a ship and detain it for me. Can you do it?"

"Piece of cake. Come on down, Ron. I'll find your ship. I'm sure it has something to do with Mac Daniels."

Ron took the elevator down to the sub-basement level. Mike's was one of the windowless offices, with specially lined walls; sound didn't come in or go out. There were several large screens on the wall and a desk cluttered with keyboards, wires, and flight sticks that looked like they'd been taken from a jet fighter. Ron entered without knocking.

Without turning around Mike asked, "What do you know about the ship?"

"It is the Sails of Allah, somewhere between the island country of Palau and Yak on the east and the Philippines on the west, and heading for North Korea. It's registered in Panama."

Mike started typing, his fingers flying over the keys. The computer screens came to life.

Ron watched with fascination as lines of data popped up. "Can I ask what you're doing?"

Mike smiled. "Hacking into the Panamanian registry computers to see what we can find out about this ship."

A few minutes went by, and then Mike turned and looked at Ron Haig. "Ship is a Syrian flag." He hit a few more keys. "This is the first Syrian flag company. I don't think they ever had a line."

"How new is it?"

Golef went back to his keyboard. A few more taps and clicks, "Holy shit, Ron this is a very new company, less than a year. The corporate office is located on the Isle of Jersey, but playing around here, it seems that the money and directions for the company came out of a Raqqa bank."

"Raqqa!" Haig almost shouted.

The self-designated Islamic State (IS), which previously called itself the Islamic State of Iraq and the Levant (ISIL), or the Islamic State of Iraq and Syria (ISIS), had claimed Raqqa as its capital. Raqqa was also the capital of the Ar-Raqqah Governorate, home to a few large banks.

Golef's fingers flew over the keyboard again.

Haig called upstairs to the ISIS desk. He told them about the shipping line and told them to notify the Jordan, Lebanon, and Turkish desks at the embassies. Haig's next call was to the cultural attaché at the Office of Cultural Affairs at the Israeli Embassy located at 3514 International Drive, Northwest, Washington.

A woman who announced, "Office of Cultural Affairs," answered the phone. "How may I help you?"

Haig asked, "Fran, what are you doing answering Rami's phone? Where's the boss?"

"Ronny," said Fran Parkski, recognizing Haig's voice, "The boss, as you call him, is on the phone with his boss. Besides you know who the real boss is, don't you? You know who runs this place."

"Yes, madam boss, I know who runs the place. Please tell Rami to patch me in with Moshe. This is urgent."

A few seconds later, Rami Willis said, "What is it, Ron? Moshe is on the line with us."

Haig had called in on a secure line. He had the phone number for the Mossad officers in his permanent memory, as they had his. Rami Willis was in charge of the operations in the United States, although they would never admit it publicly. In the intelligence world, it was a known fact.

The Mossad literally means "the Institute," which is short for, "Institute for Intelligence and Special Operations." It is the national intelligence agency of Israel. It is one of the main entities in the Israeli Intelligence Community, along with Aman (military intelligence) and Shin Bet (internal security).

The Mossad is responsible for intelligence collection, covert operations, counterterrorism, and protecting Jewish communities. Its current director Tamir Pardo, reports directly to the Prime Minister.

Moshe "M", as he was known, was the director of operations for the Kidon, the counter-terrorism unit. Not much was known about this mysterious unit, details of which were some of the most closely guarded secrets in the Israeli intelligence community. The Kidon works closely with the agency's clandestine service, especially the Special Activities Division (SAD) and the Special Operations Group (SOG).

It was Rami who had informed Haig that agents were in the U.S., purchasing material for improvised explosive devices. Before any damage could be done, they had been arrested. Again, in 2001, the Mossad warned the FBI and CIA that 200 terrorists were in the United States planning a major assault. A month later, terrorists struck at the World Trade Center and the Pentagon.

"ISIS has a ship," said Haig, giving them the details. Then he asked, "Do you have assets?"

"Yes, I will see what we can find out. Why the hell do you think it is going to North Korea?"

"I'm scared to guess," answered Haig.

"What are you doing about it?"

"Officially, nothing. Unofficially, I think Mac will be on that ship."

"Tell Mac to sink the fuckers. Remember what David Ben Gurion said, 'History is not written, history is created.' Let Mac create history and let the papers report a sunken ship. Keep us posted. I'll see what we have. Good luck." The line went dead.

Ron turned to Golef, "Where's the ship?"

"From what I can figure out, this ship has to be between the Philippines and Palau. It wouldn't be west of Palau, that would take it too far out of the way for a turn north to Korea." He played with the keys, ran the mouse over some charts, and said to Haig, "According to its manifest, carrying food and I would guess oil. Ah, here's the little fuck." Mike turned back to the keyboard and a few seconds later, the map of the Pacific Ocean appeared on the screen and in the center of the screen was a flashing dot. "There's your ship."

Mike played with the keyboard for a few more minutes and the ship appeared on the screen, this time so large you could read the name clearly on its lifeboats. "There it is Ron, in real time. It's sitting low. Must have a full cargo."

"Oil?" asked Haig.

"Probably."

"Keep looking. Get all the intelligence you can. Mac will need it. Where is the ship exactly Mike?"

"About three hundred miles west of Palau."

"Shit. Can you get Mac on the speaker?"

"Sure Ron." A few seconds later, the encrypted satellite phone rang on the speaker.

"Mac Daniels," came over the speaker.

"Mac, Ron and Mike Golef here."

Golef's fingers flew over the keyboard and on another screen, there was another blip and after a few more keystrokes, the blip was the hotel where Mac and Astrid were staying. He picked up the signal from the satellite phone and honed in on it.

"What do you have?" asked Mac.

Ron told him what they'd found out about the ship and its possible ISIS connection. "By the way, Mac, the ship is headed for North Korea."

There was silence. Finally, they heard Mac say, "I have to get on that ship. What can you do to help me, Mike?"

"As long as you keep your satellite phone on, I can track you. I wish you were wearing your beacon, it would be a lot easier but the satellite phone will have to do. I have you on one screen and the ship on another. I can bring you alongside, but I don't know how you're going to board."

"What about the boat with the sarin? You think you can find it?" asked Daniels.

Mike thought for a moment. "Well, it has to be between Palau Island where he picked up the sarin and the ship's current position. There is about 300 miles of open water, but taking a heading off the ship's bow and using the island as a reference point, I can get a heading. With a deviation of a few degrees on either side, I should be able to pick the boat up. If your bandit turns on his GPS to get to a mid-sea meeting point, I'm sure we can lock onto the signal to reverse back to his position. But what do you want me to do?"

"I have an idea. Give me the coordinates of the ship. I'll head out toward it and keep an eye open for another boat. I have a feeling it's a cabin cruiser, probably not more than thirty or thirty-six feet. You keep looking for him and I'll intercept the cruiser and destroy the gas. Then I'll make the rendezvous and board the ship. I'll make up some bullshit story as to what happened to the gas."

"I have an idea," said Golef. "Power down your phone. You're going to need a full charge. Use Astrid's phone and dial in. I'll plot the course from here and walk you to the ship."

"Good idea," said Daniels. "Hold on for a second."

Daniels opened the hotel safe and grabbed a handful of passports. He decided to take the Canadian passport that identified him as John Mac Brown. It was valid and legitimate except for the name. "Ron, I'll be traveling as John Mac Brown, a Canadian citizen with reported ties to extremist groups. Make it happen, Mike. When they punch my name into the computer, be sure I look like a Canadian volunteer. Tie me in as an Afghanistan and Iraqi fighter. I can do the rest. This should keep me on the ship until we get to Korea. By the time we reach Korea I'll know what they're really carrying and I'll try to find out what's going on. I suspect they'll be trading cargo for some type of munitions. Once we leave Korea, I'll sink the ship. Just be sure to get someone to pick me up."

"What do you have for explosives, Mac?" asked Haig.

"Nothing. Don't even have a weapon, just my knife. I'll think of something."

In the background, Haig could hear Astrid. "Mac," she said, "Without a backup plan or method of exfiltration, you could spend a lot of time in some rat-hole or in front of a firing squad. I don't like this. Where's plan B?"

"She's right Mac. What's plan B?" asked Haig. You could hear the concern in his voice.

"When you have a plan B you don't work at plan A," Mac said with a smile. "Let's just stay with plan A. Give us about a half hour—we'll be out in the Scarab. You'll pick up Astrid's signal."

"Hold on, Mac. Astrid cannot go with you. Astrid, you stay put. You hear me, Astrid?"

"Fuck you, Ron," was her reply. "You don't tell me what to do."

"Mac, you cannot do this."

"Listen Ron, there is no way Mac can board that cruiser while trying to pilot a Scarab at sixty miles per hour. Okay? Do you understand?" Astrid stood there, hands on her hips, her green eyes glaring at the phone.

Mac recognized the look. She was a mother bear and no one was going to fuck with her cub. "Ron, I need Astrid to pilot the Scarab. Once I'm in control, she'll turn back to Palau. Mike, try to find out the cruiser's position. It'll make my job a little easier. Can you delay the ship?"

"Mr. Daniels, with this technology we can do anything. I'll send a ghost signal to the ship. The automatic pilot or the helmsman will keep compensating to stay on course. The more he compensates, the more they will be off course. That will give you extra time. At the right time, I'll shut the signal off and the ship will correct itself and go to the rendezvous point. We can watch it and guide you to the ship. I'm going to move a few more birds into orbit so we can tag you."

Ron said, "I'm sure when you set foot in North Korea, the shit will hit the fan."

"I'll disable my phone. It will appear to be broken, but it will still broadcast a signal. I'm hoping they let me keep it. You can jam it if necessary, Mike."

"Not a problem."

Mac took out his duffel bag and threw in some clothes, toiletries, money, his knife, and his passport. He then stripped out of his bathing suit. Astrid was already out of her bikini, staring at him. She threw her arms around him. Her body felt good against his.

"Babe got time for ..."

"A quickie," Astrid interrupted him.

"Was going to say sandwich, but I can do a quickie. Not such a bad idea, babe."

"Just hold me, Mac. Just hold me. I don't like this."

He put his arms around her and they fell back onto the bed. They just lay there. He could feel the tears running down her cheeks onto his face. He whispered into her ear, "You're plan B."

CHAPTER 16

HART SENATE OFFICE
BUILDING ROOM 219

Senator John Bartlett IV, chairman of the Senate Intelligence Committee, banged the gavel. In a loud voice to an empty room, he called the meeting to order. Dr. Jon Cornaci and Admiral Eugene Charko stood up, raised their right hands, and swore to tell the truth.

The Senate Intelligence Committee oversees the Intelligence Community. The 94th Congress established the committee in 1976 and the committee is comprised of fifteen members. Eight of those seats are reserved for one majority and one minority member of each of the following committees: Appropriations, Armed Services, Foreign Relations, and Judiciary. Of the remaining seven, four are members of the majority, and three are members of the minority. In addition, the Majority Leader and Minority Leader are non-voting ex officio members of the committee.

The committee meets in the Hart Building, room 219, one of the most secure rooms in Washington. It has been described as a bank vault with soundproof double doors and steel casing to guard against electromagnetic monitoring, and it is routinely inspected for eavesdropping devices. What is said in room 219 stays there, except for the loose-lipped senators.

"I always find it amusing when spies swear to tell the truth. I'm sure you gentlemen will be honest and forthright with this committee," said Bartlett.

Cornaci, being the director and head of the agency, answered. "Senator, the truth will set you free." He had just quoted the agency motto.

Sitting behind Bartlett was chief of staff, Dick Edwards. Edwards had several files on his lap and a list of questions. He handed the first file up to his boss.

Bartlett put on his reading glasses and peered down. "I read in the papers about a navy pilot who crashed and ended up on a deserted island with a Japanese soldier. I was fascinated about that story. Imagine that poor soldier all these years on the island alone, to find out the war is over and he lost. My God,

I said to myself. I do talk to myself, gentlemen, but I don't answer myself. I'd probably lose the argument."

There was polite laughter from the committee members.

The senator continued: "I asked myself, John, I do call myself John, I would like to talk to that pilot but I didn't hear of any crashes. I asked Mr. Edwards to find out about the crash and the pilot. And you know what? There were no crashes and according to navy records, there is no Lieutenant Commander Bill Cody. There are a few Bill Codys but they are in the Atlantic and none of them fly. Since this was called in by the CIA, could you please explain?"

"If I may, with your permission, Director?" said Charko, addressing Cornaci.

Cornaci nodded his approval.

"Senator, Bill Cody was one of our covert operatives and that was his cover name at that time. There was no navy plane crash. The operative knew that the Japanese soldier's story would attract the news media and he quickly devised the story."

"Somehow that's what I thought. Without going into operational details, what is the CIA doing spying on the country of Palau? Why, the country has about 20,000 people. My colleague here," he said, pointing to a committee member, "from Texas, has more cows than that. Why are we spending our taxpayers' money in Palau? It is nothing but a bunch of little islands, some 250 from what the report says here. It seems that the most populous island is Koror with a population of 14,000. Please explain and tell me we are not wasting money."

Cornaci answered, "No, Senator. We were not and are not spying on the people or the government of Palau. It was truly by accident that our officer ended up there."

Edwards handed up another file and Bartlett took it and continued. "It seems the North Koreans lost a plane at sea. The reports have it that it went down near or over one of the trenches. Can't be recovered. By chance is there any relationship between the North Korean plane crash and your officer washing up on the Palau Island?"

This time Charko answered, "Yes, sir."

"Are we going to hear from the North Korean Supreme Leader with another threat?"

"I hope not," said Charko.

Looking at his notes, Bartlett continued. "According to the NSA there has been some considerable chatter over the airways that some Middle Eastern groups paid a lot of money for something they did not get. It seems our Cuban friends also are missing something. Did you run an operation that went wrong?"

"No, sir," said Cornaci. "In fact, our operation went as expected except for our officer landing on Palau."

"By chance is weapons grade uranium involved in this plan of yours?"

"The senator seems to be well informed," said Charko.

"It is my job," shot back Bartlett. "That's why I am here and you are there. I do not need a hair-brained scheme concocted by the Special Activities Division going south and causing this country more issues than it already has."

There was a long silence in the room.

Finally, the Senator spoke again. "I know about the sarin gas. I know the secretary of state dealt with President-what's-his-name of Palau to have it removed. I know that the president, our president, that is, did not want the CIA involved in removing the gas, which all leads me to believe that your plan did not go as expected and there is going to be some serious fallout. Am I correct gentlemen?"

"No, sir," said Cornaci in a loud voice, his face turning red. "You are not correct. In fact, you are wrong, very wrong about the operation of this agency. The only fallout, as you say sir, is there will be no nuclear fallout."

"What about the sarin?" shot back Bartlett.

"I suggest you ask the secretary of state. We did not handle the removal," replied Cornaci.

Bartlett turned to Edwards and whispered, "Cornaci is a feisty little son of a bitch. It must be his 'eye-talian' heritage."

Edwards whispered to the senator, "Why don't we request a non-operational report? With all the chatter on the airways, we had better have some information, which we might need to share with the counter-terrorism unit of the FBI along with Homeland Security. We don't need another surprise attack on our country and you know these CIA sons of bitches always hold their cards close to their vest."

"An excellent idea, Dick." Turning to Cornaci and Charko, the senator went on, "Gentlemen, why don't you provide us with a non-operational report? As you know, no names—call him or her agent 'x' but tell us what is going on."

Two hours later, after the report and some additional questions, Cornaci and Charko were in the Suburban with their escorts on the way to Langley. Cornaci turned to Charko, "Fucking assholes."

Charko smiled. "Jon—the f-bomb twice in one day."

CHAPTER 17

THE PHILIPPINES SEA

THAT NIGHT

Astrid pushed the throttles of the twin engine Yamaha F-300 almost to its stops once she was outside the marina. The Scarab was skimming over the sea on the heading that Mike Golef had given her. Back at Langley, Ron and Mike could see Mac and Astrid in real time on one screen, and the ship on the other. Golef hit a few more keys and Mac and Astrid turned into red figures. The satellite could read thermal images. There was nothing that anyone could do for now but watch and hope for the best.

"Astrid, keep heading due west, and I'll provide you with a course for your intercept. Tell Mac I'm looking for the cruiser. Steady as she goes, Astrid," said Golef.

Mac sat in the seat next to Astrid, quite relaxed and enjoying the ride. He noticed that Astrid had a white-knuckle grip on the wheel. "Easy, Astrid. It's a piece of cake. Just remember what I told you. Trust yourself, because I do."

Astrid gave him a forced smile. "Thanks, Mac."

"Astrid, give the phone to Mac; I got the son of a bitch," said Golef.

Mac pressed the cell phone against his ear, "What do you have, Mike?"

"I got him, it looks like a Grady-White about thirty-two feet, with a forward cabin. In the cockpit, I can see the containers of the sarin gas. He's running twin outboards. I ran an infrared. You're in luck, he's alone."

"I know the boat. The helm is center ship with one seat. Does he have radar?" asked Daniels.

"No radar but he has a GPS, which I am picking up. I'm going to fuck with him and throw him off course. Tell Astrid to keep her heading. I'll have you dead astern."

"Sounds good. What would be my ETA?" asked Daniels.

"Keeping him off course and you on the heading, you should have a visual in about forty-five minutes," replied Golef.

"Ron, you got forty-five minutes to find out what I'm supposed to do with the shit when I get it. Is it possible to screw it up so when I deliver it, it will be useless? If not, can I dump it over the side without causing a problem? See what you can find out. Once I get on the ship, I'll probably have two days until I get to North Korea. I'm going to need a little help. Can you get some explosive material to me?"

Ron Haig's voice came on. "How in God's name do you expect me to do that? Jesus Mac, you're going to North Korea."

"Improvise, Ron. Improvise."

"What do you want? C-4?"

"I need something that the dogs can't pick up. The Supreme Leader has sniffer dogs."

"You aren't going to kill him? You'll start a fucking war, Mac."

"Ron, trust me, I have a plan, I think. What about semtex or HMX? Oh, I know. Oxy? Oxy would work well, Ron."

"Where am I going to get octanitrocubane, or for that that matter HMX?"

"When Astrid gets back to the hotel, she'll call you. Get her the oxy. You get it to her, and I'll do the rest. You know what to do, you've done this before." Mac handed the cell phone back to Astrid and Golef gave her a new course. Mac sat back next to her as if he was on a Sunday afternoon joyride.

Astrid asked, "Doesn't this make you nervous?"

"I'm more nervous when you drive a car, babe," he said with a grin. "At least you're not going over the yellow lines. Hell, you pilot the boat pretty good."

"That's not what I meant, you moron, and you know it. I'll remember this the next time you want to fool around."

"You won this argument. Truthfully, I trust my training and I trust you. This part of the mission is going to be easy. The hard part will be getting out of Korea alive. We only have about an hour more of daylight. I would imagine they'd wait until dark before making the transfer. I want to take advantage of the darkness. The Grady doesn't have our speed. If we can run up on him, I'll board. He'll have to leave the helm to fend me off and most likely will cut his engines. You're going to have to be prepared for a hard stop."

"We've gone over this enough times. I know what I've got to do." She tried to sound confident but had that worried look on her face. She knew what to do in theory, but theory wasn't reality.

Daniels picked up a line and started to tie a bowline.

She looked at him. "What are you going to do with that rope? I mean line. I know there's no rope on a boat," she said.

"As soon as his boat comes to neutral, get the bowline around his stern cleat, then wrap the line around your midship cleat, the one that's in the ..."

"I know what the midship cleat is. Don't piss me off, Mac. I'm nervous already."

"Then tie off his midship cleat, then back to your stern cleat. This "X" tie will keep him rafted to the Scarab."

Golef came back on the cell phone with a new course heading and Astrid made the correction. They were about thirty minutes apart. The sun was going down quickly. Mac scanned the horizon. He looked at the water for signs of a wake. Finally, he saw the Grady-White dead ahead. He tapped Astrid on the shoulder and pointed. She nodded back.

"Cut your engines, Astrid. We don't want to run up on him until it's really dark."

Astrid pulled back on the throttles. She could see the white stern running light on the Grady-White. She checked to be sure that her running lights and dashboard lights were all off. At the slower speed, the Yamaha was very quiet. Slowly, she began to close the distance.

Haig's voice came on. "Mac, the ship is a good hour and a half away."

The sun dropped behind the horizon, and darkness fell over the ocean. It was the phase of the new moon when it's in conjunction with the sun and invisible from earth, but the heavens were filled with stars. The view was magnificent. Mac tapped Astrid and pointed up. She looked, smiled, and quickly locked her view back onto the Grady-White. If this were not a mission, it would have been a night for lovers.

"Babe," Mac said as he whispered in her ear. "You'll do fine."

"Mac, I'm scared. If I screw up, you could get ..."

He cut her off. "Wet. Stop it and trust yourself."

While it might be a night for lovers, for Amr Ibn Taher it was a night of confusion. He was not a boater by any stretch of the imagination. He could count the times on one hand when he had piloted a boat. He was dedicated and prepared to be a martyr. He hoped to die in combat, not alone at sea. He wanted to make the connection, drop off the gas, turn around, go back to the marina, and go to bed. He'd had enough of playing sea captain. It was nerve-racking enough when he'd run over to the island in daytime, but this nighttime run had him quite scared.

Something was bothering him. Though he'd been following the GPS, the stars were not right. Amr was not a celestial navigator, but he knew his stars. From his home village of Arar, in the Northern Province of Saudi Arabia, he often spent hours gazing at the heavens. His father said it was his Arabic ancestors who had named many of the stars. Tonight Alpha Orionis was not in the right place. Amr Ibn Taher knew the star as its name was from the Arabic *Yad al-Jauzā'*, meaning "the hand of Orion."

Taher cut the engines to idle speed and shifted the gears to neutral. He stood there holding the wheel until the boat settled down. His compass was pointing in a southerly direction and Orion was on the port side or the starboard side. *One of the fucking sides,* he thought. He settled on the left side of the boat. He frowned. The compass should be pointing west and Orion should be on his right side, but the GPS gave him a different direction. Without the GPS working properly, he would not meet the ship and he would never find his way back.

Astrid came back on the throttles slightly above idle speed. The Yamaha F-300 was almost silent. The distance closed slowly.

Amr thought he heard something. He looked around. He walked to the stern and peered over the side. His eyes opened wide. There was something—a boat. He turned to run back to the helm.

Astrid pushed the throttles full open. The Scarab was alongside the Grady before Amr could engage the gears. Mac leaped off the gunwale into the cockpit of the Grady-White. The helm station was two feet higher than the cockpit and Amr turned and jumped down onto Daniels. Both of them fell to the deck of the cockpit, rolling around. Astrid cut the engines, pulled the gears into reverse, and gunned the engines to stop the forward momentum. She went to idle speed and neutral. She was in position and dropped the bowline around the Grady's stern cleat. She quickly tied the boats together.

Amr was up first and tried to kick Daniels. Astrid put the Scarab into gear, cut the wheel and hit the throttle. The Scarab turned sharply and pulled the Grady-White, causing Amr to lose his balance and fall back, hitting his head. He didn't move. As Daniels got to his feet, Astrid cut the engine. Daniels looked at the still body of Amr.

Astrid peered into the cockpit of the Grady. "Did I kill him?"

Daniels shook his head. "No. That was fast thinking."

"What are you going to do with him?" she asked.

"Throw him overboard."

Astrid screamed, "Mac."

He looked at her.

"You can't just kill him."

Mac shot back, "Why not?"

"He may be just a local, hired to make a delivery. He may not know what he's carrying."

Daniels just shook his head. If he were alone he would have thrown the guy overboard. For Astrid's sake, he would tie him up. "Ok, Astrid. It's this man's lucky day, thanks to you."

Daniels took a line and wrapped it around the man's ankles. He then pulled the his arms behind his back and tied them as close to his ankles as possible. It was a very cramping, and after a while, a painful position. If the man were to get loose, it would be difficult for him to get the circulation in his legs moving quickly and Astrid could handle him. Daniels dragged the body over and threw it into the Scarab. He climbed back into the Scarab after the unconscious man, and then secured his body through a couple of the rod holders. "If the son-of-a-bitch gets loose, hit him with the fire extinguisher, and I mean you hit him and you hit him. Don't let him get up. Astrid, he is not as nice as you."

Astrid nodded. She understood. She handed Mac her cell phone.

"Ron, have Golef guide Astrid back to the island. She can dump the delivery boy on the deserted island. I'm sure in a few days someone will be going over there. Watch her all the way. Keep the camera live. I'm switching on my cell. We've got work to do." He handed the phone back to her. "Astrid, drop this piece of shit off at the island."

Looking at his watch, he said, "It's almost three in the morning. By the time you drop him off and get back to the marina, it should be close to six. Go back to the hotel and call Ron, then get some sleep. You did good, babe."

"Be careful, Mac."

He smiled at her. "You're getting pretty good at this. You know what to do."

She shook her head no. "I was scared shitless. I love you."

"Love you too. Now get going."

She leaned over and kissed him.

Mac untied the boats. Astrid engaged the gears and pushed the throttles forward. She heard Mike Golef in her ear, giving her directions. *North Korea,* she thought. *Oh my God.*

CHAPTER 18

THE PHILIPPINES SEA

EARLY MORNING

Daniels powered up his satellite phone. "Ron, you there?" he asked.

Back at Langley, they immediately picked up Daniels' signal and focused the overhead satellite on him. On the screen, Haig and Golef could see Daniels in the cockpit of the Grady-White.

"Not only do I hear, Mac, I can see you quite clearly," said Haig.

"All right, you can see me, you can hear me, now what the fuck do I do with the shit?" asked Daniels.

"Mac, open the bomblets. There is a thin membrane between the two agents, be sure they don't mix. Throw out one of the agents, then reassemble the bomblets; they'll be harmless. By the way, salt water can neutralize either of the agents. Then when they mix together they'll be harmless and useless."

Daniels opened the first crate. It contained thirty bomblets. He picked one up. *How the fuck am I supposed to open this?* he thought. "Shit, Ron, there's a sealant around these. Any suggestions?"

"Hold one up," responded Haig.

Daniels lifted one of the containers and held it over his head. Golef focused in on the container. They could see it on the screen as if they were holding it in their hands. Haig and Golef looked at each other. Haig shook his head. "Is there anything on the boat that you can use for sealant?" he asked Daniels.

"Hold on for a second," said Daniels. He scoured the boat from top to bottom. He found nothing. "There's nothing here. Any suggestions?"

"Sorry Mac. From here, I don't have a clue. Not sure what I can do. Why not just throw them overboard?" said Haig.

"I need to have something to put on that ship if I'm going to get on it. We don't need an ISIS Korean alliance," said Daniels. "I'm going to open these fucking containers and pour salt water in. I'll try to pull off as much of the sealant as possible. That's the best I can do under the circumstances."

Daniels started to tear at the sealant with his knife and twisted the first top off. He repeated it for the row of six. He took a bucket, filled it with salt water, and then poured the saltwater on to the bomblets and resealed them. He had started on the second row when he heard Golef.

"We have a problem, Houston. I can see the ship's bridge and it looks like several people have joined the helmsman. I think someone may have figured out they're off course. Hold on."

Daniels picked up the pace on the second row.

"Mac, it looks like we're going to have to cut this short," said Haig. "Looks like the officers are on deck and someone is on the bridge with a sextant. If they disconnect the automatic pilot we'll have no way of controlling the ship."

"I'm going to have to cut the ship loose," said Golef. "Let the automatic pilot take a fix on the correct GPS and I'll guide you toward it. If necessary, I can play with it a little later but I can't keep the ship off course." Golef played with the keyboard and killed the false signal.

Daniels looked up; he could see the ship's lights in the distance. "How far am I from the rendezvous point?" he asked.

Haig looked at Golef. "What's your call on this, Mike?"

"Little more than an hour, depending on the wind and current."

"There's no way I can finish this and be there on time. I finished two rows in only one crate. I have to shoot crap. Give me a heading and the details on the ship, the captain and everything else I need to know."

Golef gave Daniels a heading. Daniels engaged the gears, pushed the throttle forward, and set the course for the rendezvous with the ship. Golef then provided all the details on the ship; the ports of call, cargo, final destination, and the name of the captain. The only piece of missing information was the name of the person who'd organized the operation and that of the messenger, who Daniels hoped was dead.

"That's all I have for you, Mac. Good luck," said Golef.

"Ron, be sure to touch base with Astrid. I may need help getting out of there. I'm going to disable my satellite phone now. It will appear to be broken, but still be transmitting. I hope you guys can keep an eye on me."

"You are tagged, Mac. Good luck."

Daniels disabled the satellite phone and maneuvered the Grady-White toward the ship. He turned on his running lights and as he closed in, he was sure the ship's crew picked them up on their radar. Back at Langley, Haig and Golef watched the ship close the distance with Mac. Mac's speed in the Grady compensated for the fact that the ship was off course. The faster he got to the ship, the less chance that anyone would have figured out that they were compromised.

Mac stood at the helm, looked forward, and pushed the throttles as far as they would go. The Grady-White zipped along, going through the swells as if it were on a lake. It was a good, strong fishing boat. He thought about Astrid and felt confident that when she cut the prisoner loose, the man would have been so cramped up it would not be a problem for her. He didn't like letting the man live. It was a loose end and could come back and cause him a problem. Astrid, he thought saw good in people. She didn't realize the people in this business were not as good as she thought. He had no doubt this man knew what he was carrying and if possible, he would use it on them. *Remember the old cliché; what is done is done and can't be undone,* he thought He hoped it wouldn't be his undoing.

Haig and Golef continued their watch as Daniels closed in on the ship, and that's all they could do…watch. They both realized that Mac was going to end up in North Korea. What he was going to do when he got there and how he would get out, if he got out at all, no one knew. Haig had to report to the director and bring him up to date about this operation. He also hoped someone would have an idea how to get Mac out of North Korea.

Daniels pulled the Grady-White alongside the starboard side of the ship. He brought his engines to neutral after he stopped his forward motion. The floodlights from the ship came on, illuminating Mac in the cockpit of the boat. He could hear the yelling on board. He yelled in Arabic, "Drop in net."

A few minutes later, he heard the winch and slowly the cargo net came over the side of the ship into the cockpit of the Grady-White. Daniels took the lead line off the cargo net and tied it around one of the cleats. He started to load the cases into the cargo net. When he was done, he opened the drain plug and water started to come into his boat. He untied the cargo line, jumped onto the net, and yelled in Arabic to take it up. The winch pulled up the cargo net with Mac Daniels holding on.

From Langley, Golef saw this and turned to Ron. "Hold on, look at this."

Haig was about to leave the room to go up and meet with the director. He saw the net going up with Mac Daniels hanging on. "I wonder," he said, "what's more dangerous; the sarin gas or Mac Daniels?"

Golef replied, "That's easy. Mac Daniels."

CHAPTER 19

LANGLEY, VIRGINIA

SAME DAY

Haig went directly to Admiral Charko's office. He bypassed the admiral's secretary Lila Cooper and let himself into the admiral's office. Charko looked up from his desk. "Did you forget how to knock, Ron?"

"I apologize, sir. I have something on my mind. I just wasn't thinking, sir. It's Mac."

Charko put down his pen and leaned forward in his chair. Haig had his attention. "What about Mac?"

Haig took a breath, and finally said, "He's on his way to North Korea."

"What in good God's name, do you mean he's on his way to North Korea? Have you both lost your minds? I'm in charge of covert operations—not you, not Mac Daniels—me. What don't you understand about that? I can't believe what you just told me. Are you both fucking nuts?"

"It just happened, sir. It was one of those things. Mac was right about the additional cases of the sarin gas. He found them. In fact, he's in possession of them now."

"So why not just destroy them?"

"Because they were supposed to be on the way to North Korea on a ship belonging to ISIS. And Mac..."

The admiral cut him off midsentence. "ISIS has a ship? How the fuck did this happen? Who knows about this?"

Haig took a deep breath. "Please let me fill you in on the details." He gave the admiral a briefing on what had happened and what they'd found out. He told him that most of the sarin had been destroyed. But Mac wanted to find out what ISIS was doing with the North Koreans, and he thought it was just too important to let the opportunity slip by.

"So he thought it was just too good an opportunity, so he hops on a ship to North Korea? What was he thinking? Let me rephrase that, Ron, what the fuck were *you* thinking? I expect something like this from Mac, but not from you. What's the plan to exfiltrate him? Or haven't you two thought about that? Let's go and talk to the director. This will make his day."

Haig said nothing to the admiral. He hadn't been chewed out like this for a long time and the admiral was visibly upset. Mac had been in tough spots before, but there'd always been a plan. There was no plan here. Mac was winging it, and if anythinghappened to Mac ... Haig stopped and tried to put the thought out of his mind. He followed Admiral Charko out of the office and down the long corridor toward the director's office.

Charko stopped in front of Helen Benton's desk. She stopped typing and looked up. "He's on the phone. I'll tell them you're here," she said.

"Thank you," replied Charko.

Helen typed a message on her computer and hit the send button. On the director's computer screen, the message appeared that Haig and Charko were outside. Cornaci cradled the phone receiver and typed a message. On Helen's screen the message popped up, "Send them in."

In his office, Cornaci signaled for Haig and Charko to sit down. They settled into the large leather chairs directly across from the director's desk. "Very good, General," said Cornaci as he hung up the phone, sat back, and tapped his fingers on his desk. "That was General Bellardi. The General wants to meet with me," he pointed at Haig and Charko, "and you two. He wants to discuss the operation and what happened. Seems he's getting calls from the senator's office inquiring about what happened and why the DIA was not involved. Since this apparently had something to do with the navy."

"May I say something, Jon?" said Charko.

The directed nodded.

"Tony Bellardi is an okay guy, real standup. He is a good man and does his job well. Talk with him. You can trust him. He's one of the good guys and he is Mac's uncle. Mac's mother is Tony's sister."

Cornaci typed something on his computer, hit a button, and then said, "Just told Helen to set up a meeting with the general as soon as possible."

Charko said, "There's been a development and we have to talk about it."

"What happened?"

"To put it simply, Jon, Mac is on a ship on his way to North Korea and I do not know how we are going to get him back."

The director looked at Ron Haig. "Okay, Ron. Let's hear it."

Haig told the director the entire story—everything from the intercept and the transfer of the sarin to the cargo ship, with Mac going aboard attached to the cargo net. He had been going to hold back on Astrid's role in this, but he thought better of it and decided to tell the truth. "Astrid was on the boat with Mac when they intercepted the courier, and she took the prisoner in her boat."

Before he could go any further, Cornaci and Charko blurted out, "Astrid!"

"Is Mac totally nuts?" asked Admiral Charko.

Jon Cornaci just sat there too stunned for words.

Ron held up his hands in a sign of surrender. "Please, Astrid and Mac were on vacation. There was no way he could have done this without help. We have no assets on the ground there and there was no way I could stop him. I tried. Admiral, you know Astrid better than the director and you know when she makes up her mind, there's no stopping her."

"Please God, what has gotten into you two?" asked Charko.

"Admiral, I have been here at Langley all day. I was giving Mac the assistance he needed from here with the aid of the staff as best we could. He was supposed to sabotage the sarin and go back to Palau. The last thing he told me was to talk to Astrid, and I am waiting to hear from her. When I say Astrid took a prisoner, let me correct myself. Mac tied the prisoner and threw him in the back of her boat. From what I saw, the prisoner was unconscious when Astrid left Mac."

No one said a thing. The room was very quiet with each man deep in his own thoughts. Finally, Haig broke the silence. "The question is, what's on that ship and what are they getting in return from the North Koreans. Director Cornaci, Mac will find out and let us know. We may have to take drastic action depending what's on that ship when it leaves North Korea. You may have to sink the ship."

The director put his thumbs on his temples and started to massage them. As if he were talking to himself, under his breath he said, "Life at the university, I thought, was hard. It was a piece of cake compared to this." He looked at both of them and said, "Mac did what he had to do. I understand. Putting his life on the line," he paused again, "and I understand why. What did you do about this Ron?"

"I notified the appropriate desks here, sir. I had the various embassies notified and I spoke to our Israeli friends. They have a few assets in Raqqa and maybe they can pick up something. As Rami Willis said to me, 'It's really simple, sink the ship.'"

"Do what you have to do, Ron. Keep me posted."

"Thank you, sir. I can't make any meetings with General Bellardi in the next few days, sir. I apologize, but I've ordered up the Citation. I want to get to Palau as soon as I can."

"Ron, listen to me carefully," said Charko. "Under no circumstances whatsoever are you to go to North Korea. Do you understand that? This agency cannot have my deputy director falling into the hands of the North Koreans under any circumstances. I know how close you are to Mac, but you cannot jeopardize this agency and its operations with the knowledge you have falling into the wrong hands. Do I have your word on this?"

"This is hard to say, Admiral, but you have my word. I do understand the risk and won't go."

Cornaci nodded his approval. "One more thing Ron, take a couple of bodyguards with you. I do not want you on some deserted island without a chaperone. You know what I hate about this job? It makes me curse, something I usually don't do. So in keeping with the job Ron, now get the fuck out of here."

CHAPTER 20

SAILS OF ALLAH

NEXT DAY, EARLY MORNING

Several of the deck hands were waiting for the cargo net and two others were waiting with their AK-47s for the man who was holding onto the cargo net. On deck was Captain Anas Anka, pacing back and forth with his arms folded across his chest. From the look on his face, he was not a happy man. As the cargo net came down, Mac Daniels' reception committee grabbed him before he had a chance to let go. He did not resist. The captain watched as they searched Daniels and rummaged through his duffel bag. One of the crewmembers handed the captain Daniels' knife, cell phone, and passport. The captain glanced at the passport then pulled the knife out of its sheaf. He touched the blade with his fingers. In Arabic he said, "Sharp enough to cut off his head."

The crewmembers laughed and the captain said, "Kneel down."

Daniels knelt on the deck.

The Captain had a surprised look on his face. "You understand Arabic?" he asked.

Daniels responded in Arabic. "Of course I do. I was born in Arar, the capital city of the Northern Borders Province of Saudi Arabia, in the Khaldiech section, at 98 Salman Road."

"Are you a believer?"

Without looking at the captain, Daniels replied, "There is no God but Allah. Muhammad is the messenger of Allah."

The captain thought for a second. He was not sure. Daniels did not move. The captain came closer, putting his hand on Daniels' chin, lifting it up. Their eyes met. The captain stared into Daniels' dark eyes. He saw no fear in them.

"I am sure you could recite the Pillars of Islam. Anyone who would dare do what you did would be trained to know them. You probably could recite the Koran better than I could. Why are you here?"

"Because I am the only one who knows how to handle that," he said pointing to the sarin.

The captain nodded. "Aswas never mentioned that you were coming on board. All he said was that Amr was going do make a delivery and asked that I drop that off when I get back to port."

Daniels immediately picked up on the names. "May I stand?"

The captain signaled with his hands for him to get up. Daniels stepped closer. The two holding the Kalashnikov started to relax and slung their weapons over their shoulders. Daniels saw the butt of what he thought must be a Russian Makarov sticking out of the captain's waistband. The Syrian army used the semi-automatic pistol. Based on what Haig had told him, the crew was most likely Syrian and part of the ISIS movement. For all that he had heard about the military training that the ISIS soldiers received, these two and their captain had made a crucial mistake. They'd dropped their guard.

He was close enough to grab the pistol, squeeze a shot into the captain, and then take the other two. He would use their weapons and clear the deck. Next step would have been to take the bridge and control of the ship. But he didn't think it was necessary. He thought he would press on with the charade a little longer. He had an idea.

"What is your name?" asked the captain.

"Banee," replied Daniels, "which as you know, means Brown in Arabic."

The captain smiled at that. "Your passport says John Mac Brown," he said in heavily accented English. "That is not an Arabic name and your passport is Canadian."

"My father took a job with a Canadian oil company and we moved to Toronto. My mother sent me to the Canadian schools and I learned to speak English, but my father saw to it that I had the proper religious training."

The captain looked at Daniels' cell phone and saw that it was broken. He handed the phone and passport back to Daniels but put the knife into his side pocket.

"I would like my knife back, Captain."

The captain studied the knife for a second and said, "I'll hold onto your knife for a while. Let us see what Allah wills us to do."

As the sun began to rise the captain said, "It is a new day. Let us say our prayers."

Daniels nodded his approval and got down on his knees facing the sun. The captain moved behind him, drew out the Makarov, knelt down, and aimed it at the back of Daniels' head. Daniels crossed his arms in front of his stomach and started to pray. The captain put his pistol away, joining Daniels in prayer.

When they were done, they rose to their feet and the captain extended his hand to Daniels and said, "Allāhu Akbar."

Daniels responded in kind. Then he said, "Captain is there a place I can sleep? Then with your permission we can talk some more."

The captain instructed one of the deck hands to take Daniels to the crew quarters and find him a room. "Ibn Banee, sleep well and stay in your room. When you want to come out, call and you will be escorted to my quarters. I don't want to see you walking around this ship."

"I understand, Captain."

As Daniels followed the crewmember, the captain said to another deckhand, "Watch him. Don't let him out of his room. Lock him in."

"Captain, may I ask a question?" asked the deckhand.

The captain nodded, "What?"

"I thought you were going to shoot him when he was done praying. What made you change your mind?"

"He was a Sunni."

The deckhand was confused. "How can you tell?"

"The way he prayed. Shias and Sunnis offer prayers differently. The Sunnis fold their hands or cross their arms in front of their stomachs. The Shias pray arms extended out, their palms resting on their thighs. If he had prayed with his palms on his thighs he would have died."

CHAPTER 21

DESERTED ISLAND

SAME DAY EARLY MORNING

Astrid cut the engines, letting the Scarab drift toward the beach. The hull came to a gentle rest on the sand. Amr Ibn Taher was now conscious and in discomfort. His tied-together hands and ankles arched his back as if he were a bow. The pain and discomfort from the position was further exacerbated as the boat had bounced over the waves. He bounced on the hard deck like a rubber ball. His face was bruised and his nose was bleeding. Astrid untied Taher from the rod holders and propped him up onto his knees with his stomach against the gunnel. She then grabbed the lines that bound him, and lifted and pushed him over the side. He landed face down—his head was underwater. Astrid jumped in and pulled him by his bindings onto the beach. She untied the line that was holding his ankles to his wrist and loosened the other knots. Then she got back in the boat and waited. When she saw that he was safe on the beach, she put the boat in reverse and slowly backed away. Mike Golef watched the whole thing as it happened.

Amr Ibn Taher painfully rolled his body away from the water. He lay there on his back, his hands still tied behind him. His body was sore all over, but he tried to put the discomfort out of his mind. He had to get out of these ropes and reach Aswas as soon as possible. His cell phone was in his back pocket. It was not wet, and he didn't think it had sustained any damage, since for most of the trip he'd been lying on his stomach with his face on the deck. He rolled over onto his side, bringing his knees up to his chest, and he worked his hands around his feet until they were in front of him. He then rolled onto his stomach and up onto his knees, and he finally stood up. He was still stiff but managed to walk up toward the tree line. He was tired, thirsty, and hungry. He cursed the white bitch who'd thrown him off the boat without any water. He would remember the fucking whore and some day he would get even. "American whore," he said aloud to himself.

He put his hands up to his face, and with his teeth he started to pull at the knots. It took him about a half an hour until he was completely free. He took out his cell phone, which was still on. His battery was low. He did not know where Aswas was. For safety's sake, he assumed Aswas was somewhere where it would be the middle of the night and he might not answer the phone. He thought about his message before he dialed. He pressed the speed dial button and the call went into voice mail.

Following the protocol, he had been taught, he left the simple message, "Call me at nine o'clock morning, my time. I will leave my phone on for five minutes beginning at nine o'clock and on every half hour thereafter to conserve battery strength. Important. The cargo was hijacked."

He decided to look around for some water and something to eat. He was not concerned about getting off the island, only concerned about getting the message to his leader. His fate was in the hands of Allah, which he willingly accepted.

■ ■ ■

"Astrid."

"Yes, I'm here. I can hear you."

"Astrid, it's Mike. I'll give you a course to get you back to the marina."

"I'm good, Mike. I know where I am and can find my way back to the marina. More importantly, how is Mac?"

"Everything seems to be okay. I watched him all the time from when he left you until now. He's apparently in a cabin. There's no movement from the cell transponder. Perhaps he's sleeping. I will try to keep the ship on watch all the way to port. Ron is on the way to meet you. He said to give him a call on the satellite."

"Thanks, Mike."

Astrid pressed the speed dial and Ron picked up on the first ring. "Are you okay, Astrid?"

"I'm fine, Ron. I'm on my way back to the marina. Where are you?"

"On my way to you. Should be there late evening, your time. I have the items that Mac wanted, but how is he supposed to get them?"

"We'll talk about that when you get here."

"What are you two up to, Astrid?"

"Ron, it's not the time to talk. When you arrive, I'll tell you. I have to disconnect now." With that, Astrid ended the call.

Astrid then pressed another speed dial and she was connected with her assistant Vivian. Vivian was always available, not that it was part of her job, but it was her love for Astrid. "You two having a good time?" asked Vivian.

"We're having a ball Viv, but you know with Mac there's always some little surprise. I need you to do something."

"What is it, honey? Whatever you need, I'll get done for you."

Astrid told Vivian what she needed and what she wanted.

"I'll get it done but this sure is crazy, Astrid. I sure hope you know what you're doing."

"I should be in my room in about thirty minutes. I'm going to try to get some sleep. I'll call you later."

CHAPTER 22

ON BOARD THE SAILS OF ALLAH

After several hours sleep, Daniels woke up and looked at his watch. He felt good and was ready. After he took a shower, he wanted to eat, wondering if this was going to be his last meal. As he suspected, the door was locked when he tried the handle. About to bang on the door, he spotted the phone. *What the hell,* he thought and picked it up. To his surprise, he heard a male voice speak. "Communications," the voice said in Arabic.

Responding in Arabic, Daniels said, "Can I talk to the captain or can you get somebody to let me out please?"

He heard the phone click. "Fuck," he said.

He looked at the handset and banged it back into place. He looked around the room for a way to escape. The ceiling, floor, and walls of the room were steel. Daniels decided the only way out would be the porthole. The portholes were fastened to their closed positions by hand tightening several pivoting threaded devices, commonly referred to as dogs. The dogs were tight but after a few minutes of twisting, they began to give. Finally, Daniels pulled the porthole up, securing it to the overhead hanger on the ceiling. He leaned out the porthole and estimated that he could make it to the upper deck. The only question was whether he could do it without being observed. He knew he had a better chance at night and that's when he would move. He dropped the window back, securing the dogs.

He had sat back down on his bunk to plan his next moves when the phone rang.

Answering the phone in Arabic, he said, "Yes."

"Ibn Banee," said the captain. "Please join me in my cabin for some breakfast. Someone will escort you."

Before Daniels could answer the captain, his cabin door opened and standing there were two crewmembers. Both were short and thin but one held a thirty-inch metal billy club and the other held a leather-wrapped lead weight attached to the end of a leather-wrapped coil spring. "Tueal maeana, ya Ibn el Sharmouta," said the one with the billy club as he slapped the end of it into his palm.

Daniels looked at the man and thought, *He wants to pick a fight.* The man had said, "Let's go, you son of a bitch," which was an Arabic slight against him and his mother. Daniels decided not to respond.

The man with the blackjack slapped it against the metal door, making a clanging sound that was deafening.

Daniels just shook his head. "That must hurt," he said, nodding toward the door. "You dented it."

The one with the billy club poked the end at Daniels, saying "Tueal maeana ya Khara."

Daniels did not move. He thought, *this man is really trying to provoke me, calling me a shit.*

The man with the billy club poked Daniels and shouted, "Sharmouta, tueal maeana."

"Touch me again with that, and I will break your arm. And don't call me a bitch or shit again, or you will eat shit, you dog." Daniels smiled as stepped back away from the door and stood there. He knew he'd insulted the billy club man and he knew what was going to happen. The two crewmen looked at each other.

The man with the billy club moved into the room, followed by the other man. He pointed the billy club, touching Daniels with it. Looking at his arm he laughingly said, "It's not broken, you shit."

Daniels' right hand grabbed the billy club and his left hand locked onto the man's wrist and twisted it, bringing the elbow up. He brought the club down hard onto the man's elbow, crushing it. The man screamed.

"It is now, bitch."

The man with the blackjack pushed past the first man and raised the blackjack. Daniels hit him in the groin as hard as he could. The man's knees buckled, and his eyes rolled back into his head. As he fell to the floor, Daniels hit him in the back of the neck, and then he turned on one foot, wheeling the club to the back of the head of the first man. Both were now on the floor, unconscious. Daniels shut the cabin door and searched the two men, finding their keys, which he hid in the false bottom of his duffel bag.

Opening the cabin door, he looked up and down the passageway. It was clear. Dragging the two crewmembers, he went along the passageway toward the bow, to the emergency exit door, and he pushed them overboard. He threw the billy club and blackjack into the ocean, and then he continued up the companionway to the bridge deck where he thought the captain's quarters would be. He passed the entrance to the bridge, followed the passageway toward the stern past the radio room and the electric locker, found the captain's quarters, and knocked on the door.

From behind the door, he heard the captain: "Enter."

Daniels did.

"Good morning, Mr. Brown," said the captain in slightly accented English.

Answering in English, Daniels replied, "Good morning, Captain. You speak English."

"And so do you. I trust you had a pleasant sleep," he said.

"I slept well, thank you. The ship sails smoothly. It's about one hundred meters in length overall, isn't it?"

"You have a good eye. It is 106 with a breadth of sixteen meters," replied the captain. "And before you ask, the engines were refitted with Wartsila Vasa and we are running at seventeen knots."

Daniels smiled at the captain.

"You know your ships. I hope you didn't have any difficulty with the crew. Sometimes they are a little impatient with strangers."

"Patience is a virtue that has to be learned, Captain. Your men are a little wet behind the ears."

"I'm sorry we had to lock you in, but your presence on the ship was unexpected and it is a matter of caution."

"I understand. It's not a problem and I'm here now. I am pleased to join you for breakfast and answer your questions, Captain."

"I only have one question for you: Why are you here?"

"Captain, I told you last night. I am the only one who knows how to handle the poison gas. If it is mishandled and it vaporizes, this ship will be a ghost ship. I want to see it delivered and hopefully you will give me a ride back."

"To where?" asked the captain.

"To the same place you picked me up. I can have somebody meet me, unless you want to share with me where you are going."

"Where I am heading is none of your business. What I'm doing is none of your business. If your story checks out, I will give you safe passage. If it doesn't, I will kill you, simple as that."

"That's fair, Captain. Now that we have the pleasantries out of the way, shall we eat? Can I have my knife back?"

"I see you have a sense of humor, Mr. Mac Brown."

"I try to, Captain. They say laughter is the best medicine. When we're done with breakfast, may I check on my cargo?"

The captain nodded his head.

"May I make another request?"

"Go ahead," replied the captain.

"Thank you, please call me Mac. It is a name that I've been called most of my life."

"Please explain to me what this Mac means, Mac."

"As you know and as you have called me Ibn, Ibn before the family name means 'son of.' When we were living in Canada, my father added 'Mac' before our family name, 'Brown'. Mac means 'son of.' It is very common in Scottish names, but as I said, my father wanted to carry on the tradition, so we became Mac Brown."

The captain nodded his head, indicating he understood, and then he said, "Funny, you don't look Scottish." He started to laugh at his own joke and then continued, "After breakfast, Mac, I will let you inspect your cargo, but I will accompany you. After that, you must return to your room and stay there until we are in port. I don't want you running around the ship for your own protection. I need my sleep and I will not be able to protect you from an overzealous crew. I was up all night trying to reach Aswas and Amr. I also called a friend of mine, who happens to live in Arar. I am waiting for his call back to see if there is a 98 Salman Road in the Khaldiech section."

"I assure you, there is such a house. Your friend will see that I am telling the truth and that this was once the home of the Banee family." Mac was certain of this. He had stayed in this safe house in many times.

A crewmember brought them breakfast consisting of halaweh (sugar and sesame paste), jibneh bayda (white cheese), laban msaffa (strained yogurt with dry mint leaves), and black olives with tea. After breakfast, the captain led Daniels down into one of the holds where the gas was stored. Daniels opened a couple of the boxes as if he were really checking that everything was okay. In reality, he was just using this as an excuse to walk around the ship. He knew the gas was perfectly safe until it was mixed. When he was done, he told the captain that no one should be allowed in this hold. The slightest leak would mean instant death. The captain nodded his understanding.

The forward hold was filled with fuel bladders. One thousand and five thousand-gallon bladders covered the deck and were double and triple stacked all the way from the hull to the decking above. Daniels thought all of the containers on deck; six abreast and six high, must be filled with bladders. It was oil, he thought. That's what they were trading. The ship had been converted from carrying fruits and vegetables as the manifest stated, to carrying oil. With this much oil they were trading for something very big.

The captain led him back to the main deck, then up the companionway to another deck, then down the passageway to his room. He unlocked the door and Daniels stepped in.

Daniels flopped on the bunk and he heard the bolt click. He would stay in the room for about thirty minutes, and then he would explore the rest of the ship. He had two things to do; determine the final destination of the ship, and if he could not disable the ship, he had to get word to the navy so they could intercept it. He didn't know what the return cargo would be, but he knew it could not be good. The other thing that he had to do was somehow disable the radio communications. He had to prevent Aswas and Amr from reaching the captain or this would be his trip across the River Styx.

CHAPTER 23

DESERTED ISLAND

Amr Ibn Taher was still stiff from being tied up, but he slowly made his way to the Japanese campsite. He explored the area but could not find anything to eat or drink. Moving off the runway, he went deeper into the jungle and found some fruit bushes, along with a pond of fresh water. He knelt down, cupped his hands, and started to drink. After he had his fill, he picked at the berry bushes. Then he walked slowly back to where the runway met the beach.

He had been up all night, and exhausted, he sat down with his back against a tree. He looked at his watch. It was 8:45. In fifteen minutes, he'd have to turn on the cell phone. He thought he would close his eyes for a few moments. He needed to rest.

Ibn Taher opened his eyes and stretched. He looked at his watch and could not believe what he saw. It was 10:05. He had missed three check-in periods. He screamed, "Khara, Khara, Khara [shit]," and kicked the sand. He had failed, and he believed he was unworthy. He should die on this island in disgrace and not as a martyr. He looked to the east and started to pray.

At 10:30, he stopped praying to turn on his cell phone. A minute later, it rang. He quickly answered it. "Aswas," he yelled into the phone.

Aswas Rajul replied, "Yes. What happened, Ibn Taher?"

"The Americans took the boat—it was the Americans."

"Slow down Amr and tell me everything. Leave no detail out."

Amr Ibn Taher reported everything in detail, from the time he'd left the marina until he ended up on the island.

"What makes you so sure they were Americans?" asked Rajul.

"I heard them speaking. They spoke American, not the English you hear in England. I saw their boat at the marina. They were in the same hotel."

"Can you describe them?"

"Yes. The man had black hair and was taller than you." Rajul was just under six feet tall. "He was thin but very strong. I could not see his face clearly, but the woman was taller than me with red hair and green eyes. She was very pretty. I beg your forgiveness. I failed you."

"You did not fail. From what you said, it must be the Americans. I will see what I can find out. I will arrange for you to travel back to the mainland, and then you are to return and complete your original mission. I will be in contact with you."

Aswas Rajul hung up and looked at his phone. He knew what he had to do. He had to get to a radiophone and get a message to the ship's captain. He did not know what the ship's true mission was and he did not care, but he did not need some American interfering with it. He also had to connect with his contact in North Korea, just in case the Americans got there. The North Koreans would know how to handle this. What's more, the handoff of an American to the North Koreans might be worth a lot. He had to get to his home where he had a radiophone so he could call the ship.

CHAPTER 24

SAILS OF ALLAH

After a half hour, Daniels decided it was time to do a little exploring, but first he wanted to fix the communication system to prevent any incoming calls. He rummaged through his duffel bag and took out his shaving kit. The contents appeared harmless enough; safety razor, toothbrush, toothpaste, shaving cream, nail clippers, dental floss, and a nail file. The toothbrush came apart. The hard plastic was honed to a point, deadly as any icepick. The nail file was razor-sharp, and the nail clippers squared off as a flathead screwdriver on one side and a Philips head on the other. When the dental floss was pulled from its case, after a couple of feet there was a fine, steel wire, which he could use as a garrote, saw, or restraint. The lining of the shaving kit came out and it acted as a sheathe for the nail file. He put the file in the sheathe and placed it in his back pocket. The toothbrush and nail clippers went into one pocket and the dental floss into another. He retrieved the key and listened carefully at the door.

Daniels opened the door, looked out, and stepped into the passageway, locking the door behind him. He knew where he wanted to go. His first stop would be the electric locker. He'd seen this earlier when he was going to the captain's quarters. Daniels retraced his steps forward toward the companionway and listened—it was quiet. He climbed up to the bridge level, assuming that there were at least two crewmembers on the bridge.

At the door to the radio room, Daniels listened. It was quiet. He thought the room might be empty since this was a small ship with a crew of no more than ten. There was a good chance that the radioman was also the ship's navigator and was on the bridge. Incoming radio messages could be picked up on the bridge. Daniels knocked on the door, stepped back to the companionway, and waited. No one answered. He opened the door and stepped into the room. It was not a sophisticated communication center. It had several bands for the sending and receiving, along with a radiophone. Taking out his nail clippers, he unscrewed the four screws holding the wall plate. He found the wires for the radiophone and using his file, he scraped the protective coating off two wires and twisted them so that the bare wires were touching. This would cause a short and hopefully an electrical fire, which would hide the evidence of his activity. He tucked the wires up in between the other wires, then replaced the faceplate and left the room.

The next room over was the electric locker, which contained the main electrical panel for the ship. There were lines of fuses and cut-off switches. He pulled out several of the fuses that powered the radios, and with the point of his toothbrush punctured very tiny holes almost invisible to the naked eye. He replaced the fuses, knowing they would short themselves out.

Daniels followed the passageway toward the stern to another companionway and went down to the next level to continue exploring. One of the rooms used by the crew was empty. He stepped in and went through the drawers and lockers. Other than a few photos of the men with their families, there was nothing useful in the rooms. The photos were of the two who had come to his cabin. It was the same two who were on deck the night he came aboard. They were part of the night shift and but for his actions they should have been in their bunks sleeping. At least they would not be missed for several hours.

He pulled down the sheets and shut the door. If someone were to look for them, they would assume that they were on duty. It was just a matter of time, though, until they would be missed.

Daniels kept on searching, looking for clues. He knew what the ship was carrying and its destination. He just wasn't sure where it was going after it left North Korea, or what it would be carrying. He would find out soon enough.

The first officer looked at the clock and asked the radioman who was acting as navigator for a position check. According to the GPS they were right on course.

"That was really strange last night," said the radioman. "I know we were off course regardless of what the positioning was with the GPS."

The first officer just shrugged his shoulders. "What does it matter?" he asked. "We are on course now and that's what matters. Go wake up the captain," he ordered.

The radioman knocked on the captain's door. "Captain."

From inside the cabin the captain said, "I'm up. I will be on the bridge in a few minutes."

Several minutes later, the captain was on the bridge. He checked the progress nodded approvingly. "How's our guest?"

"He's in his room and hasn't called for anything," responded the radioman.

"Something's strange, I can't put my finger on it," said the captain. "Any word from headquarters?"

"No sir, it has been quiet."

The captain looked at his cell phone and turned it off. "Still no service," he said. "Send a message to headquarters. Give them our position. Find out if anyone has verified Ibn Banee's address in Arar. When you're done, see if you can get Aswas Rajul on the radiophone."

A few minutes later, the radioman returned to the bridge. "Captain, I am having difficulty. I cannot pick up a signal. The radios aren't dead. I have power to the panel and static, but I just can't seem to get a band to broadcast on."

"Did you check the fuses?" asked the first mate.

"Yes sir, they all seem to be fine. I didn't see anything wrong."

The captain thought for a moment. "Never mind, just try to get Rajul on the radiophone."

On the other side of the world, Aswas Rajul turned on his radiophone and dialed the ship. In the radio room, the receiving light lit up. The radioman acknowledged the call.

"Put me through to the captain quickly—this is an emergency."

The radioman dialed the bridge. "Captain, I have Aswas Rajul on the radio."

"Put him through immediately."

"I'm putting you through to the captain, just a moment." The radioman transferred the call to the bridge. He smelled smoke.

"Aswas Rajul, what am I supposed to do with Banee or Brown or whatever you call him?" asked the captain.

"What... (static) ...you (static) ...about?"

"Say again?" replied the captain.

The radio went dead.

The radioman screamed, "Fire! Fire!" and hit the alarm.

The clanking sounded throughout the ship. Daniels started to move quickly toward his room.

The first mate ran to the radio room, grabbed the fire extinguisher, and sprayed the panel. The room quickly filled with smoke.

The captain stood by the door and looked in, shaking his head. "Quickly!" he screamed. "Get down to Brown's room now. If he's not there, find him and kill him.

The first mate ran down the companionway and to Daniels' cabin. He threw open Daniels' door. The room was empty. He pulled his pistol and had started to turn when Daniels came out of the bathroom. Before Daniels could say anything, the first mate shut the door and relocked it. He returned to the bridge.

"He is locked in his room, Captain."

"Find Raja and Aban and tell them to guard the door. They should be in their cabin sleeping. Let them sleep in the hall but watch that door."

The first mate picked up the intercom and dialed the number for the room. There was no answer. "It is not working," he said and left the bridge. Ten minutes later, the first mate was back on the bridge. "Captain, I can't find them. Their beds were empty. It looks like the fire alarm woke them. I went to their emergency station, but they were not there. I checked the lifeboats, in case they were getting ready to abandon ship, but all was in order. No one has seen them. They disappeared off the ship."

The captain shook his head, and under his breath he said, "It's got to be Brown. Who else?"

"He was locked in his room. There is no way out. There is no way Brown, or anyone for that matter, could have taken on Raja and Aban. Either one alone could have killed Brown with his bare hands. Didn't they bring Brown to you this morning? Where did they go in the middle of the ocean?"

The captain was quiet. Thoughtfully, he said, "I think Brown could have killed me, Raja, and Aban last night, and the rest of the crew. I did not let him live; he let us live. That man had no fear in his eyes. I think that Raja and Aban are in the middle of the ocean."

CHAPTER 25

KOROR, PALAU ROYAL RESORT

Haig took the elevator to the top floor and found the corner room where Astrid was. He knocked on the door and waited.

The voice from within said, "Who is it?"

He dropped his voice. "Room service."

"Just leave it, thank you."

"I really can't. I have to bring it in," said Haig.

"Leave it and go away. Thank you," Astrid said.

"Well, if you just look through the peephole, you will see that it is room service and nothing else." He was actually testing Astrid and she was doing quite well. He was very impressed.

Astrid stood to the very side, away from the peephole, and with a coat hanger pushed the cover to one side. Nothing happened. Mac had taught her never to look through the peephole. It was the best way to take a bullet to the brain. She knew not to open the door to room service when she had not ordered. "If you don't leave the tray," she said, "I am going to call the manager."

"Okay Astrid, you pass the test. It's me, Ron, now please open the door."

Astrid smiled as she recognized Haig's voice. It was now time for her to have some fun. "Okay Ron, what is the password?"

"Come on Astrid, open the door. I don't know the password."

Astrid opened the door and Haig stepped in. He dropped his bags on the floor, gave her a hug, and kissed her on her cheek. "Astrid, what was the password?"

"There wasn't any. I just wanted to see how you handled it. Did you really think I was going to fall for that old room service trick? Mac taught me better than that. It's late. You must have been on a plane a long time. Want something to eat?"

"No, thank you. The company jets are well stocked with food. I ate and had a nap. Mac gave me a list of things to bring. I'm just not sure how I'm going to get them to him."

"Ron, tell me the truth, do you have a plan to get Mac out of North Korea?"

Haig was quiet for a minute. He decided to tell Astrid the truth. "No, Astrid. He's on an unauthorized mission, there have been no preparation, no backup, no ex-filtration plan, nada, nothing. I don't know why he did it, and to tell you the truth, I don't know how he's going to get out …" He hesitated.

Astrid finished the sentence for him, "Alive."

Haig shook his head.

"Mac has a plan. The only question is: do I tell you?"

"For God's sake, yes. What has he cooked up? What can I do to help?"

"Do you know how to handle a camera?" she asked.

"I can handle most cameras. It can't be that hard. What is it with this camera stuff, Astrid? I got a feeling I don't like where this is going."

"I am plan B," she said. "I'm going to North Korea to interview Supreme Leader Kim. Kim is well aware of my company's worldwide impact, and it's a chance for him to address the world on his own terms. This is too irresistible for him to pass up. I'm also told that he has an eye for women, and I'm going to do my very best to be an eye-full for him. You're going to be my cameraman, if you want to come."

Haig let out a big sigh. "Astrid, I am the deputy director of covert operations. I know the admiral and the director would disapprove of me going to North Korea. In fact, I would say I am under a direct order not to go."

"You don't have to tell them," she said, with a big smile on her face. "It won't be the first time an order was disobeyed."

"No, Astrid, I obey orders, and Mac doesn't disobey orders, he just interprets them differently from the rest of us. To him, no means maybe, and maybe means yes."

Astrid could not help but laugh. She understood and knew Mac. What Ron said was true.

"I gave my word that I would not go to North Korea, not to mention I have two bodyguards with me and I am sure they would prevent me from going. Assuming I was crazy enough to go along with this plan B, as soon as I set foot in North Korea I would be immediately arrested. The North Koreans are not stupid, and I am sure someone would run my prints and not only would I be arrested, most likely you would be arrested and your plan B would become plan clusterfuck."

"Ron, did you travel on your real passport when you came here?"

"No, you know very well, Astrid, I very seldom travel with my real passport for security purposes. Unlike Mac, I sometimes do make the press. I do testify before Congress. I am not a covert operative like Mac. Run my name through a computer and there is my history—run Mac's name and if you really try hard the most you will find is an active duty naval officer, if that."

"I understand, Ron, but I am going. I may be the only way for Mac to get out. Did you bring all the stuff Mac told you?"

Haig nodded his head. "Okay, I can see where this is going. If I can dodge my security detail, count me in. Now, what is the plan? Did Mac tell you about his prior mission to North Korea?"

"No. Mac never discusses his missions with me. I worry enough without having to know the details. Truthfully, Ron, we were on vacation in Florida when you told him about the sarin. It just bothered Mac. I suggested we come here partly as a vacation and to take a peek at the deserted island. Everything we discovered, Mac told you. None of it is classified so he didn't break any laws by confiding in me. I'm the one who actually discovered there was another boat at the island. When you told Mac that ISIS owned the ship and it was going to North Korea, between the sarin and its mission, he had to go. Mac didn't want the sarin being traded for some other weapon. If all goes well, Mac will fly out with me on my plane."

"If all goes well, and considering you don't have a plan …" He paused. "What is the use?" He just shook his head. He knew Mac and he was sure Mac had something up his proverbial sleeves. He also knew Astrid to be a determined woman and protective (as much as she could be) of Mac. There was no way she was going to leave Mac in North Korea without trying to get him out.

Ron looked at his suitcase, picked it up, and placed it on the bed. "Might as well go through this," he said. He opened up the suitcase and took out his clothes, running shoes, a baseball cap, several envelopes, two small jewelry boxes, a satellite phone, several pencils, and a belt with a large fancy buckle.

"Is this the stuff Mac told you to bring?"

"Yes."

"Where's your knife?"

"I don't have one, and if I did I would probably cut myself. I'm not a SEAL."

"Mac told me you had an arsenal. This does not look like an arsenal to me."

"It's everything he asked for. The clothes are mine. Nothing else is what it seems to be. Most of this is well camouflaged and should pass through customs very easily. Let me show you some of the stuff. Here," he said, handing her the first jewelry box.

Astrid opened the jewelry box and in it was a pair of earrings. They appeared to have a large pearl, surrounded by small diamond chips. She looked at them. "Not quite my style but they're nice."

"When you put them on, gently press on the pearl and it will activate the radio. One earring is a receiver and the other a microphone. They broadcast on an ultra high frequency. No one should be able to pick it up."

Astrid opened the other jewelry box, which contained a necklace with a large pendant. "Let me guess," she said. "The pendant is some type of camera."

"Correct—that can broadcast to an overhead satellite. The closer you are to a window the better."

"Mac told me to stay in the gardens, if possible."

Handing her the jewelry boxes Ron said, "Put these in your suitcase. They look out of place in mine."

"What's with the belt buckle?" she asked.

"The ends of the belt buckle where the leather goes through, break off and each one is a detonator. These detonators work off a cell phone signal. Inside the buckle is also a battery. The envelope contains fake fingerprints and the satellite phone. Even when they make you shut it off, it will be broadcasting your position."

"The baseball cap, the pencils, and the running shoes?" she said with a question in her voice.

"They're for Mac. The brim of the baseball cap splits open and the soles and heels come off the running shoes. They contain an explosive. The two number-3 pencils, when you hold the eraser down, will fire a 22-caliber bullet, which at close range will be very effective. The number-4 pencil is also a detonator. Jab the point into the explosive, hit the eraser three short times, and in about thirty minutes, it will detonate the explosives."

Haig showed her how to get the bottoms of the running shoes apart. He handed her what appeared to be clay. Astrid took it in her hands, looked at it and smelled it. "Is this C-4 or Semtex?" she asked.

"No. It is octanitrocubane. It makes C-4, Semtex, or HMX look like a firecracker."

Astrid's eyes opened wide. She might not be an explosives expert, but she knew that C-4 and Semtex were not firecrackers. She was not sure what HMX was and she certainly did not know what octanitrocubane was. She wanted to get rid of it. She handed it to Ron, and he deliberately let it drop on the floor. Astrid screamed.

Haig smiled. "Gotcha for the 'what's the password' shit you tried on me before. Octanitrocubane is shock insensitive. It cannot be detonated by shock even if you strike it with a hammer. These are Mac's running shoes and he can run with them and it won't detonate."

Haig bent down, picked up the octanitrocubane, and repacked it in the shoes. He repacked his bag.

"How dangerous is this octo shit?" she asked.

"Octanitrocubane has about thirty percent greater performance than HMX. Its explosive velocity, the speed which the shock wave travels, is about 10,000 meters per second, making it the fastest known explosive. It can reach temperatures up to 6,000 °C, and pressures up to 300,000 bars can be achieved in the shock wave."

Astrid was quiet as she took in this information. She did the math. "Ron, that's about 23,000 miles per hour and earth's sea level pressure is 1 bar. My God, the pressure is 300,000 times greater than at sea level. Ron, isn't 6,000 Celsius about 10,000 degrees?"

Astrid's eyes opened wide. "Oh my God, isn't that nuclear?"

Ron shook his head. "It was the ground temperature of the first atomic bombs."

By the look on her face, he knew she was figuring it out. "Ron, nothing can be more explosive than Octanitrocubane except..."

He finished the sentence for her, "a nuclear explosion."

"How would Mac set it off and not get killed himself?"

Haig did not answer.

CHAPTER 26

FALLS CHURCH, VIRGINIA

Aswas Rajul drove his car west on route 29. He never exceeded the speed limit by more than five miles per hour and never ran a red light. He was going to Falls Church, Virginia, a small city nine miles west of the White House, where routes 7 and 29 cross. It was a pleasant drive under normal conditions, but this was not normal. Something was wrong, very wrong and he could not get his hands around the problem. He wondered why his calls to the ship would not go through. The only possible answer was that the American who had somehow intercepted Amr Ibn Taher, had managed to get onto the ship. Who was he, and the woman? Rajul knew that many of the American intelligence agencies had female agents who could handle themselves well, but what Taher had told him did not make sense. If the American managed to get into North Korea, Rajul did not want the Koreans, who were certainly paranoid, to hold him responsible. While he was not part of ISIS, he did not want their mission to fail. He did not need them seeking revenge on him or the possibility that the Koreans would stop doing business with ISIS. There would be hell to pay for that. That's why he was going to Falls Church to meet with Ki-Young Park, the owner of The Round Table Restaurant in Washington.

Park was an agent for North Korea. The Koreans had four intelligence agencies, and Rajul was familiar with two; the Ministry of State Security, North Korea's primary counterintelligence service reporting directly to the Supreme Leader, and Reconnaissance General Bureau (RGB), which is responsible for clandestine operations. Rajul had dealt with Park, who Rajul knew was the RGB operative in Washington, D.C.

He turned onto Folkestone Road, looking for Park's house. The house was isolated from its neighbors as most of the other houses are in this secluded section of Falls Church where the residents enjoy their privacy. Rajul pulled into the driveway and then into Park's garage. The garage door came down and the overhead light came on.

In the doorway that led into the house, Park stood with a cigarette in one hand and a drink in another. "Come on in," he said, as he turned and walked into his house.

Rajul followed Park into the house and into the living room. Park sat on the recliner and pushed back. Rajul sat across from him on the couch.

"How have you been, Ki-Young?" asked Rajul.

"Please, it's Ken. It's more American," Park said with a smile. "Do you want a drink? This is a real good wine. Sorry, I forgot you Muslims don't drink." He took a sip.

"I drink," said Rajul. "Do you have vodka? I'll take one."

Park pointed to the bar. "Several good brands back there. Help yourself, glasses and ice, take whatever you want."

Rajul glanced over the labels and grabbed the Chopin, pouring himself some. He threw in a few ice cubes, twirled it, and then took a sip. "Nice and smooth," he said, "I needed that. We have a problem."

"We don't have a problem. You have a problem Rajul. I am sure that's why you are here. So tell me what your problem is."

"Maybe when I am finished you might rethink who has the problem, but for now, let's move on. I have nothing to do with ISIS. To be truthful, their brutality against women and children does not sit well with my people and me. Whatever you are trading with them is your business. They think they can beat the United States with armed conflict. That is a joke. Almost as funny as you Koreans, who think you can beat the U.S. too. Go ahead, start a war and see how much China will help." Rajul took another sip of his drink.

Park took one, too. They both sat in silence for a few seconds.

Finally, Park spoke. "You know I came here as a little boy, and I have never been out of this country. When my parents came here as RGB agents I was only two. I have no real recollection of what North Korea was like. When I grew up, I learned what my parents did. They trained me and I took over for them. I like living here, and I enjoy the creature comforts that are reserved only for the Supreme Leader and his inner circle. My restaurant makes money and the cash I receive from the North, I wash through my restaurant, making me very successful. I know that we can't win a war with the United States, but the Supreme Leader thinks otherwise and my job is to keep him informed so he can be prepared for the invasion. I will do my best to keep him happy. I really don't give a shit about ISIS or Al-Qaeda."

Rajul shook his head. "The United States can be beaten. The only way to win is to cause economic havoc through cyber warfare. The most powerful country in the world militaristically is vulnerable to teenage hackers. Take out the GPS and planes, ships, smart bombs, and even the new smart cars are useless. Take out the banking system and the country stops. Can you imagine if all the traffic lights stopped working in Washington for one day?"

Park shook his head. He knew that would paralyze the city. Even with the traffic lights working, maneuvering around town was tough.

Rajul went on, "Shut down the power grids and the country stops. Do you understand where we are coming from?"

Park nodded his head. "But how do you do this and how do you fund this?"

"You may not believe this, but I do not know how we are funded. Before Bin Laden was killed, we worked out a system of cutouts and codes. No matter what they did to me, I cannot tell you what I do not know. All I do is run an ad in a paper and I get a number to call, and money will be deposited in several accounts or I will get a package containing cash. We are getting there, but we are not ready."

"Why do you want to see me? This has nothing to do with us."

"There is where you are wrong. You have more at stake than you know, and I am going to make you a hero with the Supreme Leader and ensure that you stay here."

"You have my attention, but what is the quid pro quo? You are not doing this for the goodness of Allah. What do you want?"

"Access to your country's computer network. The Chinese will not take a chance with a cyber war, as their economy is too attached to the Americans'. The Russians would love to take down the United States, as they believe that they lost a war without firing a shot. But unfortunately, the Russians use American software and equipment and they are too dumb to know that with every keystroke, someone here is reading what they are doing as they do it. The Iranians, well they have some capabilities, but the United States would find an excuse to bomb the shit out of them. You have the ability and the U.S. won't bomb you because they think you are crazy enough to launch a nuclear missile at them. The CIA knows you have between four and eight nuclear weapons. They think that your KN08 can reach California. But you and I know it can't. The KN08, which is your first ICBM, has not been tested. You do not have the capabilities needed to miniaturize a nuclear device for missile delivery."

Park sat there, stunned. "How do you know this?"

"Does it matter? I know it and you know I am right."

"Looks like General Cheon is not doing his job. Fuck him! So how are you going to make me a hero?"

Rajul told Park about the sale of the uranium and how it had been switched for the sand. He gave Park all the details about the proposed operation.

Park stopped him. "I am aware of this. One of my agents in Cuba verified that the dead Cuban was, in fact, the courier who left Korea with the sand," he said with a smile.

It was now Rajul's turn to smile. "Did you read about the Japanese airman who was living on the deserted island since the war?"

"Of course," replied Park. "Hell, it has been all over the news and everyone is interviewing him. You cannot turn on the television without seeing him."

"The only trouble is Ken, you were fucked and not even kissed. The Americans had an agent take the Cuban's place. The person in the plane was CIA and he actually landed the plane at sea near the island where the Japanese airman was. That is where the sarin gas was. A German submarine at the end of the war brought the sarin there. The Japanese were going to use it on the Allies and get General MacArthur to sue for peace. The Americans have your uranium."

"Holy shit." Then Park started to laugh. "I would have loved to have seen the look on their faces when they found out it was sand."

"Don't laugh yet, my friend. It gets better. Hold on for this. While your Supreme Leader and General Cheon were having a good laugh, the sand was switched and the Americans actually do have your enriched uranium. Someone made a switch—so you have a spy working for the Americans or the Israelis in your nuclear facility. Without the enriched uranium it will certainly slow down your nuclear dreams."

The color ran from Park's face. His agent had verified the body in Cuba. If he kept his mouth shut, no one would know there was a fuck up. He asked Rajul, "How did they trick us with the body?"

"That was easy. They caught the courier, killed him, and made a latex mold of his prints. The mold was placed on the tips of the fingers of the American agent. He deliberately left his prints, most likely on a glass or a desk, leaving a clear, clean set for your State Ministry to pick up. After that, he was careful and probably left no others. When you checked the body in Cuba, the prints matched. You did nothing wrong, Ken. No one would have known."

The room was quiet.

Rajul continued, "I know what you are thinking; should I or shouldn't I report. Listen to me Ken. Report what I told you. Be the hero. Let General Cheon explain what happened. After all, you were here, not there. You are safe. Right now, there is an American on a ship headed to North Korea. I cannot get through to the ship and I am betting that he somehow sabotaged the communications system. I have no idea why he is going or what he is up to, but between the spy in your midst and this agent on board the Sails of Allah, be warned, and be careful."

Park nodded in agreement. "You are right. I will get a message out. Why are you doing this?"

Rajul did not answer.

"If I get caught, I am a spy, and eventually they will trade me back to the North, but you are an American and a traitor."

CHAPTER 27

PYONGYANG, NORTH KOREA

The Taedong River is a major river in North Korea. Its origin is in the Nangnim Mountains of the Hamgyŏng-nam province in the country's north. The river flows southwest into Korea Bay, part of the Yellow Sea at Namp'o. On its journey through the country, the river runs through Pyongyang, the country's capital and past the Daedonggang district, which is the home of the Munsudong Diplomatic Compound where twenty-four embassies are located. In the Diplomatic Compound on Daehak Street is located the Embassy of the Kingdom of Sweden. Almost directly across from the embassy in the Taedong River is one of North Korea's museums, the USS Pueblo, an American naval ship, which was boarded and captured by North Korean forces. It is the only ship of the U.S. Navy currently being held captive.

In the absence of diplomatic ties with the United States, Sweden functions as Protective Power for the United States, Australia, and Canada.

Standing outside the embassy was Su Young, a representative of the Minister of Foreign Affairs for North Korea. As soon as the embassy opened for business, Su Young presented his credentials to the secretary of the ambassador.

The secretary informed the representative that the ambassador was in a staff meeting. "As soon as he's available, he would be pleased to see you. Would you like to wait? I am sure he will not be long. Would you like some coffee or tea?"

The representative handed her an envelope and said, "No, thank you. Please see that the ambassador or his deputy receives this as soon as possible. Please inform him that the Supreme Leader expects this letter to be delivered by midday tomorrow." With that, Su Young turned around and left as quickly as he'd entered.

The secretary looked at the envelope and put it aside. A few minutes later, the phone rang—it was the ambassador. She brought the envelope to him and stood there while he read it, shaking his head.

"Is there a problem, sir?" she asked.

"I'll say there is a problem. It's a demand by the North Koreans for the return of the uranium and the surrender of the criminal that entered the country and stole from the people of the Democratic People's Republic of Korea. They claim the actions of the United States are an act of war. If the Americans do not comply they intend to sink or capture the Reagan."

He looked out the window, saw the Pueblo, and just shook his head. He handed her the envelope. "Please make a copy for the file, then send this to the Americans and copy our foreign minister. Mark it urgent and top priority. Thank you."

"It is something that the Americans can comply with?"

"I really don't know."

The secretary started to leave, stopped, turned, and asked, "Do the North Koreans have the ability to capture an aircraft carrier like the Reagan?"

"I don't think they could capture the Reagan, but they sure have enough missiles to sink it."

CHAPTER 28

LANGLEY, VIRGINIA

They were the code-busters in World War II. In 1952, President Truman officially formed the National Security Agency (NSA). Since then, it has become one of the largest intelligence organizations. It operates as part of the Department of Defense and simultaneously reports to the director of National Intelligence. Through a discipline known as Signals Intelligence (SIGINT), the NSA is responsible for the monitoring, collecting, and analyzing of information.

The information that the NSA sent to Dr. Cornaci was not what he wanted to read. He'd already had three cups of coffee and was on his fourth when Admiral Charko and General Bellardi came into his conference room. "Please sit down. Coffee anyone?" asked Cornaci.

"You have anything stronger, Jon?" asked Tony Bellardi. "It's going to be a tough day when the president reads this shit. Admiral, want to join me?"

"I think I will. A little Scotch for medicinal purposes, please," said Charko.

Cornaci pointed to a bar in the cabinet behind his desk. Bellardi poured a scotch and for himself, a bourbon. Handing the glass to Charko he said, "You got a mole."

Charko nodded his agreement.

The SIGINT intercept had reported a transmission from the Washington area to North Korea, detailing the CIA's involvement in the uranium deception. There were too many details; someone had given information—very secret and sensitive information.

Bellardi asked, "What's your position when the Koreans make some demand or threat?"

"We are going to deny everything. We have no idea what they are talking about. Someone is trying to start trouble and we had nothing to do with this absurd allegation," said Cornaci.

"Sounds good to me. Deny, deny, and when that doesn't work, deny some more," said Charko. "We'll never admit to it. Christ, that's the worst thing you can do. They can't prove it and they can rattle their sabers as much as they want. The Supreme Leader has to save face. He's not going to let the world know that he lost his uranium and the money too. He will not want to be embarrassed. All he can do is bang a few pots together and execute a few people. We stick to the story—deny."

"The real issue here is there is a leak, and we have to find out who it is and find out fast. I called the agency's inspector general and we'll have someone from counterintelligence start snooping around. I called Director Bertone of the FBI and we'll meet with him," said Cornaci.

"This mission was so covert that only a handful of people knew," said Charko. "We started to make a list to turn over to the Feds, and by the way, Tony you're on the list."

"I would expect to be. Who else is on the list?"

"Jon, myself, Haig, the two agents who snatched the Cuban, the pilot and co-pilot of the Lear, the team leader of the SEALs, and two or three others in the support group. Who did you talk with over at Pacific Fleet Command?"

"Spoke to the admiral himself, and told him we need to land an aircraft on the Reagan. He asked me if he should know why I wanted to use a six-billion-dollar carrier to land one of my planes. I told him that he really does not want to know. That was it. I made the call myself on a secure line. You have a short list and I hate to think that anyone on it is a traitor. This really sucks."

"Wait a minute," said Cornaci, "what about the Senate Sub-Committee? Be sure the Feds have the name of everyone who was in that room, and be sure our people at counterintelligence have them too. I say start there, and that includes Senator Bartlett."

"By the way," asked Bellardi, "where is that nephew of mine?"

"I understand from Mike Golef, who has been tracking him, he is on a ship that just entered North Korean waters."

"Holy shit, why did you send him back with all this shit going on?" demanded Bellardi.

"Easy, Tony, this is not authorized operation. It is a Mac Daniels operation and we are trying to give him what support we can. Haig is with Astrid on Palau."

"Jesus, Astrid is as crazy as Mac. How did this happen?"

Charko told him what had transpired.

"Tony, there's more," said Cornaci. "We just got word that Astrid has permission to go to North Korea to interview the Supreme Leader."

"I need another drink. What about Haig?"

Charko answered, "He's under direct orders not to go to the North. We cannot have him fall into General Cheon's hands. Haig wouldn't last too long at one of his interrogation camps."

"You know how close he is with Mac," Bellardi said, more as a statement than a question.

"I know, Tony, but I hope his bodyguards will keep him under control," replied Charko.

"We have work to do for this investigation. What do you say we get started?" said Cornaci. "Admiral, get word to Haig about this. He may have a way to reach Daniels."

"You know," said Bellardi, "I want to make a prediction. When her fucking highness, Maud Evens the APNSA calls, Jon … and I am sure that will happen," he said, looking at his watch, "two minutes after the president gets the demand from the North Koreans, she starts the conversation off with, 'Looks like you boys fucked up again.'"

"I will have to thank Her Highness for calling me a boy," said Charko.

"And the worst part," continued Bellardi, "that big pussy Secretary of State Hertz …" Then in a high pitched whine, imitating the secretary, 'I think we should give the uranium back and give them their money. We are not thugs.'"

Helen Benton, Cornaci's secretary, put her head in the door. "I'm sorry but I didn't know the secretary of state was here. He didn't sign in."

With that, all three men started to laugh. The phone rang on Cornaci's desk. He picked it up and listened. Hanging up the phone he said, "The president wants us over at the White House. We just received a demand from the Koreans."

CHAPTER 29

THE WHITE HOUSE
SITUATION ROOM

They were waiting in the Situation Room for the president. The center seat at the long conference table was vacant as it was the president's chair. To the right of the president's chair was secretary of state, Terrance Hertz; to the left was secretary of defense, Al Clancy; next to Clancy was the director of National Intelligence, Frank Green; next to Secretary Hertz the seat was vacant. It was for Maud Evens, the APNSA.

Directly across from the president's chair was the chairman of the Joint Chiefs, General Patterson, the highest-ranking military adviser to the president. To Patterson's right was Lieutenant-General Tony Bellardi, the director of the Defense Intelligence Agency. To the right of Bellardi was the chief of staff of the army, the commandant of the Marine Corps, and the chief of Naval Operations, Admiral Webster. Sitting to the left of Patterson was the DCI, Dr. Cornaci, and to his left the DD, Admiral Charko. Next to Charko was the chief of staff of the air force, General Zabitski.

The door opened and all the heads turned. It was APNSA Evens sauntering in with several files. She took her seat, looked at Cornaci and said, "Looks like you boys fucked up again."

Bellardi leaned over to the chairman. "You own me twenty, General."

General Patterson reached into his pocket, took out a twenty-dollar bill, slipped it to Bellardi, and whispered, "You fuck."

"Well, Maud, I don't mind being called a boy, but I do mind your reference to 'again,'" said Charko. "What the . . ."

Cornaci put his hand on Charko and Charko stopped in mid-sentence.

Evens ignored Charko and said to the group, "Do you all have a copy of the letter that the North Koreans sent us?" Not waiting for an answer, she went on: "As you all know, the Reagan is participating in war games with the South Koreans and is definitely in range of the North's missiles. The . . ."

She stopped speaking as the door opened and the president entered the room. All stood up. The president took his seat and said, "Please be seated. I spoke with the vice-president and discussed the matter with him. Unfortunately, due to a death in his family he cannot be here. I fully intend to brief him at the conclusion of this meeting. I do not want to go to war over this," he hesitated, "but I will not allow them to sink . . . let me correct myself, *try* to sink or capture the Ronald Reagan. We have military and diplomatic options. Let's start with Secretary Clancy."

"Mister President, when we received this," Clancy said, waving the letter, "I met with the Joint Chiefs and I would like, with your permission, to allow the chief of Naval Operations to take over."

The president nodded his head. "Go ahead Admiral Webster."

"Mister President, we could order the Reagan to move to safer waters. But truthfully, I really don't see that as our first military option. It sends a message that we're scared of them and we are not. It also allows them to be bolder the next time. With the satellites, we can tell when they will launch and we'll be ready. We'll have our eyes in the sky, Super Fudd . . ."

"Super Fudd," the president interrupted.

"I apologize, sir. It is the Hawkeye E-2D. That will also give us warning and we will have the Super Hornets and Hornets in the air. The Reagan is also fitted with the RIM-7 Sea Sparrow anti-missile weapon system, which is intended for defense against anti-ship missiles and the RIM-116 Rolling Airframe Missile (RAM). Sir, the Reagan can take care of itself. Not to mention that the carrier strike group has one cruiser, a destroyer squadron of two destroyers and frigates, and in this strike group, a submarine, along with attached logistics ships and a supply ship. I would like to turn this now over to the chief of staff of the air force."

"Go ahead General Wolf," said the president.

"Sir, we have, as you know, several bases in Japan and from either Misaw or the Kadena Air Base we can knock out the radar sites and their launch sites. We can be in and out before they figure out what happened."

The secretary of Defense spoke. "Mister President, we have approximately 50,000 military personnel stationed in Japan. The Seventh Fleet is based in Yokosuka and the 3rd Marine Expeditionary Force is based in Okinawa. We are ready."

"Thank you," said the president, "but it seems like you are going to war and that's not what I want. What do you have to say about this, General Bellardi? You've been quiet."

"Well, Mister President, what we have here are defensive and offensive plans. I think it's what you would call the 'just in case.' Only the Chinese can talk with the North; as you know, they feed them. Without China's oil and food, the North shuts down. I'd suggest a call from you to the Chinese telling them about the threat we received and saying that if their North Korean buddies fire on our ships, we will take appropriate action. They will undoubtedly call the Supreme Leader and advise him if he starts a war he is on his own. Truthfully I don't think the North will take any action, especially if we deny their allegations, which I assume we will."

"Mister President, may I be heard?" asked the secretary of state, Terrance Hertz.

"Sure ,Terry," answered the president, "go ahead."

"Do you think it would be easier to give them the uranium back? Maybe we can win their confidence and prove we are not the aggressors. Give them some money and have a peaceful resolution to this potential war-like issue."

The room was dead silent. Bellardi swore he could hear his watch ticking. He could feel his blood pressure rising. Everyone waited for the president to speak. Finally, he did. "Well, do we have any comments regarding Terry's suggestion?"

"I do," said the only female voice in the room, Maud Evans.

"Go ahead Maud, let's hear it," said the president.

"The secretary's suggestion makes sense. Maybe the North won't attack one of our ships, but maybe they will cause some real havoc in South Korea or possibly turn loose some of their agents and cause some real danger here. The Supreme Leader can't lose face. He has to show he has the courage to stand up to the United States. He will do something—what I don't know. So maybe Secretary Hertz's suggestion has some merit."

"You can't appease a bully, Ms. Evens. You stand up to the bully, Terry. If you give in they will demand we turn our agent over to them and that's not going to happen," said Secretary Clancy.

"I would never suggest to Al that we turn one of our agents over to the North," replied Secretary Hertz. "But to show our sincerity we could put him on trial for . . ."

There was an uproar in the room. The entire group all started to speak at once.

The president clapped his hands loudly, "Gentlemen, gentlemen, please a little order."

The room began to quiet down. General Bellardi had a booming voice and tapped the arm of General Patterson, who nodded his approval. Bellardi leaned over toward Secretary Hertz, and said, "Go fuck yourself. How dare you suggest we put an American hero on trial for doing his job?"

Hertz's face turned red.

"Mister President, may I be heard?" asked the chief of US Naval operations.

The president nodded his approval. "Go ahead, Admiral Webster."

"Mister President, Secretary Hertz, and Ms. Evans, this intelligence officer you have been referring to is a naval officer and SEAL. He most likely would refer to himself as a SEAL and omit the fact that he is one of the most highly-decorated living naval officers. Except for the Medal of Honor, he has every medal and some doubles that this country can bestow. Because he is truly an American hero is not an excuse to break the law, but we cannot let North Korea, or for that matter anyone, allow us to put in harm's way someone who is acting on direct orders. Mr. Secretary, I know upon further reflection you didn't mean what you said."

Secretary Hertz started to stammer and finally said, "I apologize for what I said. I spoke too quickly without thinking. I am sorry."

General Bellardi offered his apology to the secretary.

Charko's face was beet red. His hands were balled into fists. He was about to come out of his seat, when Cornaci spoke. "Mister President, I am the newest member of this council and I come from what most of you know is the world of academia, so please bear with me. Before I go into the details, I would also like to point out that this man has every medal the CIA can award to a living intelligence officer. When I first arrived at Langley, I was struck by the Memorial Wall—it stands as a silent memorial to those officers and employees who gave their lives in the service of their country. There are eighty-seven stars carved into the marble of the Memorial Wall, but no names. The "Book of Honor" lists the names of fifty-four employees who died while serving their country. The names of the remaining thirty-three employees must remain secret, even in death; each of these officers is remembered in the book by a star. Being a hero in the CIA is an unsung song. Living or dead, the officers don't get the accolades they deserve for obvious reasons."

He paused to let it sink in. "We had information that North Korea was selling highly enriched uranium through Cuba to Middle Eastern organizations, terrorist organizations, and it was not for peaceful purposes. Through our intelligence sources we found out that the North Koreans had planned to stage an airplane accident so they didn't have to deliver uranium. We caused a real accident and managed to get a significant amount of the uranium and $50 million. The North has three or four small nuclear weapons. They want to build more, but by taking the uranium we have seriously put a dent in their nuclear program and set it back ten years at least. We've also managed to create issues between the Koreans and the Cubans and the Middle Eastern groups. This mission was a success. Sometimes, even though missions are successful, there are little snags and officers have to improvise, and sometimes they have to kill. This operation cost the life of the Cuban and two North Koreans; no Americans were killed or injured. Notwithstanding the accusations of the North, they have no proof that we were involved. This officer also discovered that the sarin gas was being shipped to North Korea. We discovered that ISIS has a ship, which they like to think of as their navy. That ship is on its way to North Korea and our officer is on that ship."

President Hunt leaned forward. "Tell me he's not going to assassinate the Supreme Leader, because that is a crime in this country and a crime under international law."

"No, Mister President, he is not going to assassinate the Supreme Leader. When he was in Korea the last time, he was in the same room with the Supreme Leader and I assure you he doesn't need a weapon to kill. Our first mission was to get the uranium and this mission is to prevent whatever is going to be on that ship from getting to ISIS. Mister President, he did this on his own. We have no plans to get him out and his life is at risk."

"Doctor, I appreciate everything you say and the way you approach problems. I just don't want an international incident. You know from reading his file, he has the ability to turn a Sunday church picnic into a mob riot. I do not appreciate some of his methods. I don't appreciate what I consider the murder of some of the enemy combatants, but for now let's hope he's successful and that he gets out of North Korea alive."

All around the room everyone said, "Hear, hear."

The president stood and everyone in the room rose. He started to leave but when he reached the door, he stopped and turned around. "I don't want a war. And I don't want North Korean agents running around the United States seeking revenge." Then with a smile he said, "Especially on me. Doctor and Terry, please stay here and draft a response to the Koreans. Have it on my desk today. I will approve it and send it to the Swedes for transmission to the Supreme Leader."

As they all got up to leave, Maud Evens said, "You know the Koreans are going to do something." Then looking at Charko, she said, "Don't fuck up again."

Before Charko could answer, Bellardi spoke, "Come on Admiral, I'll buy you a drink. Be careful Maud, you might be on the Korean hit list and you better hope these boys don't fuck up."

CHAPTER 30

ROMAN TMETUCHL INTERNATIONAL AIRPORT, BABELTHUAP ISLAND, PALAU

Astrid and Ron Haig crossed the tarmac to the waiting Gulfstream. The steward climbed down the stairs and ran toward Astrid to help her with her luggage. He offered to take Haig's bags but Ron waved him off.

"We're almost on the plane, Astrid. I sent my security detail off and hopefully I will be out of here before they get back."

"Let's move, Ron."

They both picked up their pace. Astrid reached the aircraft steps ahead of Haig. She looked up and standing in the door was Jack Reynolds, and behind him was Oscar Ocho. They were Haig's security detail. Oscar Ocho was the head of the detail and the older of the two men. They were not to be fooled by Haig sending them off on a fool's errand.

"Good to see you, Miss Reed," said Jack Reynolds. "Going someplace, Mr. Haig?"

"I don't know about Mr. Haig but I am," said Astrid. "If you'll excuse me, I want to get settled in and I need to talk with the pilot."

JR, as he was known, stepped aside as Astrid entered the aircraft. He came down off the aircraft, followed by Officer Ocho.

Oscar Ocho, who was called 08 said, "Well?"

Haig smiled.

"You're not getting on a plane without us," said JR. "I have been on your security detail since I joined the agency, and I will be dammed if you think you're going to fly away and leave us."

"Do you know where we're going?" asked Haig.

"We checked with the pilot and saw the flight plan," said JR. "I always wanted to go to North Korea. Right 08?"

"North Korea, South Korea, East Korea, who cares. Where you go Mr. Haig, we go," said Ocho.

"I appreciate your loyalty but I am going to deliberately break an order. I can go out on pension. You're too young. This will ruin your careers. You're supposed to prevent me from going to North Korea, not aid and abet me. If you can't follow orders, you'll be in trouble."

Ocho spoke. "Won't be the first time and as long as you work with Mac Daniels it won't be the last time."

"Okay, come on let's go. But one thing, JR if I hear you refer to me as 'Grandpa' I'm going to kick your ass. Got that?"

"Yes sir, poppy. What about our plane?" asked JR, referring to the Citation.

Haig thought for a moment. "Have the pilot fly to Seoul. We can meet the plane there." Under his breath, as if he were praying, he said, "I hope so."

"Welcome aboard, gentlemen," said Astrid. "The pilot tells me it is about 2,500 miles to Pyongyang. We should be on the ground in about four hours. By then I should be able to teach you how to handle the camera and the recording equipment."

"They can learn how to use the equipment, Astrid, but more importantly they know how to handle Octanitrocubane."

She understood.

CHAPTER 31

THE SAILS OF ALLAH

The captain sat in his chair on the bridge, staring out into the sea. He would be glad when this voyage was over. He looked over at his first officer Akram Salib and thought, *What an idiot.* Salib had never been out of the Mediterranean Sea and was a third officer at best. The ISIS commander had assigned him to the ship as first officer and he was about as useful as tits on a bull. On the ship, the captain was in command, but once they set foot on land, Salib was the commanding officer and the captain knew he would be under Salib's control. A plan was formulating in the captain's mind.

Salib asked the captain, "Why don't you allow me to interrogate the prisoner?"

The captain ignored the question. "We should be leaving the Yellow Sea. Do you know why it is called the Yellow Sea?"

Salib was clearly annoyed and losing his patience, but he knew his place on the ship. "Because all the little yellow chinks piss in the sea. I don't know and don't care, Captain."

"You should know, Akram. Someday you will be a ship's captain. Its name comes from the sand particles from Gobi Desert; sand storms that turn the surface of the water golden yellow."

"Thank you, sir," replied Salib in a most sarcastic tone. "Now may I bring the prisoner up to the bridge?"

Again, the captain ignored the question. "Check our position," he ordered. "We should be in the Korea Bay, and if I am right that is North P'yŏngan Province of North Korea off the starboard."

The first officer was at a boiling point and this showed. He checked his global position satellite, which was locked into the automatic pilot. "You are correct, Captain. We are about 200 km southwest of Namp'o. Captain, the prisoner?"

The captain looked at him for a long moment. Finally, he asked, "Why? That man is dangerous, leave him locked up until we dock."

"Captain, we should have killed him when he came on board. Raja and Aban are missing. We lost our radio communications and he's responsible. We should interrogate and kill him."

The captain let out a sigh. "Go ahead and bring him up to the bridge."

A few minutes later, Daniels was on the bridge with the captain, the first officer, and the helmsman. "What's the occasion for letting me out of my room, Captain? You have me locked up under armed guard except for the time I checked on the sarin. What gives?"

"Mac Brown, or whatever your name is, First Officer Salib has some questions for you. I suggest you answer him truthfully."

Daniels faced the Salib. "Well, what is it?"

"Answer my questions and you'll have a quick death. Otherwise, you will pray for your death. What happened to Raja and Aban, and why are you here?"

"You know why I am here. My job is to keep the sarin from killing all of you. Whatever happened to your crew, I don't know. You had me locked up in the room and . . ."

Salib drew the Makarov pistol from his belt and pointed it at Daniels.

"Be careful, you can get hurt with that," said Daniels.

"And you will be dead."

Daniels turned to the captain and said, "Do you really need a first officer?"

The captain did not answer. He looked away.

The first officer raised the pistol.

"Well, Captain, I take your silence as a no." Turning to Salib, he said, "How can you shoot me with the safety on, the hammer not cocked, and no shell in the tube?"

Salib looked at his weapon and before he could look up, Daniels grabbed it out of his hand and in one motion slipped the safety off, chambered a round, and pointed the weapon at Salib's head. "Well, now I have a question for you. Are you a member of ISIS?"

"I am. I am an officer in the armed forces of the Caliphate of the Islamic State. I am loyal to our leader Abu Bakr al Baghdadi, the Caliph of all Muslims and the Prince of the Believers."

"And you are at war with the West?"

"We are and I will kill you." Salib lunged at Daniels.

The sound of the Makarov filled the bridge. A small hole instantly appeared in the forehead of the first officer, and the back wall of the bridge was spattered with blood and bone.

"No, you won't," said Daniels. Turning to the captain, he said, "A casualty of war."

The helmsman turned toward Daniels. Daniels waved the gun in his face. "Are you a member of ISIS?"

The young helmsman shook his head. He couldn't speak.

"Good, now take this piece of shit and throw him overboard, then go down and get a mop and clean up the cabin. I have business with the captain."

The helmsman dragged the body of the first officer out of the bridge onto the upper deck and pushed his body overboard.

"Thank you, Mr. Brown," said the captain. "I believe you did me a favor."

"You're welcome, Captain. How long till we turn into the Taedong River?"

"In about four hours we should be at Namp'o, then we turn northeast into the river and in another two hours we should be at Pyongyang," answered the captain. "Who are you and why are you here?"

"Does it matter?" Daniels said as he handed the pistol to the captain.

The captain looked at the pistol and said, "I don't need this," and threw it down. "But I think it's time we had a talk. Perhaps we will find out we are truly allies and not enemies."

"Are you a member of ISIS?" asked Daniels.

The captain shook his head. "I'm a sailor, a ship's captain. I have been sailing the seas all my life. I am a Syrian. My wife, my children, and my parents live in Raqqa, which as you know is the capital of the Islamic State. I was told that I would sail for the ISIS government, or else. I am a Muslim but I am not a member of ISIS. I don't condone brutality and the killing of women and children, burning alive, beheadings, and crucifixions. This is not what Islam is. By killing the first officer you got rid of an ISIS commander. I assume you somehow killed Raja and Aban, the other two members of ISIS forces on my ship."

"I killed them and threw them overboard. When they came into my room, they started in on me. I had no choice. I would never have made it to you."

"You did everybody aboard the ship a favor."

"What are you picking up in North Korea?"

"I honestly don't know. I am to deliver the oil to a special dock on the Pot'ong River."

"Pot'ong?"

"Yes, the Pot'ong is a tributary of the Taedong River. It runs north off the Taedong. It soon becomes non-navigable to large ships. Small craft can go all the way up to the airport. A pilot boat will escort us to this special dock, where I pick up my cargo and I will deliver it to Syria. Unless you stop me."

"Syria, then where to?"

"I don't know. You did not answer me. Are you going to stop me from delivering my cargo?"

"Let me think about that. I have some things to take care of. The less you know the better, for your sake. By the way, I want my knife back."

"It's in my cabin. I will get it for you later."

"How did Rajul get in touch with you?" asked Daniels.

"My cell phone. I do not know how he got my cell number. Only one of the commanders could have given him my number. I never met him. I was told to cooperate with him. His name is Aswas Rajul. Arabic is not his native tongue. From his words and accent, I think he is a westerner, maybe even an American. I know nothing other than I was supposed to deliver the oil to North Korea and of course I wasn't expecting you. I tried to reach him to confirm your identity, but I can't. I assume you disabled the communications."

"Change your fuses, then the radio will work. Let's get the communications working. I would like to talk with Rajul."

"When you came on board didn't you take a chance that I would kill you?"

"Not really, you held a knife backwards. The cutting edge was in, not out. You would have had to switch hands and turn the blade over. I would have taken the knife away from you and killed you."

"What about shooting you?

"The safety was on and it wasn't cocked. I would've turned around, taken the pistol just the way I did, and shot you and the two guys on deck who had slung their weapons. They were not professional soldiers. Never sling your weapons; you cannot use them that way. Then I would have had to kill everyone else on the ship and I'd be stuck navigating this boat by myself."

"Who are you?"

"I'm your new best friend."

CHAPTER 32

PYONGYANG SUNAN INTERNATIONAL AIRPORT

The pilot's voice came over the intercom. "We are thirty minutes away from landing. Please be sure your seatbelts are secure and please put away all loose items, thank you. We're cleared to land on runway one and the wind is from the west so it will be a little bumpy until we touch down."

Astrid looked out the window. They were still in the clouds and there was no visibility. It must be a low ceiling she thought. Haig, JR, and 08 all checked their seat belts to be sure they were tight. No one said anything, but the clouds surrounding the aircraft seemed to have everyone's attention. The Gulfstream 650 was a good aircraft, but it was considerably smaller and lighter than most commercial aircraft and was being bounced around.

Astrid picked up a handset and keyed the microphone, "Virgil, how's your visibility?"

Virgil Pollard was World New Corporation's chief pilot and most of the time he was flying Astrid. There was a long pause before he answered. "To be honest Miss Reed, there's no visibility. I don't think we're going to see the ground until we're on it. It's pea soup fog out there. I'm flying instruments and I'm locked onto their ILS. The good news is we have plenty of runway... over 13,000 feet and all we need is about 3,000. So if I come in a little fast there won't be a problem stopping."

"I hope their IL system works better than their electric does," she said as she hung up the handset.

JR's eyebrows rose almost to his hairline. Astrid saw the look on his face. While Astrid was a seasoned traveler, she too at times was nervous when the plane bounced around or when she couldn't see the ground, especially when they were landing. She always marveled at Mac—he just put the seat back and would go to sleep, even sleeping through landings.

"Relax JR; ILS is an instrument landing system. A radio beam transmitter provides a direction for approaching aircraft. We set our receiver to the ILS frequency for precision approaches. There's nothing to worry about," said Astrid, trying to reassure him as well as herself.

"Only if the electric fails," he quipped.

"Point well taken."

The aircraft was about five miles from the runway, passing the final approach fix and the pilot extended the landing gear. Astrid turned to Haig and forced a smile. She was scared—not of the landing, but because she knew this could be a one-way trip.

Haig gave her a thumbs-up sign.

Ocho and Reynolds sat there quietly, deep in their own thoughts. They had all come into this hostile situation unarmed. They would be at the mercy of the North Koreans. As a security detail, they had no information that would be meaningful to the Koreans, but they both knew that Haig would be a treasure trove. If they were taken captive, the question would be who would kill Haig. He could not be captured, as torture would eventually win out.

The aircraft touched down. The Virgil reversed thrusters and the aircraft came to a rolling stop. Over Virgil's' headset came an order to proceed to one of the parking bays away from the main terminal. Virgil taxied over to the designated parking bay, set the brakes, and turned off the engines. From the window, he saw several vehicles approaching the aircraft.

His voice came over the intercom. "Ground control requests that everyone stay in the plane until customs officials board and clear us. Miss Reed, there are several vehicles surrounding the plane; two cars and several trucks. I'm not opening the main door and dropping the staircase until ground control tells me to do so."

From the window, Astrid saw several squads of soldiers disembark from the trucks; all armed. They circled the aircraft, but no one approached.

She turned to JR and Ocho. "Remember, if you see Mac do not acknowledge him. Let Mac make the first move. When we travel, I find it impossible not to call him Mac, so he always uses a variety of aliases with Mac in it, Mac Arthur, Mac Williams, Mac Brown, Mac Donald, it's always Mac something, and he'll tell you what to call him. Take your time and smile—remember we're a film crew."

Haig's satellite phone rang and he looked at it. "Holy shit, it's Charko."

"You better answer it Ron," said Astrid.

"Yes Admiral," said Haig.

"Two things Ron: I am reminding you, don't set foot in North Korea, you understand?" It was more of an order than a question. Not waiting for an answer, the admiral went on. "The North Koreans know about the uranium switch and want blood. They threatened the Reagan. I don't know how, but you should try to get the word to Mac. The official position is we are denying any involvement in the incident. The president will be calling the president of China to advise him of the situation. Bellardi and I are making a few calls of our own. We have some assets in Pyongyang but this is going to be difficult.

You know what this means—there's a rotten apple somewhere within our ranks. No one could have tipped off the North Koreans about the operation except from the inside. The director has already initiated investigations and notified Director Bertone of the FBI. Where are you?"

"I'm with Astrid, sitting quietly in her plane trying to talk some sense into her. She's still hell-bent on going to North Korea, but she may be the only way to get word to Mac."

"Do what you have to do, but keep me posted."

"Astrid, we have to talk." Haig unbuckled his seat belt and moved over to Astrid.

"The North Koreans know about Mac's last operation. Exactly how much they know I'm not sure. If you can, you have to give him a warning. Two words: cake burnt."

Astrid looked at Haig and repeated, "Cake burnt. I understand. Cake burnt."

"That's the most important message. He'll know what to do. If you can, let him know that the Koreans are threatening to take action against the carrier Ronald Reagan and we are in touch with the Chinese. You have to warn him. I don't know how you're going to do it but you have to do it."

"What about you?" she asked Haig. "Can't you warn him?"

"I'll do my best, but I wanted you to know. Between the two of us one of us should be able to get him the message."

Virgil Pollard's voice came over the intercom. "Miss Reed, we've been ordered to open the door, and there are two men ready to board the aircraft. One looks like some type of military officer, and the other looks like someone dressed in his big brother's hand-me-downs. He's wearing a black suit that doesn't fit."

The copilot disengaged the door and the stairway dropped to the ground. The two men boarded the aircraft. Astrid rose to meet them.

The man in the dark, ill-fitted suit spoke first. "Welcome, Miss Reed, to Democratic People's Republic of Korea. I am Sang Ji-hu, a deputy minister in the Ministry of State Security for Pyongyang. This is," he said, pointing to the man in uniform, "Captain Gil Min-Su of our customs office. He will check your passports and examine your bags."

"Not a problem, Mr. Sang," said Astrid as she handed her passport to Captain Gil.

"Who are these people, Miss Reed?" asked Sang, pointing to the others.

Pointing to Haig, she said, "This is my cameraman," then to Ocho, "this is my sound and recording man," and finally pointing to JR, "and this is my producer-director."

"Very good, Miss Reed, but they cannot enter North Korea. Only you. They do not have permission and they are not on the list. We will supply you with a cameraman and a recording man."

"That's impossible, Mr. Sang. I need these people."

"You have two choices; leave the Democratic People's Republic of Korea and go home without an interview, or stay without these people and meet Supreme Leader and see our beautiful city and enjoy a stay at one of our famous hotels."

Astrid thought for a moment. She pulled down her suitcase, and pointing to Haig's bag asked him to pass it to her. He hesitated for a second, and then handed it to her and said nothing. He hoped he'd made the right choice. He did not try to stop her.

She picked up the handset and keyed the mike for the pilot. "Virgil, as soon as I'm off the plane, leave for the most convenient airport and wait for my call. Please do a standby."

"Yes, Miss Reed. I will see if I can get permission to land in Seoul and we will be happy to do a standby for you."

Standby meant that at all times either the pilot or copilot would be on board, and the other would not be more than fifteen minutes away. If necessary, they would sleep on board waiting for her call.

Astrid picked up her bags and said, "Okay, Captain Gil. Once we're inside the terminal you can search my bags. Let's go."

JR stood up. "Miss Reed you can't go without me."

Astrid turned to face him with a surprised look on her face.

"Mr. Sang, you may have cameramen and sound recording men, but I am the producer-director of this interview. I am the one who helps formulate questions. I direct Miss Reed. You cannot have an interview without a producer-director. I worked with Miss Reed on this interview and no one else can fill in for me."

Sang was puzzled. Finally, he said, "Wait here." He exited the aircraft, and standing down on the tarmac, he took out his phone and made a call. No one could hear what he said and if they could it wouldn't matter. No one spoke or understood Korean.

From his body language, he seemed aggravated. His hands were flying through the air as if the person on the end of the call could see him. A few minutes later, he returned to the aircraft. "You can come. No one else leave this plane."

JR handed his passport to Captain Gil, who looked at it and returned it. JR picked up his bag and grabbed Astrid's suitcase. She took Haig's duffel bag. As she came up to the doorway, she leaned into the cockpit. "Put the pedal to the metal, Virgil. Wait for my call. Safe travels."

"Yes, ma'am," said Virgil Pollard. He knew what "pedal to the metal" meant. Go as fast as you can go. He wasn't sure what his boss was up to, but he understood she wanted him out of North Korea airspace as fast as possible and he was going to do that. Even before they were off the plane, he was on the radio with ground control for clearance to taxi and take off.

Astrid got into the first car with Sang and JR got into the second car with Gil. The copilot pulled up the stairs and locked the door as Pollard started the starboard engine. A few minutes later, the Gulfstream was rolling toward the runway for takeoff.

Haig and Ocho sat quietly, knowing they could do nothing.

Ocho turned to Haig and said, "How do we explain this, sir?"

"We don't."

Virgil's voice came over the intercom, "Buckle up, we are out of here. It is 142 miles from Pyongyang to Seoul; the approximate travel time is twenty-one minutes."

"Miss Reed is a civilian—we can't stop her, Oscar, but the minute JR volunteered to get off this aircraft, he was on his own. When you disobey an order, one of two things happens; you get shot or you get a medal. Let's hope JR gets a medal."

Inside the terminal, JR threw his bag up on the table. Gil opened it and went through it item by item. He carefully inspected the entire bag for any type of false compartments and spent at least fifteen minutes examining the bag. He nodded his approval. "Next," he said.

Astrid handed up her suitcase. Gil opened it and went through all of her personal belongings, examining everything. His hands spent too much time on her fine underwear. Astrid wanted to say something, but she knew better. Gil inspected the lining, looking for a false compartment. Twenty minutes later he was done. Astrid then threw up Haig's bag and Gil opened it.

"This is a man's bag," he said.

Astrid looked and acted disappointed. "Oh, I took the camera man's bag by mistake. Where's the plane? Maybe we can swap bags."

"The plane is gone. If it went to Seoul, it already landed. I don't think you can get it back," said Gil.

"Oh, well," she said shaking her head. She took the baseball cap and put it on. "I guess I can live without it." She put on a big smile. "Can I go? I would like to check into the hotel and prepare for my meeting with the Supreme Leader."

CHAPTER 33

KORYO HOTEL

From an almost deserted airport to the city, Astrid saw little signs of life that you expect to find in a city with over two and half million people. There was little traffic, and there were virtually no private cars, mostly taxis and buses. Astrid noticed that most of the stores were empty of customers. She felt Sang Ji-hu's eyes on her. She was taller than he was... taller than most of the women here and certainly bigger breasted than the Korean women were. He kept staring at her bust line.

As they approached the hotel district, Sang finally spoke to her. "I hope you enjoyed the ride, Miss Reed. The Supreme Leader has arranged for you to stay at our world-famous, five-star hotel, the Koryo Hotel. The hotel is situated along the Taedong River in Chung-kuyok, central Pyongyang. It is the second largest hotel in North Korea, but it is the nicest. The building has twin towers, and is 469 feet tall, and contains forty-three stories. Did you know that Koryo is the name of an early kingdom of our forefathers? It is where the English word Korea comes from."

"No, Mr. Sang, I did not know that. I am looking forward to touring your city."

With a big toothy grin, which showed his yellow teeth stained from smoking, he said, "Would you please call me Ji-hu."

"Only if you call me Astrid."

"Thank you, Astrid. When we get to the hotel, you will meet your official guide. The Supreme Leader has planned for you to see the wonderful sights of our city."

For the next fifteen minutes, Sang babbled on about the city and Astrid was relieved when the cars pulled up to the front of the hotel. She was worried that he was going to suggest they have a drink together, and she was not sure how he would handle rejection.

The hotel's entrance consisted of a thirty-foot wide jade dragon's mouth that led into an expansive lobby dominated by a mosaic of North Korean cultural symbols. Standing inside the lobby was a young Chinese man. He came over to Astrid and said, "Welcome to Pyongyang, Miss Reed. My name is Guozhi Sun. I will be your guide while you are here. May I help with your luggage?"

"Thank you, Go...z. I'm sorry I'm having trouble pronouncing your first name, Mr. Sun. Your English is perfect. Where did you learn to speak so well?"

He laughed. "I lived in the United States for over ten years. I graduated from Harvard. In the States, I was called Sunny. Please feel free to use that appellation. I majored in communications and your company was often a topic of our lectures."

"I'm flattered."

"I would enjoy the chance to talk with you while you are here, Miss Reed."

"Astrid, please," she said. "This is Jack Reynolds, my producer-director. We call him JR."

Sun extended his hand. "Welcome, JR."

"Pleased to meet you, Sunny."

"Mr. Sang," said Sun, "I will be pleased to take care of these two."

Sang grunted. "I think I will stay and assist you. You can take care of JR and I will attend to Miss," catching himself, "Astrid."

Sang's phone rang, and a few minutes of conversation went on. Astrid could not understand a thing, but she heard the word "Allah."

Sang finished his call. He looked at Astrid. "I have to go. Sun will be your guide. State business calls."

"I'm sorry you have to leave. I was so pleased to be escorted by someone of your rank, Ji-hu. Maybe lunch? Can't someone else go for you?"

Sang let out a big sigh. He shook his head. "Duty calls. I have to arrest an enemy of the state."

"Can I go with you? This would be a great story, to see you in action."

"I am afraid not. It might be dangerous."

"Is there something you can tell me for my story? Maybe over a drink tonight."

"I have to go out to a ship, the Sails of Allah. There is an intruder on the ship. I will tell you more when I have the details. But as you say, it is off the record."

She winked at him. "Off the record." She knew who that intruder was.

"Mr. Sun, you are in charge. Take good care of Astrid."

Sun nodded to Sang, who turned and left. Sun brought them over to the desk to check in. A young Chinese woman greeted them to handle the transaction. Astrid took out a credit card, which the woman politely refused.

"I am sorry," said Sun. "But your Office of Foreign Assets Control prevents the use of credit cards here. You need cash and if you do not have it the Swedish Embassy can help with a money transfer."

"I have some money, thank you."

A Chinese bellboy picked up her bags and led the way to the elevator. He pressed thirty-eight.

"It seems that everyone who works here is Chinese," said Astrid.

"Not quite, but almost. Japanese expatriates operate the four restaurants, including the two revolving restaurants at the top of each tower and the circular bar on the forty-fourth floor just below the restaurants. Other than that, all the employees are Chinese, even the staff of the casino, which is located in the basement."

"Are all the official guides Chinese too?"

"Most are."

They were in the south tower, which was used only by foreign tourists; the north tower was for North Koreans only. The elevator stopped and the bellboy led the way to their rooms on the thirty-eighth floor. The bellboy opened the door to Astrid's room and they all stepped in. Astrid was in a corner room with a southeast view of the Taedong River and JR would have the adjoining room. There was a connecting door between the rooms. The room had a large double bed, with a tufted, padded headboard. She immediately thought of Mac, and then realized that each of the tufted buttons could be a listening device. There was a dresser, a desk, and chairs and ornate lamps on the end tables. Across from the bed was a large, flatscreen television fixed to the wall. She wondered if someone could see her from the television. She would drape a towel over the screen as soon as she was alone. She was pleasantly surprised at how nice the room was. The bellboy demonstrated the operation of the television and the mini-bar. Astrid handed him five dollars. He refused the tip and left. JR turned to follow him.

"JR, please stay here for a moment," Sun said. "There are a few rules you should know. The first and most important rule; never leave the hotel without me. North Korean security personnel may regard as espionage unauthorized attempts to speak directly to North Korean citizens or unescorted travel without your official guide. North Korean authorities may fine or arrest travelers for exchanging currency with an unauthorized vendor. The bellboy would have been arrested had he been found with American currency. You can exchange your currency for the won at official exchange offices. You may be fined or arrested for taking unauthorized photographs, or for shopping at stores not designated for foreigners. It is a criminal act in North Korea to show disrespect to the country's former leaders, Kim Jong Il and Kim Il Sung, or to the current leader, Kim Jong Un. Any questions?"

"Sounds like fun," said JR. "At least you can drink the water. Can you?"

"The drinking water is untreated and there are reports of foreigners being hospitalized, so stick with bottled water. Any other questions?"

"Cell phones usable here?" asked JR.

"Yes, you may use them, but there are no cell towers for civilian use. I am afraid your phones are useless here. Unless," he added with a big smile, "you have CIA satellite phones."

"Damn. I knew I forgot something," said Astrid.

Astrid had a special satellite phone that Mac had given her and she knew it would work here. She did not want JR using his phone. The rooms were bugged.

"JR, no cell phones, right?"

He got the message. "Right, Astrid. What about smoke signals?"

"I don't think so. Oh well, what's on the agenda for today?" asked Astrid.

"Why don't you take some time to freshen up then meet me in the lobby? We will have lunch, then we will take a tour of the city sights."

"I'm starved," said JR.

"How about Italian? The Pyolmuri restaurant just down the block from us on Changkwang Street is the first Italian restaurant in North Korea and almost as good as Boston's pasta and pizza."

"That settles it," said Astrid. "See you in the lobby in thirty minutes."

Sun left them. JR was about to say something but Astrid cut him off. "I want to freshen up. We can go over the interview later. See you in the lobby."

When JR left, Astrid started to unpack. She knew the room was bugged and probably had hidden cameras. She could not detect them and it upset her. *If Mac were here, he would find them instantly,* she thought. She was not going to give the security team a free show. She went into the bathroom and turned on the hot water in the tub and sink. The bathroom started to steam up. The mirrors fogged except where the camera was. The ceiling light fixture also fogged up except where the hidden lens was. The tub was safe and she could use the shower curtain liner as an overhead shield. Under her breath she said, "Fuck you."

CHAPTER 34

SAILS OF ALLAH

Daniels was on the starboard side of the bridge next to the captain. He was sitting in the first officer's seat. There was no further discussion except for the navigation of the ship in the river. Off the port side, they passed the Pueblo. They both looked and neither one said anything. Daniels felt like saluting, but he didn't want to break his story that he was Canadian, so he brought his right hand up and with his fingertips scratched his eyebrows. That was the best he could do for now. A little while later, the ship turned north into the Pot'ong River.

"Mr. Mac Brown, there seems to be more than just the pilot on the pilot boat. It looks like two soldiers and a man in a black suit, most likely state security. I think they are here for you. Are you going to kill them?"

"No. I'll deal with them. Just tell them what I told you; the truth. I am here regarding the safe handling of the sarin. You can leave out the part about your dead crew. One more thing—hold on to my knife. I have a feeling they would keep it. But I will get it from you."

"As you wish, Mr. Mac Brown. For some reason I like you. Assalamu Alaykum"

"Wa alaykum assalam."

The captain brought the ship to idle as the pilot boat maneuvered into position. The captain ordered the accommodation ladder lowered so that the pilot could come aboard. The Pot'ong River had some tight twists and turns, not to mention the tricky shallow. He was pleased to have a pilot navigate the ship to its final destination.

A few minutes later, the three men, along with the pilot, entered the bridge from the port side. The two soldiers were dressed in the uniform of the People's Liberation Army Navy. The man in the dark suit spoke Korean.

The captain shook his head. "I speak Arabic and English."

"English," said the older man. "My name is Sang Ji-hu. I am a deputy minister in the Ministry of State Security for Pyongyang. We are here for your prisoner."

"What prisoner?"

"We received a report from Park that you picked up a passenger in the ocean."

"Park?" asked the captain.

"Yes, Ki-Young Park."

"There was no prisoner, Mr. Sang—only John Mac Brown, the man who took care of the sarin gas so we all did not die en route." The captain turned to Daniels and winked.

Daniels mouthed, "Thank you."

"Mr. Sang, this is John Mac Brown," said the captain, pointing to Daniels.

Sang let out a few words in Korean, most likely not complimentary.

"I do not speak Korean, only Arabic and English," said Daniels.

"You are under arrest for espionage."

"Espionage, Mr. Sang? I just got here. There must be some mistake."

Sang barked something in Korean. The soldiers carried type-56 assault rifles; the Chinese variant of the Russian-designed AK-47. They slung the weapons over their right shoulders and approached Daniels.

The captain smiled and said under his breath in a low tone, "That's a mistake."

Sang took out his Crvena Zastava M70 pistol, capable of firing a 9mm Browning Short. There was a manual safety above the grip panel. Sang kept his thumb by the safety, ready to thumb it off, and his trigger finger extended over the trigger guard and off the trigger.

"Do not make me shoot you. Believe me I will."

The two soldiers approached Daniels shoulder to shoulder, effectively blocking any shot Sang would have. With their right hands, they reached for Daniels' arms. He grabbed their arms and pulled. The action caused their rifles to slip off their shoulders. The natural reaction was for them to reach for the rifles. Daniels grabbed the rifle slings and pulled hard, causing the two to fall, and as they did he knocked their heads together, making a loud thump. It stunned them. He followed up with quick jabs to their throats, and then he kicked one in the knee, causing him to fall. Daniels kicked the other in the solar plexus forcing him to lose conscious and to fall into Sang.

The pilot started to move forward to assist his countrymen. The captain raised his hand and stopped him. "Don't do it. You will only get hurt. Watch the rest of the show."

Sang fell back and as he did, his right hand went up in the air. Daniels grabbed Sang's right arm, twisted it behind his back, and pushed Sang into the cabin wall. Sang tried to push off the wall, but Daniels kicked his legs out and he fell on to the deck, landing hard.

Daniels grabbed the pistol out of Sang's hand and tucked it into his waist-band. He took the two assault rifles, released the magazines, and ejected the shell in the chamber. He opened the starboard door and threw the magazines and cartridges into the water. He was going to toss the assault rifles too, but he changed his mind.

"Why not the rifles?" asked the captain.

"They're going to be in enough trouble. I didn't want them to get shot over losing their weapons. If they're lucky they might not be noticed."

Sang groaned. Daniels picked him up and dropped him into the first mate's chair. As Sang regained his senses, he saw the butt of the Crvena Zastava stick-ing out of Daniels' waistband. He thought about trying to grab it. When he saw the soldiers lying on the deck; one unconscious and the other rolling in pain, he thought better of it. "You will get caught, and I will personally shoot you."

"No, you won't. If you listen, I will make you a hero. If you don't listen, General Cheon will shoot you himself."

At the mention of the name General Cheon, Sang sat upright. Daniels had his attention. "How do you know of General Cheon?"

"Because I work for him."

"What do you mean?"

"I mean just that. If you do something stupid like shoot me, Cheon will kill you. When you tell him I am here, he will want to see me. He will be pleased with you for using your brains and not your guns."

Sang thought about it for a second. No one in his right mind would say what this man had said. The more he thought, the more he believed it. "I cannot take you to General Cheon. I must make several calls to arrange it. Where do you intend to stay if I let you leave here?"

"Give me a name of a tourist hote where you have eyes and ears. I will get a meal, shower, and shave and wait for you in my room."

Sang thought about it and thought of Astrid Reed. He wanted to see her again. Maybe have a drink. She was the most beautiful woman he had ever seen. *Maybe*, he thought, *who knows?* A smile began to form on his face. "I will put you at the Koryo Hotel. I will stay there with you while we wait to see General Cheon."

"Good, let's go. I suggest you leave these two with the captain. By the time he docks, they should feel better. There's no reason for them to know what I told you. You should get all the credit. Captain, is that acceptable to you?"

"Not a problem Mac, not a problem."

"Let's go, Mr. Sang. I need a shower and a shave."

Daniels took the Crvena Zastava out of his waistband and handed it to Sang. Sang looked at it then placed it in his pocket. He thought of Astrid.

"Captain, may I request a favor?" said Daniels. "Could you send someone down to my room and have him bring me my duffel bag, please?"

A few minutes later, Sang and Daniels went down the accommodation ladder to the waiting pilot boat.

CHAPTER 35

THE KORYO HOTEL

The last time Daniels had stayed at the Koryo Hotel, he was registered as Miguel Antonio Ricardo, the honored guest of the Democratic People's Republic of Korea. He had walked out of the hotel then, and he hoped to walk out of it now and not leave in a box.

Daniels and Sang crossed the massive lobby, which Daniels had to admit was impressive. It was three stories high and almost big enough to play football. The dominant theme in the lobby was mosaics depicting North Korean cultural symbols. A country so poor, but the precious metals and gems used to create the mosaics could have fed a village or two. That was why he thought there were no North Koreans working there.

At the desk, Sang told the clerk to give Mr. Brown a room. Daniels handed over his Canadian passport and the clerk looked at the photograph and at Daniels. Satisfied, she began the registration process.

"While you are at it," said Sang, "I'll need another room for another of our special guests. He should be here in a few hours. They are docking his ship now. His name is Captain Anas Anka. Put him and our friend here on the same floor and if possible, next to each other, so I can keep an eye on them."

She hit her computer keyboard and created key cards for the rooms. "Mr. Sang, will you be staying here tonight, too?"

He thought about it. "Good idea. Be sure I am near them."

The clerk went back to the computer and finally announced, "I will put you all on the thirty-eighth floor with your other guests. Miss Reed is 3800, Mr. Reynolds is 3802, Mr. Mac Brown will be 3804, Captain Anka will be in 3806, and you sir, will be in 3808. Does that work for you?"

"Yes," said Sang with a big smile, "that works well. Is Miss Reed in her room?"

The clerk checked the detailed itinerary that Sun had left with her, in case State security wanted to follow them. "No, she, Mr. Reynolds, and Mr. Sun went for lunch at the Pyolmuri restaurant. After lunch they are coming back here for a while, then Sun will . . ."

"Enough, enough. I will speak with Sun when he returns."

"Sang, is that Astrid Reed of the World News Corporation?" asked Daniels.

"Yes. She is here to interview the Supreme Leader. She is the most beautiful woman I have ever seen. Do you know her?"

"I know of her, but I do not know her. You're right. She is beautiful. I have an idea; why not invite her for dinner? You, me, and Miss Reed."

"You will eat with the captain, and then go to your room. I will tend to Astrid and wait for one of General Cheon's aides to call me back regarding you. Eat well tonight. It could be your last meal, and Mac Brown, if so, I will pull the trigger."

Daniels just smiled. "You're the boss. Before I go to my room for a shave and shower, I want to go to the gift shop and pick up a few things."

Sang nodded and Daniels went into the gift shop. He was hoping to waste time and maybe there would be a chance that Astrid would be back from lunch. He figured Sang was smitten with her and would not pass up the chance to be with her. That was probably the only reason he thought that Sang let him go to the gift shop.

Sang sat in the reception area facing the hotel entrance with his back to the gift shop. Daniels could see him from the gift shop and had to laugh to himself. Astrid had no idea of her magical charms. He did not want Astrid here in harm's way and if she could charm the Supreme Leader the way she had Sang, everything would work out . . . he hoped.

Daniels looked over the assortment of gifts and necessities that are found in most hotel shops. He decided to buy a few t-shirts and handed the cashier his Canadian currency. The gift shop was a hard currency store where foreign money was welcome.

As Daniels came out of the store, Sang sprang to his feet and moved quickly toward the main entrance of the hotel. Astrid and JR were coming in the entrance with their official guide. Sang was right, she was beautiful, but what was JR doing there? He was part of Ron's security detail. What was going on, Daniels wondered. He followed Sang hoping Astrid, and now JR, could play their parts.

"Astrid, did you enjoy your lunch?" asked Sang.

"It was a wonderful Italian meal. How did you make out with the enemy of the state?" she asked.

Astrid didn't see Mac as he walked down the perimeter of the lobby. He wanted to approach her from the side and not head-on. He was worried if she spotted him at a distance she might give herself away. It was better to come on her suddenly. There would be less chance for her to slip.

"The enemy of the state turned out to be more complex than I had thought."

"Sang, are you calling me an enemy of the state? Shame on you," said Daniels.

All turned at the sound of Daniels' voice. Before anyone could say anything, Daniels continued, "Hello, my name is John Mac Brown—please call me Mac. Miss Reed, you're certainly more beautiful than all your pictures. I'm an avid reader of your Canadian papers and I watch your World News Show."

Astrid held out her hand. "Thank you, Mac. I should thank you twice; once for my papers and once for my show. The beauty remark I'm sure is gratuitous."

"It's just the truth, Miss Reed."

"Are you the enemy of the state?" she asked.

"No, just a guest of the state. In fact, I'm a guest at this fine hotel," Daniels said, holding up his room key card.

"Well, how nice. This is my producer-director Jack Reynolds and our guide Mr. Sun."

Sun extended his hand and said, "My name is Guozhi Sun, please call me Sunny."

Reynolds extended his hand and said, "They call me JR."

"That's easy enough, JR. Pleased to meet you. Well, if you'll all excuse me, I'm going to my room to shower and shave. Perhaps I'll see you at dinner tonight."

Daniels left them standing there and went to the elevator.

"He doesn't seem so dangerous, Ji-hu," said Astrid.

"He is not what he seems, Astrid. He disarmed two soldiers, and I am ashamed to say, myself. It all happened so fast. I do not know how he did it. As you Americans say, the jury is out on him. But let him not prevent us from having a good time in our beautiful city."

"Before we tour, I would like to freshen up. That's why we came back here. If you will excuse me."

"I will escort you to your room, Astrid," said Sang.

"Astrid," said JR, "I would like to get a few gifts. My mother Lara and my sister Cindy wouldn't forgive me if I didn't bring something back. I'll be up shortly."

"I will stay here with you JR," said Sun.

Astrid and Sang took the elevator to the thirty-eighth floor, and Sang followed Astrid to her room. As she opened the door he said, "Can we have dinner tonight, Astrid?"

"How about an after-dinner drink, Ji-hu? I can't leave JR alone. It wouldn't be right. I'll see you downstairs."

Sang had an ear-to-ear smile. "Very well, drinks it is. I will be down in the lobby. I have some business to attend to."

As Astrid shut the door, a hand came around her and covered her mouth. Her eyes widened. She was turned around. It was Mac. He brought his finger to his lips. She threw her arms around him and kissed him.

He whispered in her ear. "Stay close and whisper as soft as you can."

On the other side of the world, Mike Golef, heard Daniels' words loud and clear as he recorded them.

Astrid held him tight. Her lips were by his ears. "Mac, I'm scared shitless. Don't let me go." Then she remembered, "Cake burnt, cake burnt." She knew what that meant and it scared her. Her body started to shake. Tears welled up in her eyes. "I have never been so scared, Mac. I cannot believe this place. Look at me. My legs won't stop shaking."

"It is the adrenaline, Babe, kicking in. I can't wait for those tits to start shaking. Fight or flight."

She kissed him again, and then she heard a voice in her ear. "Astrid this is Mike Golef. Tell Mac he's live."

Her face flushed, realizing she was being recorded. "Mike Golef said you're live."

"Thanks for the heads-up, Mike."

"How did you get in my room?"

"JR slipped me his room key when we shook hands. He's a smart boy, but why is he here?"

She looked around the room. "Oh my God, can they see us?"

"No. Look at the bedside table. I have a laser light aimed right on the camera, which is in the center of the ceiling. Right about now, they are looking at a red spot. They are probably trying to clear their reception. I see you covered the television, but drape a dress over it instead. It's more natural. I'm going to make a spy out of you yet."

"I found the camera in the bathroom. I remembered what you told me. I'll be damned if these sons of bitches are going to see me naked. Naked is for your eyes only, sweetheart." Finally, a smile came over her face.

"There are several microphones in the room. There's no need for you to disable them. Just carry on your normal business. Now Astrid, calm down and tell me everything, and why is JR here?"

Astrid told him about the Koreans finding out about the uranium switch and about their demands and the threat against the Reagan, and that Ron had come with her but Sang would not allow him off the plane. She told him how JR had managed to tag along.

"Where is Ron now?"

"Seoul."

"Mike, I'm going to need a conference call with Ron, the DCI, and the admiral. Can you set it up in ten minutes?"

Astrid heard one word, which she repeated. "He said, affirmative."

"Did Ron give you anything for me?"

"Ron had a bag of stuff, and when I had to leave him on the plane I took his bag. I have it here. There is some Octo something or other, along with detonators, gun pencils, and jewelry microphone. Oh, Mac, there's so much stuff and I'm so scared. What do you want me to do?"

"How about a kiss?"

She did not hesitate and kissed him. He held her and finally whispered, "I love you, babe. Everything will be all right."

Her shaking finally stopped.

"It's Octanitrocubane. In addition, I am going to make one hell of a bang with it. Be sure to wear the jewelry at all times, if possible, especially if you are going to be with the Supreme Leader or General Cheon. Get me the bag and give me your earrings."

Astrid did what he asked. Daniels transferred what he wanted from Haig's bag to his duffel bag. He held up one of the earrings to his ear. "Mike, get a couple of birds overhead if possible; camera and infra red. I'll probably have a visit with General Cheon. Try to tag me."

"They're already up. You have been tagged, so are Astrid and JR too."

"Thanks. Please keep Astrid tagged and keep her out of harm's way."

"I'll do my best, but if you don't mind I'll keep an eye on you, too. Can you activate your phone?"

"I will." Handing Astrid back her earrings he said, "Keep them on. How about inviting me to dinner or drinks? Be careful, Sang has the hots for you."

"What's a tag?"

"It's an electronic tag or spot placed on you and it follows you so those watching can easily identify you."

"What happens indoors?"

"They switch to infrared and can watch you. They see you in body heat."

She thought about that.

"Not now, Astrid." He could read her mind. If they were tagged, then they could be seen if they were making love. He did not want this conversation now. "You better get back to your guide. Everything will be all right. I won't let anything happen to you."

"When we are back home, we have to talk." She left the room, wondering how he stayed so calm.

Daniels picked up his laser light and as he turned into JR's room, he focused the light on the ceiling camera and backed out of the room. He went down the hall to his own room, turned on the television, went into the bathroom, and turned on the shower. He grabbed a towel off the rack, wrapped his phone in it and placed it inside the shower on the corner of the tub. He stripped down and stepped into the shower, standing between the shower curtain and the liner. He pressed one of the preset buttons and Cornaci, Charko, and Haig were all on the call. He spoke softly and they brought him up to date. He had a plan and he told them about it. A few minutes later, he signed off the call, and finished his shower and shave. He got in bed, watched a little television, and soon fell asleep.

CHAPTER 36

ARLINGTON, VIRGINIA

Jon Cornaci was sitting at his breakfast table with his wife Ann Marie, enjoying his first cup of coffee. There had been no middle of the night calls and his early morning calls with his deputies had no immediate emergencies. All that was on his mind was Mac Daniels and Astrid Reed. They could not stop Astrid from interviewing Kim and as for Daniels, as he had learned, the man marched to his own drumbeat. It would be a waiting game. From the morning call with Golef, he'd learned that they had positioned satellites over Pyongyang and had tagged the parties. Reed's signals were coming in strong and he'd reported his conversation with Mac.

Ann Marie sipped her coffee and studied her husband. "A penny for your thoughts?"

He smiled at her. "I'm not a very good spy. You can read me too easily."

"I live with you. Well, what is it?"

"Thinking about Mac Daniels, that's all."

"Well, I know you can't talk about it, so how about the morning news?" She flipped on the television to Wolf News, his favorite station. The morning talk show was on when it was interrupted by a breaking news development.

A young, attractive African American reporter appeared. "We interrupt this program for an important announcement. Wolf News has learned that North Korea is prepared to attack the aircraft carrier Ronald Reagan if it participates in war games with South Korea. Reliable sources state that the North Koreans have missiles that could destroy the aircraft carrier. We will keep you advised as soon as we have more information."

Cornaci called Admiral Charko, who answered the call on the first ring. No words were wasted. "I just heard it on the news, Jon. I'm on my way to the office." The connection was broken. Dr. Jon Cornaci was not going to have a good day. He signaled his security detail, kissed Ann Marie good-bye, and left for the office. From the back of the black Suburban, he called General Bellardi.

Marilyn Bellardi was trying to calm her husband of over forty years. She was patient and calm. Tony Bellardi was not after he'd heard the news. "Your blood pressure will go off the charts," she said.

"Marilyn, please, I'm fine. I just want to find that son of bitch who leaked the story. Someone is going to have my boot up his ass and . . ." Bellardi was interrupted by his cell phone. He looked down at it and saw it was Cornaci. "Bellardi here, Jon. I just heard the story."

"I'm on my way to the office. We'll see what we can find out. It looks like this was a Pentagon leak. See what you can find out."

"I'll get Denton Starges on it. On my way, I'll call you later."

Cornaci's cell rang. It was the secretary of state. "Mr. Secretary."

"Director, I assume you heard the news."

"I caught it on Wolf and I'm already on it, so is General Bellardi. What about your end?"

"Checking. The other cable outlet, World Cable, even had more details. They alluded to the North's demand for a payment. The president is blowing a gasket. He wants a conference call at four this afternoon. By then the television pundits will have pontificated on what we should do."

CHAPTER 37

THE WHITE HOUSE
SITUATION ROOM

The president's secretary announced, "Everyone is on the video conference call, just waiting for you."

"Thank you."

In the Situation Room at the White House, five of the many screens were on. On the first screen was Secretary of State Hertz; on the second screen was Secretary of Defense Clancy with Lieutenant General Bellardi, the director of the Defense Intelligence Agency (DIA), and his chief of staff, Colonel Starges. The third screen was Dr. Cornaci, director of Central Intelligence (DCI) with Admiral Charko, deputy director (DD); and on the fourth screen was the director of National Intelligence, Frank Green with Maud Evens, the assistant to the president for National Security Affairs (APNSA). The fifth screen was the chairman of the Joint Chiefs, General Patterson; and on the sixth screen was Admiral Charles Haley, the commander of the U.S. Pacific Command (CDRUSPACOM).

The president was at the head of the table and all parties could see him and each other. Sitting around him were various aides and staff members. He started, "I'll make this short and sweet. First, do we know who leaked the story?"

No one knew.

"Second," continued the president, "the media pundits seem divided, as expected. The conservatives want us to hold course and stand up to the North Koreans and the liberals want us to recall the Reagan."

Secretary of State Hertz began to speak. "Mister President, if I may, I'd like to suggest that we recall the Reagan from participating in war games. It seems to me . . ."

The president cut him off. "I didn't ask for your opinion, Terry. I have questions and I want answers. There will be plenty of time for everyone's opinion, but I will make the decision as the commander-in-chief."

"Mister President, if I may," said Maud Evens.

"Please, Maud, not now. I have to make a decision, a very serious decision, which possibly could lead to war. At our last meeting, I heard from Admiral Webster and General Wolf as to the assets we have in the Pacific. I believe the plans for the defense of the Pacific rest with Admiral Haley. Admiral are we ready?"

The United States Pacific Command is responsible for all armed forces operations in the Pacific Ocean. The combat power of the Pacific Command is made up from the army, marine forces, Pacific fleet, and air force. Admiral Charles Haley, the commander, is the supreme military authority for all the various branches of the armed forces. The chain of command runs from Haley, to the secretary of Defense, to the president.

"Yes, Mister President, we are ready. We have plans in place for the defense of the Pacific and, if necessary, plans to take out the North Korean offensive capabilities. General Bellardi and Dr. Cornaci have kept us well informed on the North's military capabilities. While they have nuclear weapons, they don't have a delivery system, Mister President. They have not yet found a way to miniaturize the weapons and to put them into a missile for delivery. From our intelligence we believe the only way the North can deliver a nuclear weapon is by using a heavy bomber. We have the ability to take out their air force before it's off the ground. If you will allow me, Mister President, I will go through some of the options available to us."

For about an hour, Admiral Haley went over the various options. At times, the president peppered him with questions. General Patterson, at times, chimed in to lend support to the admiral.

The president was quiet for a few minutes. No one said anything. Finally, the president spoke again. "Here's a tough question," he said. "Do they have missiles capable of hitting us here in the mainland or Hawaii?"

"The simple answer is no," said Dr. Cornaci. "They do have some missiles that can pose a threat to South Korea and Japan, but I believe, as the admiral said in his presentation, we have the capabilities of taking down most of those missiles in flight."

"If I am not mistaken, Doctor," said the president, "what about their KN-08? Isn't that intercontinental? "

"The KN-08 is a road-mobile intercontinental ballistic missile riding on a Russian transporter erector launcher (TEL). It was made public at a military parade on the 100th anniversary of Kim Il Sung. An analysis of the photographs that we have showed it to be a mockup. It's a fake."

"Mister President, if I may jump in here," said General Bellardi. "North Korea has currently developed a variety of short and medium-range missiles. It hasn't successfully tested a long-range missile or ICBM. We know they have plans on the drawing board but they just can't seem to build it."

"Just what do they have, General, that we should be afraid of?"

"The North Koreans have four variations of a short-range missile. The Hwasong-6 (Scud-C) is their most effective and widely deployed. It can easily hit South Korea. We believe it has an effective range of about 300 miles and can carry about a 1500-pound payload. The Rodong (Nodong-1) is a medium-range missile, which can easily hit Japan and could carry a miniaturized nuclear warhead. The Taepodong-1 and Taepodong-2 are mid-range missiles. Theoretically, they are capable of delivering small, 350-pound payloads to the continental U.S. Without extreme miniaturization, the payload capacity is too small for a nuclear weapon. The Taepodongs cannot be considered a usable ICBM.

"The Musudan-1 is an intermediate-range ballistic missile (IRBM) capable of hitting Guam. The suspected range is anywhere from 1500 to 2500 miles. We have been carefully following the development of the Musudan and it has not been tested. We strongly suspect that it is not operational. To the best of my knowledge, Mister President, that is the sum total of their missile capability. I believe that the real threat will be to South Korea and Japan."

"Does anyone have anything else to add as far as the military threat is involved?" asked the president.

No one responded.

"I take it from your silence that I have all the facts. Based upon what I am told, I believe, we should continue with the war games. Secretary of State Hertz and I will call the president of South Korea and the prime minister of Japan to tell them what the North Koreans have threatened and what we intend to do. As you all know, we have an obligation to defend both South Korea and Japan, and we will honor that obligation. General Patterson, you are authorized to notify the appropriate military commanders that we are now at Defcon 3. Will Dr. Cornaci and Admiral Charko please stay on the line? That will be all gentlemen."

The defense readiness condition (DEFCON) is an alert state used by the United States Armed Forces. At Defcon 1, nuclear war is imminent, and Defcon 5 is the lowest state of readiness.

All the screens went blank except for one. The president ordered all of his aides and staff members out of the room and turned off the recording system. "This conversation is between the three of us," he said, "no one else. I appreciate the earlier call that I had with you two. It was very enlightening. The reason for my decision to go ahead is based upon what you told me. Did you make the calls and is everyone on board?"

Both Cornaci and Charko nodded and replied, "Yes, Mister President."

The president said nothing for a few long seconds. "Do either of you know how many nukes the North has?"

Admiral Charko answered. "We believe they have between four and eight. The reason the North is reacting so violently is that its total stockpile of enriched uranium is between thirty and fifty pounds. Daniels literately took out their nuclear plans. We probably have half of their enriched uranium. They have to produce more and we know where their five plutonium centers and their uranium enrichment facilities are. With what they lost there will be no new nukes for awhile."

"Can Daniels get out of there alive?"

"If anyone can, he can," answered Charko.

"You both know that I'm not a fan of Mac Daniels. He breaks the law, and no one is above the law. However, from what you told me, if the rest of his mission is a success, I will personally thank him. I certainly hope he can prevent a war." He hesitated for a moment, and then said, "And I certainly hope he doesn't start one."

CHAPTER 38

THE KORYO HOTEL

The phone buzzed on the table next to Daniels' bed. He reached over and answered it. "Yes?"

"This is a reminder, Mr. Brown. You have a seven o'clock dinner reservation in our rooftop revolving restaurant on the forty-fifth floor."

Daniels hung up the phone. He hadn't made a dinner reservation and he thought it must have been Astrid. He looked at the clock; it was 6:45. In the bathroom, he threw some water on his face, and finger-combed his hair. He put on a pair of black slacks with the black turtleneck shirt. He didn't have a jacket, but he slipped on a black windbreaker and looked in the mirror. Satisfied with his appearance, he left his room and didn't take the elevator but walked up the stairs, stopping on the forty-fourth floor to look over the bar. At this hour, it wasn't crowded. He thought had this bar been in New York with its view, it would've been quite impressive. As he looked over the city, except for the few government buildings it was dark. The power was out again and the hotel was being run by a generator, which he knew wouldn't last for long.

Daniels entered the restaurant and was greeted by a young Japanese woman dressed in a traditional kimono. "Good evening, Mr. Brown," she said in perfect English. "I have your table ready. It is right by the window, so enjoy the view as well as our fine food."

She ushered Daniels to a table facing the window, which had three place settings. One chair faced the window with its back to the restaurant, the other two chairs were next to the window. Daniels took one of the side chairs. He wondered who his table companions would be. He knew it wouldn't be Astrid and JR. He was sure that Sunny and Sang would both be there with Astrid. Time would tell, he thought.

A Japanese waiter came to the table and asked, "Would you like a drink while you're waiting for the other guests, Mr. Brown?"

Daniels thought for moment, nodded his head, and said, "Yes, please. Orange juice and tonic water; about a half each. Thank you."

The waiter took the order and left. Daniels saw Captain Anka standing by the door being greeted by the receptionist. She led him over to the table. *Well, there is my first dinner guest,* Daniels thought.

As is the Muslim tradition, the one who is walking should greet the one who is sitting, so the captain extended his hand to Daniels. He said, "As-salamu alaykum."

Daniels replied, "Wa alaykumu s-salam wa rahmatullah." He pointed to a chair across from him and continued to speak in Arabic. "Please be seated."

The captain sat down, looked out the window, and commented to Daniels, "Dark out there. Where are the lights?"

Daniels shook his head. "Let's not go there. I'm sure," he said, lifting a finger to his lips. "Someone is listening to this conversation."

The waiter appeared with Daniels' drink and asked the captain in English if he wished for a drink. The captain looked at Daniels, frowning when he saw the drink. Devout Muslims do not drink alcohol. Daniels could tell by the look on his face the captain disapproved.

"It's nonalcoholic, Captain—just orange juice and tonic water."

"Sounds good. I'll have one, too."

After the waiter left, Daniels and the captain continued to speak in Arabic. The conversation was very guarded, as they knew that they were being monitored. Daniels had some questions for the captain, but he thought later he would be able to speak with him alone.

"How is your room, Captain?"

"I was quite surprised how nice it is. I'm on the 38th floor. I believe I'm in the room next to you."

The waiter returned with the drink. He was followed by Mr. Sun, who was dressed in a light-blue cheogori, a loose-sleeved jacket reaching down to his waist, and tied across the chest in front with a long, broad sash. He had on a white pair of paji, loose-fitting baggie pants; comfortable for sitting on floors. He sat in the empty chair with his back to his restaurant.

"Nice pajamas," said Daniels.

Sun started to reply in Chinese.

Daniels interrupted him and said in English, "the Captain speaks Arabic and English, I speak some Chinese, Arabic, and English. I guess you are fluent in

Korean since you work here, and I've heard you speak English. So, ironically, I guess the three of us will have to speak English."

"Why is it ironic, Mr. Mac Brown?" asked Sun.

"First, please call me Mac. Well, it seems to me the North Koreans and the United States are technically still at war. The captain here runs the ISIS Navy ... and me, the people I work for have some pretty big issues with the United States. So it seems ironic we're all going to speak English tonight."

"So let's enjoy the evening and for the sake of irony let's all speak English," said the captain.

The waiter was standing by and said, "Mr. Sun, would you like a drink before dinner?"

Sun pointed to the captain's drink and said, "I'll have what they're drinking."

After the waiter left, Daniels said to Sun, "I thought you would be having dinner with Miss Reed."

"I'm not that lucky. Sang took that duty. I am here to keep you company, answer any of your questions, and see that everything for you is quite acceptable."

Captain Anka said, "Mr. Sun, everyone who works here in this restaurant is Japanese and everyone else in the hotel is Chinese."

"A Japanese company runs the restaurant under a license from the government, and employs all Japanese nationals. This particular tower is run by a Chinese company and consequently is staffed by Chinese nationals. The hotel is owned by the Korean government."

The waiter returned with Sun's drink and he went through the menu with them. Sun helped them with the menu and after the waiter left, he said, "We have plenty of electricity in Korea, however, because of the imperialist aggression by the Americans we go dark as a safety measure. Everyone knows that the Americans are planning war; they started the last one, lost, and are going to start another one. We expect them to invade us. Our great military will defeat them."

Daniels smiled at the captain. Sun ha just confirmed that everything they said was being overheard and recorded. From the corner of his eye, Daniels saw Astrid, JR, and Sang enter the restaurant. They were sitting several tables away. Astrid saw Mac and came over to the table.

"I'm so sorry you gentlemen aren't dining with us," she said. "Perhaps tomorrow we can have breakfast together."

"That would be very nice, Miss Reed," said Sun.

"Yes, Miss Reed, I would like that very much," said Mac.

"Enjoy your dinner, gentlemen. Sorry I interrupted you. Have a good night." With that, Astrid turned and returned to her table.

"She is certainly beautiful," said Sun.

Mac and the Captain nodded their approval.

"I think Sang has some extracurricular ideas about her," said Sun. "I think he's in for an interesting evening."

Mac turned, looked over his shoulder at Astrid sitting between JR and Sang, and said, "Yep, I think you're right about that. He's in for a very interesting evening."

The waiter brought them their meals. They made small talk until dessert came and Sun asked the captain, "Where's your ship?"

"We sailed up a tributary off the Taedong River, the Pot'ong River. About three miles upriver, right before the railroad bridge, we put into a dock, which I have to say Mr. Sun, was quite ingenious. The dock runs parallel to the land. As we tied up, a giant tent began to extend over the ship. Once the tent was over the ship, a curtain dropped down into the water on all sides of the ship. It was impressive to watch. From the air and land you can't see the ship at all."

Daniels asked, "How long will you be here?"

"Truthfully I don't know. As soon as I am refueled and the food replenished and they have me loaded, I am leaving."

When dinner was over, the three men walked over to Astrid's table to say good night. Sang stared at Mac. In Korean, Sang said to Sun, "There's something about this man. I've seen him before, but I just don't know where."

Sun just shrugged his shoulders and led the way to the elevator. Captain Anka handed Mac a note and Sun saw this. "It is just my phone number Mr. Sun, nothing else. Mac, when you get to Syria give me a call."

The elevator opened on the thirty-eighth floor. All three stepped out, stopping in front of the captain's room first.

"I hope you enjoy your stay here, Captain. Tomorrow we will be doing the tour if you wish to join us. Otherwise, I'm sure you have been told do not leave the hotel without a guide. Some of the citizens get nervous when they see foreigners in the street and we wouldn't want anything to happen, would we? Good night."

The next room over was Daniels'. Sun stood behind him as he opened the door. "Mind if I come in for a minute?" Daniels stood aside, allowing Sun to enter, and then he turned to lock the door. When he turned back, Sun was on the other side of the room by the far window. He had pulled a Beretta nine-millimeter from under his blue cheogori jacket.

"Nice weapon. One of the favorites of U.S. military. Where did you get it? Did General Cheon give it to you? Come on out, General."

From the bathroom, out stepped General Cheon.

CHAPTER 39

THE KORYO HOTEL, DANIELS' ROOM

General Cheon stood in the corner of the room by the entrance to the bathroom. Sun knelt down by the side of the bed, his arms extended, using the bed as a rest to steady the Beretta pointed at Mac's chest.

"Sit in that corner chair," ordered Cheon.

Daniels sat in the chair and said nothing.

"Sit cross-legged and cross your arms in front of your chest," ordered Cheon.

Daniels brought his legs up, crisscrossed them, and crossed his arms in front of his chest. His right hand rested over the inside pocket of his windbreaker where he had his special pencil, which was a 22-caliber, single shot pistol. He had one shot and he was sure he could take Sun with it.

"I heard about you, Mac Brown. Sang told me what happened; you took out two soldiers and Sang. You really scared him. He was shaking when he told me what you did. I'm not sure if he was shaking because he feared what I would do or what you would do to him again. By the way, Sang does not like you. He told me to have you killed. So you stay in that chair and don't move. Sun, if he moves his feet out from under him or tries to move his hands, shoot him and empty the clip— all fifteen rounds in him, every last bullet in his chest and his head. Don't miss. Mac Brown I am not fooling, move and he will shoot you."

Sitting on his legs with his hands crossed would make it very difficult to get out of the chair and across the room without Sun shooting him.

"Before we get started, Mac Brown, or may I call you Mac?" said the general sarcastically, "how did you know I was in the room?"

"It was easy; you announced your entrance."

"How's that?"

"When I opened the door I could smell cologne. It wasn't mine."

The general nodded his head.

Mac continued, "You stood in the doorway. You must have been looking in the closet, where you found nothing, because I have nothing. I was suspicious when Sun wanted to come in. My bags were thoroughly inspected before I left the ship and I believe they were inspected when the bellboy brought them upstairs. I know you have listening devices and video devices, so I could not imagine why Sun wanted to come in the room. I'm not his charge, Reed is. I'm here to see you. I'm not here to be a tourist; in fact I'm here to help you."

Cheon smiled at that. "How do you think you can help me? What makes you think I need help?"

"I really work for you, you just don't know it. I'm flattered that you came to my room. I thought Sang would take me to your headquarters. If you want to talk here, I'll tell you again, I work for you."

"Why should I believe that you work for me? I don't even know you. I will have you sent to jail and after two or three weeks you'll tell me everything I want to know."

"I'll tell you everything you want without taking me to jail. I'm here to help you."

"I'm going to listen to you, but if what you say is not interesting, I'm going to kill you. Do you understand?"

Daniels coughed and as he did, his right hand tightened on the pen. "You have a traitor at your nuclear facility."

"Why do you say that?"

"Because you're interrogating half of the facility to try to figure out who switched the uranium. You thought you were selling sand and you actually conveyed your enriched uranium. You're threatening the Americans, claiming you'll sink their aircraft carrier if they don't return your uranium. You're heading toward war because the Americans don't have your stuff."

"How do you know all this? Who has it?"

"I told you, I really work for you. You just don't know it. Will you allow me to make a call?"

"Who do you want to call?

"My boss."

"Your boss? Just who is your boss?"

"General Lee Kem. I'm sure you know him."

There was a reaction from General Cheon when he heard the name Lee Kem. General Lee Kem was the head of the Ministry of State Security in China. The Ministry of State Security is an ultra-secret organization, the counterpart of the

FBI and CIA combined. Inside of China, state security was the secret police—outside of China, it was an intelligence-gathering organization. A powerful organization reached deep inside of North Korea. Over the years, Lee Kem had provided much information to General Cheon and more importantly to the Supreme Leader. He was the unofficial official who dealt with the Koreans.

"So may I please call him?"

Cheon thought for a second . . . a long second, and said, "It's late, how can you reach him now?"

"I know his private cell phone number."

Cheon again was quiet. All this time Sun kept his Beretta pointed squarely at Daniels' chest.

"Can I get up, and can you tell Mr. Sun here not to shoot me?"

"Make the call."

Daniels slowly got up and walked over to the phone, which was by the bed. Now he was just less than an arm's length away from the Beretta, which followed him across the room. He turned sideways, taking away the chest shot, and forcing Sun to raise the pistol up at his head. Daniels picked up the phone and dialed the number from memory.

Cheon, still standing in the corner, said, "Put it on the speaker."

Daniels pressed the speak button. The room was filled with the sound of the ringing. It rang several times before there was an answer.

"Yes," said Lee Kem in Chinese. "Who is this?" He was clearly annoyed by the late-night intrusion.

"It's Mac, General."

"You must be in big trouble to call me at night. What is it, Mac?"

"You are on a speaker, General. In the room with me are General Cheon and his bodyguard, who is holding a gun on me. The general doesn't believe that I work for him. He threatened to shoot me, so I had to tell him whom I really work for. I need your help."

"You mean General Cheon didn't want to listen to you about the traitor and the fact that the Americans don't have the uranium? Cheon, can you hear me?"

"I can hear you, sir," said Cheon in a very deferential tone. "I thought this man, this Mac Brown, was here to assassinate me."

"Before we talk, I have a question, General. How many men are with you in the room?"

Cheon looked confused. "There's just me and my bodyguard. Why do you ask?"

"If Mac Brown was there to kill you General, you would be dead. Mac!"

Sun was still kneeling by the bed. However, instead of using the bed as a rest both of his arms were extended up in the air off the bed. His left eye was closed. He was aiming with the right eye, trying to keep the gun as steady as he could. This Beretta weighed a little more than two pounds and the position Sun was in made it difficult for him to hold it steady. It began to waver. In order to compensate, he hunched up his shoulders almost up to his ears and his elbows went out far from his body. He was not in a good shooting position.

Mac was still holding the telephone receiver although the speaker was on. He dropped the receiver on the bed, and instinctively Sun looked down at it. Mac swirled and with his left hand pulled the Beretta out of Sun's hand, while in the same swirling motion, he delivered a right hand to the side of Sun's head, knocking Sun to the floor. The Beretta was now pointed at Cheon's head.

"I'm now holding the pistol," said Daniels to Lee Kem.

Cheon could hear Lee Kem laughing.

"Do you want me to kill him?" asked Daniels.

"General Cheon, should I have you shot for being stupid?" Not waiting for an answer, Kem went on. "This man works for me. He is my best officer and extremely lethal. I suggest that you arrange a meeting with the Supreme Leader as soon as possible. I cannot come to North Korea, but I will tell the Supreme Leader as I'm telling you, if you start this war with the Americans, you are on your own. Mac's information is accurate— listen to him. Give the gun back. Mac."

Mac pressed the release button, the clip fell out, and then he jacked the shell out of the chamber. He put the clip and the shell in his pocket and threw the gun at Sun, who was now standing by General Cheon. Sun made a motion toward Daniels, but Cheon restrained him. Sun glowered at Daniels.

"Mac, when you are with the Supreme Leader call me." The phone went dead.

The room was silent finally; Sun spoke, "The next time I see you, I will..."

Cheon shouted, "Enough!"

Daniels looking at Sun said, "You will do what? If you ever pull a gun on me again, I will make you eat it. General, you don't need a war with the Americans, especially on misinformation."

"How do you know this and where do you get all your information?"

"It doesn't matter. What matters is we have to get to the truth and avoid all the bullshit deceptions before you start a war you can't win and bring the rest of the world down with you. Get Director Jang and his first deputy Shin down here for our meeting."

Cheon's head jerked back at the sound of the names of the director and his first deputy-director of North Korea's nuclear research. "How do you know their names?"

"It doesn't matter. One of them is a traitor and I will prove it. Get them down here for a meeting tomorrow. Tell them the Supreme Leader wants to give them a medal. Stop interrogating the workers. You're wasting time. Do not tell them they are suspects. I will uncover for you and the Supreme Leader who your traitor is, just get them here."

Cheon was astonished. "I don't think we can get them here tomorrow. They are at the Punggye-ri Nuclear Test Site. It's over 275 miles away."

"Yes, I know, it's located in Kilju County, North Hamgyong Province. The site is located in mountainous terrain 1.2 miles south of Mantapsan, 1.2 mi west of Hwasong concentration camp. But if you check, you'll see that they are not at the Punggye-ri site but at the Yongbyon Nuclear Scientific Research Center, in North Pyong'an Province, which is only about seventy-five miles from here.

Cheon was astounded again. "How do you know this?"

"Simple, I am a spy and not for any one country. As the Americans would say, I've privatized spying. I spy on everyone and I sell information. My allegiance is to Lee Kem, and no one else. Not because of China, but because he pays me well. Send a chopper up to the research site and get those two down here. You have the MD 500D helicopter, if they're operable. They can get back and forth in no time. Half-hour up and a half-hour back. Ironically, the airframe of the 500D was manufactured in South Korea, and was assembled in the United States. You purchased them through a German export firm. Of the eighty-seven helicopters you purchased, you had sixty modified into useless gunships. How did you get them?"

"Through a deal brokered by General Kem...."

Daniels finished the sentence, "And I put the deal together for the general."

"Who are you really?" asked General Cheon.

"Your new best friend."

CHAPTER 40

THE KORYO HOTEL

Daniels was lying on the bed when the phone rang. Reaching over he picked it up. "Hello?" he said.

"I hope I didn't wake you, Mr. Brown," said the soft voice of Astrid Reed.

Daniels sat up, "No. Truthfully, I was just lying here relaxing. May I help you, Miss Reed?"

"Yes, you can, first by calling me Astrid."

"That's easy. How about dropping the Mr. Brown and calling me Mac? I'd appreciate it."

"Mac it is. What are you doing now, Mac?"

"Nothing, what do you have in mind?"

"Well, my producer JR was tired and went to bed. I was supposed to have a drink with Mr. Sang, but he had something to do so I thought I would call and invite you to join me for a drink."

"That's a nice offer Astrid, but I'm sorry I don't drink. My religion forbids it. If you're at the bar I will be happy to join you."

"I didn't realize you were a strict Muslim, Mac."

"I'm really not strict, except I don't drink and eat pork, but I do enjoy looking at beautiful women."

"Oh, I see, you like to flirt."

"Not flirting, just truthful. You're an exceptional beauty, Astrid. I'm sure you know it. If you give me a couple minutes I'll be right up."

"I'm not in the bar, but in my room. Come on over."

"That's a nice invitation, however, our host might talk, and I am sure your significant-other might mind."

"I'm sure you'll behave yourself, and my significant other happens to be a submarine naval officer. Right now he's somewhere under one of the oceans. So come on over. I'm sure there's diet soda or mineral water in the mini bar."

Daniels knocked on Astrid's door and she opened it almost immediately. She was dressed as she had been at dinner. Stepping aside, she waved him in. "Welcome to my humble abode Mac. What would you like to drink?"

"Any juice, soda, or water would be fine, Astrid."

Astrid took two bottles of sparkling water and handed them to Mac. He quickly twisted off the tops, handing her an open bottle.

"Need a glass, Mac?"

"No thank you. You need one?"

"No. The bottle is fine. Same way I drink my beer, out of the bottle."

They clinked their bottles and took a drink. Astrid sat on the bed and Daniels sat in the chair across from her. One of her dresses was over the television.

"So how was your day touring, Astrid?"

Astrid told Mac about the sightseeing tour that she had gone on with Sun and Sang. She was careful about how she described what she saw, and she emphasized the highlights and acted as if she was excited about the various sights. She could not say how she felt and how depressed she'd felt looking at all the people who were not smiling, laughing, or talking. It was a whole population without any idea of what the outside world was like. No television, no Internet, no radio, and no knowledge of anything except what the government permitted. But she played her role well. Finally, she asked Mac, "What are you doing here?"

"On business, and as soon as I'm done, I'm getting out of here. I understand you're going to interview the Supreme Leader tomorrow."

"Yes, I am and I'm looking forward to it. My World News Corporation will allow him to reach the world, and this will be a fair opportunity for him to tell his story. This is an opportunity for him to show the world just who he is."

"Well, I hope you have a good interview and I wish you well."

"I'm actually looking forward to it, Mac."

They talked for another half hour and Daniels could sense she was nervous.

Astrid wanted him to stay. The thought that she was being listened to and watched made her skin crawl. She felt violated. She wished she could get into bed and snuggle up next to him. Then she would feel safe.

Down in the basement, watching and listening to her and Daniels, was Sang. He was focusing on Daniels. There was something about him that Sang felt he knew, but just could not put his finger on. According to the records that Sang had reviewed, Brown had never been in Korea. Why did he think he met him before?

Daniels stood up, "Astrid, I need my beauty rest—you don't. I have to go to bed. Thank you for the drink. Good night."

Astrid rose, wishing she could throw her arms around him and keep him there. She walked him to the door.

As she opened the door, Daniels put his hand on her shoulder and gave it a little squeeze. "You'll do well, Astrid. Trust yourself. If I may suggest, when your interview is over, go home. Or better yet take a few days off. Go to one of the islands. By the way, I'm just down the hall."

"Thank you, Mac." She gave him a kiss on the cheek.

He touched his cheek. "Thank you."

She watched him walk down the hall and thought, *How does he do this?* As he opened his door, he nodded to her and smiled.

Sang sat facing an array of television screens located in the observation room, which was in the basement of the hotel. The equipment was recording both audio and visual activities of the various rooms where the Ministry of the State Security wanted to check on its special guests. As soon as someone entered the room, the devices automatically went on. From the control room, an observer could actually watch what was being recorded. This made for some interesting watching. Many a visiting official was not too pleased to see his sexual cavorting with some of the government prostitutes. The tapes made them very cooperative.

Sang had been hoping to tape Daniels and Reed. Seeing her naked would have been nice. He thought about her and what he could do to her, whether she wanted to or not. He felt a stirring and quickly turned on the screen for Daniels' room. He watched every step and movement of Daniels. Daniels stripped down to his shorts, got into bed, shut the light off, and said, "Fuck you Sang."

Sang recoiled at this. His face reddened, and he thought, *What kind of man does this? He has no fear. He must know that I could take him prisoner at any time and have him tortured.* Sang focused on the dark screen for a full minute, and then Sun entered the room.

"Anything of interest?" he asked Sang.

"Nothing except the slap that you got from Brown," said Sang with a smile.

Instinctively Sun's hand went to his face. He nodded as if he were planning something. "I don't know what he's doing here, but before he leaves I intend to get even. He deserves a good slap in the face and a few extra punches."

"That's all? I intend to kill him. He will not leave here alive."

Sun's face showed amazement. Sang was silent for a moment.

"I wouldn't mind killing him myself," said Sun, "but he's well protected. He's meeting the Supreme Leader."

Sang interrupted him. "I know. I watched the tape and heard him talk to General Kem. How do you know it was Kem and not some American trick? They can synthesize voices."

Sun thought for a second and finally said, "I don't know. Let's just say he seems to have friends in high places. It might be foolish to try to kill him, but a couple of street thugs jumping him to rob him and give him a beating would be acceptable."

"You might be right. Let's see what happens when he meets the Supreme Leader. He may not get out of that meeting alive. I just can't figure out where I've seen him before."

"Are you going?" asked Sun.

"No. I'm going to watch some more tapes."

Sun turned and left the observation room.

Sang started going through the tapes. In the batch of tapes was Miguel Antonio Ricardo.

CHAPTER 41

THE KORYO HOTEL

Daniels was eating breakfast at the rooftop restaurant when Astrid and JR came into the room. He motioned them over to his table, standing up as Astrid approached. "Please join me for breakfast," he said, pulling a chair out for her.

"How's the breakfast here?" asked JR as he sat down.

"There are eggs, breakfast meats, pancakes, waffles, the usual Western stuff. Not so bad, when they have it."

Instinctively, they all stopped talking when the Japanese waitress came over. After a few minutes of questions, she took their orders. When she left they resumed talking.

"Well, how did you two sleep?" asked Daniels.

"Like a rock," replied JR. "Out like a light."

"To be honest I had a rough night," said Astrid. "I'm a little nervous about my interview with the Supreme Leader."

"You'll do fine. I may see you over there. I have," he stopped for a moment, and then said, "an interview of sorts with him too."

Astrid's eyes opened wide. Both Daniels and JR noticed immediately. Mac put his hand on hers and gave it a little pat. "Enjoy your breakfast, it's going to be a nice day."

Astrid gave a loud, noticeable sigh. She was about to say something when the waitress came over with their coffee.

"A little caffeine does wonders," said JR.

Captain Anas Anka came into the room and immediately headed over to the table. Before anyone could say anything Astrid invited him to sit and join them.

"Thank you, Miss Reed. I bet you're excited interviewing the Supreme Leader."

"Excited and certainly nervous," she said. "I hope it goes well. I don't have my camera crew here."

"Do you speak Korean or Chinese?" asked Anka.

"No," she said. "Why, I thought the Supreme Leader was fluent in English. According to my research, he went to school in Switzerland. I thought he attended a private English-language International School in Gümligen."

"You're right, he does speak English. However, I was told he only speaks it on rare occasions and usually conducts official business in Korean."

"I guess you have to use a translator, Astrid," said Daniels. "But then I understand he has an eye for beautiful women and you may be that occasion when he speaks English. I certainly wouldn't worry about it." Turning to the captain he said, "How long will you be here?"

"We might be sailing late this afternoon. I understand they're loading my ship now."

"May I ask where you will be heading to?" asked Astrid.

"Eventually heading home."

"Where's home?" asked JR.

"Syria."

"Damascus?" asked JR.

"Not really," said Anka.

"He is going to the Port of Latakia, the main seaport in Syria. It is located on the Mediterranean Sea in the city of Latakia," volunteered Daniels.

The captain smiled at Daniels. "You're right. Not many people know that Latakia is the main seaport and not Damascus." Turning to JR he continued, "Latakia is a very old city. It has been inhabited since 2000 BC. You could say the modern city was founded in 400 BC. For thousands of years, one group or another occupied the city. It actually became its own state in 1922, and then finally became part of Syria in 1944. It is a beautiful city—come see it sometime."

Daniels thought, *Yes, it is a beautiful city and from Latakia on Highway 4 it is about four and half hours to Raqqa, the capital of Islamic State, ISIS.*

"It is a long trip, Captain. You are going to pass right by the American Naval base at Diego Garcia, then Yemen, up the Red Sea through the Suez Canal, past the Israelis. You have a good chance of being stopped."

"Why would anybody want to stop me; a cargo ship under the Panamanian flag?"

"You never know. You might just be a sitting duck inside the Suez Canal."

"Mr. Mac Brown, I am not a duck. The last time I looked, Panama was not at war with anyone. There is no need for the Americans to stop us."

"The next time I speak with the director of the CIA, I'll tell him to let you pass. I wish you safe sailing and the best of luck."

Laughing, Anka replied, "Why not the American president?"

"He doesn't like me."

"He doesn't like you?" he said with a big laugh.

The waitress brought them their breakfast. Astrid picked a little at her eggs; she was clearly nervous. The men all ate and had a few cups of coffee. When they were done, eating Daniels asked for a check. The waitress indicated there was no bill. They were the guests of the government.

"If I'd known that, I would have had steak," said JR.

The captain rose and said, "Going to my room to relax and wait for them to call me to return to my ship."

He shook hands with Daniels.

Daniels smiled. "Safe travels, my friend."

Astrid turned to Mac and asked, "Where do we go to do this interview?"

Mac smiled at Astrid. "You don't go anywhere. They will come and get you."

No sooner had he finished saying that, when four men in dark suits came into the restaurant. They came over to the table.

The oldest of the four men spoke in English. "I am Captain Yong-ho from the Ministry of State Security."

Daniels almost laughed. Astrid knew what he was going to say. Before he could, she asked, "Where are Mr. Sang and Mr. Sun?"

"They are busy. I will escort you to the Supreme Leader and my men here will escort Mr. Mac Brown to meet with General Cheon. Do you have your things?"

"May I stop in my room for a moment?"

"Of course. Mr. Mac Brown, are you ready?"

Daniels looked at the three men, "Let's go."

The elevator doors slid open and they all stepped in. Astrid was glassy-eyed, looking as if tears were about to run down her face. Mac reached behind her so one could see and gave her a pat on her behind. She smiled.

The doors opened on the thirty-eighth floor, and Astrid, Captain Anka, and Captain Yong-ho got off. The doors closed and Daniels was alone with the three men, who just stared at him

Daniels asked, "Did he say Hung-how?" And then he laughed.

The men just looked. They faced Daniels and one of the men took his hand out of his pocket. He had brass knuckles, the others had slapjacks. One of the men pushed the stop button.

Sang was standing in the lobby in front of the elevator, smiling. A minute later, the doors opened on the first floor. Daniels stepped out. Sang's smile turned to a look of horror. The three men were all unconscious on the floor of the elevator. Sang tried to reach for his weapon but was too slow. Daniels grabbed Sang by the jacket and threw him into the elevator. Sang tripped over the bodies and his head hit against the wall.

"Fuck you, Sang."

A bellboy looked on in horror. He knew Sang was State Security.

"Please call me a cab," said Daniels. He reached back into the elevator and pressed number 38.

CHAPTER 42

RYONGSONG RESIDENCE AND CENTRAL HEADQUARTERS

Daniels stepped from the cab and stood in the street in front of the outer perimeter wall that surrounded the Ryongsong Residence and Central Headquarters. He realized that this place had more protection than the White House. By observing the troops standing post every twenty feet, from the various insignia he quickly determined that there were several military units assigned there. He was surprised to see that there were special operation forces also assigned to protect the complex. In between each guard posting, there was a security camera on top of the wall. He had studied the reconnaissance photos and inside the wall was an electric fence. Between the electric fence and the wall was a minefield. Behind the electric fence was a heavily armed security post. The complex was over 4.6 square miles, with a series of roads inside the small city. The headquarters was connected to the other residences by underground tunnels. A private underground train station was also inside the residence compound. There were several large houses surrounded by well-manicured gardens and manmade lakes.

The complex had been built in 1983 by the former Supreme Leader Kim Il-sung. Because Kim Il-sung believed that a nuclear attack was imminent, the complex had an underground wartime headquarters, with the walls reinforced with iron rods, covered in concrete, and lined with lead.

Daniels turned his back to the wall and for a brief second looked up to the sky and smiled. He knew he was being observed and he made a gesture with his hands.

Back at Langley, his every movement was being recorded and watched. On other screens were Astrid and the Sails of Allah.

One of the observers asked, "What is he doing?"

"He's using sign language. He said to keep an eye on Astrid."

The observer turned around. Standing there watching was Admiral Charko.

"Yes, sir. We have them both tagged."

"How is the audio and video feed on Astrid?"

"Very clear, sir. Too bad there is no audio on Daniels."

Daniels had no audio devices attached to him. He had left his cell phone and anything else that could be perceived to be a transmitter or weapon back in his room. He knew they would inspect his shoes and even try to take them apart. They would check his belt and his clothes; everything by hand and x-ray. When he entered the compound, he knew that they would take him to the lower underground levels. Langley would completely lose him. He knew that Astrid, on the other hand, would be in the upstairs residence or perhaps in the gardens, and her devices would work. She would not be subject to the same inspection he would.

He turned and faced the cameras, approached slowly, and started waving. He knew this action would bring someone out. He only hoped they would ask questions first and not shoot. He had arrived there without an official escort, and that alone could get him arrested or shot. He did not mind being arrested; he just did not want to get shot yet.

Back at Langley, someone watching said, "He's nuts."

Daniels' action got the desired results. Six guards rushed toward him. He did not want to fight and he certainly did not want to be clubbed with a rifle butt. Quickly he lay down flat on the ground, his arms stretched out. He was quickly surrounded and shouted at in Korean.

Daniels yelled, "General Cheon! General Cheon!"

The guards recognized the name, Cheon. The senior guard spoke a little English. He ordered Daniels to kneel and look at the camera. He then went to his post and made a call.

Four stories below the ground, Cheon turned on the monitor and saw the man believed to be John Mac Brown. "Bring him down to me," he ordered, and he then quickly added, "All of you. In fact, take a few more guards when you bring him down here."

The guard was not sure he understood. "Sir, you want ten of us to escort one man down?"

No, I want twelve of you to escort this man down." Cheon hung up the phone. He wondered how Mac Brown could be standing in front of the National Headquarters without an escort. Where was Sang?

Cheon quickly dialed Sang, who answered on the first ring. Recognizing the number he answered, "Yes, sir?"

Cheon screamed into the phone, "Where are you?"

"I'm in the car on my way to headquarters, sir."

"Why is Mac Brown standing here, unescorted? Why aren't you with him?"

Sang thought fast. He had to have an explanation or he knew he would end up in a labor camp. "Sir, knowing my experience with him, I decided to send three of the special operation forces men to escort him there. For some unknown reason, in the elevator he beat the three of them up. He then threw me into the elevator and I was knocked out."

"Didn't you know that I expected him to be here, and he wanted to come here? Why did you have to send three of our special forces to get him? I think you just wanted to get even for the beating he gave you on the ship. You're lucky this man didn't kill you. There is no need for you to come here. Go back to the hotel and stay there until you hear from me."

Cheon hung up his phone. He knew that Sang had most likely ordered the special forces to start a fight with Mac Brown. He wondered how one man could beat three of the elite of the Korean special operation forces. These men were the best. He quickly realized that Mac Brown was exceptional, and he was glad he'd ordered a dozen guards to bring him down to his office. He had his own suspicions about Mac Brown, and all night long he'd wondered if they were really talking to General Kem or if that was some type of CIA electronic trick. He would get to the bottom of it. But he recognized the fact that Mac Brown had a lot of information and it was correct. He wanted to see who was the traitor, and he would allow Mac Brown to show him. If he wasn't satisfied, he would kill Mac Brown.

A few minutes later, Daniels was standing in front of the large ornate desk of General Cheon, surrounded by a dozen guards; all with their weapons pointed at him. General Cheon looked at Daniels and said nothing. Daniels looked around the room and without being invited, he sat down in one of the chairs in front of the general's desk.

Daniels just stared back at the general and said nothing. The staring contest went on for a full minute before the general broke the silence. "I am not sure what to do with you."

Daniels leaned forward, smiled, and said, "First, you don't need all these guards. I'm not here to hurt you or cause you any trouble. You know that. Let me help. You have a traitor in your midst, and if you attack the Reagan you're probably going to start a war you can't win."

Cheon dismissed the guards then asked, "What do you care? What's in it for you?"

"I wish I could tell you I was for world peace or some bullshit like that, but to be honest with you, just one thing; money."

"Money, I understand that. Do you expect us to pay you for your help?"

"Of course, and you will because I can provide you with very valuable information, not to mention getting rid of a traitor. If you want to start a war with the Americans, it is your business. I don't care. I was born in Saudi Arabia, grew up in Canada, and I live on a little island in the Caribbean that no one cares about, with plenty of food, water, sunshine, and beautiful women. Whatever happens between you and the Americans wouldn't affect me one bit."

General Cheon went quiet again. He was thinking about what to do with this man, when the phone rang. "Yes," he answered it. After a few minutes, he said, "He's sitting here in front of me."

"I guess they're looking for me," said Daniels with a smile. "Your boy, Sang sent three goons to teach me a lesson. I could have killed all of them but I didn't."

"I know. I had nothing to do with it. Sang thought he would get even with you. That was Captain Yong-ho on the phone telling me you disappeared from the hotel and that he was here with Miss Reed to meet the Supreme Leader. The Supreme Leader has granted Miss Reed's request to interview him in the gardens. In fact, the Supreme Leader is driving her around the residence, giving her a personal tour."

Daniels was pleased to hear this. He had instructed Astrid to request the interview in the gardens. He had told her to ask to see the beautiful gardens and man-made lakes so she could show those pictures to the world. Daniels wanted them outside as it would not impede any of her communications and would allow the satellites to watch the interview in real time.

"I would like to meet the Supreme Leader too. When I tell him what I know, you'll be a real hero. Maybe he'll give you some of that $50 million that he doesn't have."

At that remark, General Cheon leaned forward with a frown on his face. "What do you mean?"

"I mean just that. Supreme Leader thinks he has fifty million dollars or Euros in some account. He doesn't. When you find the money, you will know who the traitor is. Let's go out to the gardens, and please bring me a laptop and Director Jang and first deputy Shin for our meeting with the Supreme Leader."

"The Supreme Leader will want to verify your relationship with General Kem."

"You know what you're thinking? You're thinking that it was some kind of electronic trick and that the general was not really on the phone."

"The thought entered my mind."

"That's one of the reasons why I want the laptop. We can get the general on a face-to-face and I'm sure there's some question that the Supreme Leader could ask him that only General Kem will know the answer to. Stop being so paranoid, General. When this is over you'll be a hero, and I hope to be out of here with some of your money. I prefer Euros or dollars if you don't mind."

General Cheon just shook his head. He picked up the phone and barked a few orders. Then he said to Daniels, "I want you to change your clothes. Just to be safe we will inspect your garments with the utmost of care. Should I find one wire, communication device, explosive device, or one thread out of order, you will be shot. Do you understand?"

"No problem."

There was a knock on the door and the general's orderly entered, carrying what looked like a pair of black pajamas and sandals. He handed the clothes to Daniels.

"Nice pajamas."

Daniels stood and took off his shirt, handing it to the orderly. As he was about to slip the pajama top over his head, the general said, "That looks like a bullet wound."

"It is. The results of the jealous girlfriend."

"You must have a lot of jealous girlfriends," responded the general. "You have more than one wound."

Daniels didn't answer. He took off his shoes, socks, and pants, and then he was standing there in his briefs. "You want me to drop my draws and bend over?"

The general shook his head no. Daniels gave his clothes to the orderly, stepped into the pajama bottoms, and slipped his feet into the sandals.

"Let's go find the Supreme Leader," said Cheon. "If what you say is true, you will walk away from here, perhaps with some money so you may enjoy your island paradise, but you also could be buried in what you call pajamas."

CHAPTER 43

WASHINGTON, D.C.

Ken Park was moving between the tables of his Washington restaurant. It was one of the "in" places and as usual, it was packed with senators, congressmen, and various staffers. Park was shaking hands and pouring on the charm. Looking around, he smiled at his success. He was expecting another shipment of cash and he would wash the money through the restaurant. Thanks to his financial advisor, his 401K, his stocks, bonds, and bank accounts were growing faster than he could imagine. He was a multi-millionaire, making it to the top one percent. If he could just get out of the Reconnaissance General Bureau, life would be perfect. If he sold the restaurant, he could retire to Florida and live just as well retired as he did working. Maybe he would buy a bar in Key West, fish in the morning, and run the bar at night. He smiled as he thought of the name of his bar, *Park Here*. Yes, life was good in the United States.

The ringing of his cell phone broke his reverie. Glancing down he did not recognize the number. Puzzled, he answered. "Ken Park here."

"Ken? What happened to your real name, Ki-Young? Have you been in America too long?"

"Who is this?"

"Is this a secure line?"

"No."

"When can you get to a secure line?"

Park was getting irritated. "Who is this?" he demanded.

"This is your uncle. Now how long before you can call me back?"

Looking at his watch, Ken answered, "Thirty minutes."

The line went dead. Park called to one of his managers and said, "I have to run an errand. Be back in an hour."

A few minutes later, he was in his car working his way to Route 29. He was going to his home in Falls Church. There he could make a secure call. Uncle was a code word; a code word that he didn't want to hear. *What happened?* He wondered.

He entered his home, went right to his study, and took out his encrypted satellite phone. The phone was attached to an antenna on his roof, which appeared to be a television dish, but wasn't. It would bolster the signal, bouncing it off a satellite for a clear connection with parties in North Korea. From another drawer he took out a battery, inserted it into the phone, turned it on, and dialed the number that appeared on his cell phone. He could hear the static of the encryption falling into place. After a minute, he heard the voice of the man who'd said "uncle."

"Who is this?" demanded Park.

"I am Sang Ji-hu, a deputy minister in the Ministry of State Security for Pyongyang. Your superior at the RGB," Sang said, referring to the Reconnaissance General Bureau, "provided me with your number and file. The information you provided regarding the American on the ship was wrong, very wrong. He wasn't an American, he was a Saudi-born, Canadian citizen, a John Mac Brown, who works for General Lee Kem, the head of the Ministry of State Security in China."

The color drained from Park's face. If this were correct, this would be a major blunder. He knew the consequences for bad information. "I got this information, from a reliable source," he said. "Are you sure of your information?"

"Of course I am, you idiot. I watched this man and General Cheon call General Kem, and I heard their conversation. From your file, I see your source for this misinformation is Aswas Rajul, an American Muslim. Could he be a double agent?"

Park was quiet for few seconds and he thought before he answered. "No. Definitely not. Give me some time to make a few calls and double-check my information. I'll call you back in an hour."

"You can have several hours. I'm sure General Cheon will be reporting this directly to the Supreme Leader. Fortunately for you, the Supreme Leader is being interviewed by Astrid Reed, which should take several hours. Call me back, and I hope for your sake that you have the right information this time. Do you realize we could have killed General Kem's agent? You've been in the United States too long. It is time to come home."

The phone went dead and Park began to perspire. His whole life had just fallen apart. If he was recalled, which he thought would be inevitable unless he had the right information, he would spend the rest of his life in a labor camp.

He made his decision. If he couldn't get to the bottom of this, he would disappear here in America. He would have to call Lou and arrange for a meeting with him in New York City. This would not raise suspicions because they usually met every month, alternating between Washington and New York. Park would take the bus to New York City, buying his ticket in cash. He would have Lou sell the business and his house and invest the money. Using the subway system, he could travel anonymously to Kennedy Airport, where he would fly on a false identity to Miami, Florida. From Miami he would take a bus to the Keys.

Once he was settled in Florida, he would have Lou wire proceeds to a bank account he had set up on the Isle of Jersey. He was thankful that their banking laws would protect the account information. He would instruct his bank to wire funds to his account in Florida. He wasn't worried about United States government. He was worried about the RGB finding his money and him.

For now, he had to contact Aswas Rajul. He had to get to the bottom of this. Rajul had never given him bad information before. They had a good working relationship. Maybe this could be straightened out, but one thing he was sure of—he wasn't going back.

CHAPTER 44

THE RUSSELL SENATE OFFICE BUILDING

Senator John Bartlett IV had his feet up on the coffee table as he slouched back in an oversized leather chair. His tie was pulled down, the collar button on his shirt was open, and his jacket lay over a chair. In his right hand was a glass half-filled with Jack Daniels and ice, and in his left hand he held a Cuban cigar. This was his private conference room, which was off his office and there was no way anyone could get into it except through his office. So when he wanted to smoke, he did. Sitting across from the senator was Brian Samuels, a lobbyist who also had a drink and a cigar. Samuels' jacket was also off; his sleeves were rolled up and his tie was pulled down. Sitting between them on the couch was the senator's chief of staff, Dick Edwards. Unlike his boss, Edwards did not drink or smoke in the Senate office building. His jacket was on and his tie was pulled up to his neck. In his hands, he had pen and paper and was taking notes.

Samuels was a lobbyist representing *The American Times*, a major news organization. The *Times* was a major competitor of Astrid Reed's World News Corporation. While a publicly traded corporation, the *Times* had the Goodman family as the major stockholder. Bruce and Ron Goodman were major supporters of Senator Bartlett, and had pledged that their Super Pac would support him for the nomination of his party to run for president. The Goodmans could and would raise and donate hundreds of millions of dollars.

Samuels was meeting with the senator not to ask for favors but to complain about the World News Corporation. "John, it's not fair that World News gets government assistance and the *Times* does not. Ron was really upset about this. We're not asking for any favors, just a level playing field."

The senator turned to his chief of staff. "Dick what assistance are we giving to World News?"

Dick Edwards scratched his head, looked puzzled, and said, "There is no assistance given to them that I am aware of. There are no grants or tax benefits or any type of financial aid."

"It's not money, Dick," said Samuels, "but they are given priority access to world leaders. Haven't you seen the television for God's sake? All the cable channels that World News owns, especially that right wing, Wolf News channel, are broadcasting that Astrid Reed is interviewing President Kim, or Premier Kim or whatever the leader of North Korea calls himself. Her newspapers will have the transcript of the interview. Apparently, she's visiting him at his residence. It's hard for Ron and Bruce to compete when she gets all these exclusives with the government's help."

Bartlett took a big sip of his drink and a drag on the cigar. He blew the smoke up in the air as he was thinking.

Edwards leaned forward in his seat. An assignment was coming. He knew this.

"Dick, check with the secretary of state and find out about this visit to the North. Brian, tell Ron and Bruce whatever help we gave World News, if any, and I don't think we did, I'll find out, and assure them they will get the same help, if not more. We believe in a level playing field."

Dick Edwards stood up, excused himself, and left the conference room. He knew the senator and Brian had many things to talk about, most of which he did not need to know.

He heard Brian say, "Who's the blonde in the outer office?"

Once in his own office, he took off his jacket and picked up the phone. He knew the easiest place to get started was a call to Astrid Reed's office.

A few minutes later Vivian Berkstrom answered the phone. "Astrid Reed's office, this is Vivian, how may I help you?"

Edwards was an old hand at this game. Chief of staff to a powerful senator gave him a degree of power, but he preferred to use the soft approach, especially dealing with women. Edwards was good looking, spoke well, and by most accounts was considered very charming.

"I am Dick Edwards calling from Senator John Bartlett's office, and I was wondering if you could be kind enough to help me."

As soon as Edwards said the name, "Senator Bartlett," Vivian's fingers flew over the keyboard and there on the screen was John Bartlett's picture, along with crucial information about him on his senatorial website. She saw the senator's office phone number. "Mr. Edwards, if you will allow me, I would like to call you back from a private line."

Not waiting for an answer, she disconnected the line and immediately called back. A woman answered the phone. "Senator John Bartlett's office."

"This is Vivian Berkstrom, calling from Astrid Reed's office. May I speak with Mr. Edwards please?"

A few seconds later, Dick Edwards was back on the line. He had a big smile on his face because he knew what Miss Berkstrom had done. He had often done the same thing himself. It was a way to authenticate the call.

"What may I do for you, Mr. Edwards?"

"Well, I'd appreciate it if you would call me Dick, and may I call you Vivian?"

"Of course. How may I help you, Dick?"

"The senator heard about Miss Reed's interview with Kim Jong Un and was wondering who arranged this interview. I'm sure you're aware we do not have diplomatic relations with North Korea. In fact, you could say we have no relations at all with North Korea."

"I arranged it. We do have a bureau in South Korea, and believe it or not, there are some people in the South that still have connections with the North. A few calls later, I had made the arrangements for Miss Reed's interview with the Supreme Leader."

"I'm impressed," he said, and he was.

"Is that all, Dick?" she asked.

"How did she get there?"

"Miss Reed has her own private aircraft. Is there anything else?"

"I applaud your ingenuity, and I thank you for your time. Have a nice day."

A few calls later and Dick Edwards knew that the World News Corporation was the owner of a Gulfstream G650 with tail numbers REM 508. He knew that the aircraft could not fly from Atlanta, Georgia, the headquarters of World News, directly to North Korea and would have to stop in order to refuel. A few more phone calls and he had the flight plan and was surprised that the plane had landed at Roman Tmetuchl International Airport on Babelthuap Island, Palau several days ago. This was too much of a coincidence and he certainly didn't believe in coincidence.

A few minutes later, Edwards was on the telephone with the customs and immigration office at Roman Tmetuchl International Airport. After he identified himself, he told the superintendent in charge of the office that this was an inquiry about some Americans and that he would appreciate any help that they could give. "I believe," said Edwards, "a private jet from the United States landed there recently."

"Yes, sir, Mr. Edwards. She's a real beauty. It's the new Citation Ten, the new big X. This is some aircraft. This plane is almost supersonic. Almost can break the sound barrier. What a beauty, it's a . . ."

"Excuse me, Superintendent, I don't mean to interrupt you. Could you please tell me the tail numbers?"

"Sure. Echo Bravo 917."

Edwards was puzzled—it was the wrong type of aircraft and the wrong tail numbers. "Will you be kind enough tell me the passenger list?"

"Besides the flight crew there were three passengers; Ronald Shaljian, Oscar Ocho, and Jack Reynolds."

"That's not the plane I was looking for," replied Edwards. While he was talking, he entered the tail numbers of the Citation. The screen revealed it was owned by East West Trading Company. "Is there another aircraft on the island that recently came from the United States?"

"Yes, a Gulfstream G650, with tail numbers Romeo Echo Mike 508. And I guess you want that passenger manifest too."

"Please."

"In addition to the crew, Astrid Reed and Douglas MacArthur."

"Are the planes still on the island?"

"No, the Citation left for Seoul and the Gulfstream for Pyongyang."

"Thank you, you have been very helpful. It looks like everybody's accounted for. We truly appreciate your help. Thank you again and goodbye."

Before Edwards could hang up he heard the superintendent say, "But you know what's really strange?"

Edwards shook his head, and asked, "What's that?"

"The Citation left empty and its three passengers left with Miss Reed. Mr. MacArthur is still on the island and is probably having more fun here than they are in Pyongyang."

"You're right, that is strange. But who knows why anyone would want to leave your beautiful island and go to North Korea. Well, thanks again and goodbye." Edwards hung up and now his curiosity was getting the best of him. He called several hotels asking for Mr. MacArthur or Miss Reed. Finally, when he reached the Palau Royal Resort, he was told that Miss Reed had checked out and that there was no Mr. MacArthur there.

For the next several hours, through an online searching tool, Edwards ran all the names given to him except Astrid Reed's, and they all came up negative. He called a friend of his over at the FBI and asked that him to run the names.

He also searched East West Trading Company and that came up negative. In the aircraft registration files at the FAA, the East West Trading Company was registered as a Delaware Corporation and its address was corporate services in Wilmington.

The corporate services records showed the corporation was a wholly-owned subsidiary of Pan World, an off-shore corporation founded and headquartered on the Isle of Gibraltar. He knew that getting any information about a Gibraltar company was impossible.

His friend from the FBI called and said there was nothing on those names.

But this was not nothing—Edwards thought this was something.

CHAPTER 45

RYONGSONG RESIDENCE AND CENTRAL HEADQUARTERS

General Cheon led Daniels through a maze of tunnels, past the underground railroad station, and eventually to an elevator, which would bring them to the garden level. The general told Daniels that the private railroad connected several of the residences and government headquarters. As he walked through the tunnels, Daniels estimated that this below-ground bunker was as close to being bombproof as possible.

Daniels asked, "I realize we're below ground, but are we far enough that this bunker would protect you from a nuclear weapon?"

Cheon did not answer right away and finally said, "We believe it is, but let us hope we never have to find out."

Daniels nodded his head in agreement. They came to the elevator and the general punched in his code. The steel doors opened and they stepped in. In each corner of the elevator were cameras. Daniel noticed there were no buttons and that as soon as the doors slid shut, the elevator began to rise. He thought this would not be a good method of escape. A little while later, the doors slid open and the pair stepped out into the vestibule, which opened up into the gardens. Daniels stood there for a moment, looking. He had seen many photos of the gardens and lakes, but standing there was something else. It was hard to imagine a country so poor having a compound of about six square miles, and quite so beautiful. It reminded him of New York's Central Park.

Cheon signaled and an orderly drove up in a golf cart. The general and Daniels got into the back seat and the driver proceeded down one of the several roads. There were fences within the compound that surrounded two large houses. Daniels guessed they were the main residence for the Supreme Leader. A little farther down the path there were about eight other houses, which were also fenced in.

Several minutes later, they passed a large, man-made lake with fountains. Tied to the dock were several rowboats and a few small sailboats.

"This is very impressive," said Daniels. "When will we meet the Supreme Leader?"

"The Supreme Leader is with Astrid Reed and he's giving her a tour. When he is done with the tour, he will meet us at one of the outdoor eating areas by the lakefront banquet hall. There are tables there so we can conduct some business. I hope this is not your last meal. Meanwhile, I will show you some more of our wonderful facilities."

They drove past the track field, the shooting range, and much to Daniels' surprise, a car-racing course. They finally stopped at the horse-racing track. The racetrack had a grandstand that looked like Kentucky Downs, only smaller. It had seats for about ten to twelve people.

Daniels asked, "How big is the track?"

"One-mile around."

"Does the Supreme Leader ride in races?"

That caused the general to laugh. "Of course not. It would not be fair. He would automatically win because he cannot lose, as he has special gifts. He enjoys watching the races."

They got off the golf cart and walked over to the stables. The stables were large, housing about thirty horses. Inside the stables was an indoor riding ring.

"Do you ride, Mr. Brown?"

"No, I'm a city boy, but I do like horses," said Daniels as he patted a big pale stallion.

"That horse must like you, Mr. Brown. I understand he never lets anyone touch him but the Supreme Leader. Behold a pale horse and his name that sat on him was Death, and Hell followed him. Are you Death, Mr. Brown?"

"I don't think so, General, at least not for you."

Cheon was silent, then said, "I tolerate your arrogance because of General Kem. If you ever think of living past today, you had better have something that makes sense, because no one can protect you from the wrath of the Supreme Leader. Director Jang and his first deputy, Shin are here and will be meeting with us. Like I said, you better have something real or else . . ."

"Or else what? Why not hear what I have to say and then decide what you want to do with me." Daniels turned and walked toward the golf cart. He looked up toward the sky, smiled, and made several gestures with his hands. Daniels was trained in sign language and more than once, it had come in handy. Then he got back into the cart. Cheon was a few steps behind him and could not see what he'd done.

■ ■ ■

On the other side of the world, in a secure room at CIA headquarters at Langley, Virginia sat seven analysts, three translators, two computer experts, Mike Golef, Admiral Charko, and Jon Cornaci. They were glued to the several screens on the wall, which gave them a real-time show featuring Mac Daniels, Astrid Reed, and the Supreme Leader.

"What did he say?" asked Cornaci, who could not read sign language.

The translator stammered for a second, and then red faced he said, "Show time. Don't hog the popcorn, Admiral."

"I'll give him popcorn," said Admiral Charko. "I'll give two weeks with the resident psych."

Cornaci just smiled.

■ ■ ■

Cheon pulled up to the lakefront seating area and motioned to Daniels to sit at the table. Cheon took a seat to his right and left one space in between them vacant. The general's cell phone rang. He had a quick conversation then signed off. "That, Mr. Brown, is our two honored guests. Director Jang and first deputy Shin are being driven over here now. I have trouble believing one of them is a traitor. I hope this is not a trick or I may have to let Sang kill you."

"I'm sure he would like that, but General it won't happen."

A golf cart pulled up and Director Jang and First Deputy Shin got off and came toward the table. Cheon pointed to two seats; one between him and Daniels, and the other to his right next to himself.

Director Jang Min sat next to Daniels. His expression showed his surprise to see a Westerner sitting at the table. Daniels guessed that he was in his early sixties. Jang's hair was grey with traces of black. He was short by western standards, but of average height for North Korea; about five foot five but excessively overweight. He wore wire-rimmed glasses and was dressed in a dark suit with a white shirt opened at the neck. Over his left breast pocket, he wore a lapel pin with portraits of the reclusive country's founder Kim Il Sung and his son Kim Jong Il. The double-portrait lapel pins are given to high-ranking executives and military leaders, but not to ordinary citizens who usually wear pins with a single portrait of Kim Il Sung. There are at least ten different pins and badges with portraits of Kim Il Sung and Kim Jong Il that North Koreans are obligated to wear.

First Deputy Shin Soo was younger than his superior, Jang. Daniels estimated he was in his fifties, with a full head of black hair. He was also on the short side; the same height as Jang but very thin. He wore a dark-blue suit with a light-blue shirt and tie. He too wore the lapel pin with the double portrait. He stared at Daniels and began to speak in Korean to Cheon.

Cheon stopped him with a raised hand. "Speak English or Chinese," he ordered. "Our guest here does not speak Korean."

Speaking in Chinese, Shin Soo said, "All the more reason to speak Korean. I am sure the Supreme Leader has his reason for having an American here..."

Daniels cut him off. "I am a Saudi-born, Canadian citizen."

"Does it matter? You're from the West, you don't understand us," said Shin Soo.

Daniels was about to say something, but he stopped when he saw the procession of golf carts coming up the path. The Supreme Leader, Kim Jong-Un, drove the lead golf cart. Sitting quite close to him was Astrid Reed. Both were smiling and at times laughing. *No translator*, he thought; *she has the Supreme Leader speaking English*. Daniels noticed Mrs. Kim's absence. He wondered if it was intentional on the part of the Supreme Leader. Walking alongside of the cart was the camera operator and the sound recorder. In the second cart were JR and several other technicians. There were several more carts filled with the Supreme Leader's entourage.

Kim's cart pulled up close to the seating area. Stopping the cart, he hopped out and ran around to help Astrid out of the cart. Kim was a lot taller than he looked in pictures. He was five foot nine, but standing next to Astrid, he looked short. Astrid was a little over five foot seven but in her high heels, she was taller than Kim.

Kim appeared to have a new hairstyle. It was cropped close on the sides, about three inches over the ears. He'd grown out his hair on top and had it sculpted into a trapezoidal shape, and he had his eyebrows trimmed. He wore a gray tunic that went down to his mid-thigh with matching gray pants. The tunic was buttoned up to his neck and over his heart was the double portrait pin of his father and grandfather.

Kim Jung-Un had a strong facial resemblance to his father Kim Jong-il, the former Supreme Leader of North Korea, who'd ruled the country from 1994 to his death in 2011. Other than the facial features, there was little resemblance because Kim Jong-il had only been five feet three inches in height.

As Kim led Astrid to the table, everyone stood up. Kim sat Astrid next to Daniels and then he took the seat next to her, leaving two empty chairs to his right. Once he sat down everyone else did and started to applaud.

Kim gave a large toothy smile, which made him look younger than his thirty-two years of age. He held up his hand and everyone immediately stopped.

"Because my honored guest, the beautiful Miss Reed, does not speak Korean or Chinese we will all talk in English for her benefit," announced Kim.

■ ■ ■

"How's the sound coming in?" asked Cornaci, as he stared at the screen.

"Loud and clear, sir," replied one of the technicians. "We're going to have good visibility and sound for quite some time."

"Holy Mother of God," shouted Charko. "Is that JR sitting at the table behind Daniels?"

"Affirmative, sir," answered one of the technicians.

Charko rubbed his temples. He could feel a headache coming on. "What's he doing there? I better not see Haig on the screen."

"Last fix we had on Mr. Haig was Seoul, sir."

"Is he there now?"

■ ■ ■

Kim introduced Astrid to General Cheon and to Jang Min and Shin Soo. When he came to Daniels, he said, "I believe you know Mr. Mac Brown."

"I do, Jung-Un," answered Astrid.

Everyone at the table held back an expression of shock that she had used the Supreme Leader's first name. Daniels would have been surprised if she called him anything else. He knew Astrid and between her beauty and charm, the Supreme Leader was hooked.

"I see we have two empty places. Is someone else joining us?" asked Astrid.

"Yes, Miss Reed. We are expecting two of our information technology specialists to join us with a few of our North Korean laptops. There is something we have to do, and we may have to speak in Chinese," apologized General Cheon.

"If you need to talk freely, I'll be happy to step away from the table," replied Astrid.

"That's not necessary, Astrid," said the Supreme Leader. "We have to verify the identification of Mr. Mac Brown, and we need to do it in Chinese. Please, your presence is welcome here."

"You mean Mr. Mac Brown is not who he says he is?" questioned Astrid.

"That's what we're trying to find out," said Cheon.

"And if he's not?" asked Astrid.

"Then he must be a spy and he will be tried, found guilty, and publicly executed; all in the next twenty-four hours."

"Oh," is all an ashen-faced Astrid could say.

Daniels saw her expression. No one else seemed to notice or care. "Don't worry Astrid. Even if my name is not my name, which really doesn't matter, I'm sure the Supreme Leader will not want to execute me. But if he does, I'll have a choice of firing squad, hanging, or decapitation in the public square."

"What do you choose, Mr. Mac Brown?" asked Cheon.

"I'll take the bullet, thank you."

Astrid joined in, "Let's hope it won't come to that. Can we please change the subject?"

Kim snapped his fingers. No one spoke. Kim ordered, "Wine."

Daniels let it drop; he didn't want to upset Astrid. If she only knew that the baby-faced leader had executed eighty people for minor offenses such as watching South Korean movies, watching South Korean pornography, or possessing a South Korean Bible. Family did not matter either; the North Korean state media had announced the execution of Kim Jong-Un's uncle. Kim ruled with an iron hand and it was not necessarily in a velvet glove.

CHAPTER 46

FALLS CHURCH, VIRGINIA

Ken Park paced the floor of his home. He couldn't reach Aswas Rajul, and this was very upsetting. He'd called several times but Rajul had never set up a voice mail. It was a security device; no messages for anyone to hear. Rajul's caller ID would show the calls and the fact that there was more than one, and he would understand there was an urgency and would call back.

Park called the restaurant and told his manager he would not be back. The manager was quite capable of handling the business, and Park had done this on several occasions. The manager didn't think anything odd of this. Park wasn't going to leave the house until he spoke with Rajul. He found a pack of cigarettes and lit one. As it burned down, he lit another cigarette with the first. He was chain-smoking again. He poured himself a drink; a double Jack Daniels without ice and sipped as he smoked.

He knew he didn't have much time left—several hours had gone by since the call from Sang and he knew that Sang was expecting his call. He wondered just who Sang was. He knew he was a deputy minister in the Ministry of State Security for Pyongyang, but there were many deputies. He did not need to find out how high Sang was in the pecking order of deputy ministers, he just had to have answers, otherwise his life in America as he knew it, would be over.

Something was wrong but he could not believe it was Rajul. As Park paced the floor, he began to go over the facts in his mind. No one had questioned him about his information on the uranium. It must've been true. Sang's only issue was the passenger on the boat. He was not an American but General Kem's agent and that didn't make any sense. If you were Kem's agent or not, that wasn't a problem, but if the uranium wasn't switched, that would have been a problem. Obviously the uranium had been switched, he reasoned, that's why the Supreme Leader was threatening the Ronald Reagan. *Hell*, he thought. *It was all over the news and therefore the information about the uranium is correct.* This just didn't make sense. He lit another cigarette and took another drink.

Another forty-five minutes passed and finally the phone rang. Park knocked over the drink, lunging for the phone. He got to it before the second ring. "Yes."

"Go to the phone booth at the entrance of Memorial Park. Ten minutes." The phone went dead.

Park had recognized Rajul's voice. He did not hesitate; he got in his car and left the house with the lights on. The park wasn't far from his home—it was in walking distance. He didn't even know there was a phone booth at the park. Several minutes later, he parked his car by the entrance and sure enough, there was a phone booth. He ran over to the phone booth and waited. Several minutes later, the phone rang.

"Yes," answered Park.

"Careful, no names. You called me four times. It has to be important. I assume there is some kind of trouble, that's why I directed you to the park. What is it?"

Park thought for second before speaking. "The information you provided regarding the American on the ship was wrong. He wasn't an American, he is a Saudi- born, Canadian citizen who works for General Lee Kem, the head of the Ministry of State Security in China."

Rajul asked, "Does he have a name?"

"Yes, John Mac Brown."

It all became clear to Rajul. "Listen carefully," he said to Park, "The information regarding the uranium switch was correct, wasn't it? If it wasn't, then why is the Supreme Leader beating a war drum and threatening to sink the Ronald Reagan? Obviously, this man on the ship was a lot smarter than we gave him credit for. Somehow he bullshitted everyone. He *is* an American and his name is Douglas MacArthur. My man was making the delivery and was overtaken by this MacArthur and a woman. The woman was a tall redhead with green eyes. Do you know who that sounds like and who was recently on Palau Island?"

Not waiting for an answer, he continued, "Astrid Reed! MacArthur got on the ship, and I'm willing to bet his accomplice is Astrid Reed, the owner of World News. Reed came onto Palau Island with this MacArthur and she left without him. He is nowhere to be found on the island."

"Holy shit! And she is in Pyongyang right now interviewing the Supreme Leader."

"And I'll bet MacArthur or Mac Brown or whatever he calls himself is there, too. You better make a call before they assassinate your leader."

Park slammed down the phone and ran to his car. He had to get a call into the Reconnaissance General Bureau headquarters first, and then to Sang. As he drove, he thought that for the Supreme Leader's sake as well as his own, he would bypass protocol and call General Cheon directly. With this information, he would be well rewarded and what a story—Astrid Reed and MacArthur publicly executed for the attempted assassination of the Supreme Leader. He finally smiled.

CHAPTER 47

THE OUTDOOR GARDENS AT THE RYONGSONG RESIDENCE

Several attendants came running out with decanters of wine. They poured for everyone at the table. Kim picked up his glass and held it up. "A toast," he said, "with our fine blueberry wine from Yangang province. To Miss Reed and our interview, which she will show to the world, and to my father and grandfather—drink."

Everyone took a sip, and the Supreme Leader brought the glass up to his face, but did not drink. Daniels repressed a smile. He thought, *This guy is really paranoid*. He wondered how the Supreme Leader would handle lunch, and his question was soon answered.

As the food was being served, two information technologists appeared with laptops. Kim waved off the food and pointed to the empty chairs. The information technologists bowed their heads and took the seats. They opened up the laptops and in a few minutes, after typing in various codes, the laptops came to life.

Each keystroke was recorded at Langley, thanks to a high-resolution camera in a geosynchronous orbit. Charko gave the thumbs-up sign to his boss Cornaci. Codes were precious. The technicians plugged in a jack that was connected to earphones and a microphone. One laptop was placed in front of Daniels and the other in from of Kim. Daniels and Kim slipped on the headphones. A few second seconds later, on the screen appeared General Lee Kem.

"Good morning, Supreme Leader," said Kem speaking in Chinese.

"Good morning, General Kem," answered Kim, replying in Chinese.

Daniels, fluent in Chinese continued the dialogue. "Morning, boss."

"Mac, Mac will you always cause me such trouble?" lamented Kem. "And don't call me boss."

"It's not me, General. It's my hosts here. They just don't believe who I am."

"I don't even know who you are, Mac, but it doesn't matter. Get this over with, as I have other things to attend to."

"How do I know this man is who he says he is?" asked Kim.

"Because he's got a scar on his right wrist. A small one from an old knife wound, that I gave him."

Kim grabbed Daniels' wrist and looked. "The scar proves nothing. A good agent can do that and you could be complicit with him. The Americans are tricky. You may not even be who you say you are. I need proof."

Kem scratched his head. "I will give you proof that I am General Kem, but I suggest that you get Mac off-line. You should be the only one who can hear what I'm about to say."

Without being told, Daniels took off his headset, pulled the plug on the headset, and pushed his chair back away from the laptop. Kim smiled. What he didn't know was that on the other side of the world at CIA headquarters, they were already online with security codes and could hear every word that was about to be said.

"Okay, General, it is just the two of us."

"When you were here with your father . . .," began Kem.

Kem went on and the more he talked, the more the smile on Kim's face grew until it was a wide-open mouthed, toothy smile that led to laughter. Kim started to laugh almost uncontrollably. "Enough enough," he said. "You are who you say you are, General. Only you would know that story. Now who is this man sitting before me and why should I trust him?"

Kem asked, "Do you wish to put me on the speaker for all to hear?"

Kim thought about it for second and then said, "I will keep my microphone and earphones on so I can converse with you. I will put the other laptop on speaker so everyone can hear. We will continue dialoguing in Chinese, as we have an American at the table who need not hear what we're about to discuss."

The technician turned on Daniels' speaker.

Kim told the general who was around the table, but left off Astrid Reed. "Please begin, General," he said.

Kem began, "The man sitting at the table goes by many names, and to be honest I do not know his real name as it is neither necessary nor required. I know him as John Mac Brown and Douglas MacArthur. He's used other names in the past but those two are the most common. He is a contract agent for the CIA."

At the mention of CIA, Kim's expression changed, as did everyone else's. Kem could see Kim's face on his screen. "Don't be alarmed—he also works for me. I trust him, but he does lie and he is lethal. Right, General Cheon?"

Cheon did not answer.

"I am not sure where he lives and I do not want to know. I know he is a wealth of information, but you have to pay him." Kem paused.

No one spoke or would dare too. They waited for Kim to say something.

Kim asked, "How do you keep him honest?"

Kem went on, "Money. He works, as the Americans say, off the books. He knows what happened to your uranium, and I believe he was involved with that."

"Thanks, General," said Daniels.

"Because I trust you, it does not mean you did not act in your best interest, which may not be my Korean friend's best interest."

"Do you have it?" demanded Kim.

Cheon let his hand drop to his pistol.

"No. I do not have it, but I will tell you what happened, if you will allow me."

"Please let him speak," asked Kem. "I do not want to lose an agent. I request that you give him safe conduct out of your country. Mac, while you're in North Korea please behave yourself. If you break the law, there are some things I cannot protect you from."

Kim stared at Daniels, and said to General Kem, "Safe conduct depends on what he says about our uranium. If I'm not satisfied, I will let you watch his execution."

Back at Langley, Cornaci and Charko closed their eyes and both shook their heads. Everyone watching held his collective breath. Cornaci said a silent prayer, "Please God . . ."

Charko knew and so did Kem that Daniels would disarm Cheon and kill him and Kim before he would allow himself to be taken prisoner.

Daniels looked up at the sky and said, "It's a beautiful day. Are you ready?"

Kim was puzzled. He nodded his head.

Kem said, "Yes."

Astrid heard in her ear, "Loud and clear, scratch your nose."

She did.

Daniels nodded. "Well," he said, as he pushed back from the table and got a little closer to Cheon, "there are two stories; one being what happened to your uranium and two; why you were fed false information about what really happened. Where do you want to start?"

Kim didn't hesitate. "What happened to my uranium? If I do not like what you tell me, there will be no reason for you to say anything else. You will be dead."

"I understand. It seems fair enough," replied Daniels with a smile.

"You smile. You can be dead in the next ten minutes."

"I don't think so. I think you will be pleased to hear what I say." Turning to Astrid, and reverting to English, he said, "When you finish with your interview, would you be kind enough to give me a lift out of this country? I would appreciate it."

Astrid looked confused but played along. "Of course."

Daniels went back to Chinese. "The Cubans brokered a deal between you and several Middle East groups. They paid the Cubans sixty million Euros and the Cubans paid you fifty million for the highly-enriched weapons-grade uranium. You were selling enough weapons-grade uranium to build a dozen suitcase bombs, or a few big bombs, and a shitload of dirty bombs. Of course, you were selling sand, but no one knew that. There was no way the Americans were going let this sale go through. They hired me to stop you. Of course you couldn't allow the sand to reach Cuba, so you were going to fake an accident and let everyone know that the plane sunk with the alleged uranium on board."

Daniels paused for a moment. Everything he said was true and Cheon knew it. They did not know about the ten million commission that the Cubans made on the deal.

Daniels went on. "Your Antonov, fuselage number 645, no letters or tail numbers, landed at Ho Chi Minh City where I was waiting in a Cubana jet. I was to take the cargo and the Cuban agent and transfer it to the Cubana jet."

Cheon dialed a number, said something, and waited. Daniels waited until he hung up. Cheon reported that 645 was the number of the Antonov.

"You had other ideas and didn't allow the transfer. You took off. I called the aircraft carrier Ronald Reagan, who put up a Hawkeye to track the Antonov. We were going to shoot it down. There was no way we would allow the uranium to reach Cuba. If we'd known it was sand, we would have gladly helped it along, I know the Antonov has limited range and something was up. Before we could do anything, the plane crashed. We did not know it was sand."

Kim was quiet.

Kem broke the silence. "What he says is correct as far as our records show. We monitored the Reagan and intercepted a call from an unidentified aircraft stating the transfer had not been made, and the Reagan launched the Hawkeye."

"I don't have your uranium. If I had it, I would have sold it to General Kem, but it is on the bottom of the sea. The only trouble is that the Middle Eastern groups did not trust you and made their own deal with your people to switch the sand for the real stuff. As we say, you got fucked. They paid ten million Euros for the switch."

This statement brought a severe reaction from Jang Min and to Shin Soo.

"That is crazy," shouted Jang Min. "It was sand."

Shin Soo said nothing. He realized this was his last day on earth. He knew his entire family would be executed. His eyes started to well up with tears.

"It was sand I tell you. Tell them, Shin Soo," Jang Min ordered.

Shin Soo was silent. Before he could compose himself, Daniels spoke. "Shin Soo, do you know where the Isle of Jersey is?"

Shin Soo nodded his head.

"And do you know where it is, Jang Min?"

"No. Why would I?"

"Because that is where the ten million Euros are," said Daniels. "In the safest and most private banking system in the world." Turning to Kim, he said, "Do you want me to continue, or are you going to shoot me?"

"Go on. So far, you have your life. Make the next part as interesting and you will work for us."

"Before we get to your traitor, what happened was your Middle Eastern buyers had paid a total of seventy million Euros and wanted revenge for your deceit. They had an American by the name of Aswas Rajul call your agent Ki-Young Park, and give him the story about the Americans having your uranium. They wanted you to do something foolish like attack the Reagan. If you had, they believed the Americans would have taken drastic action against you. They had hoped for an all-out war. What they did not know was I was the CIA officer in charge of the operation and it failed. I called General Kem to inform him before it was too late."

After a long silence, Kem spoke. "If you start a war with the Americans after what you have heard you will be on your own. We will not go to war with the Americans. Whether you like it or not, they are our largest trading partner and they buy most of our goods. This is not the time for war, but the time to think and outfox the enemy."

Kim nodded, Kem signed off, and the screen went black.

Cheon's cell phone rang. He looked down but did not recognize the 703 area code. He was about to answer it, but saw that Kim was looking at him. He powered off his phone.

Cornaci said, "Mac delivered. It looks like the war drum is put away for now."

"Yes and we have the names of two operatives and I know one," said Charko.

"Who?"

"Ken Park runs The Round Table over in Georgetown."

Cornaci asked, "What do you intend to do about him?"

But before he could answer, they all heard Daniels say, "Show time."

Charko just shook his head. "Daniels is not happy unless he is living on the edge. Show time, popcorn—God help me."

Daniels took his laptop and gave it to Astrid. She was confused and had no idea what was going on. "With the Supreme Leader's permission, I am going to give you a series of numbers that I want you to enter into the computer. Just enter them but do not press 'enter,' just slide the laptop over to the Supreme Leader. Do you understand?"

"I understand," she answered.

Daniels first gave her the web address for the Royal Bank of the Isle of Jersey. A few seconds later, it appeared on the screen.

"I have the bank's home page on the screen, Mac. Now what?"

"Go to log-in."

She did, and then said, "Okay, I need the account number."

Mike Golef had set up the account, and all he needed was the number to link the account to. Daniels had requested Astrid to do this, knowing that he would have to give her the numbers verbally and Golef would hear them simultaneously. Daniels did not want to take a chance that the satellite would not pick up the numbers. Passing the laptop over to Kim would give Golef the few extra seconds he might need.

Daniels turned to Jang Min. "You have your security card, which has a special number on it. The number is unique to you and no one knows it but you. What is it?"

"Supreme Leader, do I have to be insulted by the American CIA operative? You cannot trust them."

"Give him your number," said Kim in a voice that meant business. "General Cheon, if he does not cooperate take him and shoot him."

Jang Min took out his card and began to read in faulty English, "201."

Astrid repeated the number as Jang Min said it, "201."

He continued, "908732609212718."

Astrid repeated the numbers. She slid the laptop over to Kim, who pressed enter. He waited and looked at the screen. He then erased the screen and passed it back to Astrid.

"Shin Soo," said Daniels.

Shin Soo began as had Jang Min, and Astrid repeated the numbers.

"516954561202315551."

She slid the laptop over to the Supreme Leader, who pressed enter and stared at the screen. He then erased it and closed the top down. "Thank you for your help, Astrid," he said. "Shall we finish our interview?"

"Of course," she answered, a bit flustered.

"General Cheon please see that Mr. Mac Brown or whatever his name is, is escorted to his hotel . . ." He paused. "Safely. I hold you responsible for his safety. See that he has your contact information and wire him two hundred thousand Euros. It will be a pleasure to do business with you Mac. You two," said Kim, looking at Shin Soo and Jang Min, "stay here. When I am done with my interview, we will talk. A mistake has been made."

Cheon escorted Daniels back the way they'd come in. In Cheon's office, Daniels' clothes were returned to him and he was given Cheon's private number. Daniels gave the general instructions to wire his payment.

"My driver will see you safely to the hotel. He will be at your disposal," said Cheon.

Cheon's orderly interrupted them. "Sir, there is an important call for you. He says he has been calling your cell but cannot get through. It is Pa..."

Cheon snapped and cut him off. "I told you, do not disturb me. I am on official business for the Supreme Leader. Have them call back later."

The orderly returned to his office and picked up the phone. "Park, you must call back later."

CHAPTER 48

LANGLEY, VIRGINIA

Cornaci and Charko were not smiling as they entered Dr. Cornaci's outer office. Helen Benton had worked for Jon Cornaci at the university and followed him to the CIA. She knew him well enough to recognize his facial expressions. Something was wrong. She also knew that she was not supposed to ask. "Doctor, General Bellardi called and requested that you call as soon as you are available. Admiral," she said, "Lila," referring to his secretary, "called up and said that Colonel Starges had called and asked that you call him as soon as possible."

She had the messages and numbers on slips of paper and held her hand up as the men walked by. Neither of them took the slips.

"Thank you Helen, we both know the number by heart. They're both probably calling about the same thing. Would you be kind enough to bring in pot of coffee? I'll get the general on the phone," said Cornaci.

"Please let Lila know I'll be up here for a while," said Charko.

Both men sat on the couch in Cornaci's office. Cornaci pressed the speaker on the phone that was on the coffee table in front of the couch. The dial tone filled the room. He hit a speed dial button and on the second ring, it was answered.

"General Bellardi's line, Colonel Starges speaking."

"This is Admiral Charko and Director Cornaci here," said Charko. "You're on the speaker. Is the general available?"

"Yes, Admiral. If you don't mind, I'll stay on the line too."

"Not a problem."

A few seconds later, the deep voice of General Bellardi was heard. In the true jargon of a Marine, which he was, he said, "What the fuck happened? What's going on? I'm sitting here pulling my hair out. The Joint Chiefs ordered us to go to Defcon 3."

"General, it's me, Jon. None of us have enough hair left. Stop pulling. It went very well. Mac is a master of bullshit. He spun his story and fortunately, it sounded so good the Supreme Leader hired him as an agent and paid him two hundred thousand Euros. Mac convinced them that we don't have the uranium."

"We also got some good info," said Charko. "Got the names of two agents and the security codes of the director and vice director of the nuclear program. Right now, the boys downstairs are having a field day running through Korean computers."

"Have you run the names that you picked up?" asked Starges.

"As soon as they came in we started the process, but would you believe it," said Charko, "one of the names is Ken Park, the owner of the Round Table in Georgetown."

"Holy shit, I eat there all the time when I'm in town," said Starges.

"Don't feel bad. Just about everybody up on the hill eats there. I've eaten there with Director Bertone of the FBI more than once."

"Anything else?" asked Bellardi, losing his patience. He wanted to get to the more important issue.

"Well, Tony," said Charko, "we believe we have a home-grown terrorist, an American, who goes by the name of Aswas Rajul. For some reason I got the feeling he's in this area. From what we heard, he's behind the leak. He must be connected high up."

Starges asked, "What are you doing about Park?"

"Send it over to the Director Bertone," answered Cornaci.

Bellardi gave a little laugh. "Jon, there is a lot we can do before we give him to the Feds. I'm sure you have a few boys that can get into just about any place undetected. Do a little snooping, plant a few bugs, then give it to the Feds."

"I'll defer to the admiral on the operational matter," answered Cornaci. "But right now my gut tells me we should call the director and give him a heads up. It's easier for them to do surveillance than us. After all, we're not supposed to operate inside the States. What you think, Admiral?"

"I'd like the Feds to watch him carefully. See what he leads them to. Then hammer him. He's not a diplomat so the Department of Justice can prosecute him. We step in as the good guys, turning him and making him a double agent."

They all knew there was one more question that had to be answered. Finally, Bellardi asked, "What about Mac and Astrid? Are they out of there?"

"It looks like the Supreme Leader has given Mac safe conduct. Astrid should not have a problem. She interviewed Kim and he was smitten with the love bug. She was calling him by his first name. She'll fly out and I'm sure Mac will try to hitch a ride if possible."

"I called Admiral Haley over at PaCom," reported Starges, "and they are going to try to position a sub in the Yellow Sea. There's a problem with the depth of the water, but they will try to get in as close as possible. You know we have a few tricks up our sleeves. He'll make it out."

"Truthfully, Mac is more concerned about Astrid than anything else. I'll tell you this, Tony," said Charko, "Mac certainly didn't lose his warped sense of humor. He sent me a message; 'Don't eat too much popcorn and watch the show.' God help us."

That caused Bellardi to chuckle. "That's my boy. God help the Supreme Leader if he pisses Mac off. Speak with you later."

The phone clicked off and at the same time Helen brought in a pot of coffee and a plate of cookies. It caused Cornaci to force a smile. When she left, the men were quiet for a moment and finally Charko spoke. "Jon, I'll call Director Bertone and talk with him. Under no circumstances should anything be done until Mac is out of there."

Cornaci was tired. He had dark circles under his eyes. "I guess all we can do is sit and wait. I'm going to stay here. I'll catch a few winks on the couch. I want to go downstairs to the com room and watch for a while. I want to be here, just in case."

"Good idea. I'll call Wanda and tell her I'm staying here too. Well, we have plenty of coffee and cookies."

CHAPTER 49

FALLS CHURCH, VIRGINIA

Park lit another cigarette and kept pacing the floor. He looked at his watch again and wondered why he couldn't speak to the general. Was he too late? He made a decision. If he didn't hear back in five minutes, he would call Sang. He didn't want the Supreme Leader assassinated. Other than that, he did not care. *Nothing is simple,* he thought. All he wanted to do was run his restaurant, live in Falls Church, and enjoy his life, and that's what he was doing. If he had to, he could disappear in Florida. But first he would try once more to send the information and if he couldn't get through, his next call would be to Lou.

Another cigarette later, he picked up his phone and dialed Sang.

"Sang here."

"It's me, Ki-Young Park," said Park, using his formal Korean name.

"What do you have for me? It better be good. Otherwise my next call is to your superiors over at Reconnaissance General Bureau and you will be back here to explain your stupidity."

"The information I gave you was correct. The man on that ship is not an agent of General Kem and if he is, Kem is a fool. He is an American, his name is Douglas MacArthur, and he probably works for the CIA or DIA. Rajul had arranged for the delivery of sarin gas to the ship, the Sails of Allah. The delivery was overtaken by this MacArthur and a woman. The woman was a tall redhead with green eyes. Do you know who that sounds like and who recently arrived on Palau Island with MacArthur? Astrid Reed. Reed has a connection with this MacArthur. I cannot believe that she works for the American government, but there is a connection. MacArthur flew into Palau with her, then he arrives on the ship and she flies into Pyongyang. You figure it out."

Sang was silent.

Park thought he had lost the connection. Finally, he said, "Are you there?"

"Yes, I am just putting the pieces together. If what you say is correct, this plot by the Americans could involve the Chinese. Is that possible?"

Park said nothing. He couldn't even think how to answer that question.

Finally, he said, "Wasn't the information regarding the uranium switch I reported correct?"

"What switch? I have heard nothing about this."

Now Park was silent for a minute. He wondered how Sang could not know of this. This was crazy. He had information, good information, and yet there were so many questions. The uranium information was definitely correct—that's why the Supreme Leader had threatened to sink the Ronald Reagan.

"Uranium switch? Tell me about this," commanded Sang.

Park told him the details as he had previously reported them.

There was another long silence on the phone. "I've got it. You're right— MacArthur is an agent for the Americans. I knew I'd seen him somewhere before. Now I've figured it out. MacArthur is the Cuban, Miguel Ricardo. He is the one who made the deal with us for the purchase of uranium. I have to review the tapes from the hotel, but now I know what to look for. I missed it before but I'm willing to bet if I digitize the video and blow it up, I'll see the same bullet marks on both men. I don't know what's going on, but I'm going to detain MacArthur and Astrid Reed. You did good Park, and I'll let everyone know it was you who provided this crucial information."

His phone connection went dead, and Park took the last drag on his cigarette and put it out. He took a big drink and finally smiled. He was safe for now.

■ ■ ■

Sang called Guozhi Sun. "Where are you?"

"At the hotel. Brown just came back. He is at the front desk. Looks like he is getting his key. I am keeping an eye on him."

"Very well. Watch him but be careful. He is CIA or DIA and I want to arrest him and Astrid Reed."

"Reed?!" That took him by surprise.

"Yes. She is working with MacArthur. That's his real name. I am on my way to the hotel. I want to check the videotape to prove my point. I know you have a score to settle with him as I do, but do not try to arrest him by yourself. He is much too dangerous."

"What about Reed?"

"She will be easy. She will not suspect that we are on to her. It will be easy to handcuff her and take her into custody. I don't expect much of a fight from her. But I have something to do with her before I bring her in. I'll teach her a lesson."

Sun knew what he was referring to. While Reed might be an enemy, he did not go along with rape. Knowing Sang, he would not only rape her, but allow the guards to gang rape her. This was not going to be a good day for Astrid Reed. He kept his personal feelings to himself. It was his job and whether he approved or not, it didn't matter. Things would happen and they did. This was, after all, North Korea.

CHAPTER 50

KORYO HOTEL

Daniels took his key from the front desk and headed toward the elevator.

As soon as he stepped into the elevator, Sun went up to the front desk and asked, "What did he want?"

The desk clerk told him that Mr. Mac Brown wanted to be told when Miss Reed returned to the hotel and had asked for a dinner reservation for two people at eight o'clock tonight. Sun gave the desk clerk his cell number and told the clerk that if Mac Brown called down for anything, he was to be told. He also wanted to know when Miss Reed returned to the hotel.

As he started to leave the front desk, Sun turned and said, "Call me when Sang returns."

The clerk asked, "Where will you be?"

"In Mac Brown's room."

Sun touched the small of his back and he felt the Beretta. Under his left shoulder, he had another Beretta. He intended to use both handguns on Brown. He had tried to figure out how Brown had taken the Beretta out of his hand and he'd attempted to duplicate what had happened to him. He gave one of the communication guards in the basement his unloaded Beretta and tried to pull it out of the guard's hand. The pulling effect caused the guard's finger to squeeze the trigger and the Beretta dry-fired. Had the handgun been loaded, he would have been shot. He tried to dislodge the handgun several times from both the right and left. No matter how he tried, he would have been shot every time. He just couldn't understand how Brown could take the weapon from his hand. Well, with two Berettas pointed at Brown, Sun thought that would protect him. Brown could only slap one away, and he would shoot the other. He didn't have to be a good shot at close range and the nine-millimeter would definitely stop Brown.

Up in his room, Daniels took from the closet the special duffel bag that Astrid had given him. As not to arouse suspicion, he casually changed out of his dress pants, put on blue jeans, and slipped into the special running shoes. He had a long-sleeve black tee shirt that had two pockets; one over his heart and the other several inches lower. The pockets had Velcro straps, but if he wore the shirt inside out, the Velcro straps could hold a 10"x12" lightweight armor plate. The bottom of his bag was made out of the armor plate. It would stop a nine-millimeter bullet and that was one of the most common bullets used. He did not put the tee shirt on but left it in his bag. He thought that he would give it to Astrid, which brought a smile to his face. Seeing her in a tee shirt was a great sight, but he smiled because he knew she would complain that it didn't fit or it was the wrong color. He slipped on a blue golf shirt with a unicorn embroidered on the pocket. He ran the special belt through the loops and stuck the pencils and his laser pen in his pockets. He laid his windbreaker and hat on the duffel bag. The buttons on the cuffs of the windbreaker could be pulled off the coat and would convert into an ear bud that could connect to his phone. He looked at the carry strap on the duffel bag. It had a leather shoulder protector. On top of the shoulder protector was a round metal handle. *Funny,* he thought. No one ever inspected the carry strap. The round handle was a sound suppressor that could adapt to most handguns, especially the Beretta and he knew where he could get one.

Sun carried one and he'd seen Sun watching him when he checked in. He thought if Sun decided to go with him and Astrid when they left the hotel, then once in the car, it would be easy to dispose of Sun and take his weapon. The driver would also be disposed of. He then could drive Astrid and himself to the airport. He would take the bodies on board the airplane and dispose of them. Cheon would have his car but not a driver, and to Cheon the car was more important than the driver. He hoped that he could shake Sun off, but he was ready just in case.

From his duffel bag, he took out his shaving kit, and placed it on the special duffel bag. The toothbrush with the hard plastic was honed to a point, and the razor-sharp nail file might come in handy. He was ready to go as soon as Astrid got back. He would use General Cheon's car to take them to the airport. If he timed it right, the plane would be landing as they arrived and he and Astrid would jump in and take off. The plane should be on the ground in less than a minute. If he timed it right.

He thought about activating his cell phone to put Langley on notice, but decided to wait until Astrid was back at the hotel. He would activate then. Daniels was now ready. The dinner reservation was to keep Sun and Sang vying for a seat with Astrid. He hoped that when they were upstairs, he and Astrid would be at the airport.

He lay down on the bed thinking he might take a nap. There was a knock at Daniels' door. Without getting up he said, "It's open Sunny, come on in."

Sun slowly opened the door and quickly looked around the room. He saw Daniels lying on the bed, and he stepped in. Staying away from Daniels, he went into the corner as far away from Daniels as possible and sat down. He saw the bag on the bed with Daniels' hat and coat.

"Are you leaving us?" asked Sun.

"I'm done here. Time for me to be moving on. Is there a problem?"

"What about Miss Reed?" asked Sun. "I would've thought you would be going with her."

"Well, to be honest, I plan to have dinner with her tonight and I thought I'd ask her for a ride. I'm sure she's anxious to get back home too."

"I don't think she's going home tonight. I believe Sang wants to talk with her. We have some disturbing news and I think she has to answer a few questions."

"Well, in that case, I guess I'll be leaving without her. I'm sure I can get a local flight to Beijing and from there a flight back home."

Sun thought he would push Brown. Sang had told him Brown's real name was MacArthur and he wanted to see his reaction. He decided to provoke Brown. "You don't care about her? After all she's one of your countrymen."

Before he could get another word out Daniels cut him off and said, "She's an American, I'm a Canadian; she's American-born, I'm Saudi born; she's a Christian, I'm a Muslim; she's a woman I'm a man—other than the fact that we are both human beings, we have nothing in common. What's on your mind?"

Sun started to move his hand toward his shoulder holster.

"Don't do it, Sun. I don't want to fight with you. I don't want to hurt you. Just leave me alone."

"It's not you, Brown. It's just that Astrid Reed and a man by the name of Douglas MacArthur are here, and we believe they are trying to cause harm to the Supreme Leader."

Daniels didn't flinch. He lay there in bed and didn't move a muscle. It was as if he hadn't heard what Sun said. Finally, he spoke. "She's with the Supreme Leader and I doubt she could cause him any harm. I was there myself today and when I left, they were getting along just fine. She was even calling him by his first name."

"Long legs and big tits work over here too," said Sun. "Maybe the Supreme Leader has something in mind for her. I mean she is really something. I bet you even had a few thoughts about her. Sang should be here shortly to look after her. I am sure Sang has his ideas about her."

"She probably can take care of herself. If anything were to happen to her, I'm sure the Supreme Leader would be upset. Maybe I should have a talk with Sang."

Sun looked at his watch. "Sang should be here in fifteen minutes. When he gets here he might want to have words with you."

Daniel set up in bed. "Look, Sunny, why don't you get the fuck out of here? I don't want to fight with you. Stop trying to provoke me. I'm tired and I just want to go home. You can do what you want to Miss Reed, Sang, or anybody else; just leave me the fuck alone. I'm not your enemy. In case you didn't know it, I work for General Kem and now for the Supreme Leader. I'm going to take a nap. Now go."

Sun decided he would leave. He didn't want to start a fight in such close quarters. He reached the door and started to open it, then he turned around and asked, "What's the weather in Washington now?"

"How the fuck would I know? It's snowing. How's that for an answer? Now get the fuck out of here, because if I get off this bed, I'm going to throw you out the window."

"I didn't think it snowed in the summer time in Washington."

"Okay, sunny and clear skies—now leave. I want to get some sleep."

Sun shut the door. He had a plan and this time it wouldn't fail.

CHAPTER 51

KORYO HOTEL

SAME DAY

Sun went down to the communication room. He took a seat and felt the Beretta pressing against his back. He placed the Beretta on the console next to one of the screens and started playing with the dials, trying to focus in on Brown. He was upset.

When Sang arrived at the hotel, he immediately went to the basement communication room. He wanted to check the tapes. "What is it, Sun?" he asked.

"The cameras are not working well. I'm trying to watch Mac Brown."

Sang looked over Sun's shoulder and saw what Sun was complaining about. The screen was nothing but a blur. Sang reached for the dials but could not make it work.

"Never mind," he said. "I have something more important to do. I want to run some of the old tapes. I have an idea and I'm going to prove it."

"What can I do to help?" asked Sun.

"Nothing—just look at the screen with me and confirm what you see when we speak with General Cheon."

Sun didn't answer. He just nodded his head and looked at the screen.

Sang started to run some of the tapes. "This is the tape of Miguel Ricardo when he was here." He let the tape player for a few minutes. Pausing it, he said, "Look at his back, Sun. The upper right shoulder area, what do you see?"

Sun stared at the screen and then leaned closer. He frowned and finally said, "Looks like some kind of blemish on his back."

"It is. It's makeup over a bullet hole. Now look at this tape." He ran the tape of Mac Brown getting dressed. He let it go for a few minutes then hit pause. "Look at his upper right shoulder."

Sun stared at the screen. "Yes, I see it," he said. "It's the same mark."

"It's because it's the same person," said Sang.

Sun looked at both screens and compared them. After a few minutes he said, "You're right. It is the same person. What's going on? Have you reported this?"

"No, I haven't, but I'll tell you this. I have reliable information that Mac Brown's name is MacArthur. He was on Palau Island with Astrid Reed. They intercepted the boat with sarin gas. She flew here and he hopped on the Sails of Allah. He works for the CIA or the DIA. We have to arrest him and Astrid Reed. Where is he now?"

"I left him in his room about ten, fifteen minutes ago. He should still be there. I didn't see any elevator activity or anybody in the stairwells, although the camera's been off and on most of the time. When I left him, he was in bed."

"Let's arrest him. Take the four guards from down and . . ."

"Take all the guards and leave this place unprotected?" interrupted Sun.

"I'd take half the army if I could. Leaving this place unguarded for a few minutes, what could happen?"

Sun did not respond.

Sang continued, "Before we go upstairs, let's check the cameras and tape to be sure he is still in his room."

Sun nodded his agreement.

Sang ran the tape. As it began to run, it showed Sun leaving the room, and Brown kicking off his shoes and getting in bed, pulling the cover up, and turning off the light. Sun switched to a live feed and Daniels was still in bed.

A big smile came across Sang's face. Addressing the four guards he said, "You three take your rifles and position yourselves around the entrance to the room door. Be sure you take the safeties off your weapons and be sure they are on full automatic. You," he said, addressing the fourth guard, "take the Taser and kneel down in front of the door. I will use the master key. When I open the door, Sun will be on the phone and he'll have the power turned off on the floor. With the lights off, the hall will be dark. As soon as you get a clear shot, fire the Taser and hold down the trigger for an extra jolt. Do not wait, just shoot. Sun and I will handcuff him. Then we will wait for Astrid Reed to get back here."

Sun thought about this for a second and agreed it could work. "Sounds like a good plan; let's try to take him alive. We can get much information from him."

"Any questions?" asked Sang. No one had any. "Let's check the camera once more."

Sun hit a few keys and the screen came to life again. Mac Brown was still in bed.

"Let's go," said Sang.

Carrying their weapons, the four guards followed Sun and Sang across the lobby to the elevator. No one reacted to this sight. They stood in silence as the elevator rose up to the thirty-eighth floor. As instructed, the three guards stationed themselves around the door, their AK-47s on full automatic and safeties off. The fourth took his position, and held his Taser in firing position.

Sang slid the electronic key through the slider and gently turned the knob. He gave the signal and the lights in the hall went off. The door was gently pushed open. The guard aimed and fired his Taser. It hit into the back of Mac Brown.

Sang rushed into the room with the handcuffs and Sun pulled the covers down. The electronic barbs were sticking in the back of the pillow. The men looked at each other.

"Where did he go? How did he get out?" asked Sun.

"Quick!" yelled Sang, "To the elevators. Get downstairs before he gets out."

Running down the dark hall, almost knocking each other over, they got to the elevator and pushed the button. Nothing happened.

Sang screamed into his cell phone, "Turn the power on. Turn the power on and hurry."

Almost instantaneously, the hall lights came on, but the elevator didn't respond.

Sun yelled, "The stairs! Quickly, the stairs!"

They ran down the hall toward the stairway. Sitting in the communications room, Mac Daniels was watching the show, which brought a smile to his face. He picked up Sun's Beretta and slipped it into the waistband of his pants.

Daniels had been sitting in the lobby most of the time and when he saw everyone heading toward the elevators, he went down to the communications room. He deleted all the tapes for the past month and then replaced the blanks. Until they looked, no one would know they were erased. He then turned on the elevator power, and closed the elevator and stairwell cameras. Casually, he strolled through the lobby and took the elevator all the way up to the top floor. He then took the stairway to the roof exit and let himself out onto the roof. He turned on his cell phone and made his first call.

Before the call went through, Daniels was on the screen at Langley and immediately tagged. Both Charko and Cornaci leaned forward toward the screen. Five hundred feet above the city, sitting on top of the revolving restaurant sat Mac Daniels.

"What's he doing?" asked Cornaci.

"It looks like he is eating," said Charko.

Charko's phone rang and he answered immediately. "I see you on the roof, Mac. What are you doing?"

"Eating a sandwich and enjoying the view."

CHAPTER 52

RYONGSONG RESIDENCE AND CENTRAL HEADQUARTERS

Kim Jong-un led Astrid Reed through the Ryongsong Gardens, followed closely by the Korean camera crew. The camera crew picked up every word of their conversation. It was as if two business associates were making a deal. There was no anti-American rhetoric. Kim discussed his desire to make North Korea a tourist destination. He cited all the hotels and the beauty of this country. He volunteered to provide her with footage so she could show the world how beautiful North Korea was. They even discussed an investment by her company in a radio and television station. He promised free, uncensored access to all the government officials and freedom to broadcast all the news provided, "that doesn't violate North Korean security or in any way insult the memory of my father, grandfather, or the dignity of the people of North Korea."

Reed was noncommittal with Kim. From what she'd seen, North Korea was certainly not high on her list of places to take a vacation, and it was certainly not a honeymoon haven. She knew that there was no way she would open up a television or news station, as it was against U.S.law to do business with North Korea. She did think, however, that Admiral Charko might have use for a station, and with his help, but that could wait until she was back home.

At the same time, back at Langley, Charko said to Cornaci, "Not a bad idea."

Kim, much to Astrid's surprise, had a good grasp of the business world and had this been under other circumstances, a station would have made a very interesting venture. She was following Mac's recommendations and other than the questions Kim's staff had given her to ask in the interview, she just listened.

In his office, located deep in the basement of the central headquarters building, General Cheon had the money wired to Daniels' account. The afternoon conversation had played over in his mind. Nothing about the meeting raised any suspicion. He believed what he'd been told and their ally and friend General Kem had verified it.

Cheon thought that dealing directly with MacArthur on future weapon deals would save money. He realized General Kem made money on the helicopter transaction. He was anxious to see what MacArthur would be reporting. He thought it was a wise investment to keep this man on the government payroll. Exposing the traitor was well worth the payment. The phone ringing interrupted his reverie. His orderly told him that Sang was on the phone and needed to speak with him immediately.

"Yes, Sang," said Cheon in an irritated voice.

"General, I have important information on Mac Brown, which is not his real name. His name is..."

Cheon said, "Douglas MacArthur."

"You know, sir?" Without waiting for an answer, Sang continued, "He is an agent..."

"For the CIA," said Cheon.

Sang was confused. Pressing on, he said, "He must be arrested immediately and detained and you must arrest Astrid Reed and detain her too. They're both spies. And..."

"Stop talking, you idiot," interrupted Cheon. "Do you know what you're saying? MacArthur left here and he should be back at the hotel. He is traveling under my protected supervision. Do you understand that? He is under my protection as ordered by the Supreme Leader. The Supreme Leader, General Kem, MacArthur, and I had a conference this afternoon. We know what happened to the uranium and who the traitor is who switched it. As far as Miss Reed goes, telling me she's a spy will probably get you shot by the Supreme Leader himself."

These revelations forced Sang to stop and think. It just didn't make any sense, but he knew one thing for sure; Mac Brown or MacArthur was the same man as the Cuban, Ricardo and in time, he would prove it. He would verify the fact that Reed knew him before they arrived in North Korea and that they were working together. "General, I don't know what's going on but I do know that MacArthur and Mac Brown are one and the same person who came here as Miguel Ricardo and I can prove it. I know that

MacArthur and Reed were on the Island of Palau. Together they intercepted an Arab who was delivering the sarin to the ship, the Sails of Allah. Reed flies here to interview the Supreme Leader and MacArthur shows up on the ship. Let me detain them and I will give you the proof you need. We don't have to arrest them, but we can delay their exit out of the country for a few days while I get the proof necessary. Please, I'm right and I can prove it."

Cheon thought about it and asked, "How can you prove that MacArthur and Ricardo are one and the same?"

Sang felt relief. *There's hope,* he thought. "I was reviewing the hotel tapes and both men were shot in the exact same spot. The right shoulder area. The wound was covered with some type of make-up. The showering must have caused the makeup to fade, but if you look at the tapes carefully and blow them up, you will see there is a bullet wound in the upper right rear shoulder of both men."

Cheon thought for a moment. They were both of the same height and build and he remembered that MacArthur had a bullet wound on his front upper right torso. This was not a lot to go on but it did give him concern. "Don't arrest them. I will issue an exit permit for tomorrow. We can keep them both here overnight. Time for you to get your proof." Cheon paused then, and in a sarcastic tone said, "Perhaps you can politely ask

MacArthur to take his shirt off for a closer examination." He laughed. "As to Astrid Reed, you better have real evidence, otherwise do not even think of doing anything to her. Listen carefully, Sang, get your proof first then we will deal with MacArthur. If you want to stay alive, just watch him, understand. Just watch him."

Reluctantly Sang said, "We cannot watch him, sir. He is missing."

Cheon yelled into the phone. "What do you mean he's missing? He should be at the hotel. He can't leave without an escort."

"We went up to his room and he's gone. There is no trace of him anywhere in the hotel."

Sang did not mention that he had gone up to the room to Taser and arrest MacArthur.

"Find him, you idiot. I will let you know when Reed is on the way back to the hotel. Let her go about her business as usual. She should be easy to watch."

Sang turned to Sun who'd only heard one side of the call, but had surmised what happened from watching Sang.

"What are the orders?" Sun asked.

"Watch Reed, find MacArthur. He said we could detain but not arrest. But I have a feeling once we try to detain Reed, we will end up arresting her."

Sun frowned, and then asked, "Why did you say that?"

"Because I intend to get her to react in such a way that I will have no choice but to arrest her and then I can do to her what I want."

Sun knew what that meant. He knew Astrid Reed was not in for a pleasant evening. Once under arrest there were no rules.

CHAPTER 53

KORYO HOTEL

"You're eating a sandwich and enjoying the view?" was the incredulous reply of Charko. "Jesus Christ, Mac get serious."

"I am, Admiral. I am eating a sandwich. Look," he said, holding up his sandwich so everyone could see.

"Okay, you're eating a sandwich and enjoying the view. What's your plan? How can we help?"

"I'm traveling under the protection of General Cheon and have his car and driver at my disposal. I shouldn't have any problem getting to the airport, although I have Sang looking for me. He seems to be disobeying orders, but I can deal with him."

Cornaci and Chaco looked at each other, both shaking their heads but smiling.

"Yes, Mac, it can be a problem when agents disobey orders."

Daniels didn't respond to that comment. He knew he'd put his foot in his mouth when he'd reported Sang's activities. "I'm going to stay here until Astrid's ready to leave for the airport. It's a half-hour drive from the hotel to the airport. I'll meet her there. Can you patch me into Astrid?"

Charko nodded to one of the technicians. Within a few taps, Daniels could hear Kim talking to Astrid. He listened for a while. Finally, he whispered, "Astrid, it's Mac. I'm okay. We are on a three-way. Touch your nose if you can hear me."

"She can hear you, Mac, she touched her nose."

"There is a restaurant called No.1 Boat Restaurant, located at Kim Il Sung Square. It is the only boat restaurant in Pyongyang accessible to tourists. I want you to eat dinner there, around eight o'clock. Do you understand?"

There was no signal or response. When Kim was done talking, he heard Astrid say, "Jong-un," calling the Supreme Leader by his first name, "when we are done I would like to go to one of your seafood restaurants, maybe something on the water."

Kim showed her the big toothy grin that gave him the boyish look. Before Astrid could go on he said, "I will arrange for you to eat with your producer JR at the No.1 Boat Restaurant. You will eat on the deck by the water as my guest. What time would you like to eat there?"

"Eight o'clock if possible. Then after dinner, I would like to leave for home."

"I will have General Cheon authorize your exit papers. I am sorry you have to leave us so soon."

"I want to have your interview on television. I think many people will be impressed with you and your country."

Kim smiled and nodded.

"Astrid, said Daniels, "see you at the airport around nine forty-five. I'm signing off."

Astrid could hear the phone disconnect. She let out a slight sigh.

"What's on your mind Mac?" asked Charko.

"The restaurant is in a different part of the city, and it's about a half-hour ride to the airport. If she's out of there in an hour, she should be at the airport around nine-thirty. I want to get Astrid away from the hotel and Sang. As long as she's with Captain Young-ho, she'll be safe. Sang has the love bug for her and I don't need him around her when we're at the airport. I'm sure he has other plans for me. I want to avoid him if possible."

"Why do you think Sang is after you?"

"I have an idea, but for now, suffice it to say, he broke into my room and fired a Taser at what he thought was me. If he sees me, I'm sure he'll try to take me prisoner and I have no intention of sitting in one of his cells."

"What's your plan?"

"Kill him if I have to. I managed to pick up a weapon."

"Let's hope you can avoid him."

"From Seoul to Pyongyang is about 123 nautical miles. Should take about fifteen minutes flying time. I am sure Astrid's crew is on standby. About thirty minutes after Astrid gets to the restaurant, get them airborne. Fifteen minutes after we leave for the airport, direct them to land, and time it for twenty-one forty-five. We should be getting there the same time and we can be out of here in a few minutes after they touch down."

Everyone was silent. Finally, Charko said, "I'll contact Reed's plane and Haig's. He's on the ground in Seoul too. He'll be ready just in case."

Dr. Cornaci spoke, "I'll call General Bellardi. Give him a heads-up on this and he may be able to have the navy on standby for you."

"Thanks, Doctor. I hope we don't need the navy."

"Me too," replied Cornaci, "me too."

"I'm going dark and will call in at twenty-one hundred hours."

"Good luck, Mac," said Cornaci.

Daniels' phone went dead, but he was still on the screen, sitting there eating his sandwich.

CHAPTER 54

PYONGYANG, NORTH KOREA

The Supreme Leader walked Astrid to her car, carrying on a conversation as if they were two old friends. He gave her several gifts and expressed his disappointment that she was not staying longer in his beloved country.

"I will return," she said, "and I promise I will stay longer. I hope to hear from you regarding the documentary that I'll be broadcasting."

Smiling broadly, he said, "I will be in touch with you as I have your phone number. I just hope your NSA does not eavesdrop."

"I'm sure whatever you have to say to me would not be of interest to them. Sorry I did not get a chance to meet your lovely wife. Perhaps on my next trip."

He let that statement go unanswered. "Have a safe trip. I am looking forward to watching the documentary. I know you will present our position fairly to the world."

"I will. Goodbye." Astrid got into the back of the car and the Supreme Leader shut the door. He stared through the window a little longer than was necessary looking at Astrid's legs. She knew what he was doing and she left her dress hiked up a little longer than she normally would, before she pulled it down.

Sitting in the car with a bag full of videotape was JR, anxious to leave the country and go home. He was a member of a security detail and not trained in any type of covert field activities. He'd said little during the meeting, except to hand the questions to Astrid that were necessary for the interview. "Are you ready to leave, Astrid?" he asked.

"I think so."

Captain Yong-ho was in the front passenger seat next to the driver. Astrid asked him if they could now leave for the Koryo Hotel. Yong-ho ordered the driver to go. Astrid glanced at her watch and did the mathematical calculations. She should be at the hotel at seven-fifteen and it would take her a little less than fifteen minutes to change, get her bags, and be back at the car, so she could leave for the restaurant by seven-thirty. She would be at the restaurant by eight and with luck leave there at nine for the airport. Everything was on schedule.

As usual, there was little traffic in the city. The car pulled up to the hotel right on schedule. Yong-ho got out of the car and the driver ran around to open the door for Astrid. Astrid wondered if he was being polite or just trying to take a peek up her dress. At this point, she really didn't care. She wanted to change, get to the restaurant and get out of there.

"Going to change, get my bags, and be down in fifteen minutes. JR how much time do you need?" she asked.

"Five minutes, that's it."

"Okay, let's all meet in the lobby. Captain, it's not necessary for you to follow me up to my room, but if you insist, by all means you are free to do so."

Yong-ho shook his head as he replied, "I will wait for you in the car. Please come directly down to the car. There is no need to stop at the front desk. You are a guest of the Supreme Leader. I will get you to the restaurant for your eight o'clock dinner reservation, then to the airport."

"Thank you, I appreciate that."

JR and Astrid took the elevator to the thirty-eighth floor. They made the trip in silence. JR went to his room and threw everything in his bag, not taking the time to fold the clothes. He stuffed in the videotapes, zipped up the bag, and knocked on Astrid's door.

"I'll meet you by the car," he heard her say.

He took the elevator down to the lobby and walked out toward the waiting car.

Once in her room, Astrid pulled the bedspread off and draped it over her shoulders and around herself. She let her dress drop to the floor and pulled on a pair of jeans and a light-blue shirt. She threw off the bedspread, looked at the camera and mouthed, "Fuck you." She put on white socks and running shoes and tied a kerchief around her neck. Later she would use it to cover her hair. She packed her bags and left her room.

Astrid quickly passed through the lobby, not stopping at the desk as she had been instructed. She quickly went to the waiting car, where the driver was standing by the door. The driver took her bags and put them in the trunk, then opened the door for her and ran around to the running car. JR was not there. *Shit*, she thought. She looked out the window toward the entrance hoping to see him. The driver hit the gas hard, and the car lurched forward, knocking Astrid back.

"Wait," she yelled. "JR is not here."

"Good evening, Miss Reed," said Sang.

"Where's JR?" she demanded.

"He is with Captain Yong-ho on his way to the restaurant, but first you and I have to have a little talk."

"Fuck you. Let me out."

Astrid reached for the door handle, but it was locked and would not open. Sang turned, trying to grab her. Because she was sitting directly behind him, he could not get at her easily. Astrid took advantage of her position and hit him with her right elbow on the side of his head. She moved toward the driver's side, got her left arm under the driver's neck and pulled back hard. The driver let go of the steering wheel, grabbed at her arm, and hit the brakes hard, causing Astrid to fall forward, loosening her grip. He managed to pull her arm away and as he did, he moved toward the door. Astrid, using her right hand, pushed his head into the window, momentarily dazing him. Sang too fell forward and as he came back into the seat, he turned his head toward Astrid and was met with a hard right hand to his nose. She heard the cartilage snap. Blood ran down Sang's face. He let out a yell and bent forward.

Astrid tried to hit the unlock button. The driver hit the gas pedal and cut the wheel hard to the left, forcing Astrid back into the right rear side of the seat. He stopped the car, and threw it into park, and as Astrid came toward the driver she was met with a left handed punch, hitting her in the eye. The punch knocked her back against the door.

Sang, with the blood still running down his face, got out of the car and opened the rear door. Astrid fell out of the car. As she tried to get up, Sang hit her on the jaw, knocking her back down. He turned her over, brought her arms behind her, and then handcuffed them together. The driver and Sang lifted her up, and then Sang punched her hard in the stomach. Astrid doubled over and threw up. Her knees gave way and she started to fall. The driver grabbed her again and Sang punched her again and pushed her into the car, slamming the door.

Charko, Cornaci, and the technicians just stared at the screen saying nothing. Cornaci had never seen such brutality on a defenseless person. Someone finally said, "Oh, my God."

The driver asked Sang if he wanted to go to the hospital.

"No," barked Sang. "To the warehouse. She is going to pay for this."

Charko ordered, "Keep that car under surveillance. Tag it. I want to know where it is at all times. Mac will be calling in and he'll need to know."

"What will happen to her?" asked Cornaci.

"Nothing, if Mac can get there on time. But if he doesn't you don't want to know."

Cornaci whispered a prayer.

"No matter what happens, Jon," said Charko, "Sang will pay for this and so will anyone who is with him. Trust me, Mac will not let this go. There will be blood."

CHAPTER 55

KORYO HOTEL

At exactly eight o'clock, Daniels powered up his cell phone and hit the speed dial. The phone did not seem to ring before he heard Charko's voice.

"Charko here, Mac."

"Is Astrid at the restaurant? I'm ready to roll."

There was a long silence. Mac's sensed trouble. Something was wrong. "What is it, Admiral?"

"Astrid is not at the restaurant. Apparently when she got in the car, Sang had taken it over and now he has her."

"Why would he do that? Is she okay?"

"No, she's not. We heard and saw the whole thing. She started to fight with Sang and apparently broke his nose. She fought hard but couldn't deal with Sang and his driver. The driver knocked her out of the car and handcuffed her. Sang beat her up and threw her back in the car. We tagged the car and are following it now."

Mac was silent.

Cornaci watching the screen asked, "What is he doing?"

Chaco looked for a long second. "He's attaching the sound suppressor."

"I'll take the car, you just walk me through where she is. I'll get her out."

"Be careful—there are at least three guards in the hall."

"Fuck them. If they're there, they're dead. Don't worry about me. I'll be down at the car in a few minutes. Just keep your eye on Astrid. The plans may have changed, but I'll get her and will be at the airport."

Daniels put on his baseball cap, pulling the brim down. He shouldered his duffel bag and draped his windbreaker over his right hand, which held the Beretta. He opened the roof top door and started to descend the stairs. On the thirty-ninth floor landing, he smelled cigarette smoke. He leaned over the railing and saw one of the guards smoking, with his Kalashnikov, slung over his shoulder. *Stupid,* he thought, *but good for me.*

Daniels went down to the next landing and at the foot of the stairs he said, "Hey, asshole."

The startled guard turned around and Daniels squeezed off two shots. Both bullets entered the guard's forehead directly between his eyes and exited the back of his head with brain matter and blood splattering all over.

Daniels stepped over the dead guard and walked down several more flights to the thirty-fifth floor. He opened the stairway door and peeked out. The hall was clear. Walking down the hallway toward the elevator, he tucked the Beretta into his waistband of his slacks and put on his windbreaker.

The elevator opened at the lobby and Daniels mixed in with the crowd and walked through the lobby. Once outside, he went over to Cheon's car. The driver jumped out to open the rear door for him. Daniels ignored the open door and opened the front passenger door. The driver grabbed Daniels and pulled him back. Daniels grabbed him by his tie, pulling down hard. He banged the driver's head into the car several times, and then shoved the driver into the car.

He had taken his anger out on the driver. Watching him from Langley, everyone reacted to the force and violence of Daniels' attack. The thud of the driver's head came over the speaker from Daniels' cell phone.

Someone said, "He's really mad."

Someone else said, "Wait until he gets Sang. You don't want to watch."

Daniels got behind the wheel. "Where to Admiral?"

"Two blocks down, go left."

Daniels drove quickly, weaving in and out of traffic. As he came to the intersection, he started his turn. The driver reached up and pulled at the steering wheel, forcing the car to the right onto the sidewalk. Daniels yanked the wheel hard to the left and the car jumped off the sidewalk back onto the street. The driver tried to reach for the wheel again. Daniels pulled the Beretta and shot him.

He heard Charko's voice. "You ok, Mac?"

"Just a speed bump. Where to now?"

"Stay straight."

Daniels pushed down on the gas pedal. "How far ahead are they?"

"About fifteen, twenty minutes. They just pulled into a waterfront warehouse and dragged Astrid in."

There was no response from Daniels.

"Mac? You there?"

"I'm here. Just guide me. I'm going to break every fucking bone in Sang's body and then . . ."

CHAPTER 56

WATERFRONT WAREHOUSE

Sang's car pulled up to the waterfront warehouse. The driver ran around to the back of the car and pulled Astrid out of the back seat. Standing post in front of the main entrance, two guards were taking in the scene but did not move. As Sang approached the guards, he showed them his identification. "Don't let anyone in here. If you see a Westerner, just shoot him. Do not ask any questions. Just shoot. If he gets close to you, you are dead. Do you understand?"

The guards were not about to question Sang Ji-hu, a deputy minister in the Ministry of State Security for Pyongyang.

The driver pushed Astrid through the door into the warehouse. She fell down. He kicked her and ordered her to get up. She slowly made her way back on to her feet.

The warehouse was cavernous, having a north-south length of four hundred yards and east-west width of one hundred and fifty yards. It was four stories high. Along the roof of the building ran a rail system where the overhead cranes could be directed to different parts of the warehouse. The western side of the warehouse had large overhead doors that would allow trucks to back into the loading zone, to pick up and drop off cargo. The eastern side of the warehouse also had large overhead doors that opened onto the covered dock, which ran the length of the building along the Pot'ong River. Over the dock were also overhead cranes. The office and the control center were on the top floor of the east side of the building. From the control center, all the doors were operated, along with the overhead cranes. There was a monitoring system and closed-circuit cameras provided surveillance around the building and the interior of the warehouse.

Along the northern part of the warehouse were the fuel bladders lined up in neat rows and columns. The bladders were lined up from east to west and from the north wall, halfway down the warehouse. The southern side of the warehouse was filled with various weapons and munitions. There were several Pokpung-ho or "Storm Tiger" battle tanks, several S-25 Berkut "Golden Eagle" surface-to-air guided missiles, cases of AK-47s, cases of the Zastava M76 sniper rifles, cases of RPK type 64 light machine guns, and boxes of various caliber ammunitions.

Astrid was not cooperating, forcing the driver to drag and push her through the building. She was sizing up the situation and remembering what Mac had said, always observe. She was trying to figure out how to get out of here. Astrid intended to fight them to the death, even if it was her own. She hoped that Mac would show up, as he always did. But for now, she had to buy herself some time, or she knew this would not be a very pleasant experience.

Finally, reaching the rear of the warehouse, the driver pushed her back against one of the fuel bladders. Astrid had no idea what was in them; just some type of liquid. She guessed gasoline or diesel fuel. She saw the weapons and that, she thought, was her only hope. Astrid sank down low, bringing her knees up to her chest.

The bleeding from his nose had stopped but Sang's clothes were covered in blood. Looking down at himself, he reached up to touch his face. When he touched his nose, he grimaced. Looking at Astrid, he gave her a backhanded slap across her face. The right side of her nose began to bleed. "You fucking bitch. See what you did to me." He slapped her again, and this time the left side of her nose began to bleed.

"I'm going upstairs to call for reinforcements. I want a dozen men outside," said Sang. As he opened the door to the stairway leading to the office, he turned to the driver and as an afterthought said, "Fuck her if you want but save some for me. When the soldiers get here give each one a turn." With sarcasm dripping from his voice, he added, "Have a nice day, Miss Reed."

The driver watched as Sang disappeared behind the close door. Astrid, with her knees up against her chest, could bring her arms down around her feet. She nestled her arms between her stomach and her legs and bent over. The driver might not notice, she thought, being preoccupied with fucking her.

The driver turned to her with a big smile on his face. He took off his jacket and tie. He spoke to Astrid in Korean, while grabbing his crotch. She had a good idea what he was saying. He stood over her, straddling her legs, and bent down to pick her up. As she rose, she brought her hands up and over his neck pulling his face down hard into her

forehead. She heard the cartilage in his nose break. With all her strength, she brought her right knee into his crotch. She did it again and again. She let go of him and as he fell, she punched his broken nose up, hoping to force the cartilage into his brain. For good measure, she stepped back and when he was on his way down, she kicked him in the chin, snapping his head back, and crashing him backwards onto the cement floor. When he hit the floor, blood began to flow. She didn't know if she'd killed him or not, nor did she care. She rummaged through his jacket and found the key to the handcuffs.

Freeing herself, she made her way over to the weapons. All she needed was one bullet for Sang.

From the office surveillance cameras, Sang saw Astrid running towards the weapons. He shook his head in disbelief. He thought she must be an American agent. It made sense that she and MacArthur were a team, but what was their plan?

Sang came down the stairs and took from his holster his Crvena Zastava. He drew back the slide, chambering a round, and this time he pushed the manual safety lever, located on the left side of the frame above the grip panel, forward to fire position. He wasn't going to take a chance with her slapping the pistol out of his hands as her partner had. He would kill her if he had to.

As he rounded the corner, he saw the driver lying in a pool of blood. His disfigured face was covered with blood. He reached down and felt for a pulse— there was none.

He screamed, "You killed my driver, you fucking bitch! You can't get out of here, Astrid. I'm going to get you and then I am going to beat the shit out of you until you will never want to look at yourself in the mirror again." He moved around the fuel bladders toward the weapons. "When I am done fucking you and after the troops have their piece of you, you will spend the rest of your life in a labor camp servicing the guards. The only meat you will ever eat will be their dicks."

Sang laughed at this. "Pretty funny Astrid, no? Eating their meat."

Astrid wanted to yell back and tell him to go fuck himself, but she knew better. Stealth was her ally. She made her way around the weapons, looking for one she could use. She realized the rifles and handguns were in the crates and she needed something to use to open them. She saw an ax on the wall and ran for it. As she got there, she heard,

"Don't touch it or you are dead."

Turning around about ten feet away was Sang with a two-handed grip on his pistol aimed at her head. She raised her hands.

"Kneel down and put your hands under your knees and your head on the ground," ordered Sang.

Astrid obeyed. From this position, she was helpless. She could not move fast enough to grab him or his weapon.

Sang holstered his weapon and took out a blackjack, slapping it on one of the crates. The noise made Astrid shutter. Sang kicked her in the ribs, knocking her over onto her back. He squatted on his knees pressing on her shoulders. She was trapped. He dangled the blackjack in front of her face. "First I'm going to break your nose, like you did to me. Then your jaw, then the rest of your face," he screamed at her.

He cocked his arm back, and Astrid closed her eyes. At the top of his lungs, he started to say, "And . . ."

Then nothing. The pressure was off her shoulders. She opened her eyes. Daniels had Sang's right hand in his. The blackjack was frozen in midair. There was a Beretta in Sang's mouth.

"Stand up, Sang," said Daniels.

Sang rose slowly and Daniels forced him away from Astrid. Sang's eyes were wide open with fear.

Daniels could read his mind. "It was simple. Just drove up to the front door, leaned out, and shot them," he said, referring to the two guards.

When Sang was far enough away from Astrid, Daniels took the Beretta out of his mouth and backed away from Sang, moving toward Astrid. "How are you doing, babe? You look like shit."

"You should see the other guy," she said.

"I did. Looks like you won that round."

"Mac, everything hurts. My stomach, my ribs, even my face," she replied as tears of relief trickled down her face.

"Well, at least your virginity is still intact."

Astrid started to laugh, "Oh, it hurts to laugh."

"Here," he said, handing her the pistol, "hold this. But don't shoot the little prick." He paused, "Just not yet, anyway." Daniels turned to Sang. "You have the blackjack, use it. If you beat me, you may get out of here alive. That's up to Astrid."

Sang smiled. He threw the blackjack at Daniels, who ducked. Sang went for his weapon. As he drew it from his holster, Daniels had Sang's arm bent over his own and he broke it. Sang dropped the pistol. Daniels bent down to pick it up and Sang tried to kick him. Daniels deflected the kick and slammed his foot into Sang's knee, breaking the kneecap. Sang fell to the ground. Daniels picked him up and broke his left arm. Then he let him drop to the floor. Sang was screaming in pain. Daniels dropped the clip from the Crvena Zastava, putting it into his pocket, and then he shoved the pistol into Sang's mouth to quiet the screaming. "Shut the fuck up. You're giving me a headache. Come on, Astrid. It's time to go."

She stared at Sang. "What about him?"

"He's not going anywhere. He'll end up in a labor camp."

"No," she said.

Daniels looked at her.

Astrid stood over Sang and pointed the Beretta at his head. She just stared. Finally, she said, "I can't do it, but I can do this." She fired a round into his groin. His crotch turned red.

As she turned to leave, she said, "Have a nice day, Mr. Sang."

Daniels looked at her but said nothing.

As they walked toward the front of the building, Astrid asked, "Do I really look like shit?"

"Give me my weapon back first, Astrid, before I answer that."

She handed Mac the Beretta and he tucked it into his waistband. He gently kissed her. Before he could say anything, she started to sob and then cry uncontrollably. He stood there with his arms around her whispering, "I love you. It's all over, babe. I love you, always."

It took a few minutes for Astrid to regain control of herself. Then hand in hand, they walked toward the front entrance where Daniels had left his car.

"We'll be at the airport in thirty minutes, and then we are out of here. Back to Palau, just the two of us. No cell phones, I promise."

As they got to the front of the building, there were two cars pulling up and a dozen soldiers were piling out.

They both said, "Oh fuck."

CHAPTER 57

WATERFRONT WAREHOUSE

Astrid and Daniels started to run toward the back of the warehouse. Daniels noticed the office on the top floor and had an idea. "Quick, up the stairs," he said.

In the office, over the surveillance camera, he saw that the troops were inspecting his car and the dead driver along with the two dead guards. One of them was on a hand-held radio.

"They'll be in here in a few minutes," said Daniels. "I have an idea."

"Hope it's better than your last one," she said.

"What?"

"Plan B. I'm supposed to get you out of here."

"Okay, now it's plan C."

"C?"

"Yeah, C, for let's get the fuck out of here."

Sitting at the control console, Daniels locked the front and rear overhead doors. He started the overhead crane and played with the joystick. "Astrid, open the rear window."

Astrid did this without question.

"Here's plan C," said Daniels. "When I tell you, you are going to jump out the rear window onto the tent covering the dock. Don't try to stand up, but roll down and fall into the water. Try to go feet first. You're about forty feet up and you don't want to land on your back or stomach. Take the boat and paddle it up stream. Get away from here, then start the engine and move up river. The river runs alongside the airport. When you get to the airport, go to the upwind end of the runway and wait for your plane."

"What about you, Mac?"

"I'll see you there, Astrid, I promise."

"No way, Mac. I'm plan B and we go together or not at all. Fuck'em all. There are only twelve of them and that's six apiece."

He looked at her.

"Mac, don't piss me off. I'm in no mood for your shit."

Daniels' phone vibrated in his pocket. He took it out. It was Charko. "Admiral."

"We've been trying to talk with you or Astrid."

Daniels looked at her and saw that one of her earrings was missing. He guessed it was her receiver.

"Mac we could hear everything, but couldn't reach her or you."

"She must have lost the receiver in the fight."

"Fight? Is she okay? What about you?"

"We're both fine. Her make-up is a little messed, but other than a black eye she's fine."

"Can you get out of there?" asked Charko.

"Not until I eliminate the threat. Can you lend assistance?"

"All we can do is warn you where they'll be coming from."

"That helps. I have an idea. Worst case, Astrid will be going up the river. I'll give her my cell phone and you guide her to the airport. Best case, we'll drive there. Stay tuned. Admiral . . ."

"Yes?"

"Share the popcorn."

Charko let out a sigh and said, "No popcorn until you're here to share it with me and that's after you've seen the shrink. Good luck, Mac."

Mac sat Astrid down at the console. "Babe, this knob operates the cranes. The way you push is the way the crane goes. This button lowers the hook and this one this one lifts it. Try it."

She did. "It's easy, Mac."

"I'm going to hook up a few of the oil bladders and you are going to position them over the front door about ten feet out. When they come in you can drop it and eliminate most of them or at least your six. You are going to kill some people. Can you do it?" He paused, waiting for her to answer.

Astrid was quiet. Finally, she said, "Do I have a choice?"

Looking at her green eyes, Daniels said, "Not if you want to live."

She just nodded. She understood.

"Okay babe, you do your stuff, and I will take care of the rest. If for some reason it doesn't work, you're out the window. Understand?"

"Since when do you tell me what to do?" Then she smiled. "Mac we're in this together. If I die, it'll be in your arms. So do me a favor and don't fuck up."

"Watch the screen. I don't think they can get in except through the front door so when you're ready with the bladder, hit the unlock button and let them in."

"Sounds easy enough," Astrid said.

Mac ran downstairs. He could hear the banging on the doors. Astrid followed his progress and positioned the overhead where he directed her. She lowered the crane hook and Mac hooked up the sling and waved his hand in a circular motion. Astrid pressed the up button and the crane lifted two bladders into the air. She then pushed the joystick to the left, and then forward until it was about ten feet in front of the main door. Mac gave her the okay sign. She waved back. Before Mac could signal her to unlock the door, there was automatic gunfire ripping through it.

Mac ducked behind one of the bladders to the left of the main entrance and waited. The door was kicked in, slamming against the wall. At first, no one entered. Then after a long minute, two hunched-over men slowly entered the building, holding their weapons at the ready. One went to the right and the other to the left.

This was not going according to plan, thought Mac. Four more men followed, going straight in, but stopping about six feet into the building. They knelt down on one knee, bringing their weapons up as if they were aiming. They were not under the hanging bladders. Two more came and went about twelve feet into the building, and again one went left and the other right. Astrid watched from the surveillance screen and she was worried. The two who went left were on Mac's flank.

"Admiral, I hope you can hear me," she said as if it were a prayer. "Two bandits at Mac's one and eleven o'clock. Warn him."

Four more came into the building and stopped directly under the hanging bladder. Astrid debated whether to hit the drop button—four were better than none. Her hand slowly went to the release button, and her finger was poised to hit it, then she stopped. She saw the other four move up and stop directly under the bladder. She hit the button. The men looked up at the noise and the last thing they saw was several tons of oil coming down on them. Astrid looked away.

Daniels worked his way around to his three o'clock position, knowing the crash would cause the men on his flank to turn around. He leaned out from his cover and took the shot, hitting the man. But as he went down, the man squeezed the trigger of his Kalashnikov, which must have been on full automatic, as the bullets screamed from the rifle barrel, hitting bladders. Oil started pouring out.

The man on Daniels' eleven o'clock raised his weapon and walked slowly toward the gunfire. He was now behind Daniels.

Astrid said, "Admiral, he's on Mac's seven o'clock."

Mac didn't move. Astrid stood up and banged on the window. The two soldiers who were on the right saw her in the control room and started to fire. Astrid dropped down and pushed the control to the right. The overhead crane moved. The noise of the gunfire masked the motor of the overhead. From her screen, she thought she had the crane in the right spot and she dropped the hook. The hook fell behind the soldier, who turned at the sound and let out a burst of fire. Daniels came around from the bladder and fired, hitting him.

The two who were shooting at her stopped. The firing now had their attention. From her screen, she saw that Mac was all right, but to her horror, one of the soldiers was making his way toward her and the other toward Mac.

Mac ejected the clip from the pistol and checked the rounds left. He had one in the clip and one round in the chamber. There were two targets left. He could not afford to miss. He saw the hook from the overhead crane and stepped on it. Astrid saw this and she pressed the up button. The hook rose into the air with Daniels on it. He had a clear shot at the soldier who was at the stairwell door. The hook was swaying but Daniels had no choice. He fired and missed. The shot hit the wall. The soldier turned and saw Daniels on the hook, swaying.

Shooting ducks in a pond he thought, as he raised his Kalashnikov, and fired. Astrid dropped Daniels onto one of the bladders. The soldier did not know if he'd hit his target or not. Mac was on the bladder and he saw the soldier coming down the aisle—he jumped down and fired one shot, killing the soldier instantly. The slide on the Beretta locked back, signifying that the weapon was out of ammunition. The last of the soldiers came around the corner firing blindly; raking the bladders, the overhead crane, and the ceiling. The bolt locked back as the clip was empty. Oil poured out.

Daniels heard the soldier drop his clip. He stuck his head out and yelled at him in Chinese. "Fuck you, asshole."

Daniels had the special toothbrush in his pocket, and he pulled it apart. He had his plastic ice pick. This was all he had for now. The soldier jammed in another clip and ran toward Daniels, pulling back on the bolt. Before he could let it go, he slipped on the oil and started to slide. Daniels stepped out and jammed the toothbrush into his chest as he slid by. "Don't forget to brush," he said.

Daniels took the clip he had taken from the Crvena Zastava and pushed out the shells. He then dropped the clip from his Beretta and started to fill it. While the Crvena fired a 9mm Kratak (.380 ACP), which is smaller than the Beretta nine millimeter, it would work. As a wartime service pistol round, the 9mm Kratak lacked suitable penetration for combat; it just was not as powerful, but it was better than nothing. He stuck the Beretta into his waistband.

Mac waved to Astrid. She ran downstairs.

As she reached him, she gave him a hug and felt the Beretta. She said, paraphrasing the famous Mae West line, "Is that a gun in your pants or are you glad to see me?" Not waiting for an answer, she continued, "Come on, let's go to plan B."

"One minute, Astrid. There's something I have to do."

Daniels took off his running shoes and separated the sole of the shoes. He took out what looked like clay and rolled it into a ball, placing it on the S-25 Berkut "Golden Eagle" surface-to-air guided missile. He stuck the number 4 pencil into the clay and hit the eraser three short times. The pencil was a detonator and he'd just turned it on.

"What is that?" asked Astrid.

"Octanitrocubane," he answered her. "In about thirty minutes an electric charge will ignite the explosives. Now let's go," he said.

"Isn't that the mini atomic bomb?" she said, with a worried look on her face.

"Yes, and we don't want to be anywhere near this place—between the Octo, the weapons, and the oil, the blast will shake the earth. Nothing within or near this building will be left standing. Let's go."

They started toward the door, stepping over the dead bodies.

When they stepped outside, General Cheon was standing there holding his weapon on them. "Get back in there," he ordered.

Once inside the warehouse, he ordered them to sit on the floor, legs crossed and their hands under their bodies. He looked around. "Impressive, Mr. MacArthur, if that is your real name. My driver, two guards, twelve soldiers, Sang and his driver, let me see; that is seventeen dead. You two are a deadly pair."

"Eighteen," said Daniels. "There was one at the hotel."

"I have a few questions, but I doubt I am going to get any answers from either of you."

"I can explain, General," said Daniels with a big smile. "It was self-defense. Sang kidnapped Miss Reed and I decided to save her. Simple as that. Now if you don't mind, we have a plane to catch."

Cheon laughed. "You got balls. Did you shoot Sang in his balls?"

"No, I did, General," said Astrid. "He tried to rape me, and I couldn't kill him, so I shot him in his balls."

"Well, you did kill him, and I guess you also killed his driver."

"Yes, I did, General. He too tried to rape me. As Mac said, it was self-defense."

"Funny, I do not believe you two. I think Sang was right. I don't know how you got General Kem to go along with this, unless he is a double agent himself. I will see that my suspicions are reported. I also think somehow you framed our nuclear experts and you stole our uranium. You are most talented, whatever your name is. By the way, I sent an order; your plane will not be allowed to land at the airport."

"I appreciate the compliment, General but I must be leaving. I am going to slowly stand up, and then I'm going to help Astrid up, and we're leaving. I'm tired of this bullshit."

Daniels slowly rose up and he then helped Astrid up.

Cheon looked on in disbelief. "Get down now, or you're dead," he ordered.

He raised his weapon. "I mean it," he said.

Ignoring Cheon, Astrid started to move. She wanted to provide cover for Daniels so he could draw his weapon. As she moved, a shot was fired, and then another. Astrid fell to the floor.

CHAPTER 58

HIGHWAY TO THE AIRPORT

Daniels pulled his weapon and fired two shots. Then he bent down to check on Astrid. She was bleeding from her right side, slightly below her shoulder. The blood was not gushing out, just a stream of blood. *Thank God,* he thought. *It didn't hit an artery.* He felt her back—the bullet hadn't gone through. There was not too much he could do. The bullet could be close to her lung or major blood vessels. He had to stuff the wound.

"Astrid, Astrid, open your eyes. Look at me. Astrid."

Astrid slowly opened her eyes. "Oh God, that hurts, Mac."

He tore open her blouse and ripped off a piece of material. "It hurts worst than it is, Astrid. Glad you're wearing a bra, babe. You were hit with a ricochet. Looks like it bounced off the floor."

"Oh, Mac, we've got to get out of here."

"We will." He took the torn material, folded it into a square, and pressed it against the wound. "Hold it, Astrid, and press hard. The bleeding should stop. When we get to Seoul, we'll get you to the hospital. Some antibiotics and a stitch or two and you'll be fine. A little sore but you'll be good as new."

She saw Cheon on the floor and behind him Sun. "What happened?"

"Hang on Astrid." Daniels ran through the military supplies and found a first-aid kit. The only thing in it was two 4x7 camouflage dressings and a roll of gauze. He also found a roll of duct tape and a blanket. On his way back to Astrid, he stopped and looked down at Sun. He said something then left him there, bleeding. He got back to Astrid and took her blouse off. Stuffing the gauze into the wound, he placed the dressings over it and then duct taped it tight as he could. He threw the duct tape toward Sun. Then he made a sling out of her blouse for her right arm, to take the pressure off the shoulder. He draped the blanket around her and picked her up in his arms.

"Put me down, before you hurt yourself," she said.

He couldn't help but smile. He ignored her and carried her toward the door.

"Mac, what happened?"

"In the car, I'll tell you. We have to get out of here or we'll be blown to the airport." Daniels led her to General Cheon's car and started north along the river road toward the airport. He was driving fast. He thought he had ten minutes left. If that! He wanted to be as far away from the warehouse as possible.

"Mac, this really hurts and I want to know what happened back there. Who shot me and what happened to Sun and Cheon?"

"As you started to move . . . which was a nice play giving me cover, which was not necessary, but I appreciate it . . ."

"Mac!"

"Anyway, Cheon was about to shoot either you or me, but Sun, who must have come in with Cheon, shot him. Cheon fired into the ground and the bullet ended up in you. Luckily it was a ricochet and not straight on. Cheon wasn't dead. He tried to take another shot, so I put a bullet in his head. He dropped and Sun was standing there, so I shot him too."

"Did you kill him too?"

"No. I didn't," said Daniels, as a matter of fact, "but if he doesn't get out of the warehouse he'll die."

Astrid was silent. Her head was bobbing.

"Astrid, Astrid. Talk to me. Don't close your eyes. No sleeping." He reached over and pulled the blanket tight around her. "Astrid, put your head in my lap."

"Mac!"

"Come on, put your head down, and put your feet up on the door. You'll feel better."

Normally he would keep the wound elevated but he wanted to prevent her from going into shock. She did what he said. He took out his cell phone and hit the speed dial.

"Charko here."

"Admiral, can you patch me in to Ron?"

"Hold."

A few seconds later, "Haig here."

"Ron, who's your pilot?"

"The Bak man," Haig replied, referring to Bak Johansen. "Why?"

"Give him the phone," said Daniels without answering Haig's question.

Bak Johansen was one of the top pilots on the agency's payroll and did things with the Citation that were not approved by the FAA. Tonight was going to be one of them.

A minute later, Bak Johansen came on the cell. "Mac, what do you need?"

"Bak, you got a visual on Astrid's Gulfstream?" asked Daniels.

"Affirmative. I have a visual on it. It's about a thousand feet below and a half mile ahead. What's up?"

"I need you to piggy back into Pyongyang Airport. Is the aircraft equipped with ECM and do you have NVGs on board?"

"Are you kidding? This baby comes loaded with many extras, electronic counter-measure defense, radio jammer, decoy flares, and chaff and I have NVGs for me and Lisa," he said referring to night vision goggles and his co-pilot Lisa Geluso.

"Why the piggy back, Mac?" asked Bak.

"The airport is closed to Astrid's plane. When they ask the tower for clearance, the tower will wave them off. I need you to touch down and pick-up Astrid and JR and get out of there. This is a one-pass only and she has to be on the plane. She's been shot."

"What about you?"

"Let's just say I'm flying stand-by. If I can get on I will, if not you're out of there. Understand?"

"Affirmative."

"Ron, can you hear me?"

"Yes. You've been on the speaker."

"You need to get Astrid to the hospital. She took a bullet. I stuffed the wound and duct taped her. She has bruised ribs, a black eye swollen shut, maybe a broken nose, and bruises all over. I'm trying to keep her from going into shock. Get Virgil on the line."

A minute later, Virgil Pollard, Astrid's pilot, was on the cell. "Virgil, listen up. Time is short. The Citation is going to piggyback with you. Lisa Geluso will be on the horn with you and walk you through this."

"Whatever you want, Mac. Where is Miss Reed?" asked Virgil.

"With luck she'll be on the Citation. Bak will talk to Tower Control. You just talk with Lisa. Bak will touch down and you will wave off."

"Sounds easy, Mac, what's the big deal?" asked Virgil.

"Bak will about two feet underneath you and a few feet behind your wings."

"What the fuck?" shouted Virgil. "Mac, I'm flying a Gulfstream not a fighter jet."

"It's a piece of cake, Virgil. All you have to do is follow Bak's lead and pretend the runway is twenty feet higher than it is. You'll fly with your lights on and Bak will fly dark. When Lisa tells you to pull up, do so. Kill your landing lights and get the fuck out of there. Understand?"

As Virgil spoke, his voice cracked. "I never did this before."

"Bak has and he and Lisa will walk you through. You can do it."

"You can do it, Virgil," said Lisa reassuringly.

"Bak, when you touch down, hit the ECM and jam the radio. I'll kill the runway lights on a three count . . . and Lisa."

Lisa's voice came over the cell, "Yes, Mac."

"On the three count, have Virgil pull up."

"Will do," she replied.

"Bak, you've got to bullshit the tower. Drop the Supreme Leader's name, keep them talking so they don't call out their air force. If you do this right, you and Virgil will be one blip on the radar screen."

"Mac, I can do this. Will you be on board?"

Daniels didn't answer. "Bak, at the end of the runway, turn right to the taxiway. Keep your port side to the outer perimeter. Drop your door while you're doing a slow roll. Don't stop. JR will be able to get Astrid into the plane. Ron, anyone else on board?"

"Oscar Ocho."

"Good! Between him and JR there should be no problem."

"Bak," said Daniels, "I'll clear the runway for you. Taxi back, roll on at max taxi speed, and go. Please just get out of here as fast as you can. The shit may hit the fan. I can buy you at worst case, ten minutes—at best, twenty."

Bak knew Daniels and for the first time, there was urgency in his voice. He knew it was not for his own safety but for Astrid's.

Lisa was one-step ahead and calculated a short field takeoff. "Mac, with a rolling start I can be off the ground quickly and with the Citation can climb 3,650 feet per minute. I can achieve max cruise altitude in as little as fourteen minutes once airborne, and with any luck I'll be at seven hundred miles per hour. I'll be in South Korean air space before they know I was here."

"Admiral, I need you to coordinate their arrival and mine. Can you see me?"

"I have you on the screen. Keep driving and I'll coordinate the aircraft. Mac," said Charko, "I heard you're flying stand-by. I wish you would buy your ticket and reconsider."

Jon Cornaci's voice came on. "Mac, this is the director. I am ordering you to get on that plane."

"Too much static. I can't hear you. Sorry, sir. Admiral." There was a pause, and then Daniels continued. "The Sails of Allah set sail before I could stop it. You have to track and if necessary sink it. It's got to be loaded with tons of military hardware." Daniels paused.

"Mac," shouted Charko.

"Sorry, sir, I have to do some groundwork, Admiral. Astrid has to get out of here and to a hospital. I have to cover her. She took the bullet for me. It's not supposed to be that way, Admiral."

"Yes," said Charko, "yes, I understand." He knew this could be a one-way trip for Mac.

"Admiral, do me a favor."

"What is it Mac?"

"Save some popcorn for me."

CHAPTER 59

WATERFRONT WAREHOUSE

The thin wire in the pencil detonator was holding back the spring-loaded striker from hitting the percussion cap. When Daniels hit the eraser on the pencil, he broke the vial releasing the acid. The acid was soon doing its job, eating away at the wire. Finally, the tension on the spring was too great for the thin wire, and snapped it. The spring drove the striker into the percussion cap, which exploded, triggering the octanitrocubane.

In less than a millisecond, the octanitrocubane detonation velocity was at 23,000 miles per hour, causing the initial blast wave to tear apart the building. The explosion created a fireball rising hundreds of feet into the air and burning everything it touched. The heat from the explosion—6,000 degrees Celsius—was so powerful that it could be felt for miles away, in a "heat blast." The high temperatures melted the steel in the building, the tanks, the missiles, and the weapons, and it incinerated all the bodies in and around the building. The Pot'ong River by the warehouse was turned to steam. Nothing was left. From the cockpit of the Citation Bak saw the fireball. "Holy shit."

"Did you see that?" said Virgil from the Gulfstream.

"That must have been some explosion," said Bak. "Christ, that fireball must have been several hundred feet high."

"At least," said Virgil.

On the ground, Daniels thought that the evidence was destroyed, and if all went right, he would be considered dead, too. "Rest in peace, Douglas MacArthur."

CHAPTER 60

PYONGYANG AIRPORT

The Pyongyang Airport is divided by the Pot'ong River. On the west side of the river is the terminal and the tie-down areas for the parked aircraft and a few maintenance hangers. On the north end of the terminal there is a taxiway about one-mile long, which goes north of the terminal, then east across the river, then north about five hundred yards where it begins to run parallel to runway 1, the only runway which runs north-south. Seven hundred and fifty feet across a grassy area to the west of the taxiway is runway 1. In the center of the runway and fifteen hundred feet to the west are an army barracks, the motor pool, and the maintenance garage.

Sochon Street runs on the east side of the river and divides at a fork; the left leading over a small bridge to the airport terminal and the right leading to the taxiway, which was about two miles north of the fork. The road stops at the taxiway. To get to the runway you have to drive on the taxiway. Two hundred feet south of the runway is the electrical panel that supplies the power to the airport. There is a large, diesel-powered generator next to the electrical panel that provides the backup power when the electric goes out.

Daniels, driving General Cheon's car, sped up Sochon Street. On the fenders of the car were the general's personal flags. The car was easily recognized by anyone.

About a half mile before the fork, at a bus stop sitting on a bench, was JR. Daniels pulled over. Stopping the car, he sat Astrid up then got out. Daniels got in the passenger side and put his arm around Astrid, holding her left shoulder.

"Get in and drive," he ordered JR. He handed JR the driver's hat. "Take the right fork and don't stop."

JR followed the orders and took the right fork. He didn't stop for the guards, and they did not try to stop the car.

The road ended at the taxiway.

"Pull over to the right and stop," said Daniels. JR stopped the car. Daniels got out and leaned into the open window. "Follow the blue lights. That's the taxiway. Take it to the end. Try to stay as far over to the right as possible. If the airport lights go out, you have to drive dark. No lights. The Citation will land and turn right. The cabin door will be facing you. Have Astrid out of the car. She may need to be carried. She took a bullet to the right side. When the Citation turns, it will do a slow roll. They will drop the door. You get Astrid on the plane. Understand?"

"Yes, sir. What about you, sir?"

Before Daniels could answer, Astrid tried to open the door. Daniels leaned against it.

"I'm staying with you, Mac."

"Not this time, Astrid. I'll have to move quickly and even without the bullet, you couldn't keep up with me. Get on the taxiway and go. Go," he ordered JR, "Go now."

"Yes, sir. Shit, this is just like the movies, Mr. Daniels," said JR pressing down on the accelerator.

Daniels stood there for a few seconds, watching the car drive away. He then walked back to the diesel generator and turned off the flow valve that fed the diesel fuel to the generator. He knew that when he killed the electric power, the generator would automatically turn on and run but for less than a minute before dying out. The power outage happened often, and would not spur any concern, but the generator failing would. The tower command would have one of the mechanics sent over and when he did not come back or the power didn't go back on, the tower would dispatch the army unit assigned to the airport. Daniels had to keep the mechanics and the military unit away from the generator.

"Virgil, you ready?" asked Lisa.

"Ready." There was hesitancy in Virgil's voice.

Lisa wanted to reassure Virgil. "You're doing fine, Virgil. We're right behind you."

"Lisa, my warning systems are buzzing, the red lights are flashing, believe me I know you are close."

"Well, isn't it good to know the Gulfstream systems work?"

"You're not funny, Lisa." Finally, there was a sense of relief in Virgil's voice.

"Ok, Virgil, here's the plan: Bak is going to land the Citation mid-runway to limit his time on the ground. When we touch down, you should be thirty feet above the ground. You'll hear me talking with Bak as we approach so you can gauge yourself. Bak has been on with the tower and they are waving him off. Good luck."

"Tower, I'm telling you I have permission to land," insisted Bak. "This is Astrid Reed's plane and she just left your Supreme Leader. I suggest you talk with his office. Please call them."

The tower was confused. Cheon had said no one was to land. This pilot was insisting that they call the office of the Supreme Leader.

"Make the call, tower. I'm at nine thousand feet and 250 knots."

"Go round, go round," ordered the tower.

"Go around. My throttle is now at idle. 180 knots, flaps five," said Bak referring to the degrees.

"Flaps five," repeated Lisa. "Virgil, you okay?"

"We're good, Lisa," replied Virgil.

"140 knots, flaps fifteen," said Bak.

Lisa set the flap and repeated the command, as it was procedure and for Virgil's benefit. Virgil had to reduce speed to stay with the Citation but had to use an imaginary runway thirty feet off the ground.

"130 knots, lower landing gear," Bak ordered.

"Gear down and locked," replied Lisa.

"Tower, I passed the middle marker. I need to land. Did you call the Supreme Leader's office?"

"Go round," responded the tower. "Waiting for permission. Must go round."

"125 knots flaps thirty-five. 120 knots landing speed."

Daniels saw the planes, and he started his count.

"Virgil!" yelled Lisa.

Over the speaker they heard Daniels count down. "Three, two, one."

The lights went off. The generator kicked on.

"Now, Virgil," yelled Lisa.

Virgil pushed the throttle to ninety percent and flew down the runway.

Bak radioed, "Going around," as the Citation landed. Bak hit the electronic countermeasure defense and radio jammer.

The radar screen blurred in the tower and then the generator stopped. The tower and field were black. The only lights were Virgil's Gulfstream climbing into the night sky. Bak and Lisa had on their night vision goggles. As the Citation's nose wheel touched, Bak deployed the spoilers, then the reverse thrusters. At sixty knots, he canceled the reverse thrusters and applied the manual brakes. "Lisa, bring the flaps up to five, be ready for takeoff."

"Flaps five," she echoed.

Bak taxied a little faster than the maximum taxi speed of twenty knots. At the end of the runway, he turned right and slowed down. There was JR with Astrid over his shoulder, running toward the plane. Lisa opened the door. Oscar came to the door and stepped down onto the stairs. As JR stepped up, Oscar pulled Astrid into the cabin. JR followed, the stairs retracted, and the door shut and locked. Bak moved the throttle up as he guided the plane down the taxiway with his night vision goggles.

Daniels had worked his way toward the maintenance hangar. He wanted to take out the mechanics, and then if necessary, the army unit. Although he was not sure how he was going to do this. Next to the barracks, there were propane tanks, which provided the fuel for heat. A bullet piercing the propane tank would cause an explosion. Probably kill a few before they got to the two Ural-375 troop transports parked outside the barrack. The Ural was a Russian-made four-and-a-half-ton truck and was an ideal platform for the BM-21 Grad rocket launcher. If they got to the Ural, they could stop the Citation. Daniels looked across the field and the Citation was still on the taxiway.

He had the Beretta still loaded with the 9mm Kratak. He had to get close, he thought, to pierce the propane tank and he didn't have enough ammunition to shoot out all the tires. There were over twelve; each truck having six tires. He knew that the Kratak would not pierce the motor block.

From the maintenance garage came a motorcycle heading toward the generator. Daniels jumped in front of the motorcycle, causing the driver to brake hard. The driver yelled at him but Daniels only imagined what he was saying. Daniels grabbed the driver, pulling him back off the motorcycle, and the man went down hard, headfirst. Daniels turned toward the downed driver. He didn't move. Daniels thought that he was either dead or unconscious. "You should wear a helmet," he quipped.

Daniels jumped on the motorcycle and drove toward the barracks. He took a position so he had a clear shot at the propane tank and the door of the barracks. When the lights didn't come on, the barracks' door opened. The tower must have called. Two men came running out. Daniels squeezed off a shot at the propane tank, and then at the two men. The tank exploded but it was not as devastating as Daniels had hoped. "Fuck."

It must have been almost empty, he thought. They probably didn't keep it full in the summer months. The door burst open and men came running out. There was no way he could hit them all. He had a shot at one of the Urals and decided to take out the front tires. At least he would have only one truck to deal with.

When the officer in charge saw the bodies of the two downed men, he sent six men off to check the field and the generator. Two men headed for the generator on the run. Two went down field and two went toward Daniels. The Citation was turning onto the runway.

Go, thought Daniels. *Go.* As the men approached, Daniels fired off two silenced shots, hitting the mark and both men fell. He picked up one of their Ak-47s, checked the clip and then took the AK-47 bayonet and scabbard and got on the motorcycle. The Citation was rolling. The airport lights came on.

The truck started after the Citation, cutting across the field on an angle. It would intercept the Citation mid-runway before the plane had liftoff speed.

Bak had the thrust set to ninety-five percent take off power. The Citation was picking up speed—it was at fifty knots.

From the rear of the truck, one of the men stood and brought a rocket-propelled grenade to his shoulder. Daniels was close but from the moving motorcycle, he was not sure of the shot. He didn't want to stop but he did. He raised the rifle and fired off a three- round burst. It hit the man and as he fell back, he fired the grenade. It arched up. Daniels watched as it sailed toward the plane. It came down on the starboard side away from Daniels' view. He heard the explosion and just watched. There was no way to know what damage the Citation had sustained. He only hoped it could fly. The three other men stood to fire at the airplane and Daniels shot at them, hitting two. The motorcycle raced alongside the truck.

The Citation was at eighty knots, and pulling away from the truck. Daniels got close to the truck and kept on firing. The Citation was at 130 knots. Bak pulled hard on the yoke, and the nose wheel came up off the ground.

Daniels fired into the cab of the truck, hitting the driver. The driver lost control and the truck started to swerve away from the runway toward the west. Daniels cut away and headed down the runway. He calculated that there were two men in the truck; one in the back and one in the passenger seat of the cab; two at the generator; and two down at the end of the field. He needed to be in position.

The Citation reached 140 knots and the rear wheels lifted off the ground. As soon as they were airborne, Lisa retracted the landing gear. At fifteen hundred feet, she raised the flaps. Bak pushed the climb out and exceeded the 250 knots while below ten thousand feet. At ten thousand feet, he leveled off and pushed for maximum cruise speed.

"You're up against the barber pole," reported Lisa.

Bak glanced down at the airspeed indicator with its red/white striped bar resembling a barber pole, indicating the Citation was at the maximum safe velocity. In a few minutes, he would be in international air space.

What about Mac? he thought.

CHAPTER 61

PYONGYANG AIRPORT

SAME TIME

Daniels managed to cross the runway and lie down on the grass strip that separated the runway from the taxiway. He knew that once they saw his position they could outflank him and eventually surround him. He didn't have to check the clip; he knew he had eighteen rounds left of the original thirty rounds. *Not much ammunition,* he thought, *when you're against six men armed with the same weapon.* But he did have the bayonet. He had to get them somehow in one part of the runway and away from him, if he was to have a chance.

Two men that were downfield started coming toward the runway. Daniels took out the Beretta, which still had the sound suppressor attached. He thought if he could take out a few of the runway lights down toward the south end of the field, he hoped that the officer in charge would reason he was down there trying to provide cover for himself.

He took aim and squeezed off the first shot. While a sound suppressor doesn't truly make the weapon completely silent, the cracking sound was not heard on such a large airfield. The first light went out, then the second, the third, and the fourth. The slide on the Beretta locked back. He was out of ammunition. He released the slide and stuck the Beretta in his waistband.

His plan had worked, almost. The officer who was in the cab of the truck with the soldier was moving south, and the two who were at the generator started moving west, but the two who were on the runway were coming straight at him. *Can't get a fucking break,* he thought. Daniels was only a few feet off the runway on the grassy area. He had to take them without shooting. He needed stealth for the other four. He drew out the bayonet and readied himself. *The best-laid plans,* he thought. He took the Beretta and threw it, hitting one of them in the chest. It didn't hurt as much as it caused them to lose focus and look down at the ground.

Bending down to find what had hit him, the soldier laid down his Kalashnikov and started to look around and pat the ground. Daniels lunged. The standing soldier instinctively swung the butt of his Kalashnikov toward the rushing man. Daniels was close enough to fend off the attack by grabbing the stock of the Kalashnikov and pulling on it, causing the man to come closer to Daniels. Daniels thrust the blade of the bayonet almost to the hilt into the man—all fifteen inches. Without his weapon, the other soldier came up with his bayonet drawn. Daniels pulled his bayonet out of the chest of the dead soldier and turned to face his new adversary.

They circled each other, and the Korean slashed at Daniels. Daniels blocked the slash with his bayonet. The Korean lunged, Daniels sidestepped the thrust, and grabbed the Korean's right wrist with his left hand, lifting it up and twisting it back, exposing the man's right side. He drove the bayonet into the man's right side through the lung. Then, he let go and the Korean fell to the ground.

Now Daniels had to deal with the others. He turned to look downfield and felt a pain in the right side of his leg. Looking down, he saw the bayonet sticking out. With his last breath, the Korean had swung the bayonet toward Daniels, cutting him in the mid-thigh area of his leg. It was not a fatal wound, but it would bleed and it hurt like hell. Fortunately, the blade had not gone too far in and the weight of the bayonet caused it to fall to the ground.

"Fuck, fuck," yelled Daniels, as he touched his wound. He had to end this quickly. He stood up and yelled, attracting the other four at the south end of the airfield. They could not tell who it was. Waving his hands frantically, he deliberately fell down. He picked up his Kalashnikov, putting it on full automatic and lay there. The four men came running. Daniels just lay there until they were about ten yards away. Standing, he fired; killing them all.

Daniels took the leather bootlaces off one of the dead Koreans' boots and with the bayonet he cut a piece of material off the dead man's shirt. He folded the material into a square. On one end of the shoelace, he fastened a bowline knot, to form a fixed loop at the end of the lace. He wrapped the shoelace around his leg and brought the free end of the lace through the loop, allowing it to hang freely. He placed the material on the wound and then he pulled the free end of the lace, causing the shoelace to tighten around his leg. He pulled hard and then he tied the lace off with two half hitches. That would be all he could do for now.

His car was still down at the end of the taxiway where JR had left it. He would drive over to the terminal area and take a life vest and a valise raft out of one of the airliners. The Yellow Sea was eighteen miles west of the airport. If he made it there, he could paddle out and make it to the south or get picked up by a friendly. He ran down the taxiway to the car and started to drive south toward Sochon Road.

"Admiral," he called on his cell.

"Yes, Mac. Are you okay?"

"Leg wound—I'll live. Where's Astrid?"

"The Citation is in international airspace on its way to Seoul-Incheon International Airport. There's an ambulance waiting for her."

Daniels said nothing just nodded his head approvingly. "Admiral, I'm going to drive to the Yellow Sea. I hope to have a raft and with a little paddle power and a favorable current I should make it to the open sea and maybe you can have me picked up."

"Mac, you have a problem. There are two truckloads of troops on Sochon, heading toward the airport."

Daniels was quiet. Finally, he said, "Fuck! Admiral, I'll be at the Yellow Sea. Be sure to pick me up."

Charko looked at Cornaci, shaking his head. "We have you covered, Mac."

Daniels drove the car down the taxiway to where it met Sochon and parked it slightly south of the intersection. He then ran back cutting across the field toward the truck. A hand grabbed at his ankle, tripping him and he went down hard. Before he could react, there was someone on his back, grabbing at his neck and trying to bang his head into the ground. Daniels brought his right elbow back into his attacker's ribs knocking him off his back. Managing to turn over, he grabbed the pencil, jamming it into the man's ear. He hit the eraser. There was no reaction at first then blood began to run from the man's nose, his gripped loosened, and he fell over dead. The twenty-two had done its job.

It was the mechanic. Daniels left him there with the pencil sticking out of his ear. Looking at the dead man, he said, "You should have worn a helmet."

Finally making it to the truck, Daniels pulled out the dead driver, drove the truck to the north side of the intersection of the taxiway and Sochon, and parked it.

He took apart his belt buckle and dropped the ends of the buckle into each of the gas tanks of the truck and car. "Admiral, where are they?"

"Just past the fork, they're setting up a road block."

"I have a road block of my own."

Daniels gathered up all the Kalashnikovs he could find. He spread them out, about ten feet apart and lay on the grass, waiting for the first truck. As it appeared, he opened fire, aiming at the engine and emptying the clip. The truck stopped. The men inside jumped out and started to return fire. Daniels rolled to the right, to the next Kalashnikov, and fired. He emptied the clip. He rolled to the right, to the third Kalashnikov.

The second truck pulled in next to the first. Daniels opened fire into its engine, stopping the truck. He took out his cell and pressed send. A second later, both vehicles exploded, spewing metal and flames. The explosion killed many of the Koreans; several were on fire. Daniels picked up the fourth Kalashnikov and with the flames illuminating his targets, he eliminated the few remaining Koreans.

Finally, it was over. Exhausted and bloody he slowly walked back to the runway for the motorcycle.

Daniels heard it before he saw it. It was the sound of a plane. He had one Kalashnikov with about ten rounds left in it. He couldn't believe it. He drove over to the taxiway out of view.

The Antonov lumbered over the threshold of the runway and flew down about ten feet off the ground. It finally put down and came to a stop almost exactly where Daniels was. The pilot climbed out of his seat, moved into the co-pilot's seat on the starboard side of the aircraft, opened the window, and yelled in English. "Daniels, Daniels. Come on, let's get out of here."

Daniels drove the motorcycle across the runway, but way around the rear of the aircraft, making it difficult for anyone in the cockpit to take a shot at him. He stopped at the rear of the plane just a little to the left and aimed the Kalashnikov at the cabin door.

"Show yourself," he yelled.

The door opened and a young Korean pilot appeared.

Daniels got a puzzled looked on his face. He zeroed the Kalashnikov in on the pilot. "Who the fuck are you?"

"DIA, Lieutenant Bryan Kye, United States Navy. Until now, I was working undercover for the DIA. I was flying as a Korean air scout."

Daniels wasn't sure—he had one more question. "Who is your commanding ..."

The pilot cut him off, "We don't have time for this shit. Half the fucking army is on its way here. The admiral said he saved some popcorn for you, for after they let you out of the loony bin. So please get the fuck in here."

Daniels jumped off the motorcycle and ran for the cabin. No one knew about the popcorn. Once inside the cabin, he jumped into the co-pilot's seat on the right and Kye took the pilot's seat on the left. Kye released the brakes and pushed the throttle forward.

As the plane rolled down the runway Kye asked, "Do you really like popcorn that much?"

"What do you think? Let's go."

The An-2 moved down the runway and lifted off.

CHAPTER 62

SAMSUNG MEDICAL CENTER, SEOUL, KOREA

Daniels walked through the emergency room doors at the Samsung Medical Center, one of the largest and most advanced hospitals in South Korea. The doctor standing there stared at him in disbelief. "Quick," he yelled, reaching for Daniels. "Get a gurney!"

Daniels pushed him away. "I'm fine. Where is Astrid Reed?"

"You're fine?" said the doctor in disbelief. "You're covered in blood. There is blood all over you."

"It's not mine," said Daniels. "Where is Astrid Reed?"

"If it is not your blood what is that red stuff coming through your pants leg?"

Daniels looked down and saw his wound had opened. "I'll be all right. Now for the last time, where is Astrid Reed?"

"Mac!"

Daniels turned to the voice. It was Bak Johansen. "Bak, where's Astrid?"

"In surgery. Ron is down the hall in a waiting room."

Daniels took off, followed by a burly security guard. As he reached the waiting room, another doctor came out, followed by Ron Haig.

"Mr. Daniels?"

"How is she?"

"She is in the hands of one of our best surgeons. Let's go some place private where we can talk. And let me look at that wound, if not for your sake at least for the hospital because you are bleeding all over the floor."

"You look terrible, Mac," said Haig, "and with that blood running down it won't do Astrid any good. I'll get you some clean clothes. Go with the doctor."

The doctor led Daniels into a small examining room. "Please take off your pants and lie down and take off that shirt."

Daniels did what the doctor asked. The doctor untied the shoelace and pulled off the dressing. "This doesn't look too serious. It is in the muscles. A tetanus shot, some antibiotics, and a few stitches and you should be fine."

The doctor called the nurse, who came in with a tray of instruments. "I will give you something that will . . ."

"Never mind, just stitch me up. I have to get back to work."

Looking at this man covered in blood with a knife wound, the doctor wondered what kind of work he did, but knew better than to ask.

However, curiosity had the better of the nurse and she asked, "Just what kind of work do you do?"

"I'm a piano player in a whorehouse," said Daniels with a straight face.

After a few minutes, a few stitches, a tetanus shot, and some antibiotics the doctor was done. "Why don't you let the nurse wash off some of the blood and clean you up so when you go to see Miss Reed you won't scare her half to death. You do look like shit."

Daniels nodded.

"Nurse, please get this piano player a set of scrubs so he can walk around here until his friend gets him some appropriate clothes." Turning to Daniels, he said, "Why don't you lie down and as soon as Miss Reed is out of surgery I'll come and get you."

"Fair enough, Doc. Doc . . ."

"Yes?"

"Thanks."

The doctor left and the nurse helped clean Daniels up. He dressed in blue scrubs and was looking like a doctor. He was exhausted. He lay there a few minutes and his exhaustion finally caught up with him.

About hour later, the doctor woke him. "She's out of surgery and in recovery. We need to talk. Can I call you Billy Joel?"

Daniels let out a sigh. "How is she?"

"There is some good news and some bad. On the good side, the bullet missed her lung and did not do any damage to the nerves or any major vessels. They got it all out and she is on antibiotics. There will be a small scar but a good plastic surgeon can fix it. It is nothing major. Her nose was not broken and she has bruises to her face and body. She has a black eye, which is swollen, but it will go down. There was no damage to her eyes or eyesight. She has a couple of bruised ribs. In short, it looks like she was in a boxing match. I'd hate to see the other guy.

Daniels nodded his head and thought, *The other two guys are dead.* "What's the bad news?" he asked.

"The beating caused her to miscarry."

"Miscarry!" The look on Daniels' face told it all. He'd had no idea. He just stammered, "She was pregnant?"

"We did not tell Miss Reed. We thought you might wish to do so."

"How pregnant was she?"

"It was early. I can see by your look that you did not know. Once she was here, she started to bleed. She said that her period was late. But from the color of the discharge, it was a miscarriage. She's been through a lot. "

"I guess she was going to surprise me." Daniels looked away. "Can I see her?"

The doctor brought over a wheelchair. "Let me push you to her room. I have a feeling you are going to walk in anyway, but let me keep you off your leg for a few more minutes. I know you have to get back to work. You must play in some fancy whorehouse. There must be a half dozen armed guards here. It is your protection detail? Hop in, let's go."

The doctor pushed Daniels down the hall. Ron Haig was standing outside the recovery room; he looked down and said nothing. He saw Mac was glassy eyed and he knew to step aside. Mac and Astrid needed their time. Daniels just nodded as he was wheeled past Haig. He then saw Bak, Lisa, and Virgil. They took their cue from Haig. No one said anything. Lisa stepped in front of the wheelchair, leaned down and kissed Daniels on the cheek. She said nothing.

The doctor stopped outside Astrid's room. There were two armed guards posted in front of her door. There were two more at each end of the hall. Daniels stood, ignoring the pain. Opening the door slowly, he peeked inside.

Stepping into the room, he quietly closed the door. Astrid lay in bed with an intravenous drip in her left arm and her right side bandaged. He leaned over the bed and gently kissed her. She opened her eyes, saw Mac and smiled. "Mac, you're here," she said softly.

"Of course, I promised and you know I always keep a promise, especially to a beautiful woman in a hospital gown opened in the back. That's just inviting."

She smiled. "Not now, Mac. I'm too tired." She fell asleep. Mac was here.

Daniels pulled up a chair, looked at her, and started to cry. The tears ran down his face. He was relieved and he felt guilty for what he'd done to her. She was breathing heavily, in a drug-induced sleep.

He whispered to her, "I love you, and I'm sorry I did this to you. Please forgive me. I should not have involved you. I endangered you and I'm sorry. Never again. Please Astrid, forgive me."

He bent over the bed, put his head down, and fell asleep.

Some time later, he felt a hand on his hair and fingers running through his thick black locks. He opened his eyes. He was stiff from the position he had fallen asleep in. Astrid was awake. He sat up.

"You were tired," she said.

"Yes, Astrid, more importantly, how are you feeling?"

"As long as I don't look in the mirror, I think I'm ok."

"You look great, honey. Well, almost great. It's the black eye."

"Yeah, but did you see the other guy/" she quipped and then the smile fell from her face. "Mac, I killed many people. Oh, my God."

"You only killed people who were trying to kill you. You couldn't shoot Sang in the head, but you shot him in the balls. He deserved it. I killed Sang," he lied.

"And the driver you laid out with the kick wasn't dead. I killed him." Again, he lied.

"But let's talk about something else. Two things: where are we going to go to finish our vacation and …" He hesitated, looking for words. "Astrid . . ."

"Yes, Mac."

"Astrid, can I get in bed with you?"

"Mac, here? Are you nuts? Does all this adrenalin stuff make you horny? Not to mention I'm not in the best shape."

He could not help but laugh, "I want to hold you. We have to talk."

She moved over and he climbed onto the bed next to her. Turning on his side, he held her. "Babe, I'm sorry for what I did to you. Please, I beg you to forgive me. I never would hurt you and I love you with all my heart. You're my reason for being. I should have protected you better. I'm so sorry." He let out a sigh. "Babe, you were pregnant and you miscarried. Why didn't you tell me?"

"Oh, Mac," she said, as tears filled her eyes. "There's nothing for me to forgive you for. I really didn't know I was pregnant."

He cut her off. "Astrid, you're fibbing to me. You know your cycle runs like clockwork. You were late and you didn't say anything, because you knew I wouldn't let you go to Korea, and I shouldn't have let you go, regardless, and I'm so sorry for that."

"Mac, I love you. What would a child be without you? I wasn't about to find out. I started to bleed when I got here and I suspected as much. Hey, you know there's no back to this hospital gown. I can get pregnant again."

"Not now, Astrid. I think you're out of commission for a while."

"Mac, isn't there a ship you have to catch?"

"Yes, but not now. I'm sorry for what happened."

"I'm not. You're alive and tomorrow is another day. I'll call Lexye and have her find us the quietest, most romantic place for us, after you get that ship."

They fell asleep together.

CHAPTER 63

SAMSUNG MEDICAL CENTER, SEOUL, KOREA

SAME DAY

The next evening there was a knock on the door. Astrid opened her eyes to see that Mac was gone. She had no idea when he left. "Come in," she said.

The doctor came in. "How are you feeling?"

"Stiff and sore," she said. "How bad do I look?"

"Did you see the movie *Rocky*?"

"Which one?"

"The first one."

"That bad. Oh, shit."

"Nothing was broken, Miss Reed. You will be fine. Let's take a look at your wound." The doctor removed the bandage, examined the wound, and then re-dressed the wound. "Looks good, no sign of infection. I'll get that I.V. out of your arm. We will keep you on antibiotics and depending how you feel, you can be released tomorrow morning. Do you have any questions?"

"My mis . . ."

He cut her off. "Miss Reed, your reproductive system is fine. You and the piano player can resume your normal sexual activities in about two or three weeks. You're fine. It really depends on how you feel mentally."

"A few weeks, Doctor? The piano player, as you call him, is a sailor. You better give me a written note."

"A note?"

"Never mind—he can't read."

"You have a visitor, Miss Reed."

"Please let him in," Astrid said, thinking it was Ron Haig.

"It is not a him but it's a her and your guards won't let anyone in without your permission."

"My guards?"

"Mr. Shaljian had guards posted here. He seems to have quite a bit of power."

She smiled at that. Ron Haig was using Shaljian as his cover name.

"Please tell the guards to let the person in. I'm curious."

"I'll see you in the morning."

A few minutes later, Vivian Berkstrom came through the door.

"Oh my baby," Berkstrom said, giving Astrid a hug and a kiss. She stepped back and gave Astrid a hard look. "I won't ask what happened. What can I do to help?"

"I'm hungry. Maybe you can get me some food."

"I'm on it honey. Be right back."

The phone rang. Astrid leaned over and answered it. "Hello."

"Astrid, how are you feeling?"

She immediately recognized the baritone voice of General Bellardi. "Uncle Tony, I'm doing better today than I was yesterday."

"Thank God you're okay. How's my nephew?"

"He's fine."

"Good. I hope the two of you are going to take a few days off."

"Believe me Uncle Tony, we are. And I'm not telling you or the admiral or Ron or the president or anyone where we're going."

He gave a big laugh. "I believe you, Astrid. Aunt Marilyn sends her love. Tell that idiot nephew of mine to call his boss."

"I will. Thanks for calling. Bye Uncle Tony."

A few minutes later, Viv was back with the nurses' aide with a food tray for Astrid. The phone rang and Viv answered it out of habit. "Miss Reed's office."

There was silence on the other end for a few seconds as if the caller had the wrong number. Finally, the voice said, "Vivian?"

"Yes."

"It's Admiral Charko. How is Astrid, and what are you doing there?"

"I flew out immediately when Ron called. I just arrived. Here's Astrid."

"Hello."

"Astrid, it's Eugene Charko, how are you?"

"I'm doing fine, Admiral. It was a tough day yesterday but I'm fine."

"You did well. You certainly held up your end and the country owes you a debt of gratitude. If you don't mind, is Mac there?"

"I'm sorry, Admiral. He's not here and to be truthful, I have no idea where he is."

"He sustained a wound, so where the hell is he?"

"A wound?"

"From the tone of your voice, I can see he didn't tell you. I would appreciate it if you see him, to have him call me. He seems to have disappeared off the radar. Be well, Astrid. See you when you get back. Goodbye."

"Goodbye, Admiral."

Astrid went back to her meal. Vivian took out an envelope from her purse.

"Here," she said. "Ron told me to give this to you after the Admiral called."

Astrid opened the envelope. It was from Mac. She read it and smiled.

"I love it when he thinks he's in the doghouse. He says the nicest things."

"Doghouse? What could that hunk of man do to be in the doghouse?"

"Well, in a nutshell, besides getting me pregnant . . ."

"Pregnant!"

"And getting beat up, I had a miscarriage. Mac is beating himself up over it. The truth is I hadn't told him about it. I wasn't one hundred percent sure, but I knew. But I'm okay, Viv. The doctor says in a few weeks Mac and I can get back to normal."

"A few weeks! Doesn't that doctor know Mac is a sailor?"

What Astrid did not say was that Mac had told her he was going after the Sails of Allah.

CHAPTER 64

SAILS OF ALLAH

Captain Anas Anka was in his cabin when there was a knock on the door.

"Enter."

The door opened and Mac Daniels entered the cabin.

Anka had a surprised look on his face. "I did not expect you so soon. Do I ask how you boarded my ship in the middle of the ocean?"

"I dropped in. I'll show you in a few minutes, but first, you have my knife."

Anka opened his desk drawer, took out the Ka-bar, and handed it to Daniels.

"You really didn't come here just for your knife."

"Sure I did." Daniels unsheathed the knife and examined the blade. "You didn't use it. Thank you."

"Can you tell me how you knew where I was?" asked Captain Anka.

"The satellite tracked you and we have other methods of watching you," answered Daniels.

"Other methods?"

"Yes, but now, I have to talk with you. I have a feeling you have a few S-25 Berkut "Golden Eagle" surface-to-air guided missiles on board and some sarin."

Anka nodded. "You're right."

"You know I can't allow you to deliver them."

"I suspected as much. What are you going to do?"

"Well, I can sink the ship and kill all of you, or I can sink the ship and put you all in a lifeboat, but there is one more choice."

"What is that?

"How about you work for me?"

The captain was puzzled. "I don't even know your real name and you want me to work for you? Who are you and what am I supposed to do?"

"Look, Captain. Do you remember what you said to me when I had that incident with your first officer?"

Anka nodded his head. "You mean when you killed the first officer. Yes, I remember. I told you that I had to sail for ISIS or else. I am a Muslim but I am not a member of ISIS. I don't condone brutality or the killing of women and children, the burning alive, the beheadings, or the crucifixions."

"What about the rest of your crew? Will they work with you?"

"What is left of my crew, thanks to you, are all family-related and they will work with me. All of my crew are good men, men of peace. None of them condone what ISIS is doing."

"Then here's my offer . . ."

A half hour later, Anka and Daniels shook hands.

"Now let's go up to the bridge so we can finish what we have to do."

When Anka and Daniels were on the bridge, Daniels made a call on his cell phone and about fifteen minutes later, like a big whale, a Los Angeles-class attack submarine, the USS Cheyenne, breached the surface, one hundred yards off the ship's port side.

The Cheyenne is designed to seek and destroy ships and submarines and to carry out special operation missions, among other military activities.

The sight of the silent giant so close to the ship had the crew worried. The captain announced over the intercom that there was nothing to fear. From one of the hatches, several of the submariners started to launch rafts and row over to the ship. The captain had the gangplank lowered, in order to allow them to board.

Captain Anka looked at the Cheyenne, "Very impressive, the other method, Mr. . . ."

"William Barney, yes the other method."

"William Barney?" questioned Anka.

Daniels smiled. "I have to leave."

"How did you get here?"

Daniels pointed to the sky.

Anka looked up. "What is that? It looks like a World War One warplane, a bi-plane."

"It's a troop transport."

They were looking at the newly painted, blue and white An-2, which Bak Johansen held level at 500 hundred feet, cruising at one hundred knots, and circling the Sails of Allah.

"I bailed out with a MC-6 parachute. It's what we call a steerable parachute. You can land it on a dime, which I did on top of your bridge. Now the pilot will pick me up. If you would keep the ship turned into the wind and give me twenty knots I can get out of here."

"I'll try."

Daniels climbed up on top of the bridge. He packed his parachute into the harness, strapped it on, and called Bak, "Pick me up please."

Turning to Anka, Daniels said, "Watch this. What he's about to do, not too many pilots can do. Fly backwards."

"Backwards! I may be a ship's captain but you can't fly a fixed wing aircraft backwards."

"He can, and he will literally hover the airplane over me so I can easily get in. Watch." said Daniels.

Anka looked up as Bak made a wide turn downwind and then turned into the wind. He was three hundred feet directly behind the ship about ten feet over the bridge. He dropped the slats on the upper wing and managed to get the airplane down to thirty miles per hour.

Daniels continued, "A good pilot of the An-2 can fly in full control at thirty miles per hour. This slow speed makes it possible for the aircraft to fly backwards if the aircraft is pointed into a headwind of thirty-five miles an hour. It will actual travel backwards at five miles per hour, still under control. That's my ride out of here."

The headwind was twenty miles per hour and the ship was doing twenty knots. It looked like a movie stalled in time. The airplane was traveling about ten miles per hour over the ground. Bak played with the throttle, increasing the power to close the distance. He was slightly forward of the bridge and he reduced the power and the plane began to slowly come to what looked like a standstill. Bak gently pulled back on the yoke and the nose of the airplane lifted slightly up, causing the airplane to lose more airspeed and a few more feet of altitude. He had the plane almost sitting in the roof of the bridge. Haig lowered a rope ladder, which dangled by Daniels.

"Captain do me a favor," yelled Daniels.

"Of course, what is it?"

Pointing to the submariners who were aboard the ship, "Feed them well. They are going to be here for a time."

Anka replied, "It will be my pleasure."

Daniels grabbed the ladder and started to climb the few steps to the cabin. When he was in the cabin Bak pushed up the throttle. As the plane picked up airspeed, he gradually pulled away from the ship and gained altitude.

At fifty knots, he raised the slats, then climbed up to one thousand feet, and finally disappeared.

Back inside the bridge, Anka made an announcement; he instructed the crew to cooperate with the submariners and ordered the cook to feed them.

Looking toward the sky, Anka just smiled.

CHAPTER 65

CIA HEADQUARTERS

TWO WEEKS LATER

"You're most welcome, Mike," said Jon Cornaci as he hung up the phone.

Admiral Charko just then had entered the room. "Mike Bertone?" he asked, referring to the director of the FBI.

"He called to tell me that they had court-ordered wiretaps on Ki-Yong Park's house and business phones, and a few listening devices in the home and his business office. Mr. Park is under surveillance. Since Mac had that . . ." he paused, looking for the right word, ". . . episode in North Korea, Mike said that the satellite calls between the Reconnaissance General Bureau (RGB) and Park have been hot and heavy. When the time is right, Mike will bring him and try to turn him."

"Any word on this Aswas Rajul?" asked Charko.

"Unfortunately not. From the information Mac gave us and from what we could piece together, he's the one we need to catch. Bertone has his agents on it and they do a good job. I'm sure Rajul will slip up and Mike will catch him. But for now, the question is, where is Mac?"

"Jon, I truly apologize, but I have no idea where he is. I know I'm his boss for whatever that means, but I'll be damned if I can find him."

"What does Haig have to say about this?"

Charko just shook his head and closed his eyes. "I spoke to Ron, who swears up and down he has no idea where Mac is and I believe him. I placed a call to Astrid's personal assistant, Vivian Berkstrom, who practically raised Astrid, and she told me that even if she knew, which I believe she does, she wouldn't tell me. I had Ron call Lexye and that led nowhere."

"Lexye?"

Lexye Aversa, she's a friend of Astrid's and Mac's and runs a travel service. She plans their trips and if anyone could find a get-a-way spot, she could and she probably did. She told Ron that she had no idea where they were. Astrid's airplane is back in the United States and neither she nor Mac were on board."

Cornaci scratched his head. "Admiral is something wrong with this picture? We're the CIA and we can't find one of our officers. Maybe we should call the FBI."

"Jon, that's not funny and besides, it's not one of our officers, it's Mac Daniels."

There was a knock on the door and Ron Haig entered. He looked at both men and asked, "Have you found them?"

Both men shook their head no.

"When Mac and I returned from his naval excursion," Ron said, "he went to the hotel where Astrid and Vivian were staying. I was at a different hotel with Oscar and JR. The next morning we flew back here. Mac said they were staying for a few days. He wanted Astrid to rest before traveling."

No one said anything.

"Well, anyway I have some news. Just picked up a release from North Korea. The head of their nuclear program, Director Jang Min has been executed for treason and his family is in a labor camp. First deputy Shin Soo is now in charge of the nuclear program and Moon Il-Sung is now the first deputy and in charge of the nuclear miniaturization program."

"Well," said Cornaci, "that's very interesting. Very interesting."

The intercom rang. "Yes, Helen?"

"Sorry to interrupt you, Doctor, but you will never guess who just landed at LAX," she said. "Astrid Reed and Douglas MacArthur. What do you want me to do? Have them picked up?"

"Do nothing. The prodigal son is coming home."

Charko's cell phone rang. He answered on the first ring. "Charko here."

"I'm back, Admiral."

"Are you and Astrid all right, Mac?"

"We're both fine, Admiral. I'm sorry I was off the grid, but I needed time for both Astrid and myself. I had to do some soul searching. To be honest, I am thinking of resigning."

Charko was calm and understood. He knew what had happened to Astrid. "Mac, you have served your country both as a naval officer and a distinguished, no as the most exceptional officer of clandestine service. I understand how you feel. Whatever you do, I'll respect your wishes, but for now the president would like to see you. I told him you were on medical leave. When can you be in Washington?"

"We're on our way to Atlanta. We should be there late tonight. I can fly up to D.C. anytime you want. When does the president want to see me?"

"I'll check with Tim Harris, his special assistant, and leave word for you with Vivian. Harris told me as soon as you're back the president will make time for you and I'll send the Citation down to pick you up."

"When we're finished can I have some leave? I'd like to run up to Jersey and see my parents."

"Of course. I'll take care of everything. One favor please—wear your service dress whites. Please."

"Yes, sir. May I bring Astrid?"

"Yes, the president requested her presence also. There will be two meetings; one with us in the Situation Room and one with you and Astrid in the Oval Office."

"See you, Admiral."

The phone went dead. Turning to Jon Cornaci and Ron Haig, Charko said, "He's thinking of quitting."

Ron looked down at the ground and in a soft voice he said, "He's blaming himself for Astrid's beating, and of course the miscarriage."

The room was silent.

CHAPTER 66

ATLANTA, GEORGIA

THAT NIGHT

Astrid and Mac entered the lobby of The World News Corporation building. Mac had Astrid's suitcase and his duffel bag. They crossed the lobby, acknowledging the night security guard. The guard offered to help with the luggage, but Mac waved him off. Astrid went to the end elevator and pressed her thumb against the fingerprint reader of her private elevator. The door opened.

Her elevator made only five stops; the basement parking, the lobby, the seventy-ninth floor, her office, her eightieth floor apartment, and the heliport on the roof. The buttons were in a row, not up and down, and were unmarked. She pressed the center fingerprint reader with her thumb, the doors shut, and the elevator rose nonstop to her penthouse apartment.

A minute later, the doors opened, Mac and Astrid stepped out, and the motion detector turned on the hall lights.

"Want coffee, Mac?"

"No thanks, babe. I'm tired. Let's go to bed. We can unpack in the morning."

"Sounds like a plan," she said leading the way toward the master bedroom.

On the bedroom door was taped a note. Astrid opened it.

Reading it, she said, "It's from Viv. Admiral Charko called and said the president would like to see you and me at the White House tomorrow at three. He'll have the Citation pick us up at noon. It also said for you to wear your dress whites. I love you in the dress whites."

"I didn't know the admiral loved me in my dress whites."

She let out a sigh. "You're hopeless. Let's go to bed."

"Astrid, let's talk for a minute. I have something on my mind and we need to talk."

Astrid had a puzzled look on her face. "Sure, Mac," she said sitting down on the side of the bed and kicking off her shoes.

They started to get undressed. Mac pulled off his golf shirt and tossed it onto the chair. Astrid took off her blouse and he looked at her and could see the small scar where she was shot. She saw what he was looking at.

"Hey, sailor, stop looking at my boo boo, and start looking at my boobs."

"Astrid, I'm going to resign from the agency and the navy. I've served and maybe I can . . ."

Astrid jumped up so fast she actually startled Daniels.

"Bullshit Mackenzie Daniels. You're not quitting because of me. I knew the risk when I agreed to go. Hey, you forget, I gave it as good as I got. No, *fuck* no, I gave it better than I got. I put that asshole driver's balls in his mouth and if his head were a football, I would have kicked a field goal. And for Sang, I broke his nose and gave him a good kick. What did I get; a black eye and some bruises? Nothing broke. A fucking bullet—shit, Mac, it wasn't a shot, it was a ricochet and I would have stood in front of you and taken a bullet. And by the way, that really hurt. Stand up when I'm yelling at you. You really pissed me off. Put'em up. Come on, let's go a few rounds."

"Calm down, Astrid."

"Don't tell me to calm down," she said throwing a few air punches. "I'm no pussy. Stand up."

With that remark, Daniels started to laugh. "Babe, I think you're . . ."

Astrid took a swing and Daniels stood up at the wrong time. The hard right hit him in the eye.

She screamed, "Oh Mac, I'm sorry. I didn't mean to hit you. I'm sorry. Oh I'm sorry."

Daniels fell back on the bed holding his hand over his eye.

"What can I do? What can I do?" she asked.

"Can you get me a cold compress? Please."

Astrid ran into the kitchen and came back with some ice covered in a cloth. "Here, Mac."

Mac pressed the compress to his eye. "Astrid, please calm down and let's talk, and no more boxing. Babe, you were great out there. You really helped me and you have no idea what we did. I'm sorry I can't tell you, but trust me what you did was awesome and I could not have done it without you, but I shouldn't have put you at risk."

"You didn't put me at risk. I put myself at risk and I would do it again. Look, it was an early pregnancy and as I understand it, there is always a risk of a miscarriage during the early weeks. Many women don't even know they're pregnant." She sat down next to him. "Hey, Mac, I'm fine and I can get pregnant. So stop this quitting shit. Look sweetheart, every time you go out the door I worry. I worry until I see you. Yes, I wish you had a desk job, but Mac I can't have you quit because of me. I don't want you moping around the house thinking that but for me you would still be in the service. You'll know when it's time to leave the clandestine service and take a place at Langley running the service. But not today and not because I had a miscarriage."

Mac said nothing as she took off her bra and the rest of her clothes. He looked at her and smiled.

"What's so funny? Why the silly smirk on your face?"

"Nothing, you're just amazing."

She got in bed. "Are you going to sit there with that rag on your face all night or are you coming to bed, sailor. By the way, the two weeks are up, are you?"

Daniels stripped and got in bed. He moved next to her and kissed her. "I love you, Astrid."

"Mac, I love you more than life itself. Please don't quit for the wrong reason."

They kissed some more and there was no need for extended foreplay. She wanted him and he her. It was love making. She pushed him onto his back, threw her leg over him, and lowered herself onto him. She was hot and moist and he slid into her. She rolled her hips gently at first, making a circular motion. She pressed herself down hard on him and moved back and forth. Starting to hold her breath, she moved faster and faster. She could not control herself. The intensity of her orgasm seemed to take over her whole body as she shuddered. She let her breath out and screamed, "Oh Mac, my love."

A few seconds later, he followed her, arching his body up.

She pressed herself onto his chest, her breasts pressed tight. He held her. Her lips were next to his ears and she whispered into his ear, "I love you. Please don't quit."

He held her as she extended her legs and let her body rest on his. Her breathing grew heavy and she fell asleep. Daniels just let her lie there on him. Finally, sleep began to overtake him. He gently moved her off to his side, keeping his arm around her and her leg over his. He fell asleep.

CHAPTER 67

ATLANTA, GEORGIA

NEXT MORNING

Daniels woke first and crawled out of bed as not to wake Astrid. There were two bathrooms off the master bedroom; his and hers. Mac closed his bathroom door, brushed his teeth, and shaved. He turned on the hot water, stepped into the shower, and stood there. letting the water beat on him. He thought about what Astrid had said and he knew she was right. He shook his head. *She's always right.* He finished showering and toweled off. Wrapping a towel around himself, he tiptoed out of the bedroom and went into the den. He sat behind the desk, picking up the phone to call Ron Haig, and then his parents. Astrid's desk was covered with photos of herself and Mac. There was a keyboard on the desk that activated a screen across the room on the wall.

About a half hour later, Astrid came into the den. She had a towel wrapped around her hips and her hair tied up in another towel. Mac had swiveled in the chair and was looking out the window while he talked on the phone.

Astrid asked, "Who are you talking to?"

"My mom," he replied as he turned toward her.

"Oh, Mac, I'm sorry," she said looking at his black eye.

"Mom, Astrid is here." He paused and then said to Astrid, "Mom wants to talk to you," handing her the phone.

Astrid sat on Daniels' lap and took the phone. "Mom," said Astrid, as she always called Marie Daniels, "How are you and Dad?"

Fifteen minutes later, she hung up. "Your mom wants us to come up for the Fourth of July weekend. She said the whole family would be there, Aunt Sarah, Uncle Tony and Aunt Marilyn. Sounds like fun. What do you say?"

"Sounds good to me. I had planned to run up and see them. So after our meeting let's drive up to the shore and spend a few days."

She thought about that and said, "You go up and I'll come back here. I need to spend some time at the office. I'll be up in five or six days in time for the long Fourth weekend."

"We can stay longer. You know Mom and Dad love you and would be thrilled to have us around for a while. Let's see what I can work out with the admiral. After all, I am a naval officer in the employ of the CIA."

She kissed him. "I'm glad—you know I was right."

"Yes, dear."

"You two decent?" came Viv's voice from the hall. "I have coffee."

Astrid adjusted her towel to cover her breasts.

"Come on in, Vivian," yelled Mac.

Vivian walked into the den and stopped. Astrid was still sitting on Mac's lap, and both were dressed only in towels. "You two need some privacy?"

"No, Viv, we need some coffee," said Mac.

"Here's your coffee. What happened to your eye, Mac?"

He took a sip of coffee, and then said, "Would you believe a tennis ball?'

"No."

"Door knob?"

"No."

"Astrid punched me."

Viv thought about that for a second. "Possible, but not very likely. Never mind."

"Enough," said Astrid. "If you must know, I hit him. We're flying up to Washington for a meeting, and then I'll be back here tonight. I need to spend some time at the office. Mac's going to his parents' shore house."

"I'll set up a series of meetings with the division heads for tomorrow. Things are fine here."

"Thanks, Viv."

"I have some mail for you to go over. Why don't you get dressed and come down stairs," said Viv referring to Astrid's office.

Viv left them. Astrid went into the bedroom to dress and Mac played with the keyboard, turning on the screen to check on the news. He was still on the computer when Astrid came out dressed in shorts and a tee shirt. She kissed him and went to the elevator.

Mac yelled as Astrid stepped into the elevator, "Watch your time. It's nine-thirty and we have to be at the airport by noon."

"I'll be up in an hour. It won't take me long to dress."

At eleven, Astrid was dressed in a blue dress and Mac was in his summer whites, shoes, pants, jacket, and hat. They took the elevator to the rooftop where the helicopter was ready to take them to the airport. Astrid looked at Mac and beamed. She was so proud of him and he was so handsome in his dress whites. She put her arm through his and walked to the helicopter.

CHAPTER 68

HARTSFIELD–JACKSON ATLANTA INTERNATIONAL AIRPORT

It was a fifteen-minute helicopter ride from the downtown office building to the Hartsfield-Jackson Atlanta International Airport. The helicopter put down next to the parked Citation at General Aviation. Standing in the doorway of the Citation was co-pilot Lisa Geluso. Daniels stepped out of the helicopter and extended a hand to help Astrid. Holding his cap under his arm in an effort to fight the rotor wash, he led Astrid toward the Citation. Lisa stepped off the Citation onto the apron and was followed by Admiral Charko, who was also in his dress white uniform.

When Daniels saw Charko in uniform, he quickly saluted. The admiral returned the salute and extended his hand. "Glad to see you, Mac. Who hit you?"

Daniels shook his head. "It's a long story."

The admiral nodded to Astrid. "I'm pleased you're well, Astrid. Wanda was worried about you," he said, referring to his wife.

"Thank you. To be truthful, at times I was worried about myself, too. Please give my best wishes to Wanda. I hope I have a chance to see the both of you on a social occasion."

Astrid and Mac climbed the few steps to the Citation and took seats. Lisa raised the stairs and locked the door. She said, "As soon as we're airborne if you need something I'll be happy to get it. Bak Johansen is the pilot in command."

Johansen radioed the ground control for permission to taxi and the Citation's two Rolls-Royce engines were spooling up. The Citation began to roll. In a few minutes, they were airborne. Lisa came back to the cabin and asked if anyone needed anything. Daniels took something from his pocket and handed it to her.

"You dropped this," he said.

Looking at her credit card, she thanked him and returned to the cockpit.

Astrid said to Charko, "It's been a long time since I've seen you in uniform. You look very handsome."

"Don't believe her, Admiral, she says that to all the boys in white. She goes crazy for the ice cream man."

"You're jealous, Mac," said Charko. Turning to Astrid he said, "As a retired Naval officer I may wear my uniform, provided it conforms to the same standards of appearance as prescribed for active duty members. Retirees are authorized to wear the appropriate uniform prescribed at the date of retirement or one of the uniforms currently authorized for active duty personnel, including the dress uniform. And since the president requested some type of formality and he requested that I wear it, I did."

"So what's the occasion, Admiral? Am I being court-martialed or shot?"

"I suspect neither, although I would highly recommend long-term psychiatric care for you. I'm not sure what the president has in mind, and I'm sure we'll find out when we get to the White House. I have a question for you, Lieutenant Commander."

Daniels knew when Charko addressed him as Lieutenant Commander it usually meant that he was in trouble. The only problem, thought Daniels, was in trouble for what. He knew he had broken so many rules in the last several weeks he just wasn't sure what he'd done this time.

"Would you please explain to me how you ended up in Papeete without anyone being able to track you? Hell it's the capital of French Polynesia. Two weeks in Papeete and no record of you there. Share your secret, please."

Astrid started to speak. "We weren't in Papeete for two weeks, Admiral. We were . . ."

Daniels interrupted Astrid. "Excuse me, Astrid. I think I'd better deal with this. You don't want the admiral or the president getting mad at you. Since it's entirely my doing and my fault I'll explain."

"Go on, Mac, I know this is going to be interesting."

"Well, Admiral, I stayed in Seoul for a few days with Astrid until she was ready to travel. While I was waiting I had the Annie . . ."

"Annie?"

"Yes, sir, the Annie, the An-2 we borrowed from the North Koreans."

"Don't you mean stole?" asked Charko.

"No, sir. Borrowed—someday I intend to return it. I'm just not sure when. Anyway, I had it painted blue and white, then I added a few tail numbers, and I hopped from place to place, island to island, until we got to Bora Bora and that's where we stayed for most of the time. Before you ask, Astrid's friend Lexye made the arrangements for all the hotels and charged everything to one of her companies, that is one of her foreign companies and she emailed Astrid the bill, which I'll be submitting for reimbursement . . ."

"Reimbursement! Are you nuts? Since when does the agency pay for vacation and gas for your Annie?"

"Just the hotel and food not the gas . . ."

"That's big of you."

I charged the fuel to Lisa's credit card. I knew you would be tracking Astrid's and mine so I took Lisa's. She didn't give it to me. I took it. She had nothing to do with this.

When we flew out of Faaa International Airport in Papeete on Air Tahiti Nui to Los Angeles, I charged that on my company credit card. By the way, the Annie is tied down at Faaa International under Lisa's card. You might want to pick it up. "

"Can you give me one good reason why I should reimburse you?"

"How about the $50 million the agency picked up, not to mention the two hundred thousand Euros that I was paid for my services by the Supreme Leader? A few more missions like this and I'll help balance your budget."

"What am I going to do with you, Daniels?" asked Charko rhetorically. Then he smiled, "You're worth it, this time. Send the bills to me. I'll see that they're paid, this time. No more, do you understand?"

"Yes, sir."

Astrid just smiled. The rest of the trip was small talk, no business and soon the Citation landed at Joint Base Andrews. Waiting for them was the black Suburban with two Secret Service agents.

CHAPTER 69

THE WHITE HOUSE
SITUATION ROOM

The Suburban pulled up to the side entrance of the White House. The two Secret Service agents jumped out, opening the rear doors. Charko exited first, followed by Astrid and then by Daniels. As they approached the side entrance door under the portico, Tim Harris, the president's special assistant, stepped out to greet them. Harris had been the voice of President Hunt during most of Hunt's second term. A lawyer by training, he was recognized as the one person who could field the hard questions and come up with the right answers. He was wearing one of his trademark custom suits with his handmade British shirt displaying his initials on the left cuff right below his cufflinks.

Following the appropriate protocol, Harris addressed Charko first. "Good to see you again, Admiral, and welcome to the White House Mr. Daniels. We have never had the pleasure of meeting before. The president speaks of you often."

"Does he talk about the firing squad for me?"

Harris thought for a second and smiled. "That's hard to answer. If I say yes, well you can figure the rest out, but if I say no, you can only assume he doesn't discuss the firing squad with me. Perhaps I should object to the form of the question. It's a leading question."

"I thought you could ask leading questions of a hostile witness," replied Daniels.

"Please, Mr. Daniels, I'm not hostile, however, if you insist, he has not discussed with me your firing squad, but perhaps he has discussed it with others."

Turning to Astrid, "I know you've been to the White House on several occasions during the prior administration, but allow me to be the first to welcome you to the White House on behalf of President David Hunt."

"Thank you, Mr. Harris. I'm looking forward to my visit."

They followed Harris through the door and through the metal detector. Astrid placed her purse on the belt for the x-ray machine. They then followed Harris down the hall toward the elevator, where he stopped and said, "Miss Reed, would you be kind enough to follow me? We will go to the president's private conference room off the Oval Office until he finishes with a meeting. He should be up within a half hour. Gentlemen you are wanted in the Situation Room. I will have someone escort you downstairs. After your meeting you will join Miss Reed and the president in the Oval Office."

Harris signaled for a Secret Service agent to escort Charko and Daniels to the Situation Room. Waiting for them inside the Situation Room was General Tony Bellardi, Frank Green, Al Clancy, Mike Bertone, Maud Evens, and Dr. Cornaci.

When Daniels entered the room, everyone stood up and started to applaud except for Maud Evens. As Daniels approached the conference table, they gathered around him, shaking his hands, and giving him slaps on the back. When he came to his uncle, General Bellardi, he gave him a bear hug and a kiss on the cheek.

"Am I glad to see you," said Bellardi. "Mac, you gotta stop this shit, you're fucking crazy and you're making the rest of us nuts, too. Who the hell hit you?"

Daniels shook his head, "It's a long story," he said. Then he took a seat directly across from Evens. Next to her on her left was Director Green, and on his left was Secretary Clancy, and on his left was Director Bertone. Next to Daniels, on his right, was Director Cornaci, on his right was Admiral Charko, and to his right was General Bellardi. The seat at the head of the table was left empty for the president.

"Mac, I have something for you," said Charko. "I've been waiting to give this to you. Something you really deserve." He handed Daniels a bag of popcorn.

Daniels let Charko explain to the rest of the room what it meant.

The door opened and the president entered the room. Everyone stood up. The president took his seat at the head of the table and said, "Please be seated." Turning to Daniels, he offered his hand saying, "I understand we owe you a very big thank you. Unfortunately, no one will ever know what you did, but on behalf of all Americans, I do thank you. I'm anxious to get the full report. Then I'd like you to go upstairs with me to the Oval Office as I have something to say to Miss Reed."

Daniels was glad that the president didn't ask about his black eye.

Dr. Cornaci spoke first. "Mister President, everyone in this room has the highest security clearances but what we're about to discuss can never leave this room, even to others who have high security clearances. We know there's a traitor working for the other side. Which side we're not sure, but working against us. I've ordered the inspector general of our agency to investigate, and according to procedures we've turned over all the information to Director Bertone for his investigation. We haven't found out who this traitor is, however, Director Bertone is actively investigating the matter. So until we find out who this traitor is, this conversation absolutely must be confined to this room and the people in here. Other than Admiral Charko and General Bellardi, no one else has all the pieces of this puzzle. Even at Langley, those who worked on this only know certain parts. This is that sensitive, that secretive, that we must be protected at all cost. When Mac tells you the story you'll understand."

The president looked around the table. "Maud, Frank, Mike, Al are we all on the same page?"

Everyone agreed. The president turned to Daniels. "Please tell me what happened."

"Mister President, with all due respect to you sir, and everyone sitting around this table, I will leave out of my report certain names because there are people right now whose lives are on the line and they are living in a most tenuous of circumstances. I need to protect them. You'll understand what happened without all the names. I hope that is acceptable, sir. No disrespect meant to you or anyone here."

"That's fair, Commander Daniels, I have no problem with that."

Daniels did not want to correct the president. He was not a commander but a lieutenant commander. He didn't want the president to think he was insulting him, so he let it go.

"Well, sir, everyone knows the Reagan participated in the war games and not a shot or missile was fired. The Supreme Leader was satisfied with my explanations and the backup I provided him proved it. I told him there was a traitor in his government who was responsible for the uranium being switched. I explained that there was a ten million Euro payment. In order to prove this to him, we had some fancy wire transfers and created a bank account for Director Jang Min, the head of the nuclear program. When the Supreme Leader saw the account and the money, he was convinced he had been betrayed. As you may or may not know, Jang Min has been executed for treason and his family is in a labor camp. The first deputy, Shin Soo, is now in charge of the nuclear program and there is a new first deputy, Moon Il-Sung."

Daniels paused and then continued, "I'm pleased to tell you that their nuclear program has been reorganized and we now have someone working for us on the miniaturization program. As you know, their long-range missile has poor tracking capabilities and cannot fly with a heavy load and without this miniaturization program they're not able to deliver nuclear weapons."

Evens interrupted "Who is this person that's working for us in the program and for what agency does he work?" she asked.

Daniels looked at her and didn't answer. He just stared, his dark eyes focused in on hers until she looked away.

"Is the name necessary, Miss Evens?" Charko asked and answered his own question. "I don't think so. Point being, through Mac's efforts we've set back their nuclear program by years. We've depleted their weapons-grade uranium, which will take years to produce and the terrorist groups are a bit wary of buying products from the North Koreans because they really wonder whether there was an accident and is their uranium at the bottom of the sea or still in North Korean vaults."

Daniels continued, "We managed to discover the names of two spies here in D.C. and that information was turned over to Director Bertone. The third person, Amr Ibn Taher is a Saudi, born in Al-Ahsa in Saudi Arabia's Eastern Province. He is known to the agency and we are working on finding him. I understand from the Admiral that Ibn Taher is a recruiter, and I believe he works for Aswas Rajul."

Bertone spoke in a soft voice. Prior to being appointed director of the FBI by the former president, he was the U.S. Attorney for the Southern District of New York.

"Mr. Daniels provided us with the names, Aswas Rajul and Ki-Young Park, the owner of The Round Table Restaurant here in Washington. Park is the head operative for the North Korean Reconnaissance General Bureau (RGB), which you all know is responsible for clandestine operations. From the information that was provided to us by Mac we know that he was working either with or for this Aswas Rajul."

"Holy shit," exclaimed Director Green. "Secretary Clancy and I eat there often."

"I think we all do," said Bertone.

"I don't," said Evens with a big smile.

Under his breath Bellardi said, "Fuck you."

Charko nudged him with his elbow as if to agree with his comment.

Bertone went on. "We have court-ordered wiretaps and listening devices in Park's home and business and he is under twenty-four-hour surveillance. Since Mac's return from Korea, we've been getting a lot of traffic from and to him. But I'm sorry to say nothing on Aswas Rajul. We can't find anything, and the other agencies have nothing either. We believe he is an American, a home-grown terrorist, but highly sophisticated— not a bomb maker but a planner. We believe that his name is a cover. It's Arabic for "brave man." In Osama bin Laden's papers and on his computer there was reference to this Rajul but that's all we have so far."

The room was quiet until the president spoke. "What is your plan?"

"When the time is right I'm going to drop in on him," said Daniels. "I'm going to offer him a job with us. I'll explain the benefits of working for us rather than in some maximum-security prison. I'm going to be the good cop."

Daniels paused for a moment. "I want him to give me Rajul."

Bertone went on, "Mac, your efforts have been invaluable. Thank you."

Daniels continued, "I intercepted a ship, and I managed to turn the surviving crew into agents for us."

The president interrupted him. "You intercepted a ship by yourself?"

"Well, not quite by myself. My pilot flew me over the ship and I jumped onto it."

The president looked at him as if he didn't believe him. He asked, "You parachuted from a plane onto a moving ship in the middle of the ocean? What would have happened if you missed?"

"Swim, Mister President," said Bellardi.

They all laughed.

"I gave the captain three choices. I told him I could sink the ship and put the crew in lifeboats, or I could sink the ship with him and his crew on board, or he could work with us. The captain and the crew decided to work for us."

Evens interrupted again. "You trust him?"

"Yes, Miss Evens, I trust them. When I was on the ship, the captain helped me and he gave me several bits of information that helped me through this mission. Believe me, I trust him."

Evens didn't stop, "If you trust them, we have reports that ISIS has North Korean surface-to-air missiles that were actually delivered by your captain. Why didn't you stop the shipment? Don't you think you're putting our pilots in danger?"

Daniels let out a sigh. "No."

Evens continued, "What about the sarin?"

Bellardi jumped in, "Ms. Evens, for your information those missiles are useless. If you check your DIA reports, you'll see that several of them blew up on the launch pad, killing many of the ISIS soldiers. Many of the missiles had no guidance system and could not lock onto any of our planes. They actually fell back to the earth harmlessly or landed in ISIS territory, killing more of their soldiers. ISIS is really wondering whether or not to buy more equipment from the North Koreans. They have no patience for defects."

She looked surprised. "I hadn't received that report."

"It was a DIA report that was circulated," retorted Bellardi.

"How did all the missiles become defective?" she queried.

"Well," replied Daniels, "when the captain and the crew agreed to work for us, General Bellardi contacted Pacific Command and the USS Cheyenne popped up, forgive the pun, you know the Cheyenne is a submarine, and some of its crew boarded the ship, did some maintenance work on the missiles, and neutralized the sarin. That's why I let the ship go. Now we have agents working for us who will report their movements, and depending what's on the ship we can take appropriate action."

Cornaci spoke "Mister President, in a nutshell, we set back the North Korean nuclear program due to a lack of weapons-grade uranium, and the miniaturization program will not go forward quickly. We caused a major rift between the North Koreans and their customers, we picked up the names of two spies, and we have new agents inside. All in all, it was a very successful and very dangerous mission that ended without a loss of our officers or agents."

The president looked at Daniels "Commander, how did you get out?"

Daniels was quiet for a moment. "Mister President, the short answer is General Bellardi had one of his agents pick me up and get me to Seoul. The details are not important and would be very upsetting. Suffice it to say many people died."

The president nodded his head, and then asked, "Now what is your position with the North Koreans? I understand you're working for them."

"I don't know as of yet. I have to do some inquiry. When I figure it out whether or not I'm alive or dead as far as they're concerned, I will act appropriately and accordingly."

The president had noticed the bag in front of Daniels and finally asked, "May I ask what's in the bag?"

"Popcorn."

"Popcorn?"

"Yes sir. Would you like some?"

The president reached over, put his hand in the bag, and took out some popcorn. "Thank you."

Daniels popped a few pieces in his mouth, turned to Charko, and said, "Thank you for saving me some popcorn. I appreciate it, Admiral."

The president stood and everyone else stood. Addressing the room, he said, "Thank you all for attending. I appreciate your efforts, and please keep up the good work. Frank and Mike, please keep me in the loop on this Rajul. Let's put him away." He was about to leave but turned around, looked at Daniels, and started to clap. Everyone else started to clap too, and so did Maud Evens.

Turning to Daniels the president said, "Let's get up to the Oval Office. Miss Reed is waiting for us, and we have some more business to conduct."

Bellardi, Cornaci, Chaco, and Daniels all stood and followed the president.

CHAPTER 70

THE OVAL OFFICE, THE WHITE HOUSE

The president's Oval Office is just that, an oval-shaped room. At one end of the oval is the Resolute desk, a large, nineteenth-century partners' desk that was a gift from Queen Victoria to President Rutherford B. Hayes in 1880. It received the name "Resolute" because it was built from the timbers of the British Arctic Exploration ship, Resolute. It was Jackie Kennedy who first brought the desk into the Oval Office in 1961 for President Kennedy. It was removed from the White House only once, after the assassination of President Kennedy in 1963, when President Johnson allowed the desk to go on a traveling exhibition with the Kennedy Presidential Library. President Carter brought it back to the Oval Office, where all the presidents used it except Bush 41, who kept it in the private residence.

At the opposite end of the room, directly across from the Resolute desk were two armchairs, and between the armchairs and the desk were two couches, one on each side of an oval-shaped coffee table. The president leaned against the desk and directed the men to be seated on the couch. Charko and Cornaci were on one couch and Bellardi and Daniels were on the other. The president remained standing.

"I have several questions," he said. "First, how did you get that black eye? It looks fresh."

Bellardi and Charko looked at him; it was the same question they had asked.

"This is embarrassing, especially in front of General Bellardi. You know sir, he's my uncle."

"Yes, Commander, it is a well-known fact. I believe his loyalty and love for you caused him to tell the secretary of state to go fuck himself," replied the president.

"Uncle Tony, you used the "F" word?"

"I'm going to use it again if you don't answer the president."

"Oh well, Astrid Reed punched me. She was shadow boxing and my face got in the way."

"I knew it," said Bellardi. "Why can't you two kids be normal, like holding hands. Wait till I tell your mother," he said with a laugh, which caused everybody to laugh, even Daniels.

"Now," said the president. "Tell me why you said that the North Korean miniaturization program will not go forward quickly."

"When we started this mission we had two purposes; one was to deplete the weapons-grade uranium to prevent the manufacture of more nuclear weapons. We believe they have only three or four bombs. We also wanted to disrupt the miniaturization program. Their missiles can't carry the nuclear payload. So they need to shrink the payload."

The president nodded, and then said, "I thought they had an intercontinental ballistic missile."

Daniels continued, "Not quite sir. The KN08, which is their ICBM, has not been tested. It was made public on the 100th anniversary of Kim Il Sung, at a military parade. However, an analysis of the photographs that we have seen showed it to be a mockup. It is a fake."

Charko jumped in, "They have one medium-range and two mid-range missiles. The Rodong is a medium-range missile and the Taepodong-1 and Taepodong-2 are mid-range missiles. The Rodong can easily hit Japan and the Taepodong could reach the West Coast. But they can't carry their current size nuclear weapons."

"So," said Daniels, "our plan was to leak information regarding the switch through Chinese sources. We expected a purge of the personnel at the nuclear program. We also had the ability to set up a few key players with disinformation—a deception. Whoever leaked the fact that we had their uranium threw a wrench into the works. We managed to create a deception that was magical and when Kim saw that Director Jang Min had a secret bank account, we knew what would happen to him and his family. The new first deputy Moon Il-Sung works for us and is in charge of the miniaturization program. As long as we can keep him safe, the program will drag its feet and we can be one step ahead. That's why, Mister President, I did not reveal his name. Only you and the four of us know his name. Someone high up who must have clearance blew our original story. That's why we have to find Aswas Rajul—to get to the traitor."

"Fascinating. How about we get Miss Reed in here? She's with Tim Harris in the Oval Office dining room. He gave me notice that he is returning to the practice of law. I'm going to lose one of my best."

Through a small corridor off the Oval Office is the Oval Office Dining Room. It is the room the President uses as a small office or to have a casual meal.

The president picked up his phone and asked that Astrid Reed be shown in. A few minutes later, there was a knock on the door and Harris and Astrid Reed came in.

"Welcome, Miss Reed. I am sorry to have kept you. Come, please sit down."

The president led her to the armchairs across from his desk and sat down next to her.

"Not a problem at all, Mister President. I had a lovely chat with Tim and a very good cup of coffee. Thank you. I've been here before but never in that private dining room. I enjoyed the artwork too, especially the painting of Abraham Lincoln with General Grant, Major General Sherman, and Admiral Porter with Lincoln sitting holding his chin in his hand listening to his generals. Interesting that the painting is called *The Peacemakers*."

"You know your art, Miss Reed. Many of my critics think I should listen more to my generals. What do you think?"

"Do I have to answer that? How about I pass the question off to my new director of news, Tim Harris."

"What! Tim? Congratulations," said the president. "I didn't know you two knew each other."

"We didn't, Mister President," said Harris. "We just met and after talking, Miss Reed made me an offer I couldn't refuse. Director of News and my own show, *The Wolf's Den*."

"Will I get a fair shot, Tim?"

"Miss Reed promised me academic freedom. Do what I want and say what I want. I'm looking forward to this. Looks like I'm not getting back to the law office any time soon. I'll stay with you as I promised until Congress goes on summer recess."

"Wonderful," said the President. Turning to Astrid he said, "You have a good man there. Miss Reed, on behalf of all Americans I want to thank you for what you did. You helped keep the peace and probably prevented a war. I have a request, if possible; please run that documentary you made over there. You can tell the world that the questions were scripted but it is important that Kim knows you are trying to show us a better side. Just maybe we can break down the barrier without force or arms."

"I intend to run it, Mister President, for many reasons."

The president and the entire group spoke for about fifteen more minutes and finally the president said to Astrid. "You know why I asked you here?"

"Yes, Mr. President I do," she said with a big smile.

"General, if you will," asked the president.

"My pleasure, Mister President."

Bellardi stood up, and barked, "Room. Attention."

All the military men jumped to attention. Cornaci and Harris rose to their feet. Astrid opened her purse and took out two shoulder boards. She stood in front of Daniels and smiled at him. She reached up to his shoulders, unpinned his lieutenant commander boards, which were three gold bands; two bands surrounding a thin band, and replaced them with new boards of a commander, three gold bands of the same size.

"I am so proud of you," she said, and she handed him his silver oak leaf; the insignia of a commander, replacing the gold oak leaf insignia of a lieutenant commander. "Commander Daniels, congratulations on your promotion. I love you."

Daniels took it, smiled, and kissed Astrid. "Thanks, Astrid, this is a surprise and I do love you."

"Congratulations, Commander," said the president. There were echoes of congratulation and handshakes.

The president asked, "You never corrected me when I called you Commander. Why?"

"I didn't want to correct you in front of everyone, sir. If you ever call me Admiral, I'll just smile."

"Now Miss Reed, your turn." The president had a box on his desk and he picked it up. As he opened it he said, "On behalf of the citizens of this great country, I am proud and pleased to present you with the Presidential Medal of Freedom. This is the highest civilian award of the United States. It recognizes those individuals who have made a meritorious contribution to the security or national interests of the United States, world peace, cultural, or other significant public or private endeavors. Congratulations."

They shook hands. He held up the badge.

The badge of the Presidential Medal of Freedom is in the form of a golden star with white and red enamel. In the center of the star is a disc with thirteen gold stars on a blue enamel background. A golden American bald eagle with spread wings stands between the points of the star. The medal is worn around the neck on a blue ribbon with white-edged stripes.

The president placed the ribbon around her neck. "This is for what you did in Korea, but Tim's assignment will be to document and issue a press release for your efforts in world peace and your significant public endeavors."

"I don't know what to say."

"Say thank you, babe," said Daniels.

Astrid turned to the president and said, "Thank you, babe."

That got a laugh out of everyone.

"Actually," said Bellardi, "you got the award for giving Mac that black eye. That's something many people have tried to do."

"Mac, you told on me."

"I was ordered to speak," answered Daniels, "a presidential order."

"I have several meetings," said the president, "Tim will show you out. Thank you both for what you have done. God bless you."

They all began to leave and the president said, "Just one more minute, Commander. Is it true you managed to get into the White House and serve my predecessor breakfast in bed?"

With a big smile Daniels said, "Mister President, Yogi Berra once said, 'I didn't say all the things I said,' and I didn't do all the things I did."

CHAPTER 71

MANTOLOKING, NEW JERSEY

Mantoloking is situated on one of the barrier islands, in Ocean County, New Jersey. It is less than four hundred yards wide, in most parts, separating the Atlantic Ocean on the east from Barnegat Bay on the west. The township has a total permanent population of 296, although the summer population is approximately 5,000. The main street is Highway 35, dividing Mantoloking down the middle. Driving from the north, highway 35 is only two lanes wide; north and southbound. In other parts of New Jersey, route 35 is a highway but down the shore, it is the "Main Street" of many shore communities. In the summer time, it is quicker to walk than to drive on Highway 35. Many houses in Mantoloking are of the shingle style and seashore colonial designs with cedar shakes and white trim. Mantoloking is considered part of the Jersey Shore's "Gold Coast." The name Mantoloking is derived from the language of the Lenni Lenape Indians who once inhabited New Jersey. It means "land of beautiful sunsets."

The Daniels home is on the Atlantic Ocean side of 35, set back off the road. The front of the property is lined with a neatly trimmed, high hedge. The driveway is in the center of the property, cut through the hedges. The driveway is composed of sand and crushed seashells. Off the sides of the circular driveway are parking aprons. The house is multi-level with front and rear porches. The front porch is lined with wicker rocking chairs. The family would sit there, and enjoy watching the beautiful sunsets over the bay. The back porch was also lined with rocking chairs, overlooking the ocean. Daniels and his father would have their morning coffee watching the beautiful sunrise. The back porch opened to the beach and down to the ocean.

It was seven-thirty when Daniels drove the agency Suburban, the admiral had arranged for him, into the driveway. He climbed up the five steps to the porch. Looking around the porch, he saw that nothing had changed. Everything was there in the same place as it had been last year. He lifted the flowerpot and laughed; the house key was there. He decided against letting himself in. Instead, he rang the bell and he could soon hear his mother coming.

The door opened. Marie Daniels let out a scream of joy. Mac Daniels picked his mother up. She yelled, "Bob, Mackenzie is home. Bob."

Bob Daniels came running. He grabbed his son and hugged him. The three of them stood there for a while just holding each other.

"What happened to your eye? Come inside," said Bob Daniels. Looking around, he asked, "Where's your gear, son?"

"My eye, Dad, is a long story—my gear is being sent over. I'm sure Mom still has some of my clothes in my room. How about some food? I'm starved. Been on the road for three-and-a-half hours."

Bob Daniels spotted the new shoulder boards. "Congratulations, Commander. When did that come through?"

"Today."

"How nice," said his mother. "You two go sit on the back porch and I'll make something for you to eat. Dad and I ate supper already. Why didn't you call? How long are you home for, Mackenzie?"

"Beer, son?" asked his father.

"Sure, Dad," Mac answered. "Mom, I just got in, and I'll be here at least through the Fourth of July and maybe a few days longer. Astrid is coming up."

His father grabbed a couple of beers and went out the back door. Mac was on the beach looking over the ocean. His father joined him and handed him a beer. "How have you been, son?"

"Well, I'm feeling fine and looking forward to doing a little fishing with you."

"Me too. I'm glad you're home for a while. How's Ron doing?"

"He's well. Maybe we can run over and visit with him and Cathy."

They talked for a while until they heard his mother call, "Come and get it."

When they were sitting down, his mother said, "Where's your ship parked?"

"Mom, parked? It's docked and it's not a ship, it's a boat. Submarines are called boats."

Daniels' mother believed he was a submariner, which explained his long absences and lack of communications.

"Well, ship or boat, parked or docked, whatever, you should transfer out into a better job. You go away for six months, and we have no way of reaching you when you're underwater. When I see your commanding officer, I'm going tell him what I think."

"Well, I was thinking about joining NASA. Hey Dad, can you call me when I'm my way to Mars?"

"Oh, Mackenzie," his mother said, leaning over and giving him a kiss. "I'm so glad you're home. How is Astrid?"

CHAPTER 72

MANTOLOKING, NEW JERSEY

TEN DAYS LATER, FRIDAY, JULY 1

Astrid had called. She was in New Jersey. She arranged for a car service and was on her way to the shore house. It was 11:30 and everyone in the Daniels' household was asleep except for Mac, who sat on the front porch in the rocking chair, waiting for Astrid. He was trying to enjoy the evening and looking forward to seeing her.

There was a lot of traffic on Southbound 35. It seemed as if the whole world was coming to the shore for the July Fourth weekend. It had become a standing tradition with his family and Mac enjoyed it. He hoped the weather would be nice and Astrid and he would spend some time at the beach. Monday would be the parade. Every year whenever possible they went to the parade. His mother insisted that his father wear his uniform, and Astrid would insist that Mac wear his dress whites.

He saw the lights turning into the driveway. It was Astrid. He got up and went downstairs to meet her. The car stopped at the foot of the steps, and the driver ran around to open the door for his passenger. Astrid got out of the car and ran into Mac's arms. There was a long kiss and embrace.

The driver finally said, "Excuse me, what about the luggage?"

Mac said, "Leave it, I'll take it in. Thank you very much."

As the car pulled out of the driveway, Mac followed Astrid up the steps, suitcases in hand. "Why all the luggage? You're only staying for a few days, aren't you?"

"I don't know. I might stay all summer. I like it here and I love your parents."

"Aunt Sarah's here."

"Great, how is she?"

"She's fine and she never changes. I'm sure she'll start in on us over breakfast."

"Oh, Mac," she said. "Come on, let's put this in the room and go down to the beach. I have much to tell you, and wait till you see what I bought."

Mac and Astrid went upstairs to his bedroom where he dropped the suitcases on the bed. Astrid quickly got undressed and grabbed a towel, wrapping it around her.

He said, "I thought we were going to the beach?"

"We are, come on."

He just shook his head, stripped down, and grabbed the towel, following her down the stairs, out the back door, and down to the beach. The minute Astrid felt the sand beneath her feet she started to run. As Mac followed, his towel began to fall off. He wondered why the woman's towel never fell. As they got closer to the water's edge Astrid dropped her towel, and that brought a smile to Mac's face. He dropped his and followed her into the water.

"It's cold," he said

"It's great," she said.

For about ten minutes, they played in the water and then walked up the beach to the white dry sand. They lay down on the towels and began to kiss.

Mac heard the sounds behind him getting louder. Someone was coming. Standing around, balls naked, was not the best way to enter into a fight. Then he heard that distinctive laugh.

"Mac, what are you doing," asked Aunt Sarah.

Quickly wrapping themselves in the towels Mac and Astrid stood up.

"Did I interrupt something?"

"No," snorted Mac.

"Aunt Sarah," yelled Astrid, throwing her arms around her. "How are you?"

Mac shook his head; he knew where this was going.

"Come on in the house, kids, I'll make some tea and we can have cake."

Sarah and Astrid locked arms and started to walk toward the house. Mac stood there for a second. "Tea and cake, Aunt Sarah?" he said to himself. "I had something else in mind."

"Are you coming?" asked Sarah.

"Don't mind him," said Astrid. "He gets that way."

NEXT DAY, SATURDAY, JULY 2

Daniels opened his eyes and looked at the clock; it was almost eight, time to get up. Astrid was still sleeping, her head on his chest, her long legs over his. "Astrid," he said in a soft voice, "rise and shine."

Opening her eyes, she smiled. "What time is it?"

"Time to get up. I can smell the coffee and I'm sure Aunt Sarah will be here in a few minutes."

Astrid kicked the sheet off her and sat up in bed. She was naked. He looked at her, but before he could say anything, there was a knock on the door.

"You kids up?" They heard Sarah's voice.

"Hold on, Aunt Sarah," yelled Astrid.

Astrid grabbed Mac's boxer shorts and put them on with his tee shirt. Her clothes were still packed. She flipped him a bathing suit and went to the door. "Come on in," she said to Sarah, who entered with two cups of coffee. "Perfect, just what the doctor ordered," said Astrid.

"Aunt Sarah, did you ever think we might want to be alone?" asked Daniels.

Before Sarah could answer, Astrid said, "Ignore him, he's a sailor."

"Marie and Bob are anxious to see you," said Sarah, "and Uncle Tony and Aunt Marilyn will be here shortly. Marie is making a big breakfast. We can all eat on the back porch and you, Mac, can run in the ocean and cool off your jets, or testosterone, but Astrid and I have much to talk about and it is certainly not about you. See you two downstairs."

Sarah turned and left.

Mac stood there shaking his head.

"I love her, Mac."

"So do I, so do I. How about you put on a bathing suit and get out of my shorts. My mother might figure something out. And don't put on that dental floss, postage stamp thing you call a bathing suit. Just a normal bikini and no thong. Christ, you'll send my dad and Uncle Tony into cardiac arrest."

Mac placed her suitcase on the bed, and Astrid unzipped it, opened it, and fumbled around for a moment. She threw off his shirt and he put in on. She dropped the boxer shorts and pulled something out of the suitcase. Daniels could not see what she had.

Standing there naked, she said, "I have something to show you."

"That's an understatement."

She pulled out a Chiappa Rhino and held it up.

Daniels immediately recognized the weapon, pushing the barrel away from himself. "Never point a gun, Astrid. What in good God's name are you doing with a 357 Rhino? Christ, this is one very powerful hand gun."

"I want you to know I have a license for this. After what we've been through, I decided it's better to carry."

"First of all, your license is no good in Jersey. So for the time being I'm going to hold on to this. Second, we'll go to the range, to be sure you know how to use it. When you shoot a weapon, you have to know your target and what's beyond your target, just in case you miss. But, honey, this gun will go right through me and through the wall and through the next wall. This is serious firepower. So for now, let's put it away, enjoy your weekend and perhaps we'll go to the range later."

The doorbell rang.

"It must be Uncle Tony and Aunt Marilyn."

A few minutes later, Astrid and Mac joined the family on the back porch. There were hugs and kisses. They all loved Astrid as much as she loved them. Marie Daniels had her usual family spread, eggs, with all the assorted meats, pancakes, toast, and her famous coffee cake.

"Mom," said Astrid, "your coffee cake is delicious. Dad, how do you stay so slim, with all this food?"

"Let's not talk about weight," said Marilyn, looking at her husband who tipped the scales at 250 pounds. Everyone laughed.

"Let's change the subject," said Tony. "Astrid, one question, if I may, what does a beautiful girl like you see in this?" pointing at Mac.

Before she could answer Mac blurted out, "What do you mean? She has a tattoo on her butt that says, 'Hi sailor.'"

They all laughed.

"Well, to tell you the truth, Uncle Tony, it's the good home cooking and it's an excuse to see all of you. You are my favorite uncle—sorry Aunt Marilyn."

"Honey, give me the three dollars, I paid for the license and you can have him. When I married that jarhead, he was so poor I paid for the license."

"Best three bucks you ever spent," said Tony.

Marilyn smiled. Astrid reached under the table, grabbed Mac's hand, and gave it a squeeze. She was home and she was happy.

Mac looked around the table and smiled.

"What are you two up to, today?" asked Marie.

"It doesn't look like a beach day, so I'm taking Annie Oakley here to the shooting range. She just purchased a new handgun."

"What did she buy?" asked Bob Daniels.

"A .357 Rhino."

"Holy shit, Astrid, that's a cannon. Don't piss her off, Mac," said Tony. "Pass the coffee cake."

■ ■ ■

NEXT DAY, SUNDAY, JULY 3

Sunday morning, after breakfast, Tony and Mac were huddled in the den. Tony held the package of papers. The phone interrupted their conversation. From the hall, Mac heard his mother say, "It's for you, Tony."

Tony picked up the phone in the den. It was Colonel Denton Starges, his chief of staff.

Starges wasted no time. "Ki-Young Park is dead."

"What happened?"

"One of his employees at the restaurant went nuts and shot him to death. When the police came, the shooter killed himself."

"Is it linked to what happened in North Korea?"

"No. I think it's linked to Rajul," answered Starges. "The killer called out 'God is great.' The Feds are on it but jurisdiction for murder is with the D.C. police."

"Speak with you later."

"One more thing, General."

"What is it, Denton?"

"Dick Edwards, the chief of staff for Senator John Bartlett has been nosing around. He wants to see you when you get back to the Pentagon."

"Fuck him. Tell him I'm busy. He and his boss are fucking anti-military trouble makers."

"I told him I would see what I could do. He knows about Commander Daniels' promotion with the president presiding and that Miss Reed was awarded the Presidential Medal of Freedom. He was asking me about the commander's promotion. I told him to ask the president."

Bellardi laughed at that. "Denton, I have an idea. Have a nice July 4th. See you back at the office." Hanging up the phone, he turned to Mac and told him the news.

"Fuck," said Daniels. "It's related to Rajul. He needed to close the door on Park. If we'd pushed Park, he would have given up Rajul. Are you going back to D.C.?"

Bellardi thought for a moment, and then shook his head. "Nothing we can do. Besides, Dick Edwards, Senator Bartlett's chief pain in the ass is looking for me. Let's enjoy the weekend, and I'll keep you posted. Enjoy your time off, you earned it."

There was a knock on the door and it slowly opened. Astrid put her head in, keeping her body behind the door. "Are you two staying in all day? It's really nice out."

"That's the best offer I had all day," said Bellardi.

"I hope she was talking to me, Uncle Tony," said Mac.

"I'm talking to anyone who wants to see my new bathing suit." She stepped into the room wearing a very small bikini that showed off all of her assets.

Tony Bellardi put his hand on his heart. He shook his head. "Obviously Mac, that invitation is for you."

Mac smiled and got up, "See you later, Uncle Tony, and if I'm not back don't look for me."

CHAPTER 73

JERSEY CITY, NEW JERSEY

THREE WEEKS LATER

It was ten o'clock and Len Tucci, Ken Park's financial advisor, sat in the conference room of Margulies and Wind, his attorneys. The corner room faced New York City with breathtaking views. He enjoyed the view even though he had seen it many times before. But this time, as he nursed a bottle of water, he was upset and very nervous. He had received a call from the Newark office of the FBI and they wanted to talk about Mr. Park. They'd told him this was routine and had nothing to do with him. He arranged to meet them at Margulies' office at eleven. Tucci was not talking to anyone without his attorneys.

His lawyers of many years, Bob Margulies and Jack Wind, sat across the large granite conference table from Tucci. Margulies, the older of the two lawyers, sat back in his chair with his hands crossed over his stomach and asked, "Did you know that Mr. Park named you as his executor in his will?"

Len shrugged his shoulders. "To tell the truth I had no idea," he said. "But he gave me a letter that was to be opened in case of his death."

Wind held up a paper. "Is this it?"

"That's it."

Margulies asked, "What did you do?"

"When I saw on television that Park had been murdered, I was stunned. He was shot to death in his restaurant on Sunday July 3rd. He was such a nice guy and so young. I got to my office on Tuesday, opened the letter, and read it. I was to call attorney Pat Lytle in Arlington, and then I was to call Park's brother Hwan in Seoul and break the news of Park's death. He left instructions regarding the funeral. He wanted to be cremated and his ashes spread into the ocean. So I called the attorney as I was instructed."

"Then what happened?" asked Margulies.

"The attorney spoke with me for awhile and I made arrangements to go to Arlington to meet and do the legal stuff, so I could administer the estate. I called Korea and reached Hwan Park. He spoke English very well and said to call him Harry. I told him all I knew about his brother's death and that he was the sole beneficiary of the estate, which was quite substantial. He thanked me for the call and I gave him my numbers and he told me he would be in touch."

"Then what happened?" asked Jack Wind.

"I had Park cremated and took over the administration of the estate. I secured his home and had the manager of the restaurant continue running it. I transferred all his holdings into an estate account and called an accountant friend of mine, Richard Gironda, who's here in Bayonne, and I told him to do the tax returns. Then I received instructions from Harry Park that he wants the business and house sold and after all the expenses, to wire him the money. I called Pat Lytle to sell the house and he told me that there was someone interested in buying it. Shit, it wasn't even listed yet. The offer was for fifty thousand more than the appraised value. Of course, I told him to sell it. He said it was a cash deal and he took care of it, and yesterday he wired me the money. Then I received an offer for the business from a Japanese company," he said, handing the offer to Margulies. "Look at that offer, two million—all cash."

Margulies crossed his legs, leaned back and glanced up at the ceiling, "Okay, what do you want us to do?"

"Handle the transaction, sell the business and wire me the net funds, and most important, deal with the Feds."

"This is strange," said Wind.

"Strange, is an understatement. Two unsolicited offers for properties that are not even listed for sale and at a price greater than they are worth. Then the Feds call me up. What the hell is going on?"

There was a knock on the door and Bob's secretary Marie entered the room, and said, "Agents Glover and Hand are here."

"Please bring them down," Margulies replied.

Two hours later, the agents were done with their interview. Tucci had gone over everything he knew about Park. Margulies asked, "What is this about?"

Glover said, "I can't discuss an ongoing investigation. The request for this interview came from the Washington Field Office. They picked up Mr. Tucci's name from the will and we were asked to do an interview. I assure you Mr. Tucci, this has nothing to do with you. I doubt you will ever hear from us again. Thank you for your time."

CHAPTER 74

50,000 FEET OVER THE PACIFIC OCEAN

SAME DAY

The Citation X zipped along at 600 miles an hour, cruising at 50,000 feet over the Pacific Ocean. Haig was going through reams of papers and making notes. Daniels was on a recliner, sound asleep.

Lisa came out of the cockpit to check on her passengers. "Mr. Haig, can I get you something?"

"If it is not too much trouble Lisa, could I have a peanut butter and jelly sandwich on white bread and a glass of milk?"

She smiled and said, "I'm sure we can do that for you. By the way we have plenty of chocolate on board, your favorite, Ghirardelli's milk chocolate."

A big grin came across Haig's face. He loved chocolate.

A few minutes later Lisa put a tray down in front of Haig with a peanut butter and jelly sandwich, glass of milk and a half dozen pieces of chocolate. She returned to the cockpit.

Daniels' satellite phone rang. He immediately woke and answered it. "Yes."

"Mac, Charko here. Where is Haig?"

"Sitting next to me, sir."

"Put your speaker on so Ron can hear."

Daniels pressed the speaker button and leaned toward Haig. "Go ahead, Admiral."

"We received an update from Mike Bertone. Park's business was sold to a Japanese company, and so was his house. The entire estate went to Park's brother Hwan. We had our office in Seoul do some checking and his alleged brother, Hwan Park, happens to be the Reconnaissance General Bureau (RGB) resident agent in South Korea. Park orchestrated the sale of the business. The money is being circulated. The North Koreans funded the Japanese company, who paid the estate, who sent the money to Park, who returned it to the North."

"So I guess the new operator of the restaurant will be the RGB agent in Washington. It'll make it easier for the Feds," said Daniels.

"Do you want us to drop in on Hwan Park?" asked Haig.

"No. The South Koreans have him under watch. Let's see what happens."

"Any word on Rajul?" asked Daniels.

"Unfortunately not. He's dropped from sight. Maybe when the new RGB boy gets here, he'll make contact and the Feds can pick up on it."

"Don't count on it, Admiral. Rajul had Park killed. He's closing the circle. I would have done the same thing."

"You're probably right, Mac. For the official record, it seems that the murder was committed by a disgruntled employee. Unofficially, the investigation shows that the employees were well paid and happy to work there. The report, which is being kept under wraps, states that the killer was a martyr and had prepared for this in detail. This killer knew that Park was under surveillance. He killed Park in the kitchen after the restaurant closed and tried to escape out the back door. The FBI agents heard the shot and saw that he was covered in blood. When they approached he cried out, 'God is great' and shot himself."

Daniels shot up in his seat. "Why did the report state that the killer knew Park was under surveillance?"

"Because he said before he died, 'I waited until you could not see us.' There has to be a leak."

"No," said Daniels. "No, I think Rajul is plugged in. We have to get him."

"Check in with me, Mac, when you're done."

"Yes, sir."

The phone went dead. Daniels reached over and grabbed half of Haig's peanut butter and jelly sandwich and a couple of pieces of chocolate.

"Well," said Haig.

"I know this Japanese company. And I'm going to use it to get Rajul."

CHAPTER 75

BEIJING, CHINA

NEXT DAY

It was a warm summer's day in Beijing and the beautiful weather had brought out the masses. The parks were crowded. Even General Lee Kem, the head of the Ministry of State Security in China, left his office, saying to his secretary that he was going to the Monument of the Peoples' Heroes.

The park was a few short blocks from the Great Hall. General Kem walked slowly toward the Monument, allowing the sunshine to warm his face. It felt good to be outside.

The Monument is a tall marble obelisk with the names of those who had given so much for the Great Revolution chiseled in the stone. This was a place where many Chinese paid their respects. The general stayed away from the crowd. There were too many that were milling around the public tombstone. He thought there were some names that shouldn't even be there. But that was politics.

"Nice day, General," the voice said.

The general didn't turn around. He recognized the voice. "Yes, it is a nice day. At my age every day is a nice one."

The general moved toward the many picnic tables, picking one that was being used by a young family. He noticed that they were almost finished eating. *Perfect,* he thought. They would leave soon. "May I sit here?" he asked. It was common for strangers to share the tables.

The man gestured with his hand. "Please be seated."

Taking an apple from his pocket, the general brushed it against his sleeve, shining it. The family had no sooner left when his friend sat down across from him. As was the custom, both men nodded to each other. Had anyone been watching, it would appear as if to strangers were sharing a table.

"Do you play chess?" asked the general.

"I do."

The general took from his pocket a chess field, opened it, and ironed it with the flat of his hand. Then he took the chess pieces from his pocket and the two men set up the field. The general had more than chess on his mind.

Several minutes into the game the General spoke, "Am I safe?"

"I think so, unless you piss me off," said Mac Daniels.

"Is that the way to talk to an old man?" asked the general.

"No, but it's a way to talk to an old war horse, who almost threw me under the bus."

"Am I safe, Mac?"

"You are and only because I like you. You know, you could've been a little more convincing with the Supreme Leader. I didn't appreciate your description of me as being a liar who can't be trusted. And that I like the money. Thanks for nothing; a little support would be helpful."

"I only told the truth. You do lie."

"Almost as much as you," retorted Daniels.

"I have but one name— you know how many names I have for you? Let's see; Mac Daniels, Mac Arthur, Mac Brown, Mac Johnson, Mac Smith, Mac Williams, and then there's a few others without the Mac. Bill Cody, Bill Barnett, Bill Boyd, Bill Hitchcock and I'm sure there's more names than I know. I'm not even sure what your real name is."

"Does it matter? John Doe, okay?" said Daniels with a big smile.

"No, but I told them the truth as I knew it. Now for the big question, do you have the uranium?"

"Of course not, General, I don't have it. I told you that before you got online with the Supreme Leader."

"Why don't I believe you?"

"Because you're a spy and believe no one. Believe what you want. It makes no difference to me. Look, we prevented a war and that's what counts. You know if they fired on the Reagan we would've taken action and you would've had your hands full trying to prevent your country from getting involved."

"You are right," said the general. "You know some people in my government may not appreciate what I did for you, but when Admiral Charko told me of the situation, I agreed to help."

The general paused and thought about his next chess move.

Daniels studied the board, and thought, *the general is a sly fox in life and in games*. He made a move to counter the general then asked, "Would your government appreciate a war? We buy what you make. If we don't buy, then who, the North Koreans? If you didn't feed them, they would starve. War is no good for the economy and it sure is no good for life. You're a hero and your name belongs on the monument."

The general held up his hand. "Don't rush it. I can wait."

"Your buddy General Cheon and one of his subordinates, Sang, were very suspicious. Apparently, they viewed some tapes and put two and two together. Sang figured out that I was someone else, and Cheon was going to report you to your president on suspicion of treason. I wanted you to know for sure that before they could act they were both dead and the tapes destroyed."

"You are still lethal."

"No, not lethal, just alive. Has there been any inquiry about me from the North?"

"No. What about their bodies?"

"What bodies? They weren't found. They were incinerated. Not a trace of anything. You're safe, but there is just one loose end and I will take care of that. The next time I call on you, you could be a little more enthusiastic in supporting me. Do me a favor."

"What?"

"Let's finish our chess game."

CHAPTER 76

THE WHITE HOUSE

ONE WEEK LATER

The President woke at five, his usual time. He quietly rolled out of bed so as not to wake his wife, and slipped on his robe and slippers. The president opened his bedroom door. Standing there was a Secret Service agent, who handed him a coffee mug along with a stack of reports reflecting the night's activity.

The president moved to a little office off the master bedroom and turned on the desk light. He flipped through the security reports and the threat assessments from the office of the National Security Director.

He had a report from Mike Bertone's office indicating that they'd still had no success on tracking down Rajul and that they expected a replacement for Park. It had been in all the papers that the restaurant was being renovated and would be opened for Labor Day.

He turned on the television to watch a taped show. He was watching *In the Wolf's Den*, with the Wolf news director Tim Harris. He liked Harris and was pleased to see his success, and true to Tim's promise, the President felt he was getting a fair shake. Harris had adopted a line that the president liked, "Pundits have opinions, and newscasters have facts." He thought he even might consider doing an interview with Tim for the holidays. That would be a first.

At six o'clock, the president's wife woke up and took her morning coffee with her husband. They took this time to talk about the children and family. Once the president left the private residence, his life was not his own. Every minute of the day was planned and scheduled.

The president excused himself and went into the bathroom. A few minutes later, the first lady heard him laughing. She wondered what he could be laughing at in the bathroom.

The president came out and held up a piece of toilet paper—written on it was, "Have a nice day, Mister President. Commander M.D."

He looked at his wife laughing and said, "I actually could get to like that guy."

CHAPTER 77

FALLS CHURCH, VIRGINIA

LABOR DAY

Exhausted, he had been working late into the night so his restaurant would open on Tuesday, the day after Labor Day. Congress would be back in session and the city would be alive after the August doldrums. Turning onto Folkestone Road, he was almost home. Finally pulling in to the driveway, he stopped before hitting the button to open the garage door. He sat there, surveying the neighborhood to be sure there was nothing unusual. There were no cars parked in the street; it was a no-parking block. No one was walking about at this late hour—nothing out of the ordinary. Satisfied, he pulled into the garage of his home, the former home of Ken Park. Opening the side door of the house, he heard his alarm beep. *Safe,* he thought. On his entering the code, the beeping stopped. Passing through the kitchen, he decided he was too tired to eat and would go upstairs, shower, and go to bed. He wanted to be fresh for tomorrow's opening.

As he started up the stairs, he heard a voice. "Come on, have a drink, Sunny."

Startled, Guozhi Sun jumped, turning toward the voice. His heart was racing—he was scared. Flipping on the light, he saw Mac Daniels sitting on the recliner, with his feet up, a drink in his left hand, and a 1911 Colt 45 with a sound suppressor in his right hand.

"You're alive," Sunny blurted out.

"So it seems, and so are you. Are you a tour guide here too?" asked Daniels, with a big smile on his face. He answered his own question. "I don't think so. Let's see, you worked for the Ministry of State Security in North Korea, and now I would bet you are on the Reconnaissance General Bureau's (RGB) payroll, taking over for the late Ken Park."

Sunny didn't answer, he just pointed to the pistol and asked, "Is that necessary?"

"Depends," said Daniels as he sat up looking at the Colt. "Wonderful weapon. It makes a small hole going in, but a really big hole coming out."

"Depends on what?" Sunny asked.

"Your answers."

On the table next to Daniels was what appeared to be a Smartphone, except this one had a small antenna.

"What's that?" asked Sunny.

"A jammer and right now, the Feds are going crazy trying to override it. It's safe to talk."

"The Feds?" he asked in surprise.

"Of course. They've been watching you since you arrived here."

"I think I'll have that drink," he said.

"You have some really good vodka," Daniels noted.

"I'm glad you're enjoying my vodka," Sun replied as he went to the bar and grabbed the bottle of Chopin. Pouring himself some vodka, he threw in a few ice cubes, twirled it, and took a sip. "Nice and smooth," he said. "Now what?"

"Question and answer time," said Daniels. "First question: Are you their agent or ours? Tell me you're not a double agent."

"Double agent, fuck you."

Daniels lifted the Colt up so it was pointed at the man's head. "Wrong answer, I'll shoot you. Now are you a double agent?"

"I guess you will shoot me. You already shot me once. No, I'm not a fucking double agent."

Daniels smiled. "Truthfully, I didn't think so, but I thought I would ask. Just to see your reaction. 'Fuck you' was the right answer. Why did you wait so long to identify yourself to me? I could've killed you."

"Because I wasn't given specific details about who was coming. No clue whatsoever. It all happened so fast. I thought that JR was the contact person. When I gave him the identification code, he didn't have the right answer. Since you had General Lee Kem, the head of the Ministry of State Security in China, vouching for you, I certainly didn't think it was you. To be honest, I was confused and I was playing my cards close to my vest. Just trying to play it safe."

Daniels shook his head. "JR is a bodyguard and shouldn't have been there in the first place."

"Can I ask a question?"

"Go ahead," said Daniels.

"Who are you, Mac Brown, MacArthur and who do you work for?"

"My name doesn't matter, but if you really want to know, it's William Cody and I'm a contract employee for the CIA. Like I told the Supreme Leader, I spy for money."

The room was silent for a minute. Both men took sips from the drink.

Daniels went on, "Just for the record, that was not General Kem. It was a computer-generated image. We had many voice recordings of him so it was easy for our synthesizer. It worked well."

"Worked well is an understatement. That's what had me fooled."

Daniels asked, "What gave me away to Sang?"

"The video films of you and Miguel Ricardo that were taken in the hotel. When you showered, some of your body makeup must've washed off and he noticed there were two identical bullet-wound scars."

"I'll have to remember that." Daniels took another sip of his drink. "And did they question my disappearance?"

Sunny nodded. "You certainly were a topic of conversation. I saw you leave the warehouse but how did you survive the airport massacre?"

"What massacre? I went to the airport and just flew out. Anyway, go on," said Daniels, "fill in the details."

Sun took a long sip of his drink, let out a big sigh, and began, "There was a major firefight at the airport. Somehow, some agency or some special forces shot the place up and killed quite a few soldiers."

"It certainly wasn't me," said Daniels. "Go on."

"When I was questioned, I told them that Sang had taken Miss Reed hostage. They were very surprised to hear this. I explained that Sang believed she and you were spies. Sang brought Miss Reed to the warehouse to question her and was going to have her gang-raped. You showed up and then Cheon showed up and a gun battle erupted. I told them that you managed to get Miss Reed out of there, but you stayed on and after Sang shot Cheon and me, you shot Sang. I managed to get out of the warehouse before the place exploded. I think they thought it was all the rocket fuel and weapons that caused a massive explosion, not to mention the oil. By the way what did cause the explosion?"

Daniels shook his head. "Go on."

Sunny continued, "I told them I really don't know whether you were alive or dead. So if you want to resurrect yourself you can, because it's apparent that the Supreme Leader liked you and was looking forward to doing more business with you. He was very upset about Miss Reed's treatment and I believe he was trying to contact her. I think Sang's family is paying for it."

Daniels nodded his head.

"I have a question. If you knew I was on your side, why did you shoot me?"

"To save your life. If you left the warehouse without a scratch, you would've been tortured and told everything you know. I had two choices; kill you or wound you, and wounding was a better way to go. I'm sure you will agree. You followed my advice and told them that Sang shot you and you gave them the right cover story. When they took the bullet out of you, it was a 9mm Kratak, which is fired from a Crvena Zastava; Sang's gun. You're a hero."

"Fuck you, it hurts getting shot."

"Don't I know it, and so does Miss Reed."

"How is she?"

"I understand she's doing fine, not really sure. I don't exactly hang out with her. She's above my pay grade."

"Do you know who I work for?" Sunny asked.

Daniels smiled. "Sure I do. You're with the Defense Intelligence Agency and you are Captain Guozhi Sun ..." Just then, Daniels' phone vibrated. "The Feds should be here in a little while. My people are outside and will try to keep the Feds out until we're done. A few more questions and I'll get out of here. I want a favor, Sunny. I want Aswas Rajul. He'll know that you are the resident RGB operative and will contact you. Give him to me, not the Feds. When he contacts you, and he will, call Langley and ask for the DD Admiral Charko and give him the message, and he will get it to me. I want that fucking son of a bitch."

Daniels put his weapon away, and as he did, the door burst open. In came several special agents along with Ron Haig. They had their weapons drawn and they looked at Daniels and saw the jammer. Daniels had his hands up.

The first agent asked, "Who are you?"

Daniels answered, "I am going to take out my creds very slowly, so don't get a nervous trigger finger." He slowly reached into his shirt pocket, took out a folder, and flipped it to the agent.

The agent caught it, opened it, and looked. He tossed it back to Daniels. "Okay," he said to the other agents, "stand down. This is William Cody, CIA and I'm sure he's going to tell us that he jammed the signal because of national security." Looking at Daniels, he asked, "Why did you jam the signal?"

"Because of national security."

"Wise ass."

"Sorry, boys, that's the fact; national security. I'll take my jammer and leave. By the way, if you want to check it out, I suggest you call Director Bertone, who knows I'm here and why. So please feel free to call the director."

As Daniels started to leave, he asked Sunny, "What's the weather in Washington now?"

Sunny laughed, "How the fuck would I know? It's snowing."

"I didn't think it snowed in the summertime in Washington," said Daniels. "I'm glad you know the identification code, Sunny."

Turning to the special agents, he said, "Gentlemen, and I use the term loosely, this RGB agent is Guozhi Sun, who I know as Sunny, Captain, United States Army, serving in the Defense Intelligence Agency. He works with us. I suggest you boys work out the protocols because he's going to be the best asset you've ever had. The whole North Korean RGB will be working through him, so let's keep him alive, not like Park."

"Fuck you, Cody. You and your agency fucked it up and we had to clean it up."

Daniel stood and before he could say or do anything Haig grabbed him and said, "Come on Bill, let's get out of here."

As they walked to Haig's car, Daniels asked, "Did you hear everything?"

"Loud and clear. I have one question, why did you tell him that Kem was a computer-generated image and not the truth?"

"Because if he ever goes back to North Korea and they torture him, he'll give it up. I promised Kem I would protect him, and Sunny was the last open piece."

Haig asked, "Do you think he can help with Rajul?"

"He's our only hope. I don't care if he runs an ad in the *Post*. He's got to make that connection for us. Ron, my gut is telling me this Rajul can do some real damage."

"Where to now, Mac?"

"I'm flying down to Atlanta. I have some extended leave. See what Astrid has planned. What about you, Ron?"

"I'm taking some time. Cathy has the honey-do list. Maybe some golf. Then we start over again. Does it ever get easy, Mac?"

"Ron, the only easy day was yesterday."

EPILOGUE

ARLINGTON MEMORIAL BRIDGE, WASHINGTON, D.C.

NEXT DAY

It was a warm September day and Aswas Rajul, like so many other Washingtonians, was taking a leisurely stroll. He had left the Lincoln Memorial and was walking across the Arlington Memorial Bridge, which crossed over the Potomac River and connected Washington, D.C. to Arlington, Virginia. Like many other tourists, he took out his cell phone and appeared to be snapping pictures of the Lincoln Memorial and taking pictures up and down the river. What people didn't know was that he had actually dialed a number. Holding the phone over the bridge he started to speak. "Amr."

Amr Ibn Taher answered, "Yes, Aswas Rajul."

Aswas Rajul immediately dropped the phone into the river. Taking another phone, he dialed again.

"Amr, say nothing just listed and never, never say my name again. The NSA has every device scanning for my name. Every forty-five seconds I will hang up and redial. Do you understand?"

"Yes."

Rajul could see his watch. He said, "You did well. Park is dead. Your man died a martyr. He enjoys Paradise. We have to move on, to the next phase."

"What must I do? I am always ready to serve you and die for our cause."

"You are to go to Saudi Arabia with the recruits . . ." Before he finished the statement, he dropped the phone in the river. He took out another phone and began the ritual all over again.

At Fort Meade in Maryland, the headquarters for the NSA, the computers were buzzing. Someone shouted, "We have a hit."

Someone else yelled, "Do you have a location?"

On a new phone, Rajul continued, "Have your men take the jobs that were assigned. You are in charge. The water and oil must be destroyed and the king must die. Do you have any questions?"

"No, I know what we must do."

Again, Rajul dropped the phone in the river. Repeating the ritual, he said, "I will give you a contact number for me. My name is Mohammed bin Al Tar."

"That is a good name, 'son of vengeances' suits you well, bin Al Tar."

"Even better, because we have an opportunity to purchase uranium from our Russian friends. When I call again, I will give you a number for me."

He dropped the phone into the Potomac. As he turned around, a black Suburban pulled up. The doors opened and a Secret Service agent jumped out. The agent walked up and said, "Mr. Edwards, the senator wants you to hop in."

Inside the car, Edwards could see Secretary Terrance Hertz and Senator John Bartlett.

As Dick Edwards got into the Suburban and drove away, he thought, *this isn't over yet Mister Daniels.*

To be continued . . .

Printed in Canada